Expert Witness

A Josie Bates Thriller
Book 4

By

Rebecca Forster

Expert Witness

ISBN: 0615605486
ISBN-13: 9780615605487

For Bruce & Carole Raterink

Many thanks to Jenny Jensen for keeping this story on track, and to friends with good eyes:

Nancy McClain, Julie Mandarino, and Jay Freed.

Your help, cheerleading and friendship is so greatly appreciated.

CHAPTER 1

Day 1
An Outbuilding in the California Mountains

He touched her breast.

He hadn't meant to. Not that way. Not gently, as if there was affection between them. Not as if there was suddenly sympathy for her, or second thoughts about the situation. To touch her so tenderly – a fluttering of the fingers, a sweep of his palm – was not in the plan and that, quite simply, was why he was surprised. But he really couldn't find fault with himself. There must have been something about the fall of the light or the turn of her body that made him do such a thing.

Taking a deep breath, he closed his eyes not wanting to be distracted by her breasts or her face or her long, long legs. For someone like him, it would not be unheard of to be moved by the frail, failing light filtering through the cracks in the mortar, pushing through the hole high in the wall. This was a desperately beautiful light, heroically shining as the dark crept up to capture it, overcome it, extinguish it.

There were smells, too. They were assaultive, musty smells that reminded him of a woman after sex. Then there were the scents of moist dirt and decaying leaves mixed with those of fresh pine and clean air. There was the smell of her: indefinable, erotic, unique.

Breathing deep, turning his blind eyes upward, fighting the urge to open them, he acknowledged the absence of sound. The sounds of civilization were white noise to him, but in this remote place his heart raced at the thump of a falling pinecone, the shifting of the air, the breathing and twitching of unseen animals, the flight of bugs and birds.

God, this was intimate: sights, smells, silence. His head fell back against the rough concrete. He understood now what had happened, why he had crossed the line. Oh, but wasn't his brilliant objectivity both a blessing and a curse? He saw life for what it was and people for who they truly were. He was so far superior in intellect and insight – and hadn't that just messed him up at a critical juncture in his friggin' life because of her-

He stopped right there.

No wandering thoughts. No anger. He was better than that. It had taken years to master his hatred, and he would not throw his success away on this pitiful excuse for a woman. He closed his eyes tighter, banishing the bad and empty words that were simply the excrement of exhaustion. He breathed through his nose, lowered his heart rate, and returned to his natural, thoughtful state before realizing that he had neglected to acknowledge her blouse. It was important to be thorough and sure of his conclusions, so he opened his eyes, pushed off the wall, and balanced on his haunches. He pressed his fingers onto the cool, hard-packed earth.

Ah, yes. He saw it now. The dart. The tailor's trick of construction intended to draw attention to a woman's breast. The widest part hugged the graceful mound, the tip pointed right at the nipple. There wasn't more than one man in a thousand who would notice such a thing, much less understand its true purpose. That dart, so absurdly basic, was a subliminal invitation to familiarity. Confident and in control again, he touched her purposefully. He didn't grasp or grope yet she moved like she didn't like it.

That pissed him off just a little so he squeezed her hard and hoped it hurt. He would never know if it did and that was more the pity. He liked the symmetry of cause and effect. Certainly that's what had brought them to this place. She was the cause of his torture, and she would have to deal with the effect of her actions.

Disgusted that he had wasted precious time, he pushed himself up and kicked at her foot. She didn't move. She was no better than a piece of meat. He worked fast, pushing her on her side. He cradled her finely shaped skull. When it was properly positioned, he dropped it on the hard ground.

Leaning over, he grabbed the stake above her head with both hands and pulled as hard as he could. It didn't move. No surprise. The hole was deep, the concrete was set, and the wood was too thick to break, too wide at the top for the rope to slip off. His hard work had paid off: the bag of concrete dragged half a mile uphill, the water carted from the creek a mile in the other direction, the patient whittling of the wood itself. He had battled the thin air and the crushing September heat that rested atop the mountains and smothered the city below. Now that it was done, though, he realized how much he hated this place. There was a spiritual residue here that fanned his spark of uncertainty. He shivered. He hoped God wasn't watching.

Gone. Banished. Think on it no more.

Sin, immorality, cruelty were not words he would consider. He had chosen this place precisely because it was ugly and horrid. No one had a better purpose for it than him. Pulling his lips together, he put his knee into her stomach, crossed her wrists, and yanked her arms upward. They slipped through his grasp.

"Good grief," he muttered.

Practice had gone smoothly, but the reality was that limp arms and smooth, slender wrists slipped away before he could get the rope tight enough to hold her. She groaned and that made him afraid.

Beads of sweat became rivulets. His shirt was soaked. He would throw that shirt away. He would cut it up and throw it away. That's what he would have to do. Maybe he would burn it.

Working faster, he leaned his whole body against her and pushed her arms up, not caring if the rope cut her or anything. Task completed, he collapsed against the wall and mentally checked off the list that had been so long in the making.

Engage.

Subdue.

Transport.

Immobilize.

Punish.

Only one remained unchecked. It would come soon enough, and with it would come satisfaction, retribution and redemption. He didn't know which would be sweeter.

A water bottle was placed near enough for her to drink from if she didn't panic. Food – such as it was – was within biting distance. Bodily functions? Well, wouldn't she just have to deal with that as best she could? Humiliation was something she needed to understand. Humiliation and degradation.

He was starting to smile, when suddenly she threw herself on her back and her arms twisted horribly. He pulled himself into a ball, covering his head with his hands. When no blows fell, when she didn't rise up like some terrifying Hydra, he lowered his hands and chuckled nervously. He hated surprises. Surprises made him act like a coward, and he was no coward. And he was no liar, as God was his witness.

He looked again and saw it was only the drugs working, not her waking. Catching his breath, he stood up. It was time to go. He paused at the door and entertained the idea of letting her go but knew that was impossible. What was done was done. Justice would finally be served.

With all his might, he pushed open the metal door, stepped out, and put his shoulder into it as he engaged the makeshift lock. He wiped his brow with a handkerchief and composed himself. Next time all this would be easier. Next time he would bring water for himself. Next time he would bring the woman in the cement hut something, too.

He would bring her a friend.

Josie Bates' House, Hermosa Beach

Max slept on the tiled entry near the front door while Hannah Sheraton marked off the hours by the sound of his dog dreams; timing his snuffling and whining like labor pains.

Eight o'clock.

Nine.

Ten.

Eleven o'clock.

At midnight Hannah went for her meds, but it was the razor in the medicine chest that caught her attention. She touched it, cocking her head, narrowing her eye. It would be so easy to break it open, take the blade and slice away her fear and anxiety. Another scar would be a small price to pay for relief. Her fingers hovered over it just before she snatched the pills and slammed the door. She wouldn't disappoint Josie.

At one a.m. Hannah stepped over the old dog, eased outside, counted off twenty paces, and stopped exactly one step from the gate. She stood arrow-straight with her feet together and her knees locked. Whippet thin, lush chested, graceful and gorgeous as only a sixteen-year-old girl could be, Hannah paused. A breeze came off the ocean and fussed with her long black curls but did nothing to cut the heat. She scanned one side of the tiny walk-street where Josie's house anchored the corner, and then scanned back the other direction to the beach. The neighbors' houses were dark.

Suddenly her ears pricked and her heart beat faster. Someone was coming, walking on the Strand that paralleled the beach. That person wore hard shoes. Their steps sounded forlorn. That person stumbled once. Alert in the silence, Hannah waited. The steps started again. Hannah saw it was a man walking and an unhappy one at that. The moon was bright enough to see that his hands were stuffed into the pockets of his pants. He was hunched over like Sisyphus eternally, wearily, fruitlessly pushing that rock of his. Hannah's shoulders fell as he went by, disappearing into the early morning dark without ever looking her way. Her nerves prickled under her skin and her gut roiled with disappointment. She wanted that to be Josie walking home to her. Her head nearly split in two with wanting that.

At two a.m. Hannah turned on her heel, went back up the walk, took the key from inside, locked the front door, jiggled the knob four times, and moved away. Then she went back and did it all again. Dissatisfied still, she forced herself to leave.

Quickly, silently, Hannah went down her walk-street, turned north on the Strand and hurried toward the big pink apartment building half a mile away. The breeze kicked up to a hot wind as if the beach itself was suddenly as unsettled as she. Narrowing her eyes against the sudden dusting of sand, she caught her hair in her fist. It was sticky with the salty mist.

Hannah hurried past Scotty's Restaurant. The wall facing the beach was made of glass. Inside, a neon beer sign glowed yellow. If a thing could look lonely it did. On her left she passed the statue of the surfer perpetually crouched under the curl of a bronze wave, forever beached at the foot of the pier. If the artist had a soul, he would have at least faced the surfer so he could see the ocean. Hannah shivered as she glanced past the statue to the pier itself. It looked like the road to hell, reaching into the sea, swallowed by the black water.

To her right was Pier Plaza. The walking man had tired and now sat outside Hennessey's at a table bolted to the concrete. Whatever pain kept him up so late it was his alone. He wouldn't let it loose on her the way men liked to do. This was Hermosa Beach, after all. This was the safest place on the face of the earth. That's what Josie said. But Josie wasn't here, so the truth of that was suspect.

Breathing hard, unaware that she had been running, Hannah reached her destination and slid into the shadow of the awning over the front door. She pressed her fist against her chest as if this would keep her thumping heart inside. If anyone saw her they would think she was still sick instead of just afraid. Everyone was afraid of something, even if they didn't admit it.

Letting a long breath curl through her lips, her numbers tumbled out with it. She touched her fist to her chest five times, ten, fifteen and twenty, whispering the number that went with each one. Ritual complete, Hannah opened the outside door of Archer's apartment building and ducked in.

Quickly, lightly, she went up the first flight.

Heart pounding, numbers rattling inside her head, she made the second landing.

She caught her breath. There was one more flight to go.

She made it to the third floor with barely a sound.

A shudder ran down her spine before branching out to wind around her waist and clutch at her stomach. Her chin jerked up and then down again. Slowly Hannah opened her palm and looked at the key. She never thought she would touch this key much less use it. Not that she'd been forbidden to be here, it had just worked out that way. The man and the girl had not easily taken to one another, but they had staked out acceptable territory in Josie's life. Tonight, there was no choice. Hannah had to cross the boundary.

Putting the key in the lock, she turned it slowly, sure that the tumblers sounded like the crack of a gunshot. It was only her imagination. Inside, Archer slept on. That was a good thing. Hannah didn't want to wake him; she only wanted to see if Josie slept beside him.

The door swung silently. She stepped inside. A full moon illuminated the deck and half the living room. Hannah closed her hand around the key, her fist went behind her back and then her back went against the door.

Her courage was small, so she moved fast when she found the kernel of it. She went past the couch, past the chair, past the bookshelf with the rosary hanging from the neck of a beer bottle. She stopped just to the side of the bedroom door, peered around the corner and looked at the bed.

Her heart fell.

The covers were piled too high for her to see who was underneath them. Biting her bottom lip, knowing she couldn't turn back now, Hannah inched into the room. No harm done if she was quiet. A quick look and she would be satisfied.

Three…

Four…

Five steps…

Suddenly, an arm was at her throat, a gun was at her head, and Hannah was pulled back against a man's half-naked body.

CHAPTER 2

Archer's Apartment, Hermosa Beach

"Jesus Christ, Hannah. You're damn lucky I didn't shoot you."

Archer paced, he lectured, and Hannah sat on the couch with her knees together, feet out, hands clasped, and head down. He probably thought she was ashamed, but she wasn't; she was embarrassed by the sight of a shirtless, shoeless Archer wearing only his raggedy robe and sweat pants. His hair was mussed and he needed a shave. The only reason she was upset was because he had been sleeping alone.

"Hey, are you listening to me? I could have hurt you. I could have..." He pulled his hands through his hair and stopped right in front of her, splaying his legs, bending from the waist, barking at her like a drill sergeant. "Look at me when I'm talking to you."

Hannah's head snapped up, she raised her sharp green eyes to his keen dark ones. He couldn't intimidate her. Sixteen years of her life was like sixty for a normal person, but he'd forgotten that. All he saw was a kid sneaking around his place.

"Stop yelling. I can hear you."

"And I've got a telephone," he barked. "You could have called."

"And I didn't because you'd be pissed at me. You think I don't know when Josie is here she's off limits?" Hannah came back strong, but her bravado was a beat off. "She might have forgotten to tell me she was staying here, you know. It's not like either of you is used to having a kid around."

Her stunning, dark face tightened with indignation. She picked at the upholstery, looking more like a child than Archer had ever seen her look. Finally, she pushed her chin up and shook her hair back.

"When my mother didn't come home all I had to do was look in some dude's bed to find her. I'm sorry if I'm just doing what comes natural."

Archer opened his mouth only to close it again. What could he say to that? The girl had a point. Sixteen-years-old, she had been framed by her own mother for murder, a mother who slept with anything that moved, who abandoned Hannah for days on end when she was little, and kept doing it until the day they put her in jail and threw away the key. Yeah, Hannah had cause to worry when the adults who were supposed to take care of her went missing.

"Point taken," he mumbled.

"Okay." Hannah gave an inch because he had. She raised her eyes again and the fingers of her right hand methodically tapped her left. "I don't expect Josie to babysit me, but if I saw that she was here I could at least go home and sleep. But she's not here, she's not anywhere, and now I'm really scared."

Archer sat down opposite her and put his elbows on the chair arms. He covered his face with his hands then drew them down slowly as much to wake himself up as to give him time to check out this girl who had changed the way he and his woman went about their business.

Josie Bates had almost given her life for this kid – literally – then turned their world upside down for her. She made sure Hannah saw a therapist twice a week, got her into school and encouraged her art. He understood. This was Josie's way of healing her own broken heart, crushed when her own mother abandoned her. She'd been close to Hannah's age when that happened. Even Archer had to admit that Hannah and Josie were a good fit: just different enough and just alike enough to make theirs an interesting, dedicated and complex relationship.

Given all that, it made no sense that Josie would not check in with Hannah. Besides, Hannah's obsessive-compulsiveness led her to check every nook and cranny of her surroundings a hundred times a day, so logic dictated that she had searched meticulously for Josie. If she hadn't been found, something was definitely wrong.

"Okay. Okay." His hands fell to the side. "When did she leave?"

"I saw her yesterday morning."

Hannah hugged herself and shook her head. Those startling green eyes of hers never left Archer's face. For the hundredth time he admired the genetic recipe used to create this girl: not black or white, East Indian or Irish. She simply was exquisite and that, as far as Archer was concerned, added to the trouble she brought with her.

"When did you get back from school?"

"Three-thirty," Hannah answered. "Then I went to an appointment with Doctor Fox."

"And what time did you get back from the doctor?"

"Six. Max was sitting by the front door. He needed to go out." Hannah grabbed a couch cushion and hugged it.

"Did you call her cell?"

"No," she drawled. Archer raised a brow. She raised one right back. "I called the cell like maybe a hundred times. It was turned off, or she wasn't near it or something. All I get is her message."

"Could you have called me a little earlier?"

"No." Hannah did that Egyptian head thing home girls do when they are trying to be cool. It was an affectation that always amused Archer. He thought the gesture something akin to a mouse trying to intimidate a hawk by twitching its nose. "Sometimes people don't come back when they say they will; sometimes you have to wait until people want to be found."

"Josie isn't some people." Archer's voice dropped as his mind kicked into gear. Investigating was what he did, and it never helped to panic or rise to the bait of people who were on the verge of it. "What've you been doing all this time?"

"My homework. I tried to paint," Hannah answered. "I called Burt, but Josie wasn't at his place. I looked out the window hoping I'd see her. I fed Max and I took him out for a walk, but we didn't go too far. Mostly I waited. What?"

Hannah stopped talking, aware that Archer's line of vision had shifted to her arm. She was scratching it through her shirt.

"You okay?" Archer asked.

Hannah pulled up her sleeve up. The chocolate colored skin was crisscrossed with razor thin scars, none of them fresh.

"Nothing up my sleeve," she quipped.

"Good. Josie would have my balls if..."

Archer's voice trailed off. That wasn't the right thing to say to a teenager, but this girl had been abused and misused. There was no way she was going to dial back to high school sleepovers and waiting to be asked to the prom. Archer got up, retied his robe, walked out to the deck, and instantly felt clear-headed.

He loved California fall: sizzling hot days that drove people to the beach, early sunsets that sent them home again, slow night cooling so the natives slept with their doors open and covers on. Right now it was late enough that early was making itself known. The black sea was dark grey, but in a couple of hours there would be a pink sunrise. Josie should have been there with him. The fact that she wasn't by his side, or that none of the locals had heard from her, narrowed the field to possibilities that didn't thrill him. Three came to mind: Josie was with another man, something had ticked her off royally and she was on cool down, or she was hurt. He discounted the first, couldn't imagine what could cause the second, and it made him sick to even think about the third.

He swung his head and looked over his shoulder half expecting to see Josie behind him, but it was only Hannah hanging near the doorway. He gave a little snort, not to laugh at her but to express his reluctant sympathy. Doors were her obsession the way honesty was his. Both things allowed them to know exactly where they stood. She needed to see who was coming into her life and who was taking a hike out of it; he needed to know exactly what he was dealing with so he could decide how to dodge, swerve or run headlong into trouble. Archer nodded her way; Hannah raised her chin. Truce for now. Not that they were enemies, they had just migrated to the same territory and were unsure of how much of it they could claim.

"Did you two fight?" Archer asked.

"Did you?"

"Nope." Archer laughed outright and shook his head. "And you gotta cut me some slack, Hannah. I would have asked you the same thing if you were Mother Theresa."

There was only a beat while she gathered her courage to tell him what really scared her.

"Josie and I were supposed to go to court Wednesday." Archer looked at her quizzically. "You know. Court? The guardianship. Josie was going to make it legal on Wednesday. We're supposed to see the judge." Hannah's eyes were brighter, and if Archer didn't know better he would have sworn she was going to cry. "Will you help me find her, Archer?"

"No." He pushed off the wall and walked past Hannah. "But I'll find her for you.

Before she could object, he disappeared into the bedroom. Five minutes later he was dressed: jeans, a Hawaiian shirt, and a windbreaker that covered the revolver at the small of his back. They left the apartment together, went down the empty Strand and turned onto the walk-street that led to an intersection with Hermosa Boulevard. Josie's house was on the corner. Hannah had left every light burning like a beacon to help Josie find her way home.

Archer held the gate for Hannah. Without a word they went inside the house: Hannah to the answering machine to check for messages, Archer locking up. Archer took off his jacket and didn't object when Hannah made the rounds again: doors, windows, windows doors. Eventually she was satisfied, said goodnight and made Archer promise to wake her when Josie walked through the door. Archer promised knowing he'd damn well wake the whole neighborhood when she came home. That would be after he reamed her up one side and down the other for causing such worry.

Turning the inside lights off, he left the one over the front porch burning, walked through the darkened house, through Josie's bedroom and out to the adjacent patio. He pulled up a chair and settled in. Every inch of this place was as familiar to his eye as Josie's body was to his touch. This house had been a tear down, but Josie saw a diamond in the rough. She rebuilt and refurbished it with her own two hands.

The tiling was complete, and the low wall around the patio was built, raised planters were now pocked with succulents and flowers. Inside, the archway between the living room and dining room was waiting for plaster, and the hardwood floors needed refinishing.

He rested his hair on the back of the chair and closed his eyes. Josie was a heck of a woman, a lawyer, and a friend. He and Hannah were lucky to share this nest with her even if they were so strangely cobbled together, a family without joints. They moved uneasily against one another.

In the kitchen, the icemaker popped a few cubes. Somewhere an electrical circuit clicked. The silence from

Hannah's bedroom was heavy with her anxiety. Max the Dog ambled through the bedroom and across the patio, his nails clicking on the tile. He walked close to Archer's chair, and the big man let his hand slide over the dog's back. It bumped over the raised scar left after Max tried to save Josie from Linda Rayburn's murderous attack. Archer took a handful of fur and pulled him close.

"Where is she, Max?'

In answer, the dog lay down beside him. Together they kept watch while, alone in her room, Hannah Sheraton counted the minutes until Josie's return.

It was three thirty in the morning.

An Outbuilding in the California Mountains

Things Josie heard:

The creak of metal.

A swish.

A thump.

A grunt.

Something falling hard.

Things Josie saw:

Walls of grey. Waves of grey.

Early morning light. Not much of it. Coming on slow.

Someone. Hunched over. A man? A shadow of a man?

Things Josie tried to do:

Speak.

Why couldn't she speak?

Reach for him.

What happened to her arms? She couldn't feel her hands.

She must have made a noise, moved, done something to catch his attention. He turned his head toward her. Her eyes closed. A movie came to her muddled mind. What was the name?

Think, dammit.

The movie was…

The Elephant Man.

Yes, that was it! This person's head looked too big for his body. It was fuzzy and featureless like the Elephant Man with a bag over his head. The shape came close, the fuzzy head tilted. He was looking at her. She swooned. Swoon was a silly word. Her eyelids fluttered. It was suddenly dark again, but the blackness came too fast for it to be dragged in on the tail of a sinking sun.

Ah. Oh.

Her eyes had closed. That was funny. Once more, through sheer force of will, she raised those eyelids as far as she could. He was so close now she could feel his breath.

Yes. Yes. Help me.

The shadow morphed and undulated and black became grey and grey became blue. Then blue took on form for a split second and no more. The man was once again made of blurs and shades and gradations of color that she took to be hair, a face, a shirt.

Was she in a hospital? Restrained, drugged and a danger to herself? Was that why her arms hurt and her hands were numb? Was that why she couldn't stay awake? It seemed so logical but that wasn't what she remembered. The truth was, Josie remembered nothing.

Hannah!

The name was a flash-bang in her brain. Big letters. Everything fluttered: heart and head and eyes, mind winking in and out. Then she felt a hand under her head. Someone was lifting her up; caring for her.

Thank you. Thank you.

The man put water to her lips. It rushed into her mouth, bubbled and dribbled down the side of her face. The person shook her head. He wanted her to swallow. She tried. She coughed. He shook her head harder and it wasn't nice. He shook her again, roughly this time. She was trying so hard to be good. She wanted to get better, and still he was angry. Water slid down her throat. There was so much of it that she gagged. Josie's eyes closed once more.

Sleep tight.

That's what she thought she heard him say, and he said it as if he didn't mean it. Before she lost consciousness again, Josie Bates thought she heard something else.

She thought she heard someone crying.

CHAPTER 3

Hermosa Beach Police Department

"Oh, for God's sake, Archer. Give it a rest. It's not even seven. I haven't had my coffee, I need to take a leak and traffic was a bitch."

Detective Liz Driscoll straight armed Archer. She couldn't have pushed him out of the way if he stood his ground, but he knew fighting with her would hurt more than help. Archer raised his voice so it would follow her into the ladies room.

"If you can't hold it for an hour then maybe you should move closer to where you work."

Liz did an about face, ripped open the door and gave him a look that would stop an elephant in its tracks. Obviously, she could hold it long enough to give him a piece of her mind.

"This from a guy who inherited his prime piece of real estate with the ocean view? Real sensitive, Archer."

He rolled his eyes. Those sharp little teeth of hers were embedded in her favorite two-course meal: those who have and those who don't. She stepped back into the hallway, her bladder now completely forgotten.

"I'm fifteen years younger than you, been on my own since I was sixteen, and didn't have the good fortune to be born with a silver spoon in my mouth, so buying into this pricey little piece of heaven just isn't in the stars, my friend. Oh, wait. You own that pretty pink building right there on the beach. Lower the rent on one of those primo units, bucko, and I can move in this weekend."

"I'll give you the damn building if you'll get serious."

Liz's nostrils flared, her jaw set. She turned on her heel and was gone. Archer would have sat in the next stall to get her attention, but this lady wasn't like other women or other cops. No amount of begging, pleading or rational discussion could sway her to dig into work before she was ready. Only immediate and present danger could do that, and according to her there wasn't any.

The door flew open again. He gave her props for being quick and a few more for being single-minded. Liz didn't even drop a comma in the conversation as she burst out of the john and headed down the hall.

"Josie is a big girl, Archer. Just because she didn't spend the night with you doesn't mean that she didn't spend it with someone."

There were times when Liz should think before she spoke and this was one of them. A foot shorter than Archer and a hundred pounds lighter, he almost pulled her off her feet when he grabbed her arm. Her hair was so short she could be mistaken for a young man from the back. Head on she looked years younger than thirty-five unless you were up close and personal. Then you could see the set of her jaw, the creases on her forehead, and the history in her eyes. She glared at Archer, putting him on notice that he wasn't going to put the fear of God into her. Someone else had tried to do that long ago, and that was when Liz learned if God couldn't scare you nothing could.

"That doesn't feel too good, Archer." Liz gave a nod toward his hand. He let her go and stepped back.

Liz wasn't exactly his cup of tea. She carried a chip on her shoulder and thought she knew a little more than she did. Still, he didn't want to date her, he needed her help. Liz moved in tight, put her hand on Archer's back and steered him into the partitioned area she called an office.

"Little raw there, cowboy." She pointed him toward a chair. Liz planted herself on the side of her desk. "I didn't mean Josie was sleeping around on you. It's just that she doesn't exactly answer to you. How often has she gone hunting for Billy Zuni because his mom locked him out and he's sleeping under the pier? That's a lousy way for a teenager to live." Liz shook her head like she couldn't believe a mom could do that to her own child. "Anyway, Josie's been out looking for him like a thousand times. Sittin' with him on the beach 'till the wee hours, talking just to keep him out of trouble. That kid's like her own pet project, and she doesn't call you every time she's giving him some attention." Liz waited a beat. "Well, does she?"

"No."

Drained, Archer slumped in the chair. The last few hours had been a bear. He hadn't slept. He'd headed out to the police station at six only to turn around and jog back when he remembered Hannah. He wrote three notes and taped them around the house so she would know that he hadn't forgotten her; that he, at least, would be back.

"And Josie has two kids to worry about now. She wouldn't have hung all night with Billy without telling the girl who lives with her," Archer muttered.

"I didn't know she'd made it permanent with that girl," Liz mused. "Kind of weird, Josie getting all maternal like that. What's her name? The kid, I mean."

"Hannah Sheraton. She's waiting at Josie's place in case she comes home."

"Maybe it's meltdown time. Josie might have needed a break. It's hard for someone as independent as her to change her stripes, if you know what I mean."

Liz hopped down from her perch and went to her own chair behind a desk littered with papers. There were nineteen thousand people in Hermosa Beach, thirty-seven cops on the force, five of them detectives. Liz crossed her arms and rested them on top of the papers. He had her attention because one of Hermosa's own was the topic, and Archer was the one she was talking to.

"So Josie's just been gone since yesterday morning, far as you know," Liz said.

"Yes. Nothing disturbed. She went to work like any other day."

"No plans for the evening?"

"None that I know of, and she didn't mention anything to Hannah."

"You're sure the girl is clean? As I recall, she was charged with assault with intent to kill, murder, and arson. Not nice stuff. Maybe she flipped and did something to Josie."

"No way," Archer shook his head. "Hannah was willing to take a murder rap for her mother. If she were that loyal to someone who treated her like trash, she would be doubly loyal to Josie who picked her off the heap. If she had done something, she wouldn't have come to me."

"But you're such a teddy bear," Liz drawled.

"And she's scared," Archer snapped.

Liz's hands went palm up. "Okay, just trying a little levity here. Did you check with Billy Zuni?"

Archer shook his head, "I saw him hanging at the pier. He was alone."

"Did you walk up and actually ask him if he'd seen Josie?"

Archer was impatient with Liz's long and winding road. "Josie wouldn't have taken the car to go see Billy. She would have jogged, or she would have walked. Her car would be in the garage or parked on the street."

"Okay, cool your jets."

Liz sank back in her chair. She crossed her legs, foot over knee. Instead of girl- clothes, she wore biker boots, generic jeans and a too-big jacket. The pencil flipping lazily between two fingers suddenly took flight and landed in the middle of her desk. That's when Archer knew it was a no-go on any official help. If she were engaged, that pencil would be filling out paperwork now.

"I'll ask around and see if anybody's seen her, but you know as well as I do nobody is going to do a damn thing about this."

"But this is Josie we're talking about," Archer objected.

"What? Like she's the only upstanding citizen who's ever taken a powder? Any force in the country is going to look the other way 'cause ninety-nine percent of the time when an adult disappears they're just off doing adult things. Unless you can tell me there's been an overt threat, that someone's been stalking her, or she's bordering on suicidal my hands are tied. Can you imagine me going to Captain Hagarty and wanting an investigation because that girl is worried? He'd have me washing squad cars just so I could contemplate the error of my ways. Bottom line, Archer, I'm up to my boobs in work. I'm asking you to take a deep breath on this."

"Oh, come on." Archer rolled his eyes. "This is Hermosa Beach. How much work can there be?"

"Hey, hey." Liz waggled a skinny little finger. Archer saw that she bit her nails. "Don't give me that shit. I've got two assaults, major vandalism down on Twenty-Second Street, and an armed robbery two nights ago at The Mermaid. Oh, and a couple of domestic complaints that would make your head spin. And that's just my case load."

"What hat have you been keeping this crime wave under?"

"No publicity means those property values stay up. Be reasonable buddy. It hasn't even been twenty-four hours. Besides, Josie's an Amazon. She can take care of herself." Seeing he needed more convincing, Liz sat up straighter, a move that really didn't add to her stature.

"Archer, if Josie fell down and hit her head and had amnesia anybody within a twenty mile radius would know to bring her to Hermosa. Heck, anyone in the nation considering the coverage of her last few cases. Since I don't think she's got amnesia, that tells me she had something to do and she's doing it."

Archer's fingers drummed the arm of the chair. Liz was down to cooing just to get him out of her office so she could get to work. It wasn't like she wouldn't want to spend some time with him, but she would prefer it to be after hours. Even before Josie, Liz figured out nothing would never happen between them, but that didn't keep her from wanting it – or from doing her job.

"Aw, look. You know the drill. We'll give priority when it's called for. There just isn't anything for me to sink my teeth into right now." Liz's finely shaped brows arched high over her eyes. Archer always found those brows disconcerting. They were so elegant on such a pedestrian face. She dismissed him as she pulled a report in front of her.

"My gut is telling me this is solid, Driscoll." Archer put his hands on her desk and leaned close. It was a posture that put lesser humans on notice.

"You're trying my patience, Archer." She flicked her gaze his way. When she saw his face, she took pity. "Will you leave it alone if I unofficially call for a look-see on the Jeep?"

Archer pushed off, stood up, and picked up the crumbs she was dropping.

"Call me as soon as you hear anything."

"Vice-versa, buddy." Liz picked up the pencil and then had another thought. "Archer. What about the kid? You want me to have child protective services catch her until Josie's back?"

Archer opened his mouth, hesitated and finally said:

"She'll be okay."

CHAPTER 4

The California Mountains

He sunned himself like a lizard, laid back against the broad face of a boulder despite the fact that the sun was barely up. The work had been harder even though this one was smaller and softer than the first one. The pallet had seemed clumsier and the path rockier. Maybe he was tired because this part was over. There had been so much planning. So many little details to attend to. Now with the first phase not only complete but also absurdly successful, he was quite let down. That was natural, of course. Any first year student of psychology or theology or physiology or any of the 'ologies' could tell you that. And hadn't he just known enough psychologists and psychiatrists and priests and ministers to make his head spin?

Recognizing this truth, allowing the second thoughts to run through his mind, he acknowledged the physical drain. Acknowledgment of a downturn made one stronger. Even God said that. The trick was to stay on track and keep his eyes on the prize. For exactly five days he would anticipate that which could not be anticipated. He would choose the time and place of communications. Then he would lead the world here, they would recognize him as a superior human being. Those women would owe their lives to him, and he would own them forever. Timing was crucial. He would have to be smarter than smart; he would be more than brilliant. He would not be surprised or blindsided ever again.

He sat up. He was not sorry he lingered through the dawn because now he was refreshed and ready to finish. The pallet was gone. Pity no one would ever know what it had taken to build it or the lengths he had gone to dispose of it The pieces were scattered so that they looked like a natural part of this God-forsaken place. Maybe he would leave a note to be opened upon his death so people would know how darn smart he had been. Maybe not. It would just be one more thing to do and his death was not imminent. There was plenty of time to pen just the right admission or, if it was more appropriate, confession. It was now time to run through his list even though he was sure he had left nothing undone.

Drinking water within reach.

Door closed and locked.

Guests immobilized and isolated.

Nothing of him left behind.

He was so pleased with it all. But there was so much more to come. Now, though, he had to go. He mustn't be late. He was sure the real show would begin today, and he wanted to be ready.

Burt's By the Beach Restaurant, Hermosa Beach

Faye Baxter was visiting her daughter in San Diego, but a quick phone call confirmed she had neither heard from Josie nor was she privy to her full caseload. When they had decided to share office space but not form a partnership, the two women respected one another's professional space. Faye hung up the phone promising to contact Archer or Hannah if she could think of anything that would help. The last thing Archer heard was that she would pray that everything would be okay.

Archer figured that couldn't hurt. He'd done some praying of his own the night before. When Josie still hadn't shown up by dawn, he knew he would have to rely on the resources he had at his fingertips. The first stop was Liz. He hadn't really expected her to jump on a missing persons' report, but at least she was on notice. The second step was to put out a call to Josie's closest friends in the community. If need be, Archer would expand that circle but for now it was Burt, Billy Zuni and Hannah.

Billy Zuni, Josie's favorite underage, pro bono client, didn't seem to have much to recommend him except a good heart. He surfed, was truant, and mooned after Hannah when she allowed it. He always had a lid, which was a crime, but would share his weed with anyone so people looked the other way. He was a poster boy for those lost to the sun, sand, surf and his single mom's neglect. Today his bright-white grin was washed away by a wave of concern.

Burt, proprietor of Burt's by the Beach, was Hermosa's innkeeper. It was Josie who made sure Burt got what he deserved after a motorcycle accident left him close to crippled. George, the night man, was tending bar, so Burt could pow-wow on the matter at hand. He was neither as glum as Billy, nor as intense as Archer. He would be the Greek chorus, the devil's advocate, the ear to bend, or the shoulder to cry on.

Hannah sat still as a statue. Her tendency toward self-protective defiance, self-mutilation and obsessive-compulsiveness would always be under the surface, but now all that was hidden behind a composed and beautiful face.

"Okay, then," Archer said. "The cops are going to play wait and see, so it's up to us to move things along. Burt? You've got half of Hermosa coming in here and they bring the rest of the South Bay with them. I'm thinking you can chat everyone up. Josie is well known in all the beach cities. Do you still have that picture I took of her at the ATV tournament? The one she made you take down?"

"That I do, my friend," Burt said, "and it's going right back up until she makes me take it down again."

Archer smiled. He had clicked the shutter just as Josie went for a spike. Baseball cap on backwards, she was every bit as graceful and cut as when she played volleyball for USC.

"Thanks, Burt." He turned his attention to Billy. "You do the same but I want you on the sand. Go down near the pier and stick there at night if you can. No panic, just conversation. You hear anything that sounds remotely interesting, it comes back to me. Any time. Day or night. Don't try to check it out on your own. You've got a cell, right?"

"Dude." Billy proudly pulled a state of the art phone out of his pocket. Archer didn't want to know where he got the bucks for it. "I'll stay up all night if I got to."

Archer gave him the upswing of his chin to let him know that he was grateful.

"I'll wait for Angie at Josie's office and get in to look at Josie's desk," he went on. "I think that about does it."

Chairs scraped. Burt squeezed Archer's shoulder as he went by. Billy hung his head and gave Archer his hand.

"Dude," he said again.

Archer shook it and pushed his chair back toward the table as they scattered. He was about to leave when he heard:

"What about me? What am I suppose to do?"

Archer hesitated. He hung his head.

Hannah.

CHAPTER 5

They cut up Twenty-Second Street and went up a block, then turned left. Hannah walked ten steps ahead of Archer. While she ranted, Archer focused on the hem of her jeans. They were frayed and so long they almost engulfed her gold shoes.

"What did you expect me to do? Sit home with Max and wait until something happened? You even gave Billy a job, for God sake!"

"Hannah. Hannah! Hey, slow down." Archer touched her shoulder. She pulled away. It was part reaction, but there was something personal in it, too. He backed off. "Right now it's about information, and people in Hermosa don't know you yet. No one's going to talk to you the way they would Billy or Burt or Faye."

"You didn't even ask me what I could do," Hannah snapped.

"You came to me for help." Archer threw up his hands. "If there was something you could do, I figured you would have told me."

"I didn't know what it was. Now I do."

"And I didn't know you'd been working for Josie," Archer cried. "And I'm sorry. I should have. Okay?"

Hannah stuck out her hip, the little ring piercing her bellybutton glinted and Archer tried not to look at it. If Hannah was his daughter she wouldn't be dressing like that, but she wasn't his daughter or Josie's and her outrage was that of a grown woman. Heaven help the man who hooked up with her in a few years. Since there was nothing he could say to appease her, Archer did the only thing he could think to do. He walked past her and up to the door of the bungalow that Faye Baxter had converted into a law office.

Hannah caught up with him and moved him aside with a look. She flipped her hair over her shoulder as she bent forward and announced triumphantly.

"I've got the key."

The San Diego Freeway, South

Damn. Damn.

The traffic was stopped. The freeway south should have been clear this early. He'd made the run five, maybe ten times in preparation, and nothing like this had ever happened. Nothing.

He raised his hand to hit the steering wheel to relieve some of the pressure that was building, but beside him was a car and in the car was a woman who was looking directly at him. He knew it even though her eyes were hidden behind her Jackie-O sunglasses. He couldn't blame her for being interested. There was something about him that drew attention. Any other day he would have reveled in her interest, but today he didn't want to be recognized so he simply draped his wrist over the wheel. Yep, draped that wrist, let his hand casually swing a little, and offered her a smile that said 'isn't this traffic a bitch?'

She turned her head as if she found him distasteful.

Traffic, he decided, wasn't the only thing that was a bitch.

He looked back to the four lanes of cars at a dead stop. He should have left right after everything was done. It was unseemly to gloat like a drunken frat boy after a messy conquest. That was a mistake he wouldn't make again. He shifted, starting to get nervous. If traffic didn't start moving soon, and the wheels he had set in motion started to turn, he was screwed. Game over before anyone really got to play.

He lifted his fingers and stretched them. He still wanted to hit something.

Law Offices of Faye Baxter & Josie Bates, Hermosa Beach

"When did you start working for Josie?"

"Three months ago." Hannah turned on the lights.

The place was exactly what someone would expect of a California bungalow converted to office space. The living room was a reception area with a desk for Angie. File cabinets were nestled into an alcove where a breakfront probably stood when this was still a home. A bay window looked out onto a porch. In front of that were two loveseats and a table with magazines arranged neatly on top. An arched doorway led to the old dining room, now the conference room. Archer knew what kind of meetings were conducted around that table: women stunned to find themselves part of a divorce action, parents looking for help with a troubled kid, small businesses being sued by legal spammers, property disputes, parking violations, wills. Every once in a while Josie's previous life – that of a high priced, high risk defense attorney – would rear its head, and draw her back into problems that were just a little bigger than this place. He thought those days were over. Now Archer had to assume something had come down the road that was a little more serious than a DUI.

"Come on." Hannah brushed by him and led the way down the hallway.

The three bedrooms had been turned into offices. Faye had knocked out a wall between the first two and created a modest suite for herself. Easy chairs were covered in muted fabrics, flowered pillows were plumped on a small couch and bucolic paintings hung on the walls along with a formal portrait of the man who had been both husband and partner. There were photographs of her daughter and grandchildren peppered over a credenza behind her desk. Clients who walked into this room felt like their mom would make everything right.

At the end of the hall Hannah flipped on another light, and Archer paused in the doorway of Josie's office. Clients who walked into this room would feel empowered. The desk was sleek and the color of sand, like the exposed wood floors. Behind the desk were white-shuttered windows and in front of it was a black and white rug. The painting on Josie's wall was white and blue. There were no family pictures on the desk, and the file cabinets were lined up in an alcove that used to be a closet. There was a coffee table and chairs to the left of her desk. Hannah opened the shutters. Late morning light flooded in.

"I checked her personal answering machine. Angie might have other messages but all that's on this one is a call about the South Bay Bar dinner and a man who only left his number. No message."

"What's his name?"

"It sounded like Cuwin Martin. He didn't spell it. I took the number and left the message on the answering machine. He was black," Hannah said.

"Are you profiling?" Archer asked.

"Just talking about a brother," Hannah said just to bug him.

Archer moved around the desk, but Hannah took Josie's chair before he could. He pulled up another.

"She wasn't in the last two days. She was down at the Torrance courthouse day before yesterday, and then yesterday she said she was going to the San Pedro women's center. I don't know where after that. I called them, and they didn't know either. They said she left around two. When she's not here I come in and file, input invoices into the computer, and other stuff."

Hannah pulled a file out of the desk drawer.

"This is where I keep the back message slips until the end of the month, and then I archive them and take out the oldest month. There's supposed to be six months of messages in here all the time, but I haven't been here long enough to do that yet. Her calendar is on the computer and it's synced with her phone."

"Do you save the phone records?"

"Yes." Hannah answered. "But it won't have the last three weeks."

"I'll call the phone company," Archer said.

"I can get it online. I have her password."

"Okay." Archer was going to point out that Tug-o-War was for picnics, but he held his tongue. "What's in the boxes?"

"Old case files. She had me bring them from storage. She has a lot of stuff in storage."

"She defended a lot of rich scumbags before she came to her senses." Archer muttered as he scooted over to the boxes and opened them.

"Do you ever say anything nice?" Hannah asked.

"Yeah."

Archer left it at that, but was relieved when he caught sight of Hannah's slight smile. His relief turned to remorse when he opened the first box and saw the files were People v. Hannah Sheraton. He put the lid back on and pushed the box aside. Josie was probably boning up for the custody hearing in a few days. The scumbag comment had definitely been uncalled for. He opened the next one and pulled the original filing. The date showed it was a case Josie worked on long before they knew one another.

"Want to do the calendar, messages or her notes first?"

Archer abandoned the file search and turned back to the desk. Hannah was putting the messages into neat piles, trying to make them evenly stacked.

"These are just personal things, so we can probably throw them away."

"Don't do that." Archer took one of the slips.

"It's from the plumber," Hannah objected.

"You never know." Archer took the rest of them and fanned the pieces of paper. "Here. Carpet cleaner. He could be on parole. The plumber could have a beef about compensation. Maybe one of them saw something or someone that didn't look right. It's all worth looking at even though it might not be a priority. There's another from the shop where she takes her Jeep. I know those folks. Unless they've had some personnel change I won't spend too much time on them. Still, they might know something about the condition of the Jeep. What else do you have?"

Hannah slid a few more messages his way.

"These are ones from clients or potential clients. Mr. Horton is a potential new client. He asked for an appointment. Abby Wingate has a third DUI. She was really scared when she came in to see Josie. We can put her in the pile with the plumber."

Archer took those slips and put them in the low priority stack. Hannah was surprised but Archer paid no attention. When she was right, she was right.

"Okay. Judge Kramer called."

"When was that?" Archer asked.

"A week ago."

"I thought he retired when the South Bay courthouse closed. Did he say what he wanted?"

"No. Maybe they just like to get together."

"Maybe."

Archer put that message aside and then fingered the first slip in that pile.

"What do you know about this one? Horton."

"Nothing. But he said it wasn't urgent."

"Is that it?"

"No, a guy named Peter Siddon called. He didn't leave a message. He never does. He sounds creepy. Angie might know more." She handed the yellow slip to Archer who glanced at it.

"This guy is in the high desert," Archer mused. "When was the first time he called?"

"About three weeks ago, but I don't know if Josie talked to him."

"Okay," Archer muttered and put it with those he would follow up on. He was reaching for the next pink slip when his phone rang. He was quick on the draw and quicker still to hang up.

"They found Josie's car."

CHAPTER 6

An Outbuilding in the California Mountains

Someone was behind her. Josie's toes touched an ankle and then a narrow foot. A woman's foot. Sleep came again. Josie didn't fight it. At least she wasn't alone.

Peter Siddon's Home, California's High Desert

Peter Siddon pulled into his garage, turned off the ignition, and let his hands fall to his sides. He didn't move when the door closed behind him. He didn't look at his wife when she poked her head out of the door that led to the kitchen. He didn't acknowledge his five-year-old son pounding on the car door, calling for him to play.

Play wasn't what he felt like doing. What he felt like doing was sinful and he felt like doing it to Josie Bates. His mind was always on Josie Bates, and he wished he could get her out of there. She was the one who caused all this misery, and all he wanted her to do was admit it.

He rested his head on the back of the seat. He loved this crappy car and now he would lose it even though he only had two more payments to make. He loved his wife, but he'd probably lose her too now that he'd screwed up her life. He didn't know what to do. He sniffed. Tears were coming again. He didn't want his kid to see his dad cry, and he didn't want to endure his wife's defeated silence. He needed to talk to someone.

Picking up his cell, he dialed a number.

"I need help. I need to talk," he said.

In the next minute, his wife picked up their boy to keep him from running after his dad. The garage door was raised again, and Peter Siddon was speeding away from them. His wife looked after him and then went back to the kitchen, weary of his demons and his obsession with that other woman, the one who he would kill if he ever got his hands on her. Well, maybe not kill, but he would do something really bad if he got the chance.

The Pier, Redondo Beach

Archer pulled into the parking lot of the Blue Fin Grill and stopped on the far side of the black and white. The driver side door was open and there were two cops inside. It was the guy behind the wheel who got out and greeted Archer.

"Sorry we couldn't do anything," he shrugged along with his apology. "Hermosa squawked for us to keep a look out, but we didn't want to own it."

"No worries. I appreciate the effort." Archer cast a look at Josie's Jeep. "Is this the way you found it? No other cars around, nothing on the ground."

"What you see is what you get."

When the uniforms took their leave, Archer leaned against his screaming-yellow Hummer, cast an objective eye on Josie's Jeep, and resisted the urge to tear it apart looking for clues as to her whereabouts.

The black vehicle was parked in the third row, second slot from the south entrance to the restaurant lot and one space over from the steps that led down to the lower level of the old pier complex. Down there, working boats were moored to a horse-shoe shaped dock that was flanked by an outdoor restaurant, a sad excuse for an arcade, and a bunch of shops that sold kites and whoopee cushions to the tourists who managed to find their way down. Quality Seafood, the outdoor restaurant, served up lunches on Styrofoam plates, had ice beds for the catch of the day and bubbling tanks where lobsters crawled all over each other, their rubber-banded claws useless in their fight to survive.

To Archer's right was a complex designed to look like a New England fishing village. It housed the now boarded up courthouse and still functioning professional offices. More right of that were the new Redondo Beach pier, the breakwater and a stretch of beach that wasn't the nicest. A lot of rough people went to that beach after hours: drunks from pier bars, inner city types looking to cool off, gang members and drug dealers. Josie could have run into a bunch of problems down there.

Behind him was the Blue Fin Grill. Drinks were expensive, the menu predictable and the waiters distracted. Josie might have met someone there, but it wouldn't have been a friend. Friends went to Burt's or Scotty's or the Mermaid. There were lawyers, accountants and insurance offices in the small complex. She could have parked in the Blue Fin lot, walked over there and done what? He turned his attention back to the Jeep.

The ragtop was down. The windows were up. That meant it had been left while the sun still shined. Josie always closed up the car after dark, even if she garaged it. Whatever happened, it happened in the open and after three o'clock if he added in drive time to her departure from the shelter in San Pedro. Given that time frame, and the fact that it was a weekday, it would have been dead quiet around here.

"Okay, Jo, here we go. By the book."

Archer opened the back of the Hummer. He was a cop again, a cop with a camera. The fact that he loved Josie might drive him, but it wouldn't overrule his common sense. He was trying to decide between the digital or film camera when he heard:

"Hey! Archer!"

His head snapped up. He smiled a real and relieved smile sure that Josie would come sauntering toward him. His smile faded when he saw Liz Driscoll.

"Ask and you shall receive, huh?" Liz came to a halt beside him, looked at the Jeep and gave him a little shoulder bump to underscore how cool she was.

"Yeah." Archer opted for the digital camera even though he preferred to use film.

"Don't go overboard thanking me for sticking my neck out." She grinned, obviously unconcerned about her neck or much of anything else. "Brought you a present, bucko."

Evidence bags. Sweet. Archer stuffed them in his pocket without saying a word and started to circle the Jeep.

"You're welcome," she quipped and dogged his steps.

Both of them looked for signs of foul play. If they found it, Liz would make this an official missing person's case; if they didn't, Josie was just another grownup who wasn't where other people thought she was supposed to be.

An early drinker pulled into the parking lot and wanted to know if the Jeep was for sale and if Archer would throw Liz into the deal. A few chosen words from Liz – one of which was police – and the man drove on and parked at the far end of the lot. Archer looked after him, taking a minute to consider that beauty was definitely in the eye of the beholder. He gave up his musing when Liz dropped to her knees, flattened herself on her back, and checked under the chassis. She was up again a second later, brushing herself off.

"Nada."

Archer was leaning over the driver's seat when he said: "No keys. Parking brake on."

Click. Click. Click

He walked around the car and opened the passenger door, careful to cover his hand with his shirt. He snapped a few more pictures of nothing. Not even a gum wrapper on the floor.

Click. Click.

Running shoes in the back. A couple bottles of water. A jacket. All of this was standard emergency fare for Josie. She kept those things in a box next to chains and a jumper cable.

Click.

Archer paused when he saw Josie's baseball cap. The pain hit him in the gut. It took a second to put it in its place, and then he looked past the hat to the roll bar, the wheels, the tires.

Click. Click. Click.

He was shooting zilch: no dirt, leaves, new scratches or scrapes. He took five more pictures because he hoped he was just missing the one thing that would set him on the right road. The paint gleamed. The Jeep was recently washed. That could be good news or bad. Good news because there would be fewer fingerprints to check, bad news because everything would have been cleaned out of the inside. He made a note to visit the carwash. Archer slid on to the passenger seat, covered his hand again with his shirt, opened the glove box, and sat still as a statue as he peered inside.

"Archer?" Liz called. "Hey, Archer. What have you got?"

He raised those dark eyes of his, his boxer's face expressionless. He slid out of the car.

"Nothing."

"Just as well. Means we can be pretty sure she was okay while she was in the car," Liz said.

"But someone could have taken her outside of it," Archer countered.

"Yeah," Liz said. "Or she's on a bender."

"Josie doesn't drink that way."

"Everybody drinks sometime." Liz's grin indicated she knew that from personal experience. "I don't know Josie all that well, but I'd say she has a hard time getting on with her life. She's always being side tracked by one thing or another. You know, like saving the world, lifting up the downtrodden. Not like you and me."

Archer almost laughed at how off-base Liz Driscoll was. He carried every pain, every joy, and every uncertainty with him every damn day. He didn't share any of it unless someone got real close, and Josie was about as close as anyone had got to him in his whole life. Liz mistook his silence for petulance and tried again to engage him.

"I looked up the Rayburn trial. That woman? Linda Rayburn? She almost killed Josie, didn't she? And now Josie's guardian for a killer's kid."

"Is there a point, Driscoll?"

"Point being, the attack was bad."

"Broken ribs. Shiner. Cracked cheekbone. Dislocated arm." Archer filled in the laundry list he knew was coming.

"Head injury?" Liz hooked her thumbs in her belt and talked slow, but he didn't need the lead.

"I see where you're going, but no," Archer shook his head. "Clean bill of health."

"Yeah, but there was the McCreary thing, too. He had her under those waves a good long time. How long did she spend in the hospital after that?"

"Two days. Totally cleared by every doctor who saw her. Josie's an athlete. She's strong."

"That doesn't rule out residual damage. Blood clot. Something," Liz went on.

"I called Torrance Memorial and Little Company of Mary hospital this morning. No one matching her description was brought to emergency."

"Maybe she couldn't get to a hospital. Maybe she hasn't been found." Liz kept at the argument while Archer raised his camera and angled one from the passenger to the driver's side. Liz shut the driver's door to give him a clean shot, still talking as she came around beside him. "On the off chance something's going down, though, I'll have this baby towed."

"It's Redondo's jurisdiction," Archer pointed out.

"Redondo PD has no reason to take it. You want the restaurant to tow it? Let it sit in a lot and leave possible evidence unprotected?"

Archer's lips tipped. He cast a sidelong glance. "I thought there wasn't anything to be worried about."

"Just helping a friend, and protecting my sweet little butt in case there is. Don't want you suing the city because I was derelict."

Liz's wide grin transformed her face. That pug nose of hers looked way cute and the wrap-around glasses didn't look so ominous. No matter how hard she tried, though, she wasn't going to get Archer to smile back. He just wasn't that kind of guy. Archer snapped one more picture, grateful that the detective was getting a hinky feeling about this too. He dropped the camera to his side and gave Liz's arm a squeeze.

"Thanks, Liz. I'll wait for the truck. You go on and save Hermosa from itself."

She gave him a friendly slap on the rear and a 'hang in there' as she took her leave. Archer watched her go. They had been acquainted a long time but had never really gotten to know one another. Liz Driscoll, he thought, just wasn't the kind of woman who got to know anyone really well. She probably liked it that way. Then Archer just didn't think of her at all.

Leaning against the Hummer, running through the images on the camera, he formed a strategy for the next twenty-four hours: check the offices in the adjacent complex, check with the folks at the Blue Fin Grill, follow up on everyone who had contact with Josie in the last week, get a lock on her cell from the provider, get these pictures to someone who could analyze them properly. His planning was interrupted when the tow truck lumbered into the lot. The guy didn't say a word as he hitched the car with the winch. Archer stood aside as the Jeep was raised.

"Whoa!" Archer called to the driver. Then he hollered 'hold it' when it didn't stop.

Finally, the winch shut down, suspending the Jeep at a forty-degree angle. Liz hadn't shut the driver's side door tight and it was swinging. As Archer caught it, he saw the floor mat had shifted and was wedged between the door and floor. He started to adjust it but stopped. A piece of paper had been exposed when the mat shifted.

Heart pounding, Archer held the door against his backside and photographed what he had found. The color was off-white and the stock was cheap. Picking it up in his fingertips, Archer was surprised to see that it was smaller than he originally thought it would be. Closer inspection showed the paper had been cut, so somewhere there was a matching piece. It could be stationery, but he doubted it.

Archer backed away, let the door of the Jeep slam shut, and strode to the Hummer. Swinging the back door open, he put the piece of paper on the bed of the vehicle and dug two pairs of tweezers out of his camera bag. Working carefully, Archer manipulated it. There was nothing on the back and only the printing on the front. He tipped it, and saw there were no watermarks. There was absolutely nothing interesting about the paper. What was written on it, however, was intriguing.

"Hey! You done, man? I got a schedule."

Archer looked from the impatient driver to the Jeep. "Yeah, I'm done here."

Putting the paper in the plasticine envelope Liz had given him, Archer took out a Sharpie and noted the specifics of the find on the bag. The bag went into the breast pocket of his shirt as he climbed behind the wheel of the Hummer, pulled out his phone, connected with the Internet and started to type.

A second later, the cell snapped shut and the yellow Hummer was speeding down Pacific Coast Highway. The first stop wasn't far.

CHAPTER 7

An Outbuilding in the California Mountains

It was hard for Josie to swallow and harder still to open her eyes. It was impossible to move her hands, but she could move her legs if she concentrated. That was good because it meant those legs of hers were still attached to her body. And her arms were still there because her cheek brushed against her bicep when she jerked out of whatever sickness had come upon her. She could wiggle her fingers. Her wrists burned. She didn't feel afraid because sleep came and went, taking with it all opportunity to panic. She was addled. She was forgetful. At least she was awake enough and lucid enough to register the water bottle.

With great effort, she raised her head. Behind her eyes there was an explosion of light and pain. Her head fell and she landed cheek down in the dirt. She was drooling. That struck her as funny. Max drooled.

Max…

He was…

Who was Max?

Josie threw her head up, balanced her cheek between her upper arm and shoulder, craned her neck and finally managed to get her mouth on the sport top of the water bottle. Clamping her teeth down, she tilted it and dragged it closer. Counting to three, she threw up the bottle. Once. Twice. The third time was the charm, and she balanced the bottle above her. Water flowed. She gulped, and choked and the heavy bottle fell away. Using every ounce of energy, Josie kept her teeth around the top. Once more she whipped it up. The water went down her throat, and she drank like she had never tasted water before.

A Business Complex, Manhattan Beach

Archer walked toward the elegantly appointed building in an office complex peppered with identically well-appointed buildings. Each of the ten three-story structures was set at an angle and separated by well-established greenery: tall trees, lush bushes, and dense ground cover. Archer threaded through it all on a wide stone walk, noting strategically placed pools of water and benches. The only things that set the structures apart were letter designators high up near the roofline. He passed building A and B and F giving no thought as to why F came after B.

Spotting J, his step quickened as he took the three low-rise steps that led him to J's double glass doors. Archer could see straight through to a back door that led to a garden and a parking lot. In the space between the two, Archer saw an elevator, two facing couches and a coffee table with a tabletop fountain. There was a chrome-framed legend board. He pulled the heavy door open and stepped through.

The interior was serene and silent save for the little bubbling fountain. The edge of his lips tipped when he saw that someone had put a penny in the water. They were either desperate for a miracle, or their dreams were as small as the place they left their wishes. Out back there were a couple of cars in the lot: a pearl-white SUV that had seen better days, an old Toyota, two Mercedes and a Lexus. The Mercedes and the Lexus were in reserved spaces and both were black. The Toyota needed a wash.

Satisfied with the manageable environment, Archer ignored the elevators and took the emergency stairs two at a time. Exiting the second floor, he paused to get the lay of the land. Four doors. Discrete nameplates. No windows. Knowing he would see any challenge before it became a problem, Archer made his way down the hall, counting off the tenants as he went.

Brahms. General Surgery.

Cochran. DDS.

Fistonich. Gynecology.

The door of Dr. Fistonich's office opened. Archer stepped aside as a woman the size of a barn waddled into the hall. He nodded; she flashed him a beatific smile. He nodded again, flustered as only a childless man can be when faced with a woman in the throes of hormonal bliss. When the pregnant lady was well inside the elevator, Archer moved on and found what he wanted.

Young. Daniel P. Psychiatry.

Archer opened that door.

A young woman with shoulder-length, light brown hair smiled at Archer with practiced sincerity and rehearsed serenity. She spoke with a voice modulated to a perfect, peaceful pitch.

"Hello there."

Archer took a second to admire her and her surroundings. In this doctor's office there was no room divider with a sliding, frosted glass window, no clipboard for him to fill out with his name, time of appointment and his insurance information. There were no chairs lined up against the wall or old magazines to leaf through. This place was a haven for the weary, the wounded, and the worried.

Three of the walls were painted a mole color with an accent of brick red on the fourth. On that wall hung a huge portrait of a woman with moist eyes and expressive lips. A tear of white paint trickled down her cheek to her bare shoulder. Her lips were matte, her eyes sparkled with a trick of technique that made it seem as if she was daring the viewer to look closer and see inside her. Over a couch of saddle leather hung antique baskets and what appeared to be an ancient papoose. There was a walnut table cut from a giant burl. Music played. He couldn't identify it but it soothed him as intended. And then there was the receptionist, though he doubted she considered herself such.

She was young but not too young; pretty but not gorgeous; interesting without being intimidating. She sat behind a delicate desk with a carved apron that hid all but the lower sweep of her gorgeous gams. Her shoes were expensive, her posture was perfect and Archer imagined she had once been a dancer who had wisely stopped chasing the dream and settled for a regular paycheck. Her hair was stick straight and hung past her shoulders; severe bangs covered her brows so all he saw were those two blue eyes encapsulated by kohl smudges. Archer glanced at the painting. Those eyes of hers were as daring as those of the woman in the picture. Doctor Young had very specific taste in women.

"May I help you?" She smiled wider, enticing Archer's attention away from the artwork. The real thing, she seemed to intimate, was far more interesting.

Archer looked just in time to see her right hand fall gracefully to her lap. Best guess: a panic button was wired somewhere underneath. His hesitation had made her cautious, but her instincts were good. She gauged that Archer was only the possibility of a threat.

"I need to see Dr. Young," he said.

"Dr. Young sees new patients on Wednesday."

"I'm not a patient." Archer pulled out a card and put it in front of her. That errant hand reappeared. She held the card in both hands. Her nails were clipped short, filed square and buffed to a sheen. Her lips moved slightly as she read and her nude lipstick sparkled. She looked charming until she stopped smiling.

"I'm sorry, the doctor doesn't partner with private investigators. I could recommend some of his colleagues who do." She tried to hand the card back, but when Archer made no move to take it she put it aside like a Vegas dealer knowing the house would win.

"This is a personal matter."

"I see." She pulled a pad of paper out of a drawer and picked up a Mont Blanc pen. "If you could give me an idea of what this is about, please."

"I'm looking for Josie Bates."

The receptionist jotted the name. She looked up from underneath those incredibly sexy bangs.

"I'll get this to the doctor, but I doubt he can help. The name doesn't ring a bell."

"I guess I wasn't clear. I need to know if Young knows Josie Bates, not you."

Her lips pulled together in an expression of displeasure. Archer imagined many a man had seen that look at an inopportune moment.

"I would know if Doctor Young knew her. I handle all of Dr. Young's business – including his personal business."

"I still need to talk to him. I'll take a phone number. Let me know where he's playing golf or having dinner, and I'm out of here," Archer persisted.

"The best I can do is to give the doctor your card. I've put her name on the back, but if you could be more specific about the information you're looking for it will speed up the process. Otherwise, I'll have to ask you to make an appointment like everyone else."

She had the card again, and the pen was poised. It was Archer's call, and he made it.

"You can ask all you want, but I'm not leaving without a way to contact Doctor Young. This woman is missing, and I have reason to believe that he knows something about it." Archer leaned toward her. "The woman who is missing is such a good friend that I will do anything I need to do to talk to the doctor sooner rather than later."

To her credit, the receptionist didn't flinch. Either Young paid her a heck of a salary or something about the good doc made her willing to fight tooth and nail to protect him. Or, maybe she was like Josie and objected to anyone telling her what to do. Archer pushed a little harder. He pointed to the sofa.

"I can sit there and wait. I'll come back tomorrow and the next day and sit there until I get what I want."

Two high spots of color stained the young woman's cheeks. Before Archer could finish telling her how miserable he was going to make her life, she reached for the phone. Archer knee-jerked and put his big hand over hers, smacking the receiver into the cradle.

"This is no joke," he growled.

"And that is assault," she shot back.

Archer twitched. He let go of her hand, more shaken than she by his overreaction. That had never happened before, so he backed off as best he could.

"We're in LAPD jurisdiction, and the only thing I've threatened you with is malicious waiting. It would be easier just to tell me where Young is."

Obviously, he wasn't hitting the right notes because the woman's hand was under the desk again. Archer looked over his shoulder expecting security to come through the door behind him, but it was the door behind her that opened instead. Archer's head whipped around again.

"What's going on out here, Gay?"

There in the doorway was the man Archer had come to see. He knew it in his bones and was across the room in three strides, his anxiety boiling over. Young watched him come, but all Archer saw was Hannah's frightened eyes and Liz Driscoll's sharp ones and Josie's beautiful ones. He felt again the sinking sense he had as dawn broke over Hermosa and Josie hadn't come home. He felt the loneliness in the night silence as he waited for a phone to ring, or a door to open, or a step to sound. All of that had been corralled and fenced in and managed until this moment. Now the alarm roiled and mixed with anger and impotency to create an explosion that sent emotional shrapnel toward the guy standing in the doorway – the one who looked like he put talcum powder on his balls and cleaned his jackets with a horsehair brush. Without thinking, without meaning to, Archer pushed him into the doorjamb and grabbed his shoulders.

"What do you know about Josie Bates?"

CHAPTER 8

An Outbuilding in the California Mountains

Josie dreamed of sex: satisfying, wet, affectionate sex with a man who loved her. She moaned sorrowfully. She couldn't remember his name; she couldn't see his face. She wanted to wake up in his arms and ask who he was.

Office of Dr. Daniel Young, Manhattan Beach

"Dr. Young's office. Hurry!"

Archer heard the receptionist call, but he couldn't stop himself. He pushed harder against the man, oddly aware that the doctor's handsome face never registered fear. No, that wasn't it. Young wasn't surprised, but that probably came with a psychiatrist's territory. That analysis was fleeting as Archer focused on the physical. Daniel Young matched Archer in height but not bulk. Lean and narrow at the hip and waist, the man was fit and moved as smoothly as he spoke.

"Let me go. Do it now." There was a moment, a beat. Young notched his head to the left, and his lips came closer to Archer's ear. "Now, if you don't mind."

Archer blinked. The fingers clutching the man's arms relaxed, but his body was as rigid as rebar. He couldn't seem to move, to take that one step away that would bring some sanity back to the moment. Then he heard the sound of a gun being readied to fire.

"Let him go or I'll shoot."

Keeping hold of Daniel Young, Archer looked over his shoulder and saw a uniformed security guard. He was way too old to be carrying a weapon and that, more than anything, made Archer nervous. Beads of sweat dotted the old man's hairline, but to his credit his hand was steady. The woman with the bangs and the gams sat back in her chair, and put her hands flat on the desk, alert, ready to push off at a moment's notice. She chanced a look at Daniel.

"Dr. Young? What are you…?"

"I should have told you I was here."

Archer barely heard him. He and the guard had eyes only for each other.

"Let me go," Young said again as he put his hands over Archer's and eased them away.

Archer stepped back, in control of nothing. Daniel Young gave Archer's shoulder a pat and moved on. Any other man wouldn't have wanted his back to Archer, but this guy had probably seen a lot of crazies come through his door. Archer was just one more. Young had the security guard's shoulder a second later.

"Shooting a man is never a first option, is it Frank? Let's put that back where it belongs."

Syllables – not words – lingered in the back of the doctor's throat as if they had a mind of their own. His hand went to the barrel of the gun, and like magic it was pointed to the floor.

"I don't know, doc." The security guard's voice quavered.

"I'm good," Archer muttered, embarrassed to find himself in this position.

"See, Frank?" Daniel Young chuckled softly. "Lots of folks with big problems in this world, don't you know? Some are bigger than others, I dare say, but all important to the people who have them."

Frank wasn't convinced, but holstered the gun as Daniel turned him toward the door. "Do you want me to call the cops?"

"Do you think you should, Frank?" The old man shook his head slightly while he looked at the doctor for corroboration. "Ah, I didn't think so either, but it's always good to have an expert weigh in. Remember when I told you how my patients sometimes get upset, and we need to use all of our best judgment about how we handle situations like this?"

"He's a patient?" Frank asked in a hoarse whisper.

"Not yet," Daniel answered, more for Archer's benefit than Frank's. "But stay close. You'll know what to do if either Gay or I call, won't you?"

Archer rolled his eyes. What crap. Even in his darkest hours, Archer would have recognized this for what it was: Therapy 101. Frank was lapping it up like a puppy; happy to be relieved of responsibility while being led to believe he was calling the shots. What really ticked Archer off was that this had all been so unnecessary. All the receptionist had to do was call her boss out, Archer would have the information he needed and been on his way. No harm, no foul, but nothing was ever simple. When the door closed, Young walked to the receptionist who put Archer's card in his outstretched hand.

"Mr. Archer," he muttered.

"Just Archer," came the correction. It didn't surprise Daniel Young. Archer was a simple name for a simple man.

"Gay, why don't you go on down to the coffee shop and take a break." Daniel Young took a bill out of his pocket. She stood up and Archer took the time to notice that her skirt was shorter than he thought and her legs better than he had imagined. She rounded the desk and stood shoulder-to-shoulder with her boss. Her now-bitchy eyes were still trained on Archer as she spoke to Daniel.

"Are you going to be okay?"

"Give me a break," Archer muttered.

"Off you go," Young directed, and out she went.

When the door closed, Daniel Young turned and smiled. "That was quite an entrance. I can't wait to see what's next."

CHAPTER 9

An Outbuilding in the California Mountains

When Josie Bates was thirteen years and ten days old she woke up at two forty-one in the morning. She did not wake with a start or in fear. She could not identify a noise that had disturbed her sleep, yet suddenly she was wide-eyed, staring into the darkness of her room. Her heart pounded in her chest, and she knew that whatever was wrong was very, very bad.

Josie sniffed but smelled nothing. She touched her brow and the shirt she slept in. Both were sticky with sweat despite the old fan her mother had put in the corner of her room. She listened, but the silence was deafening. She turned to her side, pushed up, put her feet over the edge of the bed and got up.

Josie wanted her father, but he was gone to Asia. He wore a uniform and killed people. Even at thirteen she understood what he did and why he did it. Her mother did not.

Carefully, she opened the door of her bedroom and slipped out into the narrow hall. The living room was to her left. The front door was closed and the furniture was still in place. Like all the other houses on the base, the kitchen was beyond that. Her mother's room was eight steps away. Josie took the first step and the second. She managed two more but went no further. Much as she wanted to open that door and reassure herself that the bad thing was not behind it, she could not. She was not as brave then as the woman she would become.

Josie went back to her room, stripped the covers off her narrow bed, lay down on her back and threw her arm over her eyes. She breathed fast through her nose, pulled her lips together tight, and sweated through every pore. That night she felt every inch of thirteen years: too old to be so afraid of nothing, too young not to be. She turned on her side, crooked her knees, folded her hands beneath her cheek, and closed her eyes thinking if she made herself small enough and didn't look at anything she would not die of fright.

The next morning, Josie got up and her mother was gone. No word. No note. No sign that she had ever been there. At thirteen, Josie Bates was abandoned, alone and afraid in a hot little house in Texas.

The primal survival instinct that woke her that night, the same cloying, smothering heat she had experienced, woke her once more. She was no longer a child and she was not in Texas, yet she was in a place that felt as narrow as her childhood bed. This time she woke not with a start, but with a sudden awareness that her eyes were open and she was conscious. In front of her was a wall constructed of cement bricks. Best guess it was a little over eight feet tall. She was six. There was a brick missing up near the top.

Her chin lowered to her chest. She could see her knees. Her khakis were dirty and torn. She was shoeless. She could move her legs but they were weak. Raising her head as best she could, Josie saw that the wall at the end was about ten inches longer than she was. Okay. The place was almost seven feet long, eight feet high, maybe five feet across. It was hot and airless.

Her neck wobbled, her head crashed down. She saw stars and tasted dirt. She shook it off and looked up at the stake in the ground and the intricate knots that bound her wrists to it. The wall above her head was six inches away.

Suddenly, Josie's body jackknifed. Her mouth opened wide, her gut twisted as she dry heaved, gagging on nothing. Once, twice, three times her neck extended, her stomach muscles tightened, her head swam, her brain crumbled. The sound she made was revolting. She was nothing but a reactive shell. One more time her intestines grabbed, pushed and threw her back against her restraints. When the spasm was over, she was gasping for breath, exhausted and sweating like a pig. Her eyes closed, but she was determined not to let go of the moment. When she opened them again she saw the water bottle. Before she could maneuver to reach it, the woman behind her moved.

Daniel Young's Office, Manhattan Beach

Daniel Young's inner sanctum was a curiosity. At first glance it appeared to be a comfortable place, but Archer wasn't comfortable. It had nothing to do with his anxiety and everything to do with the furniture.

The couch against one wall was not the regulation six feet nor was it as small as a loveseat. A petite woman could lie on it with ease, but a man Archer's size could not. But if a small woman sat on the couch, her legs would dangle over the side with her feet unable to touch the floor. It was low enough that if a large man sat on it his knees would be up to his chin.

There were a couple of wingback chairs – nobody was ever comfortable in a wingback chair – and tables that weren't close enough to the furniture to be of use. Daniel Young's desk was a table that was positioned kitty-corner, facing neither couch nor chairs. The walls were painted a restful sage color, but the artwork looked like giant Rorschach tests.

Diagnosis: passive aggressive decorating that seemed so out of character for the man himself. He was relaxed and in control and concerned for Archer despite his meltdown. Archer put him in his early fifties, yet he could be ten years younger or ten years older. He had that square-jawed look of an adventurer; still Archer doubted he lifted his own suitcase when he traveled. His skin was tanned but nearly seamless. It was a toss-up whether he had good genes, an excellent plastic surgeon or an amazing dermatologist. Over near the door, which Archer assumed led to a bathroom, was a vanity wall of framed photographs and magazine covers. Young motioned to the chair in front of the desk, but Archer wandered toward the pictures. Daniel Young had made the cover of L.A. Magazine twice but the covers were old. Archer had no way of telling if the photos at celeb events were dated, but one thing was for sure: Young liked beautiful women and the beautiful women in the photos looked adoringly at him. Archer stepped closer. This kind of PR was usually reserved for Beverly Hills types, not a doctor in Manhattan Beach. His eyes went to a picture because it was the only one where the woman with Young wasn't as impressed as –

"I do remember Josie Bates. I haven't seen her in years, but I assume you think I have," Daniel Young began conversationally.

Archer turned just in time to see Daniel ease himself into a burgundy leather chair replete with manly hobnails.

"I don't know what I think, but I'll show you what I've got."

Archer dug in his pocket for the plastic bag, walked across the room and put it on the table. Young positioned it exactly in front of him, leaned over it dutifully, and took it in. When he was done, Daniel Young pushed the envelope over the table and sat back.

"Someone has very nice printing, but I can't say the artwork is too impressive."

Archer glanced at the paper. Names were neatly printed in two columns. Beside each were tiny avatars. Next to Daniel Young's name someone had drawn something that looked like a donkey.

"Do you recognize any other names on that list?" Archer took back the evidence bag.

"Almost everyone," Daniel answered. "It's a list of the people who were involved in the Xavier Hernandez trial."

"I found this under the mat in Josie's car."

"I dread to think what's under the mat in my car," Daniel countered.

"Her car was abandoned in a parking lot in Redondo Beach, and she hasn't been seen since yesterday afternoon."

"Then shouldn't you be talking to the police?"

"I already did. Missing adults aren't a priority," Archer said.

"Well, then, I don't know how I can help."

"I don't either." Archer grabbed the back of the chair, hung his head. He didn't know what he expected when he headed here.

"She was a very attractive woman; a very aggressive lawyer," Daniel said. Archer looked up. The other man smiled sympathetically. "I can understand why you're upset if you have a relationship with her. I never did understand, though, how she could defend Hernandez.

Then again, I don't understand how many defense attorneys can do what they do when guilt is so obvious."

Archer walked around the chair and stopped to lean against the cushioned arm.

"What did you have to do with it?" he asked.

"I examined Hernandez."

"A for-hire witness, huh?"

"An expert, yes," Daniel Young responded. "I assume you don't think much of that kind of testimony."

"I think the work is easy, the pay is good and if you're not talking hard science you can pretty much tailor your testimony for whichever side pays the bill," Archer noted.

"True," Daniel admitted. "That's why the jury has to be completely convinced of an expert's ethical and intellectual value. My analysis of Hernandez was impeccable, but the day was won by Ms. Bates."

"Then I guess you weren't expert enough if Josie got the guy off," Archer suggested.

"One clear and rational voice does not a defense make," Daniel pointed out. "I would never be so arrogant as to think that. And, to the point, she didn't get him off. There was no doubt he was guilty. Josie Bates' brilliance lay in maneuvering to argue the best-case scenario. Xavier Hernandez was charged with two counts of first-degree murder. The prosecutor wanted to add special circumstances. Ms. Bates got the first charge dropped completely during the preliminary hearing, and she convinced the judge to offer jury instructions that allowed for a finding of second degree murder on the second count."

"There had to be a basis." Archer pressed for more information as he moved the chair slightly and sat down.

"Technically there was, but I've never been a fan of technicalities. You might say, I abhor them," Daniel Young said. "I tried to convince the prosecutor to fight, but he was confident he could convict on first degree murder. He didn't account for the fact that jurors are human. Many find it difficult to impose the harshest sentence when another option is available."

Archer resisted the urge to point out that the prosecutor had the law degree, but he also had to give Young credit for not blaming the lawyer completely. Archer had seen enough jurors swayed by the oddest of sympathies: a pretty face, a sad childhood, or an old mother sitting in the spectator gallery. Archer never understood it, but then it wasn't his job to worry about things like that. His job was black and white: investigate, click the puzzle pieces in place, point the finished piece at the jury and hope they weren't idiots.

"Do you remember the prosecutor's name?" Archer asked.

"Rothenberg, I think," Daniel said offhandedly. "I doubt he's still with the D.A.'s office. I don't think he was cut out for public service. Is his name on that list?"

Archer shook his head, "No. I've got a Paul Rothskill listed. You sure the prosecutor was Rothenberg?"

"Positive," Young began only to pause. "Wait. Wait. Rothskill was the young man who had been with the two victims before they were abducted."

"Erika Gardener?" Archer ticked off.

"A reporter. Very attractive."

"Donald Maas?" Archer said.

"He was the judge."

"Cuwin Martin?" Archer asked. "Peter Siddon?"

Daniel Young's brows pulled together. He leaned forward and reached for the paper. "Those names aren't on the list."

Archer smiled held up the see-through envelope. "Good memory. They aren't."

"I have an exceptional memory, if I do say so myself. It's long and very clear. Pity those who underestimate it," Daniel said, seeming a little peeved at Archer's game. "Why ask me about those two?"

"They called Josie's office recently. I figured it couldn't hurt to see what you knew."

Daniel Young tented his fingers and tapped them against his chin. He dropped them when he saw Archer staring.

"Where was her car found?"

"In the parking lot of the Blue Fin Grill. Redondo Beach," Archer answered.

"My bike club was by there yesterday. That's the one thing the beach cities did well. The bike path from Santa Monica to Palos Verdes is amazing, don't you think?"

Archer's chest tightened. The guy didn't just look GQ, he lived it. The doctor was part of the cycling elite that terrorized Southern California. They rode in packs, dressed in matching Spandex, and wore helmets that made them look like raptors. The serious male riders shaved their legs to cut down on wind drag. Male or female, they all had great butts. That was the only good thing Archer could say about them. The fancy cyclists thought they owned the highways and bi-ways. They rode double-digit miles, cut you off in traffic, blew stop signs and never signaled. Knowing Young was one of those put him in perspective for Archer. Any other time, he wouldn't be spending even a minute with the doctor, but Archer didn't want to bond, he just wanted information. To his credit, Young had read Archer's initial disdainful expression accurately.

"You know, Archer, given the circumstances, you should count yourself lucky that I'm talking to you at all after your assault on my office staff and myself. A modicum of respect and a little courtesy would be appreciated."

Archer colored. That Young couched his slap down in that polite psychiatric voice ticked him off. Still, he knew he deserved it.

"Just a few more questions." Time was wasting and somehow they had veered from the problem at hand to Daniel Young. The guy wasn't that interesting, and finding Josie was imperative. "Did you stop and go into the restaurant?"

"We didn't stop. We went up to Palos Verdes, around the bend to Miraleste and came back. Beautiful ride, but I can't remember anything out of the ordinary."

"Anybody veer off and go through the parking lot?" Archer asked.

"Not that I know of," Daniel said.

"How many people in your group?"

"We have fifty members; perhaps twenty were there yesterday. It was a work day."

"Any of them stop in at the Blue Fin Grill?" Archer fired off another question.

"I wouldn't know. We're pretty focused when we ride, but someone could have stopped. I could send an e-mail and ask if anyone did." Daniel picked at his sleeve.

"I'd appreciate it," Archer mumbled, feeling more uncomfortable by the minute. Graciousness when it was uncalled for was suspect. "What time were you there?"

"Early. That's all I can tell you," Young said, and Archer knew time was running short. He wasn't asking the right questions and he was losing the guy.

Tight-lipped, Archer focused on the middle ground, his eyes resting on the books and papers on the desk, the slim computer, even Young's well-pressed shirt as he considered the minimal information he had garnered. Archer settled on a different tact.

"What can you tell me about the trial?" Archer asked.

Daniel smiled and his eyes brightened. Bingo.

"As I said, it was a murder trial. The original charges were for two counts in the deaths of Susie Atkins and Janey Wilson. Both were sixteen. Both were held for five days and both were brutally murdered. Susie Atkins might as well not have existed. Her death was dismissed in the preliminary. Janey Wilson was another matter, as I'm sure you can imagine." Daniel paused, waiting for Archer's reaction only to be disappointed when he received a shrug in response. "Janey was Isaiah Wilson's daughter. The televangelist?"

Daniel inclined his head to acknowledge Archer's dawning. When he was satisfied Archer had caught on, he continued his monologue.

"Of course, back then Isaiah was just a storefront preacher. Janey and Susie had gone to Mexico on their first independent mission. They were helping build a house in some village. Paul Rothskill was the youth minister and chaperon. Their car broke down, and

Rothskill hitched a ride to find help. Hernandez found the girls and convinced them to go with him.

"After the trial, the reverend wrote books, produced tapes based on his experience with forgiveness and his belief that retribution always comes to those who offend God." Young added dryly. "Isaiah masterfully navigated the issue. Read one of his books and you can find justification for both love and hate. I thought he came very close to condoning vigilante justice in the name of God. Very provocative stuff. We followed one another around the media circuit once he found his voice. I was commentating on the trial for CBS, appearing on talk shows, and interviewed for print articles. It was quite a time."

"Was that kosher?" Archer asked.

Young answered. "I was very careful not to cross any ethical boundaries."

"But Wilson did?"

"I didn't say that. There wasn't a gag order. Isaiah was dramatic to say the least. He was good for ratings."

"Sounds like you think he exploited his daughter's death," Archer noted, then added, "or, are you sorry you didn't?"

"You really should read Dale Carnegie," Young laughed easily. "But I'll play along. Mine was an objective voice, and the public was more entertained by the voice raised in grief. I actually empathize with Isaiah. When something you value and cherish, something that defines you, is taken away so brutally and abruptly, life is never the same. You look for ways to make the pain go away. Perhaps, Isaiah was right. Retribution is necessary to the soul."

"But his motives?" Archer pressed.

"I believe Reverend Wilson's first book was written out of a real need to come to terms with his grief and outrage. What came after that was the result of a refined business sense; he saw an opportunity and he took it."

Archer couldn't help but wonder if the man of God would be pleased to know that the most momentous event in his life was tied up neatly in one paragraph by this shrink. But Daniel wasn't finished. He broadened his horizons, covering all of mankind as he spread his intellectual plumage.

"Human beings are fascinating creatures," he went on, seemingly enamored with the sound of his own odd voice. "I am amazed at the longevity of Isaiah's celebrity. What is it that pushes some people into the spotlight when they really don't deserve it? Why do they capture the imagination of the masses when other voices are passed over?" Daniel heaved a sigh and offered Archer his beautiful smile. "But I suppose the mighty have fallen. Someone doesn't think very highly of him."

"I don't get your meaning," Archer said.

"Look at your list." Young gestured with one finger.

Archer raised the evidence envelope and looked again. Isaiah Wilson's name was in the second column, third down. Beside the preacher's name was the picture of a clown. Young turned around. When he faced Archer again he had a book in his hand. He put it on the desk.

"New York Times. Fifty-two weeks at number one."

Archer wasn't one for self-examination, self-help or self-recrimination so the book didn't look familiar, but he was curious about this turn of events. Here was a celebrity and one with an agenda that might include Josie.

Archer tilted the book, taking a moment to consider the title: AN EYE FOR AN EYE. He opened the cover. Copyright was eight years earlier. He was lowering the book, ready to ask his next question, when Daniel Young reached out and cupped his hand underneath his own. Archer's eyes snapped up. His first thought was that Daniel Young's hands were rough; his second was that the guy had crossed the line. Archer started to pull his hand away, but Daniel Young clamped down and held tight. His gaze never wavered and behind his eyes Archer saw that the tables had turned. Daniel Young was in control.

"I understand the pain you're in, Archer," he said quietly.

The book slammed back on the table as Archer stood up.

"Yeah," he said tightly. "You've got my card. Call me if you have any real information."

With that, Archer turned on his heel and took off.

Damn shrink.

CHAPTER 10

An Outbuilding in the California Mountains

"Hey, wake up! Hey! Come on! Wake up! Wake up!"

Josie's teeth stuck to her lips so the word 'wake' sounded like 'walk'. She worked her throat and brought up some saliva, just not enough to make a difference. She rolled, tipped the water bottle to her lips and clamped down on the nozzle with her teeth. She threw her head back. The bottle rose, the water cascaded down the plastic, through the nipple and into her mouth. She swallowed.

She closed off her throat and held the next gulp in her mouth. It was hard to swallow given how she was tied. Josie was thinking she would have to pace herself when suddenly she lost control of the precariously balanced bottle. It dropped out of her mouth, fell to the ground and spun away. Josie thought she heard a crack but it was hard to tell. The rabbit hole was opening again, and she sure as hell was getting tired of falling through it. To fight it, she'd focus on something else. Josie pulled her feet up and kicked the woman behind her. She kicked and kicked and kicked.

"Talk to me," she demanded, and then she slept again.

The Strand, Hermosa Beach

Hannah stormed down the Strand. She went past the five thousand square foot mansion that squatted like a Sumo wrestler next to a tiny box of a place that had been built before Hermosa Beach was prime property. Hannah fumed as she went by three men sitting on a patio drinking beer. They were dressed in shorts and well-loved logo t-shirts that reminded them of happy days spent in crappy bars. She heard their burst of laughter and that ticked her off even more. They weren't laughing at her she was just pissed that they were happy and had nothing better to do than sit around drinking.

Two women walked toward her: the big one waddled and the other was so old she toddled. A man on a beach cruiser slalomed around Hannah, and then a tall woman in running shorts and a backward baseball cap jogged past. The woman could have been Josie; that woman should have been Josie.

Hannah swiped at her hair. She climbed over the low retaining wall that separated the beach from the bike path and trudged through the still-hot sand. It filtered into the back of her gold shoes and chaffed where it got near her toes. Angrily, she ripped off her shoes and high-stepped with a vengeance toward the shore. She hated the sand, the smell of the ocean, and grown people running around like children eager to get in another hour of play before it got dark and their mothers called them home to dinner.

Hermosa Beach wasn't the real world. The real world was scary and out of kilter and not right, and if these people weren't careful they'd end up like Josie. Gone somewhere, leaving someone alone, abandoning someone again.

Hannah stopped a few feet from the water's edge and took a deep breath, surprised to hear the tremors of a sob intermixed with it. She tossed her shoes on the sand on the other side of a berm. Scrambling over it, she dug in her heels and planted her rear; she pulled her legs up, wrapped her arms around her knees, and realized it was Archer she was mad at.

Wait.

That's what Archer said as he ran out the door.

Go home. Walk the dog. Stay put.

Well screw him. Letting her head fall back, Hannah closed her eyes and, ever so slightly, began to sway hoping some part of Josie would reach out to her.

Even with her eyes closed, Hannah was aware of the blue world of Hermosa Beach. Robin's egg day faded into navy nights. The palest, palest baby blue wispy clouds hung offshore. She had tried to paint this place as a way to claim it as her home, but this kind of beauty was elusive. The colors morphed by the minute and the landscape of it was flat. Sand, sea and the sky all coexisted seamlessly. There was no drama, no conflict to focus on.

Beach people were equally hard to define. They weren't super-charged with the energy it took to pursue success. They didn't lust. Hannah could spot lust a mile away. These people simply loved without restraint and accepted that people came and went. Their souls went no further than their smiles; their worries were lost in big hearts. Their beauty was worn like God's hand-me-downs, still attractive in their faded glory. Except for Josie.

Josie's kindness was tempered by practicality. Her compassion was reserved for those who deserved it. Her beauty was strong. Josie walked beside Hannah, but stayed far enough away so that she couldn't be clung to. Josie was objective, pro-active and a problem solver. She was Hannah's friend and guardian and mentor and muse. And she wasn't here. She wasn't anywhere.

At least Archer had something to do. Well, she would do something, too. Whatever she did had to be something important, but Hannah didn't know what that something was yet. The beach was almost deserted. People were off to dinner or to the bars, and it would do no good to sit in the sand and count and tap her concern away. Max would need attention; there was no way around that.

Ten minutes later she was opening the door to the house and letting Max out into the yard. Real night was coming. There was homework to be done, but before she could do anything the phone began to ring. Hannah ran for it and grabbed the receiver.

"Josie! Hello!" Hannah cried.

CHAPTER 11

An Outbuilding in the California Mountains

Josie's eyes were dry and gritty, yet the cheek pressed into the ground was wet. It was if she had been crying in her sleep. There was only one time in her life that she had wept but that was long ago. Still, something had made her cheek wet. When she figured it out, crying seemed to be an appropriate response: the water bottle was tipped over and drained dry. The water had run from a crack in the plastic, over the hard packed ground and under her cheek. There was barely a swallow left. It didn't matter. She was truly awake, and now she was remembering things.

Archer. Hannah. Max. She knew who they were, but she couldn't remember the last time she had seen them. It was as if her life was a movie and part of it had been left on the cutting room floor. Cursing the rope, Josie pulled on it in frustration and managed to inch up, angling her body so that her arms were bent. She could look over her shoulder now, and what she saw made her sick.

She was butt-to-butt with a woman whose legs were bare and shapely, scratched and bloody. At first it appeared that she was naked. Josie strained further only to fall back when she pinched a nerve in her neck. She shook it off and tried again. This time she caught a glimpse of black lace panties and a skirt bunched around the woman's waist. Those panties weren't torn, and Josie's pants were still buttoned at the waist. Rape was out of the equation for the time being.

Looking up, Josie saw that dark was coming, but that was all right because she had seen enough to know where she was: a storage building. These bunkers had to be fifty years old if they were a day, used by crews cutting roads up and down California from San Bernardino to Malibu and beyond. No one used them any longer. They weren't usually found on beaches or in deserts, but in the foothills and mountains. Figuring this out was a small victory, but a victory nonetheless. Her lashes fluttered. She shook her head again. Stay awake. Stay alert. She needed to catalogue all the information she could.

One: Through the hole in the wall, Josie believed she had seen the light of a full day pass. While that was not a certainty, it was something to work with.

Two: the light indicated it was probably close to five in the afternoon. Twilight came around six. There was a possibility that someone might stumble upon this hut, but only if it was near a populated area. Given the planning that had gone into this situation, she doubted they were near civilization. Since school had begun, there wouldn't be vacationers.

Three: This was neither beach quiet nor beach hot, the stillness was extreme and the air silkier. This was not the desert. It wasn't dry enough. She breathed deep and decided this was mountain air. But where was she? San Jacinto Mountains above Palm Springs? San Bernardino Mountains? Both were within two hours of Hermosa, and an easy ride on a weekend when there was little traffic. But, if she and the woman behind her were taken on a weekday, it would be tough to transport them too far, keep them unconscious and do it at separate times. Add more time to get them here, tie them up, and get away. That was a huge time investment.

In the San Bernardino Mountains it would be hard to go through all that without some notice since year-round folk lived in the area.

There were other places, though, like the Santa Monica Mountains and stretches of nothing off the Grapevine. It was amazing how many wide-open spaces there were in a state full-to-the-brim with people. To figure out where she was, there was only one thing to do: get out of that building.

Archer's Apartment, Hermosa Beach

The message on Archer's answering machine wasn't what he was hoping for. A client who was paying him to check out an employee he suspected of embezzlement wanted to know if any headway had been made. Not in the last twenty-four hours since you hired me, Archer thought as he erased it. There were only bills in the mailbox. He tossed them on the bookshelf. He called Liz, told her where he had found the piece of paper, read her the list of names and told her about the Hernandez connection. He informed her that The Blue Fin Grill had no cameras and spent a few moments ragging on idiots who didn't monitor their premises. Liz listened, but it was after five and there wasn't much she could do. She promised to make some inquiries, but they would only be made at her discretion. She wanted him to understand that. No amount of pleading was going to make it anything more. Oh, and she wanted a copy of that paper with the names on it just in case. She'd run the names on the list and see what popped up. You never knew what she might run across. But, damn it, Archer; she had a whole lot to do as it was. He better get that through his head.

Pleased, Archer hung up. Liz was hooked and he needed to keep his wits about him. The day wasn't over and there was a lot to do. He took a quick shower and pulled on fresh clothes. He knew forty-eight hours without sleep was his limit, so he had to work fast. He ate the leftovers from Burt's straight from the Styrofoam box as he sat in front of his computer and searched the names on the list.

Erika Gardener. No Facebook. No Twitter. She obviously had no love for social media, which was weird for a writer. He typed in a few choice words and got her DMV records. The woman had happy feet. She had moved every two years since the Hernandez trial. San Francisco, Santa Barbara, Paris – Paris? – Venice Beach and Hollywood Hills. There was nothing after the Hollywood Hills address. Maybe she got married and dropped out of the rat race. Maybe she was raising a pack of kids. He'd drill down later on her specifically. If she wrote anything of interest on the Hernandez trial it would come up when he gathered information on the case itself.

Isaiah Wilson was another matter. There was so much information on that guy Archer was worried his computer would implode. None of it was particularly current, but if Josie's disappearance were linked to the anniversary of his daughter's death, his press would skyrocket. Archer hit up Amazon and saw Isaiah Wilson's five books held decent sales rank so the franchise was still respectable. The reverend's website was slick. His pictures were posed and retouched; his image was polished and potent: dark suit, hair waving back from a high forehead, piercing eyes, sunken cheeks, pointed chin. Add it up and you got the perfect image of a man who had suffered and survived.

Books could be bought through his website which also offered listings for his television appearances and, of course, PayPal for donations. Nothing offensive, everything seemed above board making the clown avatar seem strange.

Archer went back ten years. Wilson looked exactly the same but shabbier. He was about to navigate away when a picture caught his eye. The photo showed Reverend Wilson on the steps of the courthouse talking to a young man. Whether he was counseling him, praying with him or fighting with him was unclear. In the picture they were surrounded by people, press and parishioners who held signs imploring God for justice. Archer checked out the caption: Reverend Isaiah Wilson and Paul Rothskill.

Archer printed the picture and set it aside. He clicked out of that screen and returned to Google. Instead of typing in another search, Archer finished off his food. Fish, he decided, should be reheated. He tossed the Styrofoam box toward the trash, dialed Hannah and got an invitation to leave a message.

"It's me," he said. "The car is in good shape. It doesn't look like anything bad happened. The cops towed it. They still aren't going to investigate, but I have some leads I'm running down." He was about to hang up when he reconsidered. "When you get this, stay put 'till I get back to you."

His next call was to Josie and Faye's secretary, Angie. He needed to get back inside the office and asked if she would wait for him. She was headed home, but would leave the back door open if he promised to lock up after he retrieved the files he wanted. Archer wished Angie good night and she wished him good luck. All that done, he turned back to the computer for one last search. There was one more picture he wanted to see. He typed:

Janey Wilson.

An Outbuilding in the California Mountains

"I'm an attorney. I live in Hermosa Beach. Hannah Sheraton lives with me. She goes to Mira Costa high school. My boyfriend is named Archer. He's an investigator. A photographer. He was a cop before he retired. Do you know him? What do you do? Do we know each other? Who are you? Talk to me. Please. Just say something."

Josie Bates' House, Hermosa Beach

Hannah opened the door and there stood Billy Zuni.

"Tacos." He held up a white paper sack, the bottom of which was soaked with reddish tinged grease.

"You went to Miguel's?"

"Naw. Sean was going home with his doggie bag and told me I could have them."

Hannah nodded. Been there, done that when her mother forgot to come home or even to leave food in the fridge. Hannah had been grateful to anyone willing to give her anything. She opened the door wider. Billy walked in. No matter what time of day she saw him, no matter where, he smelled like the beach. The scent was a funny mix of sunscreen (which he didn't use) and dope (which he did) and water and sand and beach sweat which was totally different than exercise sweat or nervous sweat.

Max didn't get up but blinked his big dark eyes in gratitude when Billy reached down to gives his ears a little pet. The dog stretched and showed his belly.

"This dog sure likes me," Billy laughed.

"He likes anyone who pets him." Hannah took his greasy bag and headed into the kitchen, counting her steps silently along the way.

"He likes me especially. I can tell," Billy called after her as he scratched Max, and put his face close so the dog didn't have to reach too far to give him a kiss. He gave Max one more pat and stood up. "Heard from Josie?"

"No."

"Archer?"

"He called while I was on the phone with you. He left a message and said he found Josie's car. There's nothing weird about it. He's running down a few things. He didn't tell me what." Hannah took out the tacos. They were cold, and the grease that had looked reddish on the bag had taken on an orange glow as it congealed on the meat. "Are you really going to eat these?"

"Sure, but I'll share if you want."

"That's not what I meant."

Hannah reached for a plate, put the two tacos on it and gave it to Billy as he sat down. She opened the fridge and filled her own plate with cold chicken before making a spinach salad and taking a seat on a chair opposite Billy. He shook the bangs out of his eyes and looked at her. Annoyed she looked back.

"What?"

"Well, maybe you say grace or something. I've never had dinner at Josie's house before."

"No, we don't say grace," Hannah answered, but she said it nicely because there was some comfort in Billy thinking about praying. "You can go ahead and eat."

"Did you say grace with your mom?" he asked.

Hannah snorted. The only thing Linda Rayburn ever prayed for was more money and less responsibility.

"My mom doesn't either," Billy said matter-of-factly. "I don't even know if we're a religion. Sometimes, I go down to the services at the beach on Sunday."

"Do you know anything about your mom?" Hannah drawled.

Billy picked up his taco and bit into it. The taco didn't crunch, so it must have been in the bag a long time.

"Not much. I know she was way too young when she had me 'cause that's what she always says. *I was way too young,*" Billy mimicked and Hannah couldn't help but laugh.

"My mom used to say that, too."

They ate in silence for a while: Billy thoughtfully chewing his limp, cold tacos, Hannah picking at her salad.

"Did you talk to anyone on the beach?" Hannah asked.

"Sure did, but nobody's seen her. And Burt doesn't have everybody coming into his place, like Archer thinks. It feels like we're pissing in the ocean, know what I mean?" Billy shook his bangs back again. "Like, who's ever going to know you did it when there's so much water around you anyway?"

Hannah poked at her chicken like she wanted to kill it all over again. She put a piece in her mouth and rested her head on one upturned hand. She was looking at her food while Billy was looking at her. The end-of-day light was coming through the kitchen window and Hannah's hair was sparkling like it had been polished. Billy thought he'd never seen more beautiful hair. Hannah, on the other hand, thought Billy was right. Pissing in the ocean was kind of useless. It was the same as being a grain of sand on the beach. It just didn't get noticed and neither would a question here or there. She raised her eyes, the light pierced her irises, turning the green a cat-like golden. She looked freaky-beautiful. She looked even more freaky-beautiful when an idea started to take form.

"You want to help me with something?"

Billy's grin was dazzling. Hannah grinned back, and for the next few hours they were pretty close to being friends.

CHAPTER 12

An Outbuilding in the California Mountains

Josie put the balls of her feet on the cement wall and pushed back. Her legs weren't as strong as they usually were, but they were serviceable. She pumped and pushed herself up, lifted her rear, wiggled her shoulders. Like a pill bug, she managed to move a few inches until she was cupped around the stake, easing the rope's tension. Josie laughed. It was a small sound meant just for her, but the other woman responded.

"Can you help me?" she asked in a gravelly whisper.

Josie closed her eyes against the tears that welled when she heard those words. Regrouping, she opened them again and the tears were gone.

"Not yet, but I will."

The Law Offices of Faye Baxter & Josie Bates, Hermosa Beach

It was almost seven and Archer sat on the floor of Josie's office in a pool of light cast from the desk lamp, surrounded by boxes. He hadn't been surprised to find that the second set of boxes he had seen earlier when he was there with Hannah were from the Hernandez trial.

Someone had intended the list found in Josie's car to point in Hernandez's direction; Young confirmed the connection. But for Josie to have pulled these boxes out of storage meant someone had to have given her a heads up that the Hernandez matter was hot again.

Now Archer was an audience of one, and the curtain had risen on a show he didn't buy a ticket for. It was up to him to figure out what it was all about and the program was extensive. Luckily, Josie made it a little easier by being a meticulous record keeper.

There were twelve boxes in all. Each was neatly labeled: motions, filing, transcripts, media, appeal, etc. Archer started at the end. He opened the box labeled 'appeal'. Josie had not been the attorney of record, but she had been involved. Again, no surprise; appellate lawyers were a breed unto themselves. He flipped through the paperwork to the ruling. The appeal was denied. The conviction stood at second-degree murder.

Sentence: fifteen years to life with another twenty tacked on for various and sundry additional charges. Hernandez was remanded to state prison.

Archer re-filed the information and went to the first box.

Arrest Report:
Name: Xavier Hernandez.
Age: Twenty-six
Height: 5 feet 9 inches.
Hair: Black
Eyes: Brown
Weight: 191 lbs.
Glasses: No
Contacts: No

Scars: None

Injuries: Scratches to the right side of neck, bruise on the inside of the right thigh, puncture wounds on the palms of both hands.

Fingerprint card: That was funny to look at. These days LAPD took prints and filed this stuff digitally.

There was an inventory of the personal items confiscated during booking: keys, driver's license, three dollars and fifty-three cents in cash, a piece of gum, a heart-shaped necklace and a scrunchy.

The necklace, Archer knew, belonged to Janey Wilson. He had seen it on an Internet photo.

Booking photos:

Xavier Hernandez's mug shot showed a nice looking guy with long, thick, straight hair. His lips were narrow and expressive in repose. Not quite a smirk or a smile, they tipped up naturally as if he was thinking about something pleasant. His cheekbones were high and his gaze straightforward. There was something exotic and a little delicate about him. He looked like one of those Italian models that were so popular these days, but he was Hispanic and it showed in the tone of his skin and the color of his eyes. Archer looked further. Xavier's neck was big and short and held his head atop powerful shoulders and a broad chest. It was as if Xavier's face had been sculpted by the aristocracy of Spain, and his body by the Indians of Mexico.

There was a photo of the puncture wounds on his hands. They looked as if he had hit gravel hard. They were more pockmarked than wounded. There was dark stuff under the nails on his right hand.

The picture of his neck showed deep, obvious scratch marks. The picture of his thigh showed a large bruise at the groin. Another picture showed worn jeans, shoes worn down at heel, a suit jacket, a t-shirt, mismatched socks, stretched out tighty-whitey underwear. The shoes were especially dusty. There were dark stains on the right side of his jacket and on the pants.

The Police Report:

Suspect was observed speeding and weaving down the desert highway in a red Toyota, Camry at 3:24 p.m. Suspect crossed the centerline of the two-lane highway twice. Officer in pursuit at speeds in excess of eighty miles an hour. Officer immediately activated lights and siren and believed the suspect was both aware of pursuit and was fleeing from such. Suspect also was observed leaning toward the passenger side of the vehicle while simultaneously attempting to steer the vehicle. Officer called in license plate and was advised that there were outstanding warrants for traffic violations on registered owner Agatha M. Hernandez.

Suspect lost control of his car, veered onto the shoulder and came to a stop approximately a hundred yards off the highway. Officer followed suit, stopping behind suspect's car at twenty feet, and observed that the suspect was sitting with his back to the officer. His hands were not visible. Officer called in his position, and exited the patrol car leaving the door open per standard procedure. Officer approached the Camry observing that the car was extremely dirty.

Officer observed the driver's window was partially open, and advised the suspect to put his hands on the wheel. The suspect did not comply nor did he acknowledge the officer's presence. Officer called out again for the suspect to put his hands on the wheel. The suspect did not comply; the officer drew his weapon and approached with caution. After a third attempt at engagement, officer approached the vehicle and opened the door. Only then did the suspect look at the officer. At that time the suspect responded to directions to exit the vehicle, stood with his hands by his side, turned at direction, put his hands on the hood of the car, and assumed the position as ordered. Officer noted the suspect's unkempt appearance and the blood....

Archer set aside the report and picked up the photo of Xavier Hernandez's hands. The officer's report described blood on the thumb pad and the back of Hernandez's right hand. By the time the suspect was transported he managed to wipe away most of it. The rest had dried, leaving half-moons of what appeared to be dirt under the nails. Some had sunk into the wrinkle between his finger and thumb. Archer put that picture down and picked up the one of Hernandez as he had been dressed. It looked like he'd slept in his clothes. It was possible to see the dust on his shoes and on the hem of his pants.

Archer put all the photos and the extended arrest report aside and dug into the box marked 'evidence'. The sheer volume of paperwork was overwhelming as it always was in a trial of this magnitude. Reports, analysis, lists and comparisons. For every bit of discovery the prosecution sent to Josie, she created twenty pages of notes to discount it, motions to have it thrown out, requests for clarification, and samples for independent testing. Finally, Archer found what he wanted: analytics for evidence taken from the body of Xavier Hernandez.

He went over it fast. Blood was confirmed under the fingernails and embedded in his hands. Blood was also dried on Hernandez's pants and jacket. Archer dove back into the box and pulled out a few more pages. Initial analysis indicated blood on his pants was both his and the victims'. The scrapings taken from under his nails matched the same types that had co-mingled with his own.

Hernandez was not drunk.

He was not belligerent, nor arrogant nor in shock. He accepted the arrest.

He had offered no explanation for his state of disarray or the blood.

He had allowed the officer to search his car.

The officer found more blood evidence inside the car, cuffed the suspect, and called to have the car towed.

Archer would have convicted the guy on this alone. He couldn't wait to see what magic Josie had worked to save Hernandez's sorry butt.

Back in the box.

It took more than a few minutes to find the report on evidence taken from inside the car. Archer dug in the first box again and grabbed the full booking report. It included the detective's interview with Hernandez and the next round of booking – this time on the charge of double homicide. They had found the bodies.

It was getting late. Archer's back hurt from sitting on the floor. He wasn't hungry but he had to eat. He had to sleep. He had to stay on top of his game. He had to get help to go through this stuff, and Hannah wasn't the one to do it. She was too young, too scarred from her own trial, and too angry at him, so he wouldn't ask her to look at the gruesome things he knew he would find in these boxes. It was, after all, a trial of a man who killed two girls Hannah's age.

Standing up, Archer stretched, checked his phone and texted Hannah.

Homework done?

Hannah: No worries.

Archer: Try to sleep.

Hannah: Okay.

Archer hung up.

Hannah slipped her phone into the back pocket of her jeans. Archer's text had unnerved her. She had assumed out-of-sight-out-of-mind was Archer's way. His concern made her feel guilty and guilt made her feel angry, so she took it out on Billy.

"Hurry," she hissed. "Come on, Billy."

"Why? It's not like we're doing anything bad."

"Did I say we were?" Hannah snapped. "I just want to get home. In case Josie calls or Archer comes over."

"I think we should have waited for Archer before we did this." Billy shook back his hair and looked at her, the hammer in his hand poised to strike.

"No. It's okay. We're almost done," Hannah assured him, but inside she had the sinking feeling Billy was right. Still, what could go wrong? They were only helping.

CHAPTER 13

An Outbuilding in the California Mountains

Josie pulled herself into a ball, unwound again and curled again until she was positioned closer to the stake. Her legs now tingled with the blood flow, and even her hands felt better.

"Your hands are tied above your head, right? Just look at the knot and nothing else. See the knot?" Josie spewed orders at her companion, trying to engage her and shake her out of her lethargy.

"Yes," came the reply. Josie imagined the woman's bleary eyes trying to focus, and her brain attempting to process every bit of information. Josie sympathized, but she wouldn't let up.

"Okay. Good. We can figure this out together, but we've got to move you up. Look. Raise your eyes. Keep them open. See why? See what I'm talking about? If you move up you can get your fingers on the knot. The rope is cotton. It's cotton rope. Do you know what that means?"

"Cotton? Cotton."

"Right. Cotton," Josie insisted. "It's not jute. Cotton has some give. Whoever did this made a big mistake, I can tell you. Cotton rope. Come on. Come on! You've got to start working now. Massage the knot. I know it looks impossible, but if one of us can get the rope to relax-"

Josie stopped talking as she recognized the silence of sleep. She shoved back with her rear and made contact. A rivulet of sweat tracked from her brow to lips. It was salty. Josie spit it out. Her shirt was plastered to her body. Even when she spoke softly, her voice sounded large and harsh in this little space. She would kill for a drink of water.

"Do you remember my name? Josie. Josie Bates. What's yours? Do you remember?" Working the rope was tough so she took a break. She rested, but kept talking just to hear her own voice. "Archer won't be happy I'm sleeping with a woman I don't even know. What about you? Are you married? Will someone be looking for you?"

Josie looked at the knot. It was still tighter than tight.

"I hope someone will be looking for you," she muttered. "How about your name? You have to remember that."

There was nothing for a minute. Then she heard the woman make a great effort to breathe and out came:

"Erika."

Archer's Apartment, Hermosa Beach

Archer sat on the deck in the one beach chair too low to see over the edge. Absentmindedly he twirled the pedal of the beach cruiser that had been banished from the garage to make room for the Hummer.

He'd spent the hour since he returned home making calls. The first was to Daniel Young, but he got no answer. Then he started calling Josie's current clients. There were eight of them. Hannah had been right about the DUI being nervous. The woman almost jumped out of her skin when Archer identified himself as a private investigator. There was a woman named Linda Lopez with a number in South Gate, and another woman named Martha Vabino who was in Los Angeles. Martha Vabino was a rep for a legal journal. Archer got the message machine which announced that the offices were closed, but if he wanted to book space in the next issue the drop dead date was three days before issue. Archer tossed it.

Archer called Linda Lopez. It was a dead end. Her son was in prison, and she heard that Josie handled children pro bono. Her child was nineteen, a gangbanger and went by the handle 'Biter' because he liked to chew off body parts during a rumble. Archer told her she should probably find another attorney because Josie wasn't taking on new cases. Linda was disappointed, but not devastated. In fact, the woman didn't sound particularly sober.

He called Peter Siddon's number, got a woman who said Peter would only talk to Josie Bates and it better be soon. After what she did to him, he at least deserved to talk to her. Then the woman began to cry and hung up. Even though Peter Siddon wasn't on the list found in Josie's car, Archer put him high on his personal list of people to check out.

He was about to pick up the phone again to dial the number on Cuwin Martin's message when two things happened: the phone rang and the doorbell sounded. Archer pushed the button on the phone and held it to his ear as he crossed to the open door. One way or another, he was positive he'd be talking to Josie. He was wrong.

Standing in the doorway was Daniel Young; on the phone was Hannah. In Daniel Young's hand was a piece of paper.

"My fingerprints are on it," Young said.

An Outbuilding in the California Mountains

"Do you have a last name?"

The woman moved. She yelped. It hurt like hell when you pulled the wrong way. Josie knew that all too well. The woman whimpered, but something was changing. Whatever it was, it hovered in their hot little cell just out of reach. Finally, Josie realized what she was sensing: resolve, a gritting of the woman's psychic teeth. Before she could nudge the woman behind her to greater consciousness, she mumbled:

"What the hell happened?"

CHAPTER 14

The Hollywood Hills

Archer had a few rules he lived by. Spend your time wisely was right up there at the top of the list. Then there were the rest of the easy-to-follow rubrics that covered just about any situation that might crop up in his life. When you worked, work for people who paid well; when you played, play with people you like; when you loved, love without boundaries, expectations or tethers.

Daniel Young wasn't going to make Archer any bucks, and he sure as hell wasn't someone Archer wanted to have a beer with at Burt's, but the man was someone it would be wise to spend some time with. Archer needed help and Daniel Young had brought a most interesting little item. A Xerox of the original list found in Josie's car. This time there was a check mark next to Daniel's name. Archer took the list and dealt with Hannah at the same time.

"Everything okay, Hannah?" When he got an affirmative he said, "I'll call you back."

Archer snapped the phone shut, and his call to Cuwin Martin was put aside as he studied the list. Daniel followed him into the apartment. Archer raised his eyes, motioned toward the couch and the doctor sat down.

Young was wearing the same outfit he had on at the office and wasted no time in filling Archer in on the rest of his day. Gay had left around six-thirty and he, himself, had stopped reviewing histories at eight. The piece of paper was found on the floor of his car, passenger side, and it was face down. He thought the car had been locked. The minute he saw what it was, he got in the car, locked the doors, fired up the engine and drove straight to Hermosa. He didn't mind admitting he was afraid. Archer understood. He had seen the environment in Young's office complex. Lots of trees, plants, and places to hide. Archer assured the doctor he had been smart to be cautious. Next on the list was Erika Gardener and, since they didn't have a phone number, a road trip was the next best option. Daniel Young was going to tag along no matter what Archer said. Now Archer was driving and Daniel had spent the last forty-five minutes expounding on the Hernandez trial.

"I admit that I was intrigued after your visit. I looked back over some of the press. I had forgotten that Erika was really the go-to reporter on this thing. Her research was impeccable, her reporting above reproach, but it was clear that she was appalled when Xavier was not convicted. She wrote a book exposing the judicial system for what it was: flawed, filled with ineptitude. Not like now. Now reporters regurgitate whatever they get off the AP. No one thinks anymore. I hate that about the Times. No one makes the effort to track down those in the know. I've seen so many articles where a simple interview would put events in the proper perspective."

"Yeah. If only they had an expert." Archer tossed him a look. It was brief and expressive. Daniel Young was no dummy, nor was he put off by Archer's ridicule.

"I'm curious, Archer. You disdain expert witnesses, yet you must have surely offered your expertise in a trial or two." Daniel turned slightly, his sincere interest whacking Archer up the side of his head.

"They have their place," Archer answered. "But most of them think they are smarter than everyone else. Most of them are just arrogant and glib, and they sell out easy."

"Everyone sells out," Daniel pointed out, his odd voice catching and releasing like a fisherman teasing a big fish before he reeled him in.

"I don't sell what I do to the highest bidder, and I don't tell my clients what they want to hear."

"Ah, there it is." Daniel said energetically. He liked being engaged in an intellectual exercise. Archer figured him for a debater in high school. "You think people like me are unethical. Not so, Archer. I can't tell you how many times I have turned down requests for my services precisely because it was implied that I would provide predetermined conclusions in my testimony."

Archer countered. "And my testimony doesn't have wiggle room. Either I find what someone's looking for, or I don't. You, on the other hand, can make people believe anything. You talk out of both sides of your mouth."

"You mean like lawyers do?" Daniel suggested.

Archer tightened his grip on the wheel. Touché. Daniel was right. Lawyers sold out to the highest bidder, and it wasn't always for money. Josie had sold herself to Hernandez and he was dirt poor; she sold herself for notoriety. Now she was getting a return on her investment in spades.

"Let's just say I have reservations about your true value in a courtroom," Archer answered. "Opinion on a state of mind is subjective."

"Then I suppose I'm only here to keep you company, since I was no more than a pretty face in the Hernandez trial."

Daniel faced forward and stopped talking. The silence felt like arm wrestling, and it was Archer's psychic arm that was starting to tremble. Finally, he called uncle.

"Okay. I'll bite. What was your take on Hernandez?" Even though Archer's eyes were on the road, he knew Daniel Young was smiling like he just won something.

"Xavier Hernandez knew right from wrong, and he had no remorse when he did wrong. He was not compulsive about his urges, but he was smart enough to take advantage when a situation presented itself. He abused those girls and, realizing the trouble he would be in, killed them. He was also smart enough to hire Josie Bates and meticulously follow her advice. He never once incriminated himself. Xavier had issues, but he was not mentally ill. He relied on his mother for everything, and his mother gave it to him just to keep him away from her. Bottom line, he acted on impulse when he offered those girls a ride, but he carried out a plan once he had them isolated. He had full knowledge that what he was doing was a crime. I gave the prosecutor everything he needed to convict. I spoke to details that Hernandez provided to me during our interviews because I alone knew what to ask. I..."

Archer had heard enough about how fabulous Daniel Young was. What he spouted was standard stuff any psychiatrist could have offered, but Young made it sound like he had opened Hernandez's head and plucked out a detailed confession.

"Okay, so he was smart and you were smart. But why is someone ticked off now? And if they're avenging Hernandez's conviction, why go after Josie? She was the only thing standing between him and the needle."

"Perhaps someone thought she should have got him off Scott free. In my *expert* opinion, her performance was both brilliant and disgusting."

"And what about this woman? Erika Gardener?"

"Collateral damage, maybe?" Daniel suggested. "Although some of her articles were brutal, I don't think Xavier really cared one way or the other about his press. It might be as simple as Hernandez liking to have two women. Making Janey watch Susie being killed heightened his pleasure. That's what he told me."

"Then maybe we're looking for someone who isn't affiliated with Hernandez at all. Maybe the statement isn't that Hernandez got a raw deal."

Daniel raised an eyebrow as he chuckled. "And just who might that be making such a statement?"

Archer raised a brow right back. "The victims' families? How about someone who didn't like that the Susie girl never got her day in court? Or, what about Isaiah Wilson? It's the ten year anniversary of his kid's death, and all this guy got was second degree."

"You're not suggesting Isaiah Wilson is responsible for Ms. Bates' disappearance, are you?"

"Stranger things have happened. But hey, you're the expert, I'm just a dick."

CHAPTER 15

"There. There!"

Young shouted the command as he pointed to the street Archer had driven past. The fingers of his other hand latched onto Archer's arm, and that did it. Archer hit the brakes as he shook Daniel Young off.

"Got it, man," Archer growled. "You can just tell me I missed the turn."

In the Hollywood Hills the roads were narrow, the streets carved out willy-nilly and street signs were often hidden behind overgrown bushes or low-hanging branches that had been there since Mary Pickford was queen of the screen. All Young had to do was point the sign out. Archer rolled on his hip, dug in his pocket and passed a slip of paper to Daniel.

"Here, read me the address."

"Thirty two and a half Sunrise Court," Daniel confirmed. "I know I saw Sunrise Court. It was right back there."

Archer stepped on the gas, heading forward looking for a place he could safely turn around.

"Go the other way. Come on, Archer. Didn't you hear me?" Daniel demanded.

Archer slammed on the brakes, threw the car into reverse, and put his arm over the back of the passenger seat. He hit the gas and fishtailed into a turn only to slam on the brakes again. That sent Daniel slapping against his restraints and back against the seat again. The face Young turned his way was not what Archer expected. It was pale with resentment and moist with sweat and his expression was disdainful.

"Very nice," Daniel noted drily, and that was just enough to make Archer really angry.

"Listen to me real carefully, Young. You are here as a courtesy. You don't order me around, and you don't insult Josie or me. Got it?"

"You're right. I wouldn't want to infringe upon your territory or disrupt your work."

Archer pulled his lips together. He looked out the front window knowing they both had reason to be angry and anxious. Young wasn't the bad guy, but he shouldn't be here now. Archer owned the bad. He had bought into the urgency Young presented when he showed up at Archer's door. He should have sent the guy home. If he had, Archer could have done his job the right way.

"I apologize," Archer said, knowing Daniel's little snipe paled in comparison to Archer's own behavior in Young's office. "I'm tired. I'm worried. Josie means a lot to me."

"I know," Daniel answered. "Just remember this: right now, I'm the only one taking you seriously, and you're the only one who believes I might be in danger. That makes us rather like partners, doesn't it?"

They looked at one another, two shadows in a darkened car. Archer put his hand on the gearshift, but his eyes still held Daniel's. There was something about this all- knowing, carefully groomed psychiatrist that unsettled Archer; there was something in him that Archer both despised and admired. He had to admit that Young's determination to be part of his own salvation was admirable. Most people in his situation would be cowering behind a locked door and demanding police protection. That didn't make Daniel Young any easier to stomach.

"I'm scared, too," Daniel said quietly. "So much can go wrong if one isn't careful. People could really get hurt. I don't think Josie Bates ever thought about that."

"Yeah, well, I got it," Archer offered a curt nod.

"My name is on that list," Daniel reminded him.

"I got it," Archer mumbled.

"I want to be a part of whatever happens."

Young put out a well-manicured hand and waited for Archer to shake. Archer would rather have walked over hot coals than seal a deal with this guy, but what could he do. He took the proffered hand and shook it. They were partners. Maybe Young wasn't quite the dilettante Archer thought him to be. His hand was strong; his skin was that of a man who knew some physical work, and Archer found that comforting. He gave Young a second more and their time was over.

Archer shifted hard, put his foot on the gas and drove on, leaning over the wheel and peering through the dark. He pulled up short and made a U-turn before easing onto a small road and cutting the headlights as he coasted to a stop in front of a prime example of California architecture: the bungalow.

Erika Gardener's House, Hollywood Hills

Erika Gardener's house was yellow with white wood trim. The front door was red and the porch floor was painted hunter green. There was a rattan couch and round table under the front window. Tea roses in full bloom spilled over the porch railing. Grass grew between parallel strips of concrete that led up to a one car detached garage in the back. Pink poufs of hydrangea billowed on a monstrous bush of big, dark green waxy leaves. A yellow light warmed a room somewhere in the back of the place, but the front porch light was off.

Archer popped the door of the Hummer and stepped out into the humid heat of the Hollywood Hills. He rounded the front of the car just as Daniel Young stepped off the running board and started up the walk. Archer caught up with him and touched his arm.

"We check it out slow," he whispered.

"It looks fine," Young noted.

"So did Josie's car. So did yours," he pointed out. "Let me go. I don't want to have to worry about you."

Archer hadn't taken more than three steps when Daniel stopped him.

"Just watch out for yourself." Daniel was defiant and Archer pivoted, narrowing his eyes at this guy. Young set his jaw and met Archer's gaze. "We both bring something to this table, Archer. I might need you to use that gun you carry in the back of your pants, but you might need me to talk down whoever is in there."

"Why do you think someone might be in there?"

"Because we're being led by the nose. Eventually, we're going to meet up with whoever it is. What if that someone is Xavier Hernandez? A killer. A brutal murderer. Do you think he would tell you where Ms. Bates is if you acted the way you did in my office?"

"Young, for a smart guy you are not real bright. Hernandez is in prison."

"But he has friends. It could be one of his friends. You knew what I meant," Daniel snapped, coloring at his mistake. "I'm just pointing out that we don't know what we're walking into."

Archer gave his neck a twist and tucked his jaw down. It gave him the heebie-jeebies to have Young hanging in his literal and mental peripheral vision, but he was there. Archer wasn't going to risk some hissy fit about who was leading and who was following. Archer passed the next minute looking at the house. Right now it wasn't who might be in there that really mattered, it was the real possibility that someone might be. Archer made a decision.

"Okay, but I say down and you hit the deck. Got it?"

"And if I say be quiet, you stop talking. Agreed?"

Archer nodded and walked ahead thinking about what could be waiting for them. One: Erika Gardener dead. Two: Josie and Erika, prisoners inside that house. Three: Erika and Josie both dead. And that led him right back to, why not Young? That was the million-dollar question, but there were also good answers to it: Young was a man and more difficult to take, Young had somehow sidestepped the effort and didn't know it, or Young wasn't as enticing as two women.

Abandoning speculation, Archer walked up the narrow driveway, past the porch and stopped briefly at the side window. The living room was empty. Young peered over

Archer's shoulder. They saw nothing and heard nothing and that meant nothing. Archer had a good sense for abandoned and this place felt empty.

Young stepped away as Archer walked parallel to the flowerbed that ran down the side of the house. In the back, the raised porch was covered by a red awning with white piping and was accessible by three concrete steps. Archer knew the door he was looking at led to the kitchen. All these places were the same. The yard was manageable and framed by the driveway on one side, flower beds on the other, and a detached garage at the end of the property. There were more colossal hydrangea bushes in the back and they were covered with flowers the size of a man's head. Those plants were interspersed with lilies and ferns and other plants Archer couldn't name. There was a smiling ceramic frog squatting under one big bush, and a food dish closer to the porch than the garage. That dish was small, so the woman probably had a cat. A dog would have made noise. Although, if there were someone inside wanting to do harm the first harm would have been done to a dog.

The kitchen door window was bare. Archer looked toward the garage and then back to the porch. The porch it would be. He walked up the steps, flattened himself against the wall, waited a beat, and then looked through the paned window. He tried the door. It was locked. Daniel Young had paused at the side of the house, but Archer could feel his eagerness and curiosity.

What? What do you see?

Archer shook his head as he came back down the steps.

Nothing. Nothing at all.

Archer motioned for Young to stay where he was, and then moved quickly to the other side of the house. Around the corner he saw a fence and a locked gate. The neighbor was close, but a stand of Italian Cypress cut off the view from one house to the other and created a natural sound break. Archer went back the way he had come.

"Come on," he muttered.

Together, they retraced their steps, walked across the lawn and went up the steps to the porch and the front door. Young raised his fist to knock; Archer caught it. He wanted a minute more to think. Somewhere in the distance a dog barked, and then all was quiet again. He looked through the window into the dining room. He tried the knob. It turned. He could go in quiet or make some noise. He decided to ring the bell. If Erika Gardener showed up, he would know instantly whether she was under duress. If she were, Archer would decide what to do when he looked into her eyes; if she weren't, they would all settle down for a nice chat.

It was now approximately thirty hours since Josie had disappeared, a second night had fallen, and Archer prayed that this wasn't a dead end. When Erika didn't come, Archer rang one more time. When everything stayed still, Archer turned the knob fully with one hand and drew his gun with the other. He motioned for Daniel Young to stay back just before he crossed over Erika Gardener's threshold and into her life.

An Outbuilding in the California Mountains

Josie had it in her head that a person could die of thirst in three days. She had no idea when she had been abducted, or how often she had come to and managed to take a drink of water from the bottle before the damn thing cracked. She was going to assume that she had been there two days at least and had her last drink approximately six hours earlier. Eight tops.

She had watched the progress of the sun through the hole in the wall and noted the temperature change. Darkness came. There was nothing like mountain darkness, and in this hut, away from the moon and stars, it was all encompassing, a night unlike Josie had ever seen. This dark – this situation – terrified her. It was better when Erika was awake, but she wasn't. That was understandable. Whatever they had been given had a lengthy residual effect. Though Josie was a few hours ahead of Erika, she was still drifting in and out herself.

Still, she believed someone had miscalculated. They would both come out of it soon, and no one had returned to give them another dose of whatever it was that kept them unconscious. Unless they were being left to die. That wouldn't take long if she was right about the three-day water window. And if they weren't meant to die, what would it take to free them? Ransom? Archer would have paid it gladly. Then again, money may have changed hands, and they were still here, languishing. That meant this was personal. If it was personal, then she and Erika had crossed the same person. The question was who?

Second thought: if there were no intention of releasing them, why go to all the trouble to leave the water and the granola bar? Why tie their hands? A locked door would have restrained them long enough to allow them to die. This was about power and humiliation.

Someone gave and someone could take away food, water, and freedom. That meant there were only two other choices.

"Punishment or revenge," Josie whispered to herself. Then she raised her voice. "What do you think, Erika? Have you done anything bad enough to be punished liked this?"

But Josie was speaking to the dark. Erika Gardener slept on as easily as if she were in her own bed.

CHAPTER 16

Erika Gardener's House, Hollywood Hills

Erika Gardener liked things clean and sharp and colorful. The couch was leather and colored the deepest of purples, the walls were white, the pillows yellow and green and sapphire blue. A huge print hung on one wall; an entertainment center with state of the art sound system was in a corner. Wall-to-wall built-in shelves behind the couch were filled with books. Erika Gardener had lined them up neatly by height. The books on the square, squat coffee table were about travel and fashion. The rest of the tabletop was peppered with pottery. There was a beautiful rug on the hardwood floor, a low-slung chair and an antique set of stacking tables. Atop those tables were fresh flowers: roses that were still opening, and drinking up clear water. She'd been there within the last twenty-four hours, if the assumption was that she had arranged the flowers.

The woman had good taste and enough money to reasonably indulge it. Archer glanced toward the sparkling kitchen. A dining area sported another glass top table on a metal pedestal, and chairs upholstered in purple. The walls were white. There was a grouping of black and white photos in silver frames with red mats. He wandered toward the photos. Most were of foreign destinations, and some showed an attractive woman who Archer took to be Erika Gardener. His eyes scanned the photos – twenty or so in all – only to be drawn to one where she was dressed in an evening gown at an event that was obviously important to her. She had an impressive chest. Suddenly, Archer pivoted. His nerves spiked. Daniel was by his side and standing too close.

"She's beautiful, isn't she?"

"Assuming that's her," Archer said quietly.

"It is," Daniel answered.

"Yeah, she cleans up nice," Archer said off-handedly. She was very pretty, but beautiful? Archer didn't think so, but his touch-point was Josie. Josie with her height, her athletic body, her finely sculpted face and startlingly intelligent eyes, was beautiful. "I guess you don't forget someone who looks like that. Did she interview you?"

"I thought we knew each other well." Daniel laughed softly as if the experience had been enormously satisfying and disappointing at the same time.

"Lucky you."

Archer moved away. He took the short hallway alone. There were three open doors. If anyone were there, Archer would turn in his investigator's license and check himself into an old folk's home. Erika's place was not only empty it felt like no one was coming back.

He took a quick look in the first room. A den. Same good taste as the living room but softened by comfort things: a television, a crocheted afghan, and fuzzy slippers by the couch. He doubted Erika Gardener spent her evenings crocheting, so the afghan had to be a gift. Mom?

Grandmother? If so, there might be someone who would have seen her recently.

In the guest room there was a bed and a dresser. This room was not as well thought out as the other rooms. Erika Gardener didn't have many guests, or at least not many who spent the night in this room. There was a bed and a chest of drawers, an old printer, a treadmill and a couple of baskets that seemed to have had a purpose at one time or another. He looked at the junk for a few minutes, and then poked his head into the small, attached bathroom.

At the end of the hall was the master bedroom. Erika slept on a very expensive mattress set atop a black lacquer platform. Six down pillows were stacked neatly at the head of the bed; a down comforter was folded at the foot, European style. An original oil of a naked woman – and a none-too-pretty one at that – hung over the bed.

Archer holstered his gun as he looked into the bathroom. No 1950s bungalow had a claw-footed tub that looked quite like the one Ms. Gardener soaked in, but she had done a nice job restoring the original pink and black deco tile. There were bath oils and candles near the tub.

Archer retraced his steps to the framed pictures on the dresser. These pictures showed her as a little girl with her parents and another of her as a teenager sitting by a river. Young had been right. She was beautiful and had been since birth, but when she was young she wore it easily. In the bedside table drawer was a vibrator and birth control pills. She wasn't a hermit or a prude. There would be a man – probably more than one – in her life. If there were only one, there would have been a third picture in the bedroom. Archer opened the closet. The clothing wasn't overly expensive and almost all of it casual. He touched a fancy dress. The one she had worn in the picture in the dining room. It was long and backless and purple. He started to close the closet, but paused and touched that gown again. He didn't know why he was drawn to it, only that he was. Finally, he shut the doors. Time was flying.

Knowing now that nobody was in the house, Archer went back to the den. Daniel Young watched him from down the hall then followed him.

Erika worked in the den. Magazines were strewn about: *Bloomberg, U.S. News* and *People.* Archer stood near the computer on the desk. He fired it up. It was locked and he wouldn't waste time looking for a way in. With one finger he pushed around some papers. There was a coffee cup beside it all. Archer picked up the cup, Young looked at the papers.

"She's been working."

Archer glanced at the papers. "She's been editing for someone, this isn't her name."

"Pseudonym," Young murmured, as he read the work.

"How do you know? Could be she was helping someone out."

"I know it's hers. She has a very distinct style."

Archer half listened. He picked up the cup and sniffed the cold dark liquid in the bottom. He lost interest and put it back down.

There was no sign of a struggle in any of these rooms. Then again, Josie's car didn't exactly throw up any clues as to her whereabouts. Archer left the den light on and went into the hall. He had taken one step into the living room when suddenly he saw a dark flash out of the corner of his eye. He crouched fast and drew his gun smoothly only to hold up.

"Oh, my God." Daniel threw himself away from Archer and against the wall. Archer stood up, fighting the urge to laugh.

"Cat, Daniel. I think you're safe."

Archer left that behind for Daniel to chew on as he followed the skittish animal into the kitchen and finally to the back door. The cat wanted out, and it wanted food. He reached down and picked it up. There was meat on its bones. Archer dropped the cat and opened the door. He found a can of food, opened it, and put it in the dish. He put the can in the trash, and that's when he saw the wine glasses. Archer dug them out: the bowls were dry, but there was a ring of red wine in each of them. One was cracked. It was probably nothing, but he took them out of the trash, wrapped them in a towel, and went to find Daniel. The man was sitting on the sofa. He stayed silent while Archer put the towel near the door.

"Anything in here?" Archer asked.

"No. Not even a message on her machine," Daniel answered.

"Then if she's missing, she was probably taken sometime this afternoon after she picked up her messages."

"You can't say that," Daniel scoffed. "Maybe there weren't any."

"Women who look like her have messages," Archer noted. "And a reporter has people calling her with ideas, information, deadlines. The mail has been picked up. It came today. It's on the table. I'll find out when it was dropped."

Daniel's head swiveled as if he was looking at each of the things Archer pointed out. For a moment he considered the floor and then raised his head.

"What's in the towel?"

"Wine glasses," Archer answered.

"Why are you taking them?"

"Two glasses in the trash is kind of weird, especially when only one is broken. Maybe they can tell us something. Fingerprints. We can swab the inside for DNA in case we get someone to match it against."

"If you think those glasses are evidence of something, you shouldn't tamper with them," Daniel said. "Imagine if Josie Bates is dead, and you have contaminated evidence that would have proved who her killer was. Some lawyer as good as her would have a field day."

"I don't want to hear that again, Young. Don't even think it," Archer said.

"What?"

"That Josie is dead," Archer lashed out. "Why in the hell are you thinking about trying the guy who killed her? Why aren't you thinking of things that will help us find her alive?"

"Because I'm practical, and you're emotional."

Daniel stood up and stomped to the front door. He took the towel and went into the kitchen. Archer heard the can lid open and the careful tinkle of glass. When Daniel returned he was empty handed but full of things to say.

"I'm not assuming anything, Archer, I am simply anticipating all outcomes. If there is the slightest possibility that Ms. Bates and Erika are dead, I will not let you hobble the actual investigation before it starts. It's time we called someone with real authority."

"Who would you suggest?" Archer challenged. "You think LAPD is going to be any more responsive than Hermosa was? These are grown women. You don't know shit about how the system works, you only think you do."

Archer turned on his heel, determined to get those glasses if for no other reason than to knock Daniel Young down a peg. Daniel grabbed him. Archer spun. The two men faced off. Surprisingly, Daniel Young didn't back down. He lowered his voice as he tried to tame the situation.

"The police will listen now. We have the same list found in two cars, Ms. Bates has now been gone over twenty-four hours, and Erika isn't here. What more do we need?"

"How about some evidence that something has happened to either one of them?" Archer said tightly. "The list can't be construed as threatening. Josie isn't around, but you are. I can make a case for Josie being in trouble because I know her habits. What are we going to tell anyone about this lady, huh? The cops are going to laugh at you when you tell them you want to file a missing persons on a woman you haven't seen in ten years." Archer threw his arms out wide. "Are we going to say we're concerned because her house is too neat? We don't know if she goes out for a late dinner every night. She may be screwing her boyfriend's brains out at his place."

"That's crude." Daniel's face flooded with color. Archer almost laughed. He never would have taken Young for a stuffed shirt.

"That's life," Archer snapped. "Here's reality, Young. The most we'd get from the cops are questions about why we're trespassing."

"Alright then." Daniel's jaw set. "Since we're already trespassing, let's finish the job."

Daniel stormed past Archer, out the back, across the small yard, and up to the one car garage with Archer on his heels. He paused as if he expected Archer to do the heavy lifting.

"Go for it."

Archer let his eyes rest on the heavy door. It was freshly painted but as old as the hills and heavy as a boulder. Erika Gardener must have some guns on her to open that thing every day. When Daniel continued to hesitate, Archer goaded him.

"If she can do it, I bet you can."

The doctor took hold of the handle and yanked. Archer was about to help when Young gave it one more heave and lifted the thing smoothly. The ancient springs creaked. The door fell into place. Young stepped back and rubbed his hands together to clean off the dust. Archer took a step forward, and the two men stood shoulder-to-shoulder as they looked at the yellow VW bug inside. When Archer made a move toward it, Daniel put his arm out to block him.

"I'll do it," he said.

"Don't leave your prints."

"You're right. I'd hate to get to court and have someone tear apart my testimony because I made a simple mistake," Daniel drawled.

The garage was neat but not fastidiously kept. Erika Gardener had the same stuff in her garage as everyone else did: storage boxes, old paint, yard tools. The structure was original, the wood frame was pocked by termites and dry rot, and the rafters were laced with spider webs. The car was clean and had been washed recently. That was something Erika Gardener had in common with Josie: they both took care of their cars like babies.

Archer flipped a switch. The bare bulb gave off a dim light that turned Daniel Young's tan to yellow and his blond hair almost dark. Grabbing a couple of rags, Archer tossed one Daniel's way before going to the trunk. Daniel opened the driver side door.

"Got it," Daniel said. He was still hunched over as he extricated himself from the small car. Archer looked up. Daniel was holding what appeared to be a Xerox of the list that was making the rounds. "Erika's name has a line through it."

Archer nodded. He looked in the trunk. A bunch of empty water bottles nestled against a pile of cloth grocery bags. Erika Gardener was a schizoid environmentalist. There was another bag way in the back. Archer grabbed it. Inside were workout clothes, a make-up bag and a couple of envelopes. It looked as if she had taken the mail as she was running out to the gym. The car door slammed and Daniel came around the back.

"Anything?" he asked.

"I would say so." Archer tossed the bag into the back of the car and looked at the envelope in his hand. The return address was intriguing. It was already open so he pulled out the contents.

"That's illegal," Daniel Young advised.

"Call a cop." Archer said absently as he read the letter. He read it again and handed it to Daniel Young.

"Parole department?"

"Yeah, a little letter of release notification signed by one Cuwin Martin."

CHAPTER 17

An Outbuilding in the California Mountains

Erika breathed hard. She heaved, but there was nothing in her system to throw up. She was waking more often now. When she spoke her words were as thick as her tongue, but at least she was speaking.

"Time is it?"

Josie answered. "Eight. Nine. I don't know. Could be midnight."

"Days?"

"One at least. Probably two," Josie answered. "What were you doing before?"

"Don't know." she paused, and searched for moisture in her mouth, looking for some way out of the fog. "You?"

"Can't remember," Josie pulled on the rope. "Been in court lately? Had any legal problems?"

Josie pulled on the rope again. The knot gave. Not an inch, not even a millimeter, but Josie felt it and smiled. She had worked enough volleyball net ropes on the beach to know when a knot was giving and the rope was stretching.

"No. You?"

Josie laughed, "I'm always in court. I'm a lawyer? You?"

"I write..." Everything she said was truncated, but the last bit of information was enough to spark something in Josie's memory.

"Erika Gardener? You wrote for the Times. You wrote a book. The Broken System. I know you. You were-"

"My arms.... Blood..."

She hiccupped and cried without tears and sobbed dryly. Hysteria had crept in and wanted to lie down beside her. Josie wasn't going to let that happen.

"Take a minute. The blood might be from your wrists." Josie counted off the seconds as she tried to be patient. "Anything major?"

"My face is bleeding."

"Okay. That's okay, right?"

"Not your face," Erika mumbled.

"Got me there," Josie chuckled. "Put your legs up against the wall and push. Be careful. Anything broken?"

"No."

"Look, the knot on my rope is on the inside where my wrists are crossed. I can reach it with the fingers of one of my hands. Can you reach yours?"

"On the side. I touched -" She sighed. Josie knew Erika was fading.

"Erika, listen," Josie called, not wanting to lose her again. "That's good. You should be able to feel around the knot. Feel around and see if there's a strand that isn't pulled as tight as the others. Do you understand?"

"Yeah." She sighed again. "So tired."

"I know, but it gets better. It wears off. We're overdue for another dose, so we've got to work fast. We need to be ready when whoever took us comes back."

"Or not."

Those words hung in the air for a moment then swung like a pendulum over both of them. Josie shook her head. She'd be damned if she would think the worst.

"Either way, we're going to have to get ourselves out of this mess. Are you with me?"

"Uh-huh."

"Come on, Erika. I sure as hell don't want to die. Come on. Wake up. Wake up!"

"Trying..."

"Okay. Okay," Josie calmed herself. "You wrote for the Times. *You covered me. When. What case? Rayburn? Was that it?"*

"Hernandez."

"Hernandez?" Josie muttered. Her brow beetled. " Xavier Hernandez? That's ancient history. There has to be something else. Think, dammit."

Erika drew a deep breath and when she spoke it was with a note of pity, a trill of despair.

"You don't know, do you?"

CHAPTER 18

Archer's Apartment, Hermosa Beach

Archer took a sleeping pill and set the alarm for six. Daniel Young had gone back home, outraged by the news that Xavier Hernandez had been released and the fact that he hadn't been notified. No surprise there. A few pointed questions and Archer determined that Hernandez had never threatened Daniel Young or tried to contact him after his incarceration. Victims and/or their families were notified of bail hearings and prisoner release if the system worked right. That didn't explain contacting Erika Gardener or Josie Bates unless Hernandez had said something in prison. Still, if he had threatened either one of them he wouldn't have been released. Something wasn't kosher but they weren't going to find out what it was that night. And Archer didn't have time to read the thousands of pages of transcripts in Josie's boxes, so he did the next best thing and listened as Daniel filled him in.

"Xavier Hernandez killed Janey Wilson and Susie Atkins after picking them up on the highway that ran through the desert. Their car broke down. The young man with them – Rothskill? – he hitched a ride in order to get to help."

"Yeah, I got that. Do you remember why the Atkins count was dismissed?"

They now knew Erika Gardener had not gone to the store, she was not being wined and dined at the latest club in Hollywood; she was not visiting friends. Archer sensed that they had just missed whatever happened, that they were 'this' close to understanding it, that whatever was going on was so simple it would torture Archer for the rest of his life if things didn't work out well. Daniel talked on, so involved with his story that he didn't realize Archer was lost in thought. For Daniel, this whole thing could have happened yesterday.

"Josie Bates argued that Susie Atkins died of complications of her chronic medical problems. At best, Hernandez could be charged with gross negligence. The judge threw out that count. I think the prosecutor was relieved. He knew he was outgunned on that one given what Ms. Bates brought to the prelim."

"Do you remember what she argued specifically?"

"I'll never forget. Susie had a heart problem and asthma. The prosecution could offer no definitive evidence that the poor girl had died of manual strangulation. Josie Bates showed – with medical experts backing her up, I might add – that Susie could have died of a severe asthma attack or cardiac arrest. There was no petechial hemorrhaging, so if Atkins had died before the strangulation, Hernandez couldn't be convicted of murder. Bates convinced the judge it was a long shot for the prosecution to try and convict Hernandez on that count, and that the state would save a bundle by just focusing on Janey. There weren't any semen samples from Susie. Xavier told me he couldn't complete the act because the girl was too fat."

"And Janey?"

"Beaten horribly. Violated."

"Then no way Hernandez is out in ten on a first degree conviction," Archer scoffed.

"The judge allowed the jury to consider first and second degree, remember? Ms. Bates convinced the jury that Janey died during hard, consensual sex. Hernandez was convicted of second degree murder." Daniel shook his head as he recalled the injustice of it all. "A sixteen year old girl. Daughter of a minister. What Josie Bates did to that girl's memory was as brutal as what Hernandez did to her body."

"The victim was a kid. What could Josie possibly have argued to convince a jury that she would consent to sex with a stranger, much less an encounter like that?"

"She introduced the girl's diary," Daniel answered. "Josie Bates read it aloud and used it to cross examine Isaiah. It was hard to watch. I doubt Ms. Bates was even aware of the revulsion we all felt. She seemed to relish the attack."

"A preacher's kid had other encounters?"

"No. She had written about her fantasies and questions about sexual interaction. She was nothing but a curious girl who wanted some excitement but lived in a throwback world of God and repression. Ms. Bates was cruel and cutthroat. She took something innocent and turned it into something vile. Your friend was like a barbarian cutting a swath through a village. No one was safe."

Archer shuddered, knowing Daniel spoke the truth. Josie had been that hard; she wasn't now. Whoever wanted to punish her for what she did in that courtroom had chosen a hell of a weird time to do it. Sin had been committed, but she had gone on to make restitution. He didn't want to hear about the woman Josie had been.

Archer was about to say that to Daniel Young, but the man was staring out the window, his head turned away. The rage that poured off him was palpable. Archer had no doubt it was real, he was just surprised that he carried such indignation for Janey Wilson, a young girl he had never met. Finally, Archer broke the silence.

"What about Erika Gardener?"

"I'm sorry, what?" Daniel turned back to Archer. Even in the dark he could see that Daniel was pale and shaking with his emotions.

"Gardener. What about her?"

"I don't know," Daniel said.

"And you?"

"Me?" They had hit the freeway and the oncoming lights undulated through the interior of the Hummer. Young looked as if he were underwater, his face recognizable but changing with each little wave of light.

"Yeah," Archer said, "Why single you out for his little list?"

"I testified that he was sane, and that he acted with aforethought and malice. I faced him down in that courtroom while Josie Bates tried to trip me up. Her cross-examination was unwarranted, unprofessional and her points had no bearing on the matter at hand." Daniel's voice rose and filled the car. "That girl, me, the boy who was supposed to supervise the volunteers-"

"Paul Rothskill?

"Yes, she vilified him. He was only nineteen, and Bates tore him to shreds on the stand. If she could have, she would have convicted him of the killings to save Hernandez. And, of course, Isaiah Wilson was in her sights. Josie Bates was a sorceress suggesting theories to the jury, conniving to trip up witnesses, creating stories out of thin air that were as potent as a magic spell, but what I said was the truth and nothing after that should have mattered."

"Too bad nobody believed you," Archer muttered.

Daniel pulled back as if he had been slapped. He thought for only a second, looked at Archer for only a second longer, and then turned back to gaze out the window.

"They'll believe me now, won't they?"

An Outbuilding in the California Mountains

"Hernandez can't be out. Not possible."

"Fifteen to life," Erika said.

"Nobody who did what he did gets out in fifteen. The press would have been on it. I would have seen something. And it's only been what? Nine, ten years?"

"A letter came."

"Damn! Shit!" Josie strained at her binding. She pulled. She twisted. She yanked her wrists up and gritted her teeth and cried out in pain and frustration.

"Stop," Erika pleaded.

Josie panted with her futile efforts, and then did as Erika asked. She couldn't wrap her mind around the new information.

"There has to be something else. Hernandez might hate your guts, but he would have been executed if it wasn't for me."

"Maybe not him." Erika's voice rose but her words slurred.

"Who else then? Xavier's mother? She couldn't do this." Josie talked over her.

"No."

"The victim's families? The preacher…" Josie challenged but Erika was thrashing and mumbling.

"It's hot. It's so hot."

Exhausted, Josie put her head down, partly on her arm and partly on the ground. There was truth in that. It was hot and she had no water and –

Suddenly, Josie's ears pricked. She heard something scraping, something rolling, the sound of plastic crumpling. Erika moved and struggled, and that's when Josie realized the sound was inside the hut, not outside. She knew exactly what Erika was doing.

"Hey! Stop! Don't drink that water. That's how he's doing it."

Josie threw herself backward, threw her arms up as though she could turn and knock that water bottle out of Erika Gardener's mouth, and then she forgot about Erika altogether. Suddenly, she felt like she was floating. When she looked up, she couldn't believe what she was seeing.

"Oh my God," Josie breathed.

The San Franciscan Bar, San Fernando Valley

"One more time, Sam."

Liz Driscoll pushed her glass toward the bartender. It was the fourth time that night and the second since Archer had called. She sat with one elbow on the bar, cradling her head. She wasn't drunk, she was just thinking. When Sam slid the bourbon and water in front of her she looked at it like a crystal ball, didn't get a message from the great beyond, and took a good long slug.

Liz was a regular at The San Franciscan, choice watering hole for cops who lived out in the boonies. If you wanted someone to rail at, find someone to commiserate with, hook up someone to bounce an idea off with impunity, then this was the place to do it. Tonight, Jerry Healy sat on the stool next to her. He worked vice in the valley.

"It's not like you got anything solid, right? I mean what's this guy-"

"Archer," Liz filled in the blank as she took another drink.

"Okay, what's this guy Archer want you to do? You can't open a file. I mean, you could, but only if you tell your captain, 'cause this is an adult."

"My captain's not going to go for it. Archer likes to fly low under the radar and this woman is high profile, but she's erratic. She's ballsy. Captain'll just tell me to hang for a while but I trust–" Liz's voice trailed off into her glass.

"Archer," Healy filled in.

"Yeah, I do. He's solid. Good instincts, and now he's telling me there's another woman in the mix-"

"In Hollywood," Healy offered as Liz lost the thread of her conversation once again.

"Oh, forgot I told you. Yeah, Hollywood." Liz sighed.

"So go to LAPD, and see what you can find out. You've got a name, right? You can find out if they've got any complaints, anyone reporting her missing- "

"Yeah, and I could just poke around. You know. Doesn't cost anything to just poke around."

"Yeah, poke around," Healy reiterated and drained his beer. "Well, gotta go. Wife wants me to spend more time with her."

"Thanks, Healy."

"No problem, Driscoll." He put his hand on her shoulder. "You're a good guy."

Liz drained her glass and thought about that. Damn straight she was a good guy. The only question was what kind of cop was she? The kind who took a risk because it was right, or handed off a situation to the keep-an-eye-on-it file? Easy enough to fill in LAPD cop to cop. It was more than most would do. She wouldn't piss off Hagarty, but she wouldn't blow it off either.

Liz tossed some bills on the bar, heard the clunk of her heavy boots meeting the old linoleum floor, looked over at a man and woman in the back booth and wished, just once, that she'd be back there with someone someday. Preferably with a guy who was single. Someone like Archer. She smirked, knowing that would probably never happen. She wasn't that kind of woman. She was the kind everyone figured could take care of herself, the kind who was too smart-mouthed for her own good, too afraid to let down her guard in case someone took the opportunity to pop her one. Then again, Josie Bates was that kind of woman, and she had Archer and that kid worried sick about her. If she disappeared, who would push hard enough to get the cops to act? She couldn't think of a soul, and with that realization Liz Driscoll made a decision.

She could at least be the cop who looked into something for someone.

San Diego Freeway, North

He was disappointed it was so late. He would have preferred to make this trip earlier in the evening, but things hadn't worked out according to his timetable. Not that he was far off: three hours or four at most. And he liked the night better than the day anyway. It was very pleasant to let his mind wander while he drove, although his mind never really did wander very far. He was quite a single-minded person, after all. Only a determined person, sure of their – dare he think it? – Crusade, could juggle the balls he was juggling. He supposed he could have just stayed home, had a nice dinner, left those two women to their own devices, but where would be the satisfaction in that? That's really all he wanted. Satisfaction.

He turned off the freeway and headed toward the road that would take him to the place where he would park. He was surprised to see a car coming down the winding road toward him. He cut his eyes toward it as it passed. A middle-aged man was behind the wheel, bored, exhausted after a day at a mundane job or despondent after a fight with the wife. The man didn't turn his head to look at the car passing him. Good. The man was oblivious.

He drove another seven tenths of a mile, looked for the rock face on the left, the one with the three-mile marker near it, and the pine growing out of it at a distinctive angle. The rock itself was covered with infantile graffiti. He pulled across the road into a nearly hidden cul de sac that curved into the mountain. It was just big enough for the car. Only someone with superior powers of observation – or perhaps divine influence – would notice this place. Luckily, there weren't many of those.

When he got out he took the carefully prepared package, breathed deeply and thought 'lovely'. It was cooler up here and quiet and calming. He started to walk using only a small flashlight to show him the way. He walked a good long way, thinking of nothing in particular now that he was at his destination. Though there was no path, he knew the way well, and, when he reached the cement hut he took no care to disguise the sound of his approach. They would be asleep, his little lovelies. Asleep until he let them wake.

Josie Bates' House, Hermosa Beach

Hannah had every intention of staying awake all night, but when she heard Billy Zuni start to snore softly from his bed on the couch, when Max climbed into bed with her and curled his back into her, even those perpetual numbers running through her head stuttered and stopped. The scars on her arms didn't tighten and ache as they sometimes did when the world was dark and quiet. Sleep came and she was peaceful and that was something Hannah seldom was. It was as if God knew she would need every ounce of energy in the days to come, as if He had reached out his big and graceful hand and drew it softly down her brow and over her eyes. It seemed He cupped her cheek, but it was only Max's soft fur she felt against her face, not God's hand. Hannah put her arm around the dog and rested. No matter what happened, at least she would have known what it was like to have a home. For that she would be eternally grateful.

An Outbuilding in the California Mountains

He arrived at the hut so quickly he had to look behind to make sure that he had not unwittingly cut a path others could follow. There was nothing. He might as well have been a heavenly spirit gliding over the dried leaves and brittle sticks. It was only his exceptional sensibilities that made the journey easier each time. Or, the ease might have to do with the fact that he carried so little this time.

He whistled a little tune, softly out of respect for these lovely surroundings. Most would be afraid of nights in the forest. Not him. Not he? No matter. He put down the small flashlight he carried and took out the two bottles of water, the picture and the tape he had carried in his backpack. He would be in and out in seconds, then he would go home for a nice cup of tea, say his prayers and lay himself down to sleep.

Smiling at this little turn of phrase, he slid back the round piece of metal that locked the door from the outside and opened it wide enough to slip through. He left the flashlight pointing toward the opening. Inside it was blacker than pitch and smelled of urine and sweat. He took a moment to gaze at the silhouettes of the two sleeping women. Oh, he thought, how the mighty had fallen. But the moment was over and he went to work.

Stepping between them, he put a water bottle near the blonde. It was not laced quite so heavily with the medication. He wanted them to start coming out of their stupor slowly. Hesitating, he almost touched her but then decided the desire wasn't there any longer. How could it be when she looked like this?

He turned and stepped over the tall woman, straddling her. Leaning over, he taped the paper to the cement. She would see it when she woke up and the light would begin to dawn as to why she was there. Almost finished, he bent over and placed the water bottle by her head. Before he set it just right, Josie Bates woke.

Primal instincts drove her. She clutched at him, her hands hitting his crotch, her fingers grasping for anything to hold onto. But his reactions were good, his instinct for survival finely tuned, and he acted even more quickly than she: flinging himself away, kicking at her, flailing at her. She made sounds like the animal that she was, but he took no pleasure in it as he twirled, fell, and threw himself through the door.

Then it was his own grunting he heard, his own scraping breath as he pushed the door closed, grappled to find the metal bar, and shoved it through the lock. When that was done, he stumbled toward the closest tree, whirled around, fell onto the ground, and collapsed against the trunk. He pulled his knees up to his chest, wrapped his arms around them, and buried his face against them.

In the dark, he heard her calling for him to come back. Help! Help! Save us! He heard her make promises. Then she stopped promising and started begging. Slowly, he lowered his hands, raised his head and sat up straighter. The sound of her begging calmed him and brought him pleasure. Finally, he stood up and smiled. He was beyond pleased. He had thought she was stronger than this. In his wildest dreams he never expected to hear Josie Bates beg.

Picking up the flashlight, he turned his back and walked down the mountain. Soon, he was back to the car, starting the engine, driving away down the winding road. By the time he reached his home, he was in control once again. He showered, lamented that he had not changed clothes before going to the mountains, realized there was nothing to be done now about his favorite pants and climbed naked into bed.

Then he did what he always did when he thought of the blond woman in the hut: he touched himself. Just as he felt his manhood responding, just as he was sure he was going to end the night on an explosively satisfactory note, he stopped his pumping and caressing, and he wilted into a pitiful, pliable little mound of flesh. The blond woman's image could not keep him erect because there was something about the tall woman that made him afraid in his own bed. Finally it dawned on him. He knew exactly what it was. Josie Bates had grabbed him. She had stood up and called to him.

Josie Bates was free.

CHAPTER 19

Day 2
Hermosa Beach Police Department

"Driscoll."

Liz looked up from the printouts to find Captain Hagarty standing in the doorway of her cubicle. He was a good-looking guy; he could have gone back on the street any day in uniform and cut a fine figure.

"Yeah?" Liz hoped he didn't notice she was green around the gills.

"It's damn early." He sipped from his Starbucks cup. He hadn't taken his jacket off yet.

"Yeah," Liz mumbled.

"Anything you want to share?"

"Nope. Just being a conscientious public servant," she answered.

Hagarty nodded, sipped his coffee again, and kept his eye on her as she did on him. Liz prayed that her eyes were not too wide, her smile not as brittle as it felt, and the sweat starting to form under her arms not evident.

"Okay then. The citizens of Hermosa Beach can rest easy."

"Absolutely. On the ball, Captain."

Hagarty lingered a second longer, stepped into the cubicle and put a piece of paper in front of her.

"Do not misunderstand. That's as far as it goes on my dime," he said and then he was gone.

Liz picked up the paperwork he'd dropped on her desk. Hagarty had given permission to sweep Josie Bates' Jeep for evidence.

Mira Costa High School, Manhattan Beach

"Hannah Sheraton?"

Hannah stood up and walked past the woman who held the little swinging gate open like it was the door to the death chamber. The gate swung closed with a little thump and whoosh, and the woman hurried ahead to open the door to the principal's office. Mrs. Letitia Gray-Manning, head honcho at Mira Costa High glanced at Hannah but reserved her smile for the secretary.

"Thanks, Mrs. Taylor," Leticia Manning said even as she looked at Hannah. "Have a seat."

Hannah did as she was told and pulled her satchel onto her lap. It was Louis Vuitton, a reminder of her mother who looked darn good on the outside, but had a lot of baggage on the inside. Hannah held onto it partly because it had belonged to Linda, her mother, and partly because her artist's heart couldn't bear to part with something so beautifully crafted. In the same way, her artist's eye couldn't help but be drawn to the incredible hand stitched quilt on the wall behind Mrs. Manning's desk or the jewelry she wore. It was always the same, silver fashioned by designers who lived for their craft. Someday she'd like to talk to Mrs. Manning about art, but now Hannah was on her guard and art was the last thing on her mind.

"So, what do you want to tell me?" Mrs. Manning said.

"Other than Mr. Dreyfus doesn't know how to teach history?" Hannah responded.

"How about why Ms. Bates missed her appointment with me yesterday?"

Hannah's eyes flickered behind long lashes, but Mrs. Manning, for all her attentiveness, missed it.

"She's sick. I'm sorry. I forgot to tell you," Hannah lied easily, another talent she learned from her mother. Hannah, though, used the gift sparingly and only when absolutely necessary. Sadly, it was necessary now and she regretted it. Mrs. Manning was one of the few people Hannah trusted.

"I see." The principal clasped her hands and leaned forward. She was an attractive lady: petite, pretty, stylish, and no dummy. Hannah's gaze skated over the pictures that covered the woman's credenza: a husband, two children, and a pug dog named Homer who seemed as much a part of the family as any of the humans. It was all so normal. Hannah would kill for normal. Hannah would kill to get out of this office fast. Hannah would kill for…

"Hannah!"

The girl started, her green eyes turned back and met Mrs. Manning's dark ones. Her lips opened. All she had to do was say the word and this woman would…Hannah had no idea what this woman would do if she knew Josie was missing.

"If there is a problem," Mrs. Manning went on kindly, "I'm here to help. If you're having trouble with Ms. Bates we have counselors to help you work it out. I know your situation is an unusual one and we are..."

"No," Hannah interrupted. "No trouble with Josie. Everything is good. She just forgot because she's got this big case."

"I thought she was sick."

Mrs. Manning picked up a pencil and ran it through her fingers. Mesmerized by the action, Hannah mentally tapped a finger to keep time with the pencil's journey. It turned once, twice, four times. Eight...

Hannah's jaw clenched when Mrs. Manning stopped at nine passes. The girl desperately wanted her to turn that pencil upside down twenty times. Since the magic number wasn't meant to be, Hannah forced herself to pay attention.

"I'm sorry. She has a cold and this case. Even Josie can't do everything," Hannah answered smoothly.

"I see." Tish Manning sat back, paused and finally drew a black, plastic bound calendar toward her.

"I'm open Friday at noon or," she licked the tip of her fingers and flipped the page, "Next Tuesday. Three o'clock. Do you want to call Ms. Bates now and find out what's good for her?"

Hannah shook her head. "Tuesday at three will be good."

"Alright. I'll put her in. Don't forget to tell her." Mrs. Manning jotted the note, closed the calendar and smiled. "Thank you, Hannah."

The girl nodded, got up and slung the big bag over her shoulder. She turned toward the door. Nothing in her demeanor reflected her feeling of both relief at dodging a bullet and concern that Josie may not be able to keep the appointment. But before she could get out the door, Mrs. Manning called to her.

"Hannah?"

"Yes?"

"Cut Mr. Dreyfus some slack, okay?"

She nodded and left the principal's office. In the hall, Hannah checked her watch as she hurried toward an empty room. Ducking in, she dialed the code for the home answering machine. No messages. She dialed Josie's phone as she had done almost every hour and, once again, got Josie's message.

"Where are you?" Hannah whispered desperately. " Please call me."

She hung up quickly, hoping Josie's battery wouldn't run out before she could return the call. She hoped Archer could connect with the phone company and track that phone. She was dialing Archer just as the bell rang. There was nothing she could do but go to her next class. The last thing Hannah wanted to do was draw any more attention to herself at school. Mrs. Manning was satisfied and she would have to be, too, at least for the next forty-five minutes.

With fifteen hundred students to worry about, Tish Manning seldom wasted time wondering if she should act when one was particularly bothersome. She wasted none now as she picked up the phone.

"Gracie? I hate to bother you, but I need a favor." Tish listened to the admonition that Gracie, one of four school counselors, was not bothered by the interruption and would be happy to do a favor for the principal anytime. Anytime at all. When Gracie's assurances had run their course, Tish said, "Pull Hannah Sheraton's file? Yes. Soon as you can."

Christian Broadcast Complex, Orange County

Archer was at the church before the doors opened. Technically, he wasn't really at a church. Rather, he was at the digs of Reverend Isaiah Wilson. The preacher's show was broadcast from the Christian Broadcast Complex in Orange County. Archer had seen the place in a long shot during a newscast when a whistleblower outed Three Crosses, a televangelist network run by a guy who liked white polyester suits and his wife who sported big wigs, fake eyelashes and crocodile tears. He and Josie had watched the report. Archer couldn't understand how people could fall for that crap; Josie understood the need to clutch at straws – even ones as short as those offered by Three Crosses. The performances were as mesmerizing, curious and compelling as was the downfall of the preacher and his wife.

Archer had never seen Isaiah Wilson's shtick, but as he parked the Hummer and checked the clock he held out no hope that Wilson was any different than the Three Crosses folk. While he waited for the place to open, he dialed Liz who filled him in on the progress with the Jeep. Archer was relieved that Liz wasn't just on board, now she was ready to row. Getting out of the car, he locked it despite the fact that he had parked on hallowed ground. There were a few cars in the lot including a buttercup yellow Rolls Royce. The license plate read IBELEV.

"I just bet you do," Archer muttered as he passed it on his way toward the studios.

The outside of the complex was impressive, sort of a mix of Persian palace and Malibu mansion. It was all white save for the giant gold cross on the ornate turret at one end and little gold crosses running the perimeter of a deck on the other. Archer could make out umbrellas on the deck and they were topped with finials in the shape of baby gold crosses. Behind the main building was a huge, white inflatable revival tent. The parking lot was large enough to accommodate any and all who flocked to the Word. A wrought iron fence held up a golden gate, and that led to a golden path, and that led to a golden door. The gate and the door were still emblazoned with the three crosses logo.

The gardens through which Archer passed were beautifully tended: flowers and trailing plants and topiary shaped to look like saints and lambs and more crosses. Despite the fact that two freeways intersected close by, that a major shopping center wasn't more than spitting distance, and there was a very, very busy street running just behind, the place was silent and peaceful and comforting. Archer shook his head. He didn't want to be peaceful or comforted. He wanted some answers.

He pulled on the huge gold plate handle on the door. It swung open on well-oiled hinge, and Archer stepped into the rarified air of Three Crosses studio. The garden had been serene, but inside was downright heavenly. Directly in front of him was a mini sweep of a grand staircase that led to a golden throne. The throne was bathed in a silvery light that danced, not with dust motes, but something that looked like glitter. Archer raised his eyes, trying to figure out where the light source was, but he couldn't identify it. Beneath his feet was white marble shot with pink veins. His ears filled with celestial music. He smelled apple pie baking.

His soft-soled shoes made no sound, and he didn't call for anyone. He wasn't a believer, a sinner or a mendicant. He was on a mission, and from what he could tell today Isaiah Wilson would be filming. All Archer had to do was find him before he started.

"Can I help you?"

Archer turned smoothly and found himself face to face with a lovely girl/woman. Her eyes sparkled and her skin was polished to a luster. Her hair was caught up in two barrettes in front and hung down to her rear end in back. At least Archer imagined it hung to her rear end, but it was hard to tell where that would be since she was encased in a sack of a floral dress. A plain white Peter Pan collar circled her neck, and turned up white cuffs finished off the long sleeves. The sleeves were puffed at the shoulder, but there were no seams, no decorative stitching, and no tailoring that gave a hint of the body underneath. The fabric fell to mid-calf and her legs were covered in white stockings. Her feet were nestled in the most sensible shoes Archer had ever seen. His first thought was of the Amish; his second was that the Amish were more fashion forward.

"I'm here to see Isaiah Wilson."

"Oh, I didn't know he had an appointment." Her eyes widened as if she was ready to confess to a sin she didn't know she had committed.

"I didn't call ahead," Archer informed her. "I wanted to catch him before he started filming."

"The reverend is in contemplation before the show. Perhaps, I could give him a message."

The girl in the floral dress smiled beautifully and made a mistake. She leaned toward the hallway behind her, taking one step as if to block Archer even as she spoke of Isaiah. Archer smiled back and patted at the pockets in his windbreaker.

"That would be great. I don't have a pen or paper. Do you think you could find me something to write with?"

"Oh, certainly."

She brightened. Service was her middle name. She turned and left in a flurry of long hair and flowered cotton. Archer seized the moment and went down the hall.

CHAPTER 20

An Outbuilding in the California Mountains

Josie sat in the corner of the hut, her eyes trained on the missing brick high up in the wall. She had been awake since dawn, not that she had slept that much anyway. The adrenaline rush when she realized someone was inside the hut had been impossible to shake. Her joy at believing they were saved turned to revulsion when she realized she was grappling with their jailer.

She had thrown herself at him and tried to subdue him, but she was weary. Heat and thirst and hunger had taken their toll and she hadn't been able to change their situation. Yet, even now, Josie remained energized by the confrontation and by the fact that her hands, while still bound, were no longer tied to the stake.

Erika had slept through it all and continued to sleep as Josie worked to free her, too. Finally, she slid that rope off the stake, rolled Erika Gardener onto her side, adjusted her arms, and arranged her in a position that seemed as if it would be comfortable. She smoothed the woman's hair away from her face, touched her cheek, and, as the light dawned, Josie picked up Erika's water bottle and did what she had to do.

Finally exhausted, Josie settled down with her back to Erika and drifted off to sleep. When she woke the oblong spot of light was in her eyes and Erika was stirring.

"Morning," Josie said.

"I have to pee," Erika mumbled as she rolled over.

"Bathroom's at the end of the hall," Josie said as she smiled and held up her still-bound wrists.

Erika's eyes widened then lowered so that she was looking at her own hands. That's when Erika Gardener began to laugh and so did Josie Bates.

Downtown Los Angeles, Parole Office

Liz Driscoll had been a shitty little kid. She was the only child of an insecure, single mom who slept in her make-up just in case the house caught on fire and she had to run into the waiting arms of some burly, handsome firefighter. Her mother fantasized that she would meet the man of her dreams in the middle of a disaster. Liz thought that didn't sound like much fun, and as she grew up Liz knew that fantasy was downright weird. She didn't dislike her mother; Liz simply didn't feel comfortable with her. That was all good because her mother never felt comfortable with the swaggering tomboy she had birthed either.

There seemed to be nothing in Liz's mother's background that would account for her Perils of Pauline attitude, and there was nothing in Liz's life that accounted for her mannerisms. To her mother's credit, she recognized that fact early on. There were no attempts to dress her up in girl clothes as a child, no lamenting when Liz didn't agonize over boys in high school, and no fight when Liz struck out on her own. Her mother now lived in Chicago and they saw each other twice a year. Neither of them felt a need for more contact, and it finally occurred to them that they were more alike than they were different. They did better knowing they had each other's back than actually having it.

So it was not out of character for Liz Driscoll to be stepping a wee bit over the line without giving too much thought to what her captain would say to her field trip. She wasn't really disobeying orders; she was kind of interpreting them a little more broadly than might have been intended. Hagarty had agreed to have Josie Bates' car checked for evidence, and he had been clear that he wouldn't pay for anything else. But Liz's time wasn't exactly an out-of-pocket expense. She was on the payroll no matter what she was doing or where she was doing it.

If she got called on the carpet, she would plead ignorance and promise never, ever to overstep again. Not wanting to have to play that game if at all possible, Liz added another layer to her strategy by signing out indicating her intent to check parole on one of the guys they had questioned about an assault in Hermosa Beach. His parole officer was downtown in the same office as Cuwin Martin.

Grateful the Harbor Freeway was not her routine commute, Liz swung off the freeway, navigated the one-way streets downtown, and parked in the red zone confident LAPD would offer a little professional courtesy. She clipped around security with a flash of her badge and found Cuwin Martin's office but no Cuwin Martin. No one seemed to know where he was. Liz wandered down the hall toward the vending machines, searched for a buck and considered her choices. Damn government buildings had gone granola. The machine was filled with rotting apples and brown bananas. She would have killed for one of those buttermilk donut things that looked like a log. She put her dollar in, got a quarter and cup of bad coffee back, and put her shoulder up against the wall. She was lost in thought, calculating how long before someone from the Hermosa PD might notice she had been out a good long while, when she heard a laugh that took her back to her academy days. She followed the sound further down the hall, poked her head through one of the doors and said:

"Margie?"

The woman turned her head, saw Liz and said into the phone: "I'll call you back."

Liz offered the big woman behind the ugly desk a smile but had to fight to keep it from freezing on her face. The woman looked like three Margies.

"Lizzie! You mite. I can't believe you came all the way down here to see me."

Liz relaxed and her smile broadened as she walked into the office. Margie pushed her chair away from the desk, and then used the desk for leverage to get up.

"Don't get up!" Liz insisted, sure that if Margie actually made it to her feet she wouldn't be able to stay on them. The woman had been gorgeous when she was a secretary at the academy back when Liz was a recruit.

"Oh, you sweetie, you have no idea how much I appreciate that. Okay, then come on over here and give me a hug. How long's it been?"

Liz did as directed, putting her coffee on the desk just before Margie's giant arms enveloped her. Her ham-hands patted Liz's narrow back. When Margie released her, Liz felt as if she had been shot out of an air gun; their parting was accompanied by a *thwump* as suction was broken. Margie held tight though as she took Liz in head to toe.

"Look at you. You haven't changed a bit." Margie shook her head as she assessed her old friend. "Well, maybe a few wrinkles around the eyes, but, hey, this profession doesn't leave us unscathed, does it? You're not in uniform? Last I heard you were patrol over in Linwood."

"Long time ago. I'm a detective in Hermosa Beach now."

"Nice." Margie gave her a little shake. "Couldn't happen to a better person."

"Yep, a lot of changes over the years." Liz's lips tipped, her shoulder rose in a shrug causing Margie to let loose with a laugh that was even bigger than the one she had before.

"If that isn't the nicest way of saying 'what happened to you?'" Margie let her go and waved a massive arm at a green vinyl chair. "Sit. Sit. I'll tell you the whole sordid story. It will take all of three seconds. Gary left me. I ate a couple of Twinkies – like a box – and decided the hell with it. I liked Twinkies more than Gary, anyway. I don't really give a shit if I don't have a man in my life after what I went through with him, so what the heck? The new and happy me."

"I always liked that about you Margie. Once you decide to do something, you go all out," Liz laughed.

"Yep, always did. Remember that time we hit the bar in…"

Liz rolled her eyes, "I don't want to remember, and I swear if you ever tell anyone about it I'll pull rank."

"Oooh, I'm terrified," Margie's eyes almost disappeared into cheeks that rose and fell with her good humor.

"Yeah, I get that a lot. No respect," Liz cracked. "So, you're good then?"

"Still have a job. Got a drawer full of snacks at the office, a car that I can drive and so far the doctor says my heart can take a few extra pounds. So what brings you down to my neck of the woods?"

"I wanted to see Cuwin Martin. You know him?"

"Yeah. He gives government employees a bad name. What's your beef with him?"

"No beef." Liz took a seat and picked up her coffee. "I've got a situation in Hermosa that is linked to a woman in the Hollywood Hills and everything seems to be linked to one of Cuwin Martin's clients. Name's Xavier Hernandez. Ever heard of him?"

"Honey, if I could remember everyone who went through the system I'd be a goddess. Heck, half the time I don't even remember my own clients." She crossed her arms over her substantial belly and gave Liz her full attention. "Who are you working with at the LAPD?"

"That's the thing. I don't even know if there's an open investigation on the woman in the Hollywood Hills."

"And your victim in Hermosa?"

"Not sure she's a victim yet," Liz shrugged.

"So you've gone rogue. Oh, Lizzie."

Liz considered her coffee then raised her eyes to Margie. "Look, there are too many weird things going on for this to boil down to a couple of women taking a powder for the fun of it. I can make a case for what appears to be a threat in three jurisdictions. Written communication was left in all three cars and had the same information. Two of those receiving those notes are missing; the third has reason to be concerned. I don't have the resources to conduct a full blown investigation even if it was just a local problem, but one of the missing women is–"

"A friend?" Margie interrupted.

"A citizen of some repute and the significant other of a man I know who has good instincts. It's an attorney named Josie Bates. Ever heard of her?"

"Oh yeah, honey, I would say she's a person of some repute," Margie snorted. "I remember her from the McCreary thing. I always assumed she lived Westside. She seemed like a Westsider."

"She does seem like that," Liz agreed, even though saying so felt like speaking ill of the dead. "But nope, she's been in Hermosa a good long time now. This Cuwin guy left his number at her office. Then Archer – he's Bates' significant other and a PI – he had reason to pay a visit to the woman in the Hollywood Hills."

"What's her name?"

Liz dug in her jacket pocket and withdrew a note pad. "Erika Gardener."

Margie swiveled, typed the name and waited.

"She requested a RO a few years ago."

"Against who?" Liz asked.

"It was sealed."

"Odd, but okay," Liz mused.

"Yep." Margie typed again. "Did your guys report her missing?"

"I don't know, why?" Liz scooted forward a little.

"Missing persons opened a file," Margie said with a little smile.

"Wow, didn't know anyone would take it seriously this early," Liz whistled.

"What else you got?" Margie asked.

"Cuwin Martin sent Erika Gardner a form letter advising of Xavier Hernandez's release. We don't know when Bates or the other woman went missing, but we think under thirty-six hours."

"So Hernandez is your best guess at a hub, is he?"

"Until something tells me different." Liz raised a finger and pointed at the computer. "Got anything in that magic machine to help me out?"

Margie wiggled her fingers as if she were casting a spell, raised her eyebrows and said, "Let's see what we can come up with."

She couldn't sit back, she couldn't move forward, but Margie's typing was fast and accurate. She stopped for a minute. Her fingers hovered. A screen scrolled. She typed some more. Another window opened. Liz planted her elbows on the desk and put her chin in one upturned palm. Her other hand still held her coffee cup, but all her attention was on the screen.

"Got him, sweetie." Margie's whisper feathered into a soft whistle. "I remember this one. Those poor little girls. The preacher's daughter and her friend. If he's got your lawyer, I'd let him have her."

"Not an option," Liz laughed. "The verdict was enough to give me pause, but now I want to know why he's out. Ten years is just plain weird."

"Well, he should have fried." Margie sighed, as if to say the system was more than broken. "Just sayin'."

Liz allowed herself a little empathetic twitch, but shit happened as they said. She just wanted to know what shit was happening now. Still, patience was part of the process and she let Margie have her moment. She was back on track the next second without expounding on the failings of the justice system.

"I'll give you the high points." Margie hit print while she was talking. "Hernandez was kept out of the general population for a couple years 'cause there were any number of inmates ready to take him out given the victims: white supremacists, born-agains, neo-Nazis. Anyway, he settles in to CSP in Lancaster. Reads. Likes self-help books and porn. Since nobody was feeding him porn, he pretty much stuck with things like *The 48 Laws of Power*. But that's everybody's favorite inside."

"Never heard of it," Liz muttered.

Margie whipped the paper out of the printer, turned her chair and propped her hands on her stomach.

"You don't know what you're missing. Proverbs and myths and stuff. A con can interpret most of it as permission to screw everybody or beat the shit out of them."

"Hernandez?" Liz eased Margie back.

"Oh, yeah. Funny thing, nobody seemed to care about him."

"Wonder why?"

"I could research it if you want," Margie offered.

"Naw. Time's awastin'."

"Okay, then," she said and went back to her report. "Overcrowding put him back in the general population. Oh, here it is. This is why nobody cared about your man. Carl Potter showed up."

"Who?"

"Carl Potter. He's the one who took that little boy from his bed, dismembered him. Put him in a tree and propped up the body parts on different branches. I think that was the same time that kid, Stephen Winter, was incarcerated. He opened up with an AK47 at a grammar school in Riverside. Killed five little ones and two teachers. He was tried as an adult. They were busy over there."

"Anyway, your guy is on his own and there were no problems for the next five years. So, at that time he was already in for eight. About then, two Mexican mafia go off on a woman guard." Margie dropped the papers and looked at Liz. "I'd like to know whose smart idea it was that little itty-bitty women could be prison guards." She rolled her eyes and leaned forward. "That's just between you and me, of course. You're itty-bitty, but most women aren't you."

"Appreciate that Margie." Liz acknowledged the compliment with a little sniff and a lip tip.

"They beat her with her own stick. She should have been dead, but came away with a broken jaw, shattered cheek, dislocated shoulder, internal injuries and counted herself lucky."

"So what skin did Hernandez have in that game?" Liz drank her coffee and wondered why vending drinks never stayed hot long enough.

"He was washing down the floors when it started. Instead of stepping back, your guy steps in and dispatches one of the Hispanics. According to witnesses, he went nuts and not a peep out of him all those years. But the other one turns on him and almost kills him. By the time order is restored, Hernandez has sustained traumatic brain injury..."

Margie scanned her documents, mumbling to herself as she looked for relevant information.

"Oh. Okay," she said, "I've got it. Hernandez has saved the guard's life, put his own in jeopardy, has a clean record and he can't go back into general population looking like he's working for the man. Then the California Supreme Court decides to order the release of forty-five thousand felons because overcrowding is cruel and unusual punishment. "

"Don't remind me," Liz groaned.

"It is what it is," Margie shrugged. "Anyway, given the state he's in, his P.D. jumps on this and argues for parole. The judge is looking down the road, wanting to do her part to comply with the Supreme Court ruling. Viola! Hernandez is released. No danger to the community, a shining example of a rehabilitated, cold blooded killer – that according to the judge."

"Who was the judge?" Liz asked.

"Katherine Stella."

"Bleeding heart," Liz drawled.

"Brown appointee," Margie responded.

"Brown's first term, no less. The woman's as old as the hills," Liz sneered.

"Neither here nor there, honey." Margie dismissed her commentary.

"You're right. Okay. Do you have an address on him?"

"Sorry, Cuwin would have it." Margie confirmed. "You'll want to talk to him anyway. He'll have met the guy. Seems to me, someone who went through what

Hernandez did might not be all there, and it would take some doing to kidnap two women."

"Can I have that?" Liz reached for the printout, but friendship only went so far.

"Better you get it from Cuwin, and better you didn't tell him we've been digging around. He's a touchy sort."

"Okay," Liz stood up. "I appreciate the info. Gives me something to think about."

Liz rounded the desk, gave Margie a hug, promised not to be a stranger, and went back down the hall to find Cuwin Martin. She wasn't going to drive down again if she could help it. Before she left, Liz had one more question.

"Margie, does it say if he had any visitors while he was in prison?"

"A few."

Margie held the printout. Liz took down the names: Hernandez's mother, a woman named Cory Cartwright and Reverend Isaiah Wilson.

CHAPTER 21

Christian Broadcast Complex, Orange County

Isaiah Wilson was kneeling on the marble floor, head bowed, hands clasped when Archer found him. Archer paused in the doorway of the small, unadorned, and darkened room before easing himself in. He stood against the wall and observed the man.

Wilson wore a dark, well-cut suit brightened by the starched white of his collar and cuffs and the sparkle of gold links in the French cuffs. His hair was a tad long, luxurious and swept back as Archer had seen in his pictures. His shoes were wing tips and, because he was kneeling, Archer saw that the soles and heels were new. Archer didn't feel an aura of spirituality the way he did when he walked into a Catholic church. There was nothing like a cathedral to make a guy feel humble but not insignificant. In this bare room Archer felt only the bare room. No icons – not even a cross – hung on the walls. Isaiah Wilson was so lost in his prayer that it seemed he wouldn't have noticed any of it anyway. But he did notice one thing; he noticed Archer.

"If you'd like to pray with me, you are welcome." He raised his head but did not face Archer immediately.

Finally, he swiveled to reveal his profile, counted another beat and added, "If not, perhaps you could respect my prayer and wait in the lobby."

"I don't think this can wait," Archer said, "even for God."

Archer walked with The Reverend Isaiah Wilson down the hall, through the ornate lobby and into a studio. Wilson nodded to a cameraman, simultaneously raising a hand to someone Archer couldn't see. The studio could have held three hundred people easy, but Archer knew there would be no audience.

"I am sorry to hear that Ms. Bates is missing. God works in mysterious ways."

"You don't sound particularly surprised," Archer said.

"I have tried not to think of Ms. Bates over the years," he said as he went about his housekeeping. "Duane, could you please bring the gladiolas in from the backroom?"

Somewhere, someone went to do his bidding. Archer heard crisp footsteps, doors opening and doors closing.

"When was the last time you saw her?"

"In the courtroom." Isaiah's eyes met Archer's and Archer was taken aback. The preacher's gaze was piercing, and it wasn't an affectation. If he were to tell Archer that he had second sight and that he could see deep into a heart and soul, Archer would believe him. The other thing Archer would have believed is that Isaiah Wilson would have little sympathy if he found a heart in pain or a soul in torment. This was not a man of great empathy.

"The last time I saw Ms. Bates she was embracing the man who raped and killed my daughter. She was smiling. She was victorious."

The gladiolas arrived in a cut glass vase that Duane carried as reverently as if it held the blood of Christ. The flowers reminded Archer of a funeral but his attention to them was fleeting. He refused to be put off by the trappings of this place.

"There's been no contact? No interest in her?" Archer asked.

"I took note of her when I happened to see her written up in the press with one thing or another. I read an article that said she had adopted a young girl. A teenager." Isaiah Wilson picked up a bible and walked with it toward a Plexiglas lectern. "At the time, I wondered how she would feel if that young girl went missing."

"Probably the same way you did when your daughter disappeared."

Those eyes flicked up. Archer thought he saw a tilt of the man's wide thin lips, too.

"No, I don't think so."

Archer was the first to look away, and he did so without understanding why. A moment later he knew what it was. The look Wilson gave him was accusatory and righteous, and Isaiah was happy to hear bad news about Josie. Or was he pleased because Archer was there, and Josie's disappearance wasn't news at all? Perhaps he had been waiting for this moment, rehearsed for it, planned to have that cool attitude that said he was above this particular fray.

"Have you been in Hermosa Beach lately?" Archer asked.

Elegantly, Isaiah Wilson moved about his space, rearranging papers, opening his bible, and marking his place. Finally, he stood behind the lectern, his hands resting lightly atop it as he gave Archer his undivided attention.

"I live in Orange County."

"That doesn't answer my question."

"I know what your question is. I know what you want. You want me to tell you that I have harbored ill will toward Ms. Bates all these years. You want me to say that I blame her for standing between what was just and what is simply lawful. Is that what you want?"

"I don't want to discuss your feelings," Archer countered. "I don't want to rehash old times. Josie Bates and Erika Gardener are missing. They both had dealings with Xavier Hernandez. It is logical that I ended up on your doorstep, and it is logical that I ask if you know where one or both of them are."

"And if I had anything to do with their disappearance?"

"There's that."

"The answer is no. I have not seen either woman. I do not know where they are. Ms. Gardener was a fine writer. She was an advocate for the families."

"And Josie Bates?"

But in the end she is bitter as wormwood. Sharp as a two-edged sword. Her feet go down to death, Her steps lay hold of hell. Let us ponder her path of life – her ways are unstable. You do not know them.

ॐ

Isaiah quoted the Bible solemnly, and then in what passed for a benign smile he added: "Proverbs."

"You know where she is, don't you?" Archer challenged.

"I do not, sir."

"You know who might have done it, don't you?"

"I do not, sir."

"You know people who would like to see something bad happen to Josie, don't you."

"I do not, sir."

"If you did, would you tell me?"

"I'm a man of God, am I not?"

"You're the man who wrote the book on forgiveness and retribution. Which one would it be for Josie Bates?"

Archer was losing patience. Where did you go with someone like this? Someone who didn't react, whose eyes didn't shift, whose lips didn't twitch?

"I suppose you'll have to read the book," Isaiah answered. Archer held the man's gaze, not unaware that there was something going on behind them. "I suppose I should point out that ten years is a long time. Nothing I do could bring my daughter back, so why would I look for justice ten years after it was denied?"

"You think something happening to Josie would be justice?"

"I think whatever happens to Ms. Bates is of her own making, yes." Isaiah was patient but Archer knew he didn't have much time left.

"Did you know that Xavier Hernandez was released?"

"I received a letter."

"How do you feel about that?"

"I accept the system as it stands," Isaiah said.

"Have you seen him?"

"No, and I doubt I will."

"How can you be so sure?"

"I'm sure," Isaiah said.

"I'd like to look in your car, Reverend."

Wilson stopped what he was doing. For the first time he seemed engaged and anxious. No, not anxious. The reverend was annoyed.

"And what would you be looking for?"

"I'm looking for a message from Xavier Hernandez." The reverend raised an eyebrow.

"Reverend Wilson?" A young man came up beside the tall, older man. Archer looked at him and realized he was more than a tech guy; this one was a true believer. "We need to do sound checks."

"Thank you, Richard," Wilson said quietly. The young man melted away and those eyes were on Archer again. "I'm sorry. I have nothing more to tell you, and I can't ask you to stay. I do not preach to an audience."

"No problem. I have a few things to do. Thanks for your time."

There was nothing to be gained by pressing because this guy was cooler than the proverbial cucumber. Knowing he would have to go around the good reverend, Archer left him to preach to the camera and pray into a microphone. Daniel Young had been right about Wilson. He had exploited an opportunity when it was presented, but at what price? It didn't appear his heart had been hardened; it didn't seem that he harbored any resentment.

With Isaiah Wilson lost in the bible lesson of the day, Archer turned and started for the door only to stop midstride as he caught sight of the icon Isaiah Wilson prayed to. It was above the door, and in the preacher's direct line of sight. It was not a cross but a picture of a long-suffering virgin: his daughter, Janey Wilson. Archer's stomach lurched. A lot of people displayed huge, ornately framed pictures of their dead children, but this one was different; this one chilled Archer. Janey Wilson was not captured in a school photo, and this was not a picture of her near a lake or sitting by a tree in a happy moment. This picture was of Janey pale, pretty, young and dead. The morgue sheet was drawn up to cover her breasts, leaving her shoulders bare. Her eyes were closed and the bruises and swelling of her face evident. He could see the ragged wound where Hernandez had slashed her throat.

Slowly, Archer turned back toward the stage. Isaiah Wilson was lit with an ice-white spot. He stood straight, tall and avenging in his black suit. His silver hair glistened under the well-placed lights. His hands held his bible against his chest.

There wasn't a lot that shook Archer, but that picture did. He had never much cared for Catholic holy cards, but at least those were some artist's rendering of beatific suffering; this was suffering and death at its harshest, cruelest, and most brutal. Isaiah Wilson seemed pleased, as if he found both satisfaction and amusement in Archer's surprise and confusion.

"You're welcome to look at my car," Isaiah said again. "If you've seen everything you need to see here, that is."

CHAPTER 22

An Outbuilding in the California Mountains

Josie's fingers worked the knot in Erika Gardener's bindings. Her shoulders hurt, her butt hurt, her head hurt, but she didn't stop trying until Erika pulled her hands away and scooted back against the wall. The blond woman shook back her hair, and then did it again.

Josie stood, spread her legs and bent from the waist, stretching, trying to keep her muscles engaged, but they felt like jelly and she was light-headed. She cursed the drugs they had been given, the lack of food and water and the span of time she had lain unconscious in this heat.

It was getting harder to look at Erika because the woman was a mirror. Josie knew her own clothes were dirty and sweat stained. Her hair was matted, too. Erika had worn make-up – Josie could still see flakes of mascara – but now she looked plain and tired the same way Josie did. The difference between them was that Josie was creating a strategy for escape, and Erika was just mad.

"You should have asked me," Erika grumbled.

"What?" Josie put her back up against the bricks. She wanted to slide down to the ground but forced her knees to lock.

"You should have asked me before you dumped my water out."

"I needed you awake."

"I would rather be asleep. At least I wouldn't be dying of thirst." Erika picked at her skirt. It was cotton and tiered and had been expensive. She tired of her picking, rested her bound hands, and seemed to talk to them. "We're going to die, aren't we?"

"No. We're not."

Josie slid down the wall. Her knees were shaking. Awkwardly she swiped at her short hair, looked around the hut and thought there must be something she was missing.

"We're not tied to a stake anymore. Pretty soon we'll have our hands free."

Erika tipped her head and licked her lips. She frowned. "And when we get our hands free, what are we going to do? Dig at the grout? That'll take about forever."

"We won't have to. He'll be back."

"You don't know that."

"Yes, I do. He has a plan, and he won't stop until it's done. Imagine what he had to go through to get us up here. Nobody who's gone to that much trouble is just going to leave us. He wants something."

"What?" Erika was more than annoyed.

Josie picked up the paper beside her. It was a plain white sheet with a photocopied picture from Xavier's trial on it. Josie knew it was captured from a film clip. Still cameras had not been allowed in the courtroom, but the trial had been televised. At the time, Josie thanked her lucky stars for such exposure. It had been a PR coup. She had been so stupid back then. Still, she was grateful. She had something to use now because of those cameras. She shoved the paper in front of Erika again.

"What do you make of this?"

"I don't know," Erika shrugged.

"Come on. Look," Josie commanded and Erika Gardener glared at her. There was anger behind her tired, frightened eyes, and

Josie wanted it to stay there. She raised the paper and snapped it. "Oh, for God sake. It was left here for a reason,"

"Everybody who's anybody is in that picture," Erika answered without much interest.

"What else? Come on. Help me. I'm scared, too. I'm not thinking straight, but I'm not going to lay down and die." Josie shook the paper. "Look. Answer me."

"I don't know. It's a picture taken in court." Erika struggled to her feet. Her skirt was torn in the back and the fabric dragged on the ground. She had thrown off her one shoe and crumpled when her bare foot hit a stone. "Damn. Damn. Damn."

She raised her eyes to Josie. They were at two ends of the hut and Erika was breathing hard as she fought with herself. Finally, Erika walked back on her knees. She reached out with her bound hands and ripped the paper out of Josie's.

"Okay. Fine. The judge looks surprised. Not angry, just surprised. You're covering whoever is on the stand so I don't know who is sitting there, but you're leaning forward. You're going in for the kill. I remember that. Isaiah Wilson is half out of his chair. Rothskill is turning away. He looks disgusted."

"So it was a pivotal moment. I had hit a nerve. How do you know I was going in for the kill?"

Erika tossed the paper back to her.

"You weren't subtle. You worked up to stuff, set it up. When you went to put the knife in someone you always leaned forward. You used your height and your voice. You would have done anything to win. Whatever you were saying, whoever you were saying it to has everyone upset."

"You're there. Do you remember the day?"

She shook her head, "It was a long trial. Every day there was something."

Josie's shoulders slumped. What Erika said was true. Seconds ticked by. Had she been asked what she was thinking, Josie would have answered 'nothing'. But even at rest, even on the edge of despair, she was thinking. She thought about the tape on this piece of paper. There was a partial fingerprint on the sticky side. She would protect that. If they died at least there would be a clue as to who did this to them. There was something else, too. The picture was grainy. This was a second, maybe third generation reproduction, but there was an extra layer of something in the lower right hand corner. On her elbows, hands clasped so that she could rest her head on them, Josie bent close and looked hard.

"What?" Erika dragged herself forward another inch.

"I don't know yet." Josie looked up. "Is there anything we can use as a flat surface? It doesn't have to be big, just hard."

"Here." Erika put her arm out and pointed to the ground.

Carefully, Josie picked up the paper and crawled toward Erika. The rock she found was as smooth as slate and set so deeply it couldn't be dug out. Pity, it was probably big enough to use as a weapon, but a weapon wasn't what Josie wanted at the moment.

"Great. Perfect. Okay, then. Here we go."

"What are you going to do?"

Rather than answering, Josie put the paper flat, looked around, scooted back and got Erika's shoe. She used the edge of the hard heel and rubbed with an even pressure, careful not to tear the paper.

When she was finished, Josie sat back on her heels and stared at her handiwork. Like a grave rubbing or a child's game of secret message, the writing from a top sheet had been transferred to the bottom and along with it, a message. Erika scooted forward and saw what Josie saw. Erika began to read:

Transport

Immobilize

Punish

"He'll be back," Josie said with satisfaction. "He's not finished with us."

But Josie realized she was talking to herself. Erika had crawled back to her corner, curled onto her side and closed her eyes. Setting aside the paper, Josie sat down beside her, crossed her legs, hunched her back and started working at the knot on Erika's bindings.

Christian Broadcast Complex, Orange County

Isaiah Wilson was finished preaching. Today he had spoken about Job. He only spoke of Job 3 through 37. He argued, as had Job's fourth friend, that God uses pain to bring repentance. It had amused him to do so given Josie Bates' predicament. He hoped she was in a great deal of pain, but even he knew that hell fire would not cause her to repent what she had done to him and his daughter. Still, his sermon had been wonderful because Archer's visit had inspired him. It did not bother Isaiah that he was selective in his message; it did not bother those who listened to him. He understood that everyone took what they needed from what he said. If they wanted to look up the entire story of Job, they could.

He now walked through the complex, passing the young girl in the shapeless dress. She looked at him and then after him adoringly. When he was in her sphere, only Isaiah existed. When he passed through, her mind went back to God. It was a simple, satisfying existence that served her and Isaiah well. He assumed God was pleased, too.

He went down a little-used hallway to a door at the back of the complex. Gently, he turned the knob and eased his narrow frame through the opening. He left the door slightly ajar even though he didn't need the hall light to navigate. He had often slept here when he couldn't bring himself to go home and pass by Janey's room.

Today, though, there was someone else resting here. It was a tortured soul who had come a long way for his help. It was a sign, Isaiah believed; a sign that God was happy with his plans to celebrate the anniversary of his beloved daughter's death.

Isaiah went to the narrow bed, looked down on the young man and then leaned over and put his hand on his head.

"It's time to wake up," Isaiah said.

Peter Siddon rolled over and smiled.

CHAPTER 23

The Underground Restaurant, Hermosa Beach

It was late for lunch but Archer had been caught in traffic coming back from Orange County, and Liz had made a detour to the Blue Fin Grill on her way back from seeing Margie. They had been nonstop on the phone until Liz hit the Blue Fin, so Archer already knew about Hernandez's visitors: his mother, the Cartwright woman who ran a literacy program, and good old Isaiah Wilson. Archer wished he'd known about that before he'd talked to Wilson. He'd make another trip if he had to, but he was already on the road.

Archer asked: Did the Cartwright woman have anything Hernandez wrote?

Liz replied: She hadn't been able to get ahold of her yet. A call was in.

Liz filled him in that she'd waited two hours for Cuwin Martin. She decided the grapevine was working and he was laying low. He knew he had screwed up bad. Other interesting news: a missing person had already been activated on Erika Gardener based on one phone call.

Archer asked: Do you have a name for the caller?

Liz replied: No. It came in at midnight. Anonymous. Whoever it was must have made a good case for them to do the paperwork, just not good enough for anyone to go out to her place yet.

Archer was impressed. He couldn't even get Liz to admit anything was wrong a day ago. He would never have expected LAPD to be proactive. Since that line of thinking wasn't productive, he paid attention to Liz who continued to talk fast and make noises when the traffic ticked her off. She had tagged Gus Franklin, Hernandez's cellmate for a year and a half. She gave Archer the number she had for him, and Archer promised to follow up. Which he did while he waited in traffic. He was told Gus Franklin was a son of a bitch who hadn't been around the place for a good three weeks. Archer made a mental note to track him down, and then found himself concentrating on the heat waves that rose from the ground in squiggles that distorted everything.

He hated this heat because wherever Josie was it wasn't going to be refrigerated. If Josie was dead the temperature would exacerbate decomposition and ruin evidence, and if she was alive the heat wouldn't help her chance for survival. He was grateful when the traffic started to move. Sitting made him sick with fear, when he was moving he was able to convince himself he was making progress. Once the bottleneck broke up, he had made it to Hermosa in record time. Liz took a few minutes longer.

Now they were at The Underground Restaurant and the waitress had deposited two sodas and some fries they really shouldn't have ordered. Liz had to get back to work before Hagarty found out what she was up to, and Archer had no real appetite. All he wanted to be fed was information.

"Okay. The Blue Fin." Liz leaned over the high table so that she could keep her voice low. The Underground wasn't a favorite with Hermosa PD, but you never knew who might be around. "You know there are no cameras at the Blue Fin, but one of the servers saw Josie yesterday. He was early for work and stopped to have a cigarette. He knows some of the people who own the boats down below the parking lot and likes to check out the tourists. He was just hanging out and he sees Josie driving in and parking. Josie takes the stairs and comes out on the lower level. He didn't know who she was but noticed her because of her height. She went directly to Quality Seafood."

"Josie wouldn't eat there," Archer said.

"She checked her watch, my guy says it was obvious she was waiting. A Hispanic guy comes up to her. He's got two cups and gives her one. He sits down and they talk. My witness says it looked serious but not threatening."

"How long did your guy watch?"

"Two cigarettes. I showed him a picture of Hernandez. It wasn't real clear, but he says it could have been him. Then he goes to work."

"And?"

"I go down to Quality Seafood. One of the fishmongers down there saw them, too. The Hispanic guy was helping Josie around the dock area and toward the parking structure. The guy who works at Quality Seafood took note because Josie wasn't steady on her feet. That witness was worried she had some bad fish, but he realized that it wouldn't happen that fast and the man hadn't bought fish. He only bought drinks."

"Josie was drugged. It had to be. Nobody could have blindsided her in daylight if she hadn't been. Damn it." Archer's hands fisted and one hit the tabletop hard enough for the few patrons to look. He didn't care. Liz put her hand over his.

"Later, buddy," Liz warned. "Here's the rest. The fishmonger follows around just to make sure everything's good. The man is standing in front of the back passenger door that's open. He looks like he's helping Josie in. But there's someone else leaning through the other side. My witness figures a Good Samaritan is helping. No word on the guy leaning into the car except that he was wearing some kind of shiny blue and white shirt. My guy goes back to work, and that's all I got.

"It's all good, Liz. At least we know the how; I don't give a shit about the why. Now we've got to find out where Hernandez took her. And when we find her, when I know she's okay, we won't have to worry about another trial for Hernandez."

"I gotta go. Don't do anything stupid." Liz slid off the high stool. "I'm going to ask the captain to talk to the city council about putting cameras in the well. Three flights of stairs and no way to tell what's going down there. It's just crazy. People around here don't think anything bad can ever happen to them."

"Can you track down whoever caught the Gardener thing and see if LAPD is acting on it?" Archer asked.

"Sure." Liz said, knowing it would be dicey going back and forth with Los Angeles, but she had always wanted to be part of something big. Now that she was, Liz had no intention of stepping aside. She was about to share a few more ideas with Archer when his phone rang.

"Sorry." He gave it a glance then answered it.

"Archer?" It was Hannah. "I need you to come over."

"Not now," Archer said, knowing she was the last thing he needed to worry about. But Hannah was putting herself at the head of the line.

"No, now." Hannah said evenly. "I need you to come to Josie's house now."

CHAPTER 24

Josie Bates' House, Hermosa Beach

Archer's first thought when the door opened was that Hannah looked weird, like she was surrounded by a body halo. It was only a trick of the light combined with the architecture in Josie's home. From above the late afternoon sun shone through the skylight Josie had installed a few months earlier. Hannah wore some sparkly thing that hung off her shoulders and draped to the side of her breasts, ending in an uneven hem below her hips. Beneath that was a copper and gold tube top. Backlit as she was, the light bounced off the sparkles of her clothes and filtered through the curls and frizz of her long black hair, transforming her from petulant teenager to multi-cultural Madonna.

He tilted his head to see if that would dispel the illusion, but it was Max the Dog ambling up to her that did it. Hannah bent down to hold his collar, and when she faced Archer again the light was harsher. She was an angel tumbled down from heaven who found that earth was not the most pleasant place to be. In this new light, Hannah Sheraton looked scared and, as he knew, she didn't scare easy.

Hannah held the door a little wider, and Archer stepped over the threshold. Max's tail wagged so wildly at the sight of Archer that the old dog's entire body shook. He took Max's face in his hands and rubbed those jowls until he was sure the animal smiled.

"Thanks for coming," Hannah whispered.

"Josie here?" Archer lowered his tone to match hers, moving in far enough so she could close the door.

Hannah shook her head then cut her eyes toward the living room. He looked over casually. The room was as it always was: clean, striking in style and opulent in its simplicity. Above the modest fireplace was a painting of featureless woman. It was huge and unframed, and even Archer understood its allure for the two women who lived in this house. Hannah had painted it as a gift to Josie. Someday Archer imagined there would be a companion piece: Woman with a Face.

Then Archer saw a middle-aged woman standing near the French doors that led out to the back patio. He bristled when she jiggled the handle it as if to test the lock, as if she could go wherever she wanted in Josie's house. She clasped her hands behind her back and moved out of view. The woman was no friend of Josie's that much Archer knew. Hannah knew the rest.

"Child protective services," Hannah informed him quietly. "She's been asking about Josie. I told her she was on a business trip."

"Got it."

Hannah fell back, closed the door then walked with Archer to meet the lady. Her fingers tapped, keeping time with her internal drummer.

The California Mountains

He felt much better after a little work, some good quiet time in his own surroundings, before hitting the road again. Everything was right as rain because sometime during the night, after his initial terror, he had an epiphany: Josie Bates being free was not a problem. Even if she had managed to release her companion, that was no problem. They couldn't go anywhere. However, there were things they could do that would make all this so much more satisfying. This had never been a simple quest for justice. It was more complicated than that. Full satisfaction would only come when they were punished and degraded and humiliated the way he had been. Now, with their hands free, there was an opportunity for fun. They were animals in his own little zoo, dependent upon him for food and water. Well, they would have it. They would be rewarded as long as they danced to his tune. Why hadn't he thought of this before? Fun was something he hadn't anticipated.

The position of the hut was perfect for him to carry out his new plan. The land on the outside had moved over the last fifty years or so that he could easily stand outside and look through the opening in the wall. On the inside, the ground was a foot and a half lower. The women couldn't get up to him, but he could look down on them.

When he arrived, he put down the backpack, unzipped it and waited. They must be deaf. He had taken no precautions during his approach. He had hoped to hear them calling to him long before he actually arrived. Tiring of the wait, he jumped easily atop the little berm and peered through the opening in the wall. Even if they looked right at him they wouldn't know who he was given the way he was dressed and the light. He would look like Satan, dark and evil in the gear he had taken from the back of the car.

He needn't have worried what they would see because when he peered into the darkened interior he saw that they were asleep, face to face, curled close. They looked like Hansel and Gretel in the witch's house. Only it was two Gretel's, and they couldn't munch their way out of this place.

Wait. No. They looked like the women in that video he liked to watch when he was alone. Girls Do Girls. Maybe there was more fun to be had than even he imagined.

He tiptoed up, put his face against the hole and moved his eyes, taking in as much as he could. He saw that Josie Bates' wrists were still bound. He couldn't see Erika's, but he had to assume she had not managed to loosen the rope. By his calculations, if they had drunk all that water they might still sleep for another hour or so.

But then Josie Bates stirred. She raised her head as if she sensed him, and carefully eased herself away from Erika. She was a smart woman not to alarm her housemate until she knew what was what. It took all of his discipline – which was mighty – not to call out to her. Or laugh. No, no, bark at her like one animal calling to another animal. She was lucky he had self-control. Besides, there was immense satisfaction in seeing her try and figure it out. Her eyes were clicking to each corner as she looked for the thing that disturbed her.

No, not there.

Not in that corner.

No, not over there either.

Up. Look up.

He willed it and she did it. His will was amazing. He wanted to giggle. She was staring right at him. His dark visage filled the space that was only the size of a brick. They stared at one another for what seemed like an eternity and then, with exquisite timing, he leaned away and brought his hand up. He put a small bottle of ice-cold water on the little ledge.

"There's nothing in it," he assured her quietly. "You won't sleep anymore."

The Christian Broadcast Complex, Orange County

Isaiah Wilson held his bible in both hands at crotch level. His head was lowered. The cameras had stopped running, and as always the cameraman, producer, and sound tech remained respectfully silent. What wasn't usual was the length of time Isaiah remained stationary. The three other people in the room glanced at one another. One of them shrugged, and all of them held their breath. Another minute passed and another. They had never seen a human being stay as still as this man. When it seemed that one of them was going to have to inquire after the reverend's health, Wilson raised his head revealing a fearsome visage. His head turned to the young man in the doorway. Peter Siddon was fully awake now. His hair was neatly combed. He was calmer than when he had arrived. Isaiah smiled at him.

"I'm so glad you came to me." Isaiah opened his arms and the young man walked into them. "Let us finish what you have started."

CHAPTER 25

Josie Bates' House, Hermosa Beach

"Hello! Hello there! I'm afraid Hannah was a little reluctant to talk to me without an adult present. That is completely understandable. I didn't mind waiting in the least." The woman who had been perusing Josie's bookshelf seemed to be psychic. She popped up right in front of Archer just as he stepped into the living room. Her hand was out, her greeting chirpy and totally annoying. "Oh, I startled you. So sorry."

"This is Mrs. Crane." Hannah mumbled to Archer before raising her voice. "And I wasn't reluctant to talk to you. I told you, Josie is out of town."

The woman graced Hannah with a smile that turned Archer's stomach. One thing he hated worse than a bad guy was a sadistic good guy.

"Yes, Sarah Crane. Child Protective Services. Hannah's caseworker. Well, I'm newly assigned. Mrs. Davis quit. Not a job for a weak constitution."

With surprising grace, the woman whipped out a calling card from her standard issue government portfolio.

"Mrs. Manning at Hannah's school called me. She was concerned that, perhaps, something was wrong, and that Ms. Bates might not have the same enthusiasm for guardianship that she originally exhibited. We so appreciate that kind of concern from an educator, so I wanted to have a look-see for myself. You know, make sure that everything was hunky-dory. I've read Hannah's file, and she hasn't always had such personal attention, so I am bound and determined to make up for that."

Archer took the card and kept moving until he was standing in front of the sofa. He sat down, feet planted, arms on his knees, and his eyes still riveted on the card. He didn't need a card to tell him who this woman was because she was precise and clear about that. Archer just thought the card gave him a great excuse to think for a minute as he waded through the bullshit she was shoveling. Then he thought he should ask her to leave, and then he reconsidered. She could cause him a whole lot more grief than he needed right now, so giving her some time was the better course of action.

He flipped the card between his fingers as his eyes went to Mrs. Crane. She had taken the leather chair across from him, perching herself primly on the edge of the seat, and balancing her portfolio on her knees as she waited patiently for his attention. When she had it, Mrs. Crane opened her portfolio and withdrew a pen. Her gaze pegged Archer then clicked up a degree to Hannah who had positioned herself behind him. He applauded the girl's self-restraint. If someone were talking about him like he was a rescue animal he would have made it real clear he didn't appreciate the tone or the implications. The only indication Hannah gave that she was upset was the almost imperceptible tapping on the back of the sofa.

"So, Mr...."

"Archer."

"You're Ms. Bates' partner, I believe."

Her chin swung up as she said this. It swung so far that she looked down her nose at him. Aggravation flickered deep in Archer's eyes; satisfaction twinkled in Mrs. Crane's. He didn't like labels, and he sure didn't like them being slapped on by someone like her.

"The length of my relationship with Josie isn't relevant to why you're here, so you wasted a trip. Josie is out of town, but she's dedicated to this guardianship. No question." Archer tossed the card on the glass coffee table and gave her what he hoped passed for an expression of assurance. "You can see Hannah has a support system. She's been in school, and I live close. There's Faye, Josie's law partner. She checks in."

"Yes, yes, I do have Ms. Baxter's information. In fact, I called over to her office to chat with her. I like to cover my bases. Most people don't think government workers aren't thorough, but in my experience we are very good at covering our bases. So many misconceptions."

She flashed a grin. She might as well have tattooed 'look how special I am' on her forehead. Hannah moved her head slightly. She hated this cheery woman who was so proud of her good deeds, so damn dedicated to saving Hannah when Hannah was already saved. Archer's assessment was simpler; this woman was evil and he had to take care with her.

"It seems Faye Baxter has been out of town for some time. Business down south and seeing her daughter." Mrs.

Crane waved a little circle in the air. "So, as you say, that leaves you as Hannah's ad hoc guardian if the guardian is not on the premises. Wouldn't you imagine that would be the case, Mr. Archer?"

Archer's teeth were on a grind; the back of his neck was flushed and warm. Hannah's finger touched his shoulder as if in warning, and then he felt her tapping the back of the sofa once more. Knowing him well enough, not wanting any more trouble than was necessary, Hannah stepped in.

"Josie's not missing. She's just got caught up."

"Do you want me to call her?" Archer asked.

"Really, Mr. Archer. Do you think that would do any good?"

Mrs. Crane morphed from songbird to falcon as she called his bluff. Her eyes narrowed to mere slits in a face that had seemed narrow and fleshy, yet, in reality, was sharp boned and sunken. That beak of hers, sweetly chirping her concern only moments before was now closed tight and turned up sharply in a satisfied smirk. This, Archer imagined, was what prey saw in the instant before the predator struck. It was an ugly and fearful sight and her prey was Hannah.

"Hannah, dear, it really would be better if you didn't tell tales." Mrs. Crane's head swung away from the teenager to the man. "And Mr. Archer, I think you might do well to heed that lesson also. Especially when you are speaking to a representative of the government."

"Honesty is usually the best policy." The only way he would give an inch was if she came over and ripped it away from him. But she stayed put and smiled drily.

"Excellent." She drew the word out to a fine point. "I'm so glad we agree about telling the truth, because I picked this up on the way over. Well, not really picked it up. I took it off a telephone pole."

From her ever-so-practical portfolio she withdrew a piece of paper that was just a little larger than her case. Mrs. Crane looked at it admiringly. No matter what it was, Archer knew he and Hannah were screwed.

"I'll bet you did this Hannah, didn't you? Beautiful work. Definitely noticeable. These seem to be all over Hermosa Beach."

Slowly, Mrs. Crane turned the paper, holding it by the edges so that her hawk-like face was half hidden. Archer put his fingers to his forehead. He didn't want to look at it, but it was preferable to looking at Hannah.

In Mrs. Crane's dry fingers was a poster with Josie's picture and the word MISSING! block printed in bright red letters above it.

Hermosa Beach Police Department

"There's a reason they call it a lunch hour, Driscoll."

Captain Hagarty had noticed she'd been gone a while. He was busy and unhappy. Liz could tell by the way he shoved a message slip across his desk at her.

"Thanks." Liz snatched it up, turned and tried to make her escape only to miss her window of opportunity.

"Hand it off to LAPD, Driscoll."

"Captain, Josie Bates is a Hermosa resident and..." Liz began her argument and he finished it.

"And her car was found in Redondo and neither department has the resources to handle something this big." Hagarty sat back and clasped his hands over his middle.

"It's an inquiry at this stage," Liz insisted.

"It's a problem." Hagarty looked tired but no less determined. "The Bates thing is tied to a woman in Hollywood. Both have a history with Hernandez who was in a level four institution. He's out. The parole officer doesn't have a handle on where he is which means he could be anywhere and you playing Sherlock Holmes will just get in the way."

"It's not like that. I can help. I've tracked down people who saw her-"

"You're not hearing me Liz. You have a job and right now you have eight open files."

"Nine," Liz muttered.

"Nine," he reiterated.

"And I'm handling them so what's the real problem?" Liz planted her feet and squared her shoulders.

To Hagarty's credit, he didn't look away. She wouldn't have had much respect for him if he did.

"You don't have the chops or the back-up," Hagarty answered flatly. He sat forward, his expression softening and his talk sharpening. "I'm not saying the heart isn't there, Driscoll, but this is way out of your range of experience. We don't have the tools even an experienced detective would need for an investigation as intricate as this. A woman's life may hang in the balance for all we know, and, if it does, you don't want to be the one who tips the scales."

"Did it ever occur to you I might tip them in a good way?" Liz challenged.

"This isn't personal, it's fact. Step down. Do I make myself clear?"

"Yes, Captain. Is that all?"

"No. When you get the report on the Jeep, I want that over to LAPD before the ink is dry," Hagarty said. "That's all."

Liz turned and marched out the door, closing it behind her hard enough to make it sound pissy, but not sharp enough to express her displeasure. Even Jefferson, who was coming off the afternoon shift, turned his head and gave her a look. Liz smiled back and headed to her office cubicle hoping she looked like she had it together. Her cheeks burned, and there was a nice tight spot in the middle of her chest. She totally accepted the second part of Hagarty's argument. Hermosa PD didn't have the bells and whistles L.A. did, but they had some resources. It was the first part of his argument that made her feel sick and mad and agitated.

She never thought of herself as a second-class detective. Sometimes she wondered if she was a second-class woman, but she never questioned her ability as a detective. She had excelled at the academy. She stood up when people tried to make her back down. When it came to chops or balls or both she had more than she knew what to do with. Questioning that was like a slap in the face. No, not just a slap. A bitch slap. She kicked the damn, grey upholstered thing that was supposed to make her floor space into an office, and it shook like it was going to fall. Joe Moore was at home on the other side. He got up and looked over the top.

"Got a problem?" he asked.

Liz didn't look up. She knew exactly what she would see: a double chin, a mustache and a nose that was perpetually red.

"No," She fumed

"You in trouble?"

"No," she muttered.

"What'd you do?" he sing-songed.

"Nothing."

He lost interest, sat down again, and left her to fume. Moore started to two-finger peck on his keyboard – probably tweeting that his fellow officer was in a snit. Liz looked at the crumpled note in her hand.

"I haven't done anything. Not yet," she muttered as smoothed it out, picked up the phone and dialed LAPD.

CHAPTER 26

Josie Bates' House, Hermosa Beach

The knock on the door was timed perfectly. The three people inside Josie's house paused, and simultaneously turned their heads. Their hearts thumped in unison. Max got up and hustled to the entry on his old legs. His tail wagged low as if he, too, was afraid to hope for good news. Hannah started after him, put her hand on the knob and then stopped as Mrs. Crane insisted they pay attention to her.

"Three o'clock. I have another appointment, and since neither of you seem to want to fill me in on where Ms. Bates might be, or the particulars of why she might be there, I have no reason to extend this visit. I'm sure you're going to be busy trying to find her, unless this is some kind of prank." Mrs. Crane rustled the poster and looked at Hannah one more time. "Is this a prank?"

"No. We're figuring it out."

It was Archer who answered as he moved the woman toward the door, wanting nothing more than for her to leave so he could get back to work. Mrs. Crane paused before she got to the foyer. She lowered her voice.

"You have to understand, my job is to look after Hannah's welfare. This case is unusual, and we know that she is high risk."

"She's being taken care of. I'll take full responsibility for her."

"That's really not for you or me to say, is it Mr. Archer?" Mrs. Crane held her portfolio to her breast like a shield. "Hannah and Ms. Bates are scheduled to appear before Judge Leisinger tomorrow. I'll advise the judge's clerk that Ms. Bates will not be present. The judge will decide whether or not she'll remain here."

Archer looked at Hannah. Her hand was frozen on the knob. She didn't have to be part of the conversation to know what was going on. Archer looked back at Mrs. Crane, and did the only thing he could do; the one thing that always got him into trouble. He was honest.

"I can't be her legal guardian."

"Given your relationship with Ms. Bates, I thought you'd have some interest in the girl."

The woman was the Wicked Witch and Hannah was her Toto. She would have the girl no matter what. If Archer thought dunking this one in water would make all their troubles go away, he would do it.

"We'll be in court tomorrow," Archer said.

Whoever was outside, knocked again. No one was under the illusion that it was Josie. Mrs. Crane opened her purse and took out her keys. Archer looked at Hannah and his jaw tightened. He could see that she was stricken behind her beautiful green eyes, that she had paled beneath the chocolate colored skin, and that she shivered even though the late afternoon was hot.

"Hannah?"

She blinked, seeming surprised to see Archer in the house. He nodded toward the door. Hannah opened it and Liz Driscoll rolled into the room like a bowling ball.

"Hey, Archer. Why aren't you answering your phone?"

Hannah dropped back, Archer turned, and Mrs. Crane stood her ground. She ignored Liz and spoke to Archer.

"I could take Hannah into custody right now, you understand. Your choice, Mr. Archer."

"Hannah's choice," Archer responded.

Mrs. Crane smirked, "This is about the law, not a child's self esteem."

Archer's eyes locked with Hannah's. The two of them tied together legally, even for a few days, was not something either would relish. He tried to think of the greater good and what Josie would want. He tried not to see that beyond the pride in Hannah's expression was a deep, childlike terror. But he could see it, and he knew what the right thing was.

He said: "We'll see you in court."

Mrs. Crane swept past them all, off to do her best to wreak havoc on other lives under the guise of legislative compassion. She was a happy, content, bitter woman, unlike Liz who was as jittery as a bug.

"Archer. LAPD found Hernandez's place. Let's roll." She turned toward Hannah and stuck out her hand. "You the kid Josie took in?"

"Hannah. Who are you?"

"I'm Liz Driscoll, the cop who's gonna find her."

Liz turned on her heel and was out the door assuming Archer would follow. As he passed Hannah he put his hand on her shoulder. The girl looked at it then up at him. When her hand covered his, he expected her to brush him away. Instead, she gripped it briefly.

"Be safe," she said, her eyes never leaving his as she stepped back and put space between them once more.

Archer nodded and then caught up with Liz. Before they turned the corner onto Hermosa Boulevard, he glanced back. Hannah had followed him out to the street and Max stood beside her. In another time she would be facing to sea on a widow's walk, looking toward the horizon and hoping to see a ship bringing her sailor home. He could only imagine what she was hoping to see now: not just Josie returning but maybe him, too. It was a heavy burden. Archer didn't know how Josie dealt with it all, but he had an inkling of why she did. Hannah was worth saving and protecting.

"Archer, times awastin','" Liz called.

He looked back at her and they got into the car at the same time: her behind the wheel, him to the passenger seat. Before Archer snapped his seat belt, he saw that they weren't alone.

"I thought he might have some insight," Liz said as she fired up the car. "Ready to slay the dragon guys?"

Liz pulled out into traffic and Archer faced forward not liking Daniel Young riding along at all; not liking that Daniel's eyes were on Hannah as they drove away.

An Outbuilding in the California Mountains

"Do it, or I will."

Josie looked at Erika and then at the small bottle of water that was still perched on the little ledge. It was so close and yet so far away. For the last two hours, Josie had talked Erika out of wanting that water. They both knew it was probably drugged, but in the end Erika didn't care if it was poisoned.

"Do it." Erika demanded. "We share it and neither of us will get enough to knock us out."

"No, we have to be ready when he comes back."

"Who died and left you God?" Erika cried, her voice shaking. "I want that water, but I'm not tall enough to reach it. You are, and I want it now."

Josie wanted it, too. In fact, one more day in this place and she might have taken it all for herself. But it would take more time for her to trust the person who left it. If she could have seen his eyes she might feel better about drinking from that bottle. But his eyes were hidden behind some sort of glasses: big glasses that covered part of his brow and some of his cheek.

"Do it," Erika snapped.

"Okay. Okay."

Josie struggled to her feet. Even at her full height, she was still a foot and a half lower than that missing brick. But arms up, pushing herself off the way she would on the volleyball court, she should be able to reach it. She took a deep breath, and put her bound hands on the wall.

Eyes up and focused on the little bottle that had long ago ceased to sweat, she bent her knees, balanced on the balls of her feet, and jumped. Tied as she was, there was no way to actually grasp the bottle. The best she could hope for was to tip it into the hut. Her fingertips touched plastic. In the next split second, Josie had that bottle in her grasp, and in the second after that it was gone. The plastic was slippery, the bottle small, her hands bound and her aim skewed. The bottle tipped and toppled, and disappeared on the wrong side of the cement hut.

Next thing Josie knew, she was crumpled on the ground, on her knees, the heel of her hands balancing her. Her head was bent, her breath labored. She had failed.

"I'm sorry," she breathed and when she turned her head to look at Erika, all she saw was a blur of color, and raised fists.

"You did it on purpose. I'm going to kill you!"

CHAPTER 27

Xavier Hernandez's Place, Los Angeles

They drove the last five miles down the Harbor Freeway in silence broken only by the crackling of Liz's radio. Archer prepared himself for evidence that Josie was dead, Liz tried to tamp down the sense that she was nearing detective glory, and Daniel? Who knew what Daniel was thinking? Archer checked the rearview mirror. He could see a sliver of Daniel Young's face and what he saw told him nothing. More than likely, the vibes Archer felt from the guy were worry. He had to be wondering when it was his turn to be the target.

Archer's phone vibrated. He checked it and saw a text from Hannah. Peter Siddon had called again. He texted her back: *Ignore him.*

Archer already had planned to track him down the next day, but tomorrow's court date might change that. Then again, this trek might change everything. Instead of chasing a guy down in the high desert, he might be bringing Josie home and they would both see Hernandez behind bars again.

He pocketed the phone just as Liz exited on to Martin Luther King Jr. Boulevard, and they were dumped into a part of Los Angeles few beach people knew existed. Archer had seen it before, though. All those years with the LAPD had sent him into every nook and cranny of this sprawling city. The nooks off the freeway weren't worth a second thought. Not because it was the poor and the illegal who lived behind barred doors and windows, but because nothing could protect them. It was fate, bad luck that the people who ended up here were born ignorant and forgotten. Best thing was to get in, take what you came for, and get out. Today, they came for Xavier Hernandez or Josie and Erika Gardener – not necessarily in that order.

"Here we go, boys," Liz muttered.

She swung her vehicle down Rose Street, and then took a hard left onto an unpaved, unmarked road. It led to a duplex squashed between a triplex in front and the rise of the Harbor Freeway in back. An LAPD black and white, a van and an unmarked unit were already there. Liz pulled up behind the Crown Vic and set the parking brake, stopping in what was technically a front yard but was in reality a junkyard that happened to have a duplex built smack in the middle of it.

The ignition went off. Seat belts clicked. The heat sucker punched them the minute the door opened. Liz hitched her pants, touched the rolled up sleeves of her button down oxford, and then the badge and gun at her waist. Today she wore brown cowboy boots instead of her preferred biker footwear. She looked, as always, formidable for such a compact woman. Archer planted his feet and looked hard at the landscape: the duplex, the building in front, and the one on his left.

Windows were open and curtains drawn back to catch any bit of breeze. But cool air seldom found its way down here, and if it did it would have to squeeze through along with the constant roar of traffic, the gulag-light from hovering police helicopters at night, the screams of faceless neighbors and the crack of gunfire.

"Guess we're not in Hermosa anymore," Liz said wryly.

"Simply the cycle of civilization," Daniel added.

"Shitty luck," Archer wrapped up the discussion, his eyes constantly moving.

Five kids hung out in the yard behind the house on the left. The same dirt that was under Archer's feet was cropped into a private yard by a rusted and bent chain link fence. There was scruffy dead stuff that had been a bush once upon a time and a mattress that had probably been ten years old when it hit the Salvation Army, been put to good use for another five, and then tossed out back. Archer wouldn't let a dog sleep on it, but the dog penned in with the kids looked like it would sleep any damn place it pleased.

The animal was a hellish looking thing. A scar ran diagonally across its fist of a face. The kids kept their distance, and the pit bull kept its eyes on Archer and Liz. Those eyes were black and naked, as if the thing had no eyelids. In the middle of the night, that creature's eyes would still be open and glittering. All a bull like him knew was viciousness, and such limited knowledge needed no storage space in a brain.

What made the animal even more frightening was his stillness. He didn't strain at the chain that held him to a rusted tetherball pole, but Archer knew they weren't safe.

That animal could snap any damn thing if it wanted; chain, pole or a neck.

Beside him, Archer felt Daniel Young move close and look over his shoulder. Archer would have laughed except he knew the guy had good reason to be scared.

Archer's eyes moved from Daniel Young, skated over the brutish dog and noted the woman who looked out the window of the house on his left. Another click and he was looking over his shoulder at a woman pushing a stroller, head down as she hurried along. Two little kids bobbed in her wake: one in a first communion dress of cheap white lace and petticoats that had belonged to a much bigger girl, the other a boy who lingered, fascinated by all the cars. The pious little girl ran back to tug on her brother's arm. He pushed her and she fell in a cloud of petticoats. The mother hurried back to herd her brood away. Across the way, a shirtless young man lavished with tattoos lounged against the hood of a car. Whatever had brought the cops to his part of the world was no worry for him that day, so he watched to see who or what they would drag out of the duplex.

"Daniel," Liz said, "do you want to wait in the car until we get the lay of land?"

Archer knew Liz was giving an order more than asking a question, but Daniel seemed unsure.

"It's a hundred degrees inside that car," Daniel objected. "And these people…"

"They're more afraid of you than you should be of them," Archer said flatly.

Liz added: "Look, Doc, here's the thing. If they've got Hernandez, I want to see if it's better if we keep you out of sight or bring you in. I gotta check out his state of mind. It's for your safety. Okay?"

"I see. That makes sense. Yes."

Liz and Daniel peeled off. The door of Liz's car opened as she put Daniel inside. On her way back, Liz tapped Archer's arm as she passed. Archer took the cue and started to walk.

"We're here as a courtesy," Liz reminded Archer.

"I know."

"I don't want Hagarty's notice."

"Figured."

"My butt, Archer, so be cool," Liz insisted.

"I hear ya, Liz," Archer responded.

Liz picked up the pace. She'd given him the company line and knew neither of them was going to tow it if push came to shove.

Together they kicked up a little dust before stepping inside Xavier Hernandez's abode. Daniel Young watched until all he saw was the dark doorway then he put his head back, closed his eyes and rested.

An Outbuilding in the California Mountains

Josie's fist met Erika Gardener's jaw. It was a glancing blow, but it stopped them both cold. They separated, each to a corner, breathing hard, unable to believe what had just happened.

Erika was shaking. Her blouse was ripped and Josie could see the rise of her breast and the soiled lace bra that encased it. Her face was a map of tear-rivers cut into dirt and blood and dust. Her hair hung over her eyes, and those eyes of her looked through the dirty, lank mess.

Josie put her hand to her leg and it came up bloody. Without a word, she ripped the lower leg off her pants and wrapped it around the ragged wound as she spoke.

"I want to get out of here alive. I'll do it with or without you." Josie raised her blue eyes so that Erika could see she was serious. "You ever come at me like that again it will be without you."

Xavier Hernandez's Place, Los Angeles

Xavier Hernandez's living room was barely big enough for the love seat that had seen much better days and the chair that listed backward. There was a rusting electric heating unit built into one wall. To the left was a doorway to a bedroom. In front of Archer and Liz was a counter about two feet long and a foot wide. It separated the kitchen from the living area. That was where the LAPD staked out their territory. One detective stood in front of an olive-green stove that was missing a few knobs; the other was at ease, hands behind his back, at the end of the counter.

The guy at the stove was tall and thin with a hint of a belly. He wore a white short-sleeved dress shirt, a tie that looked like a clip-on and a wedding ring. The other was super-buff, narrow of waist, broad of shoulder, tight of ass, but lacking the height of his counterpart. He was turned out in a neatly pressed, long sleeved dress shirt and a tie that was surprisingly sophisticated for a cop. That one didn't wear a ring. Either he was a player with a wife at home or didn't want to get tied down. Liz decided the first guy was the lead, but the second detective was moving up on the track fast. Satisfied she knew who she was dealing with, Liz interrupted since they seemed to have lost their manners. They knew damn well she and Archer had arrived.

"Afternoon, gentlemen." Liz hailed them.

"Hey." The tall one pushed off the stove and put his hand out as he came around to meet her. "Detective Arnson."

"Levinsky." The guy without the ring put his hand out and gave a macho squeeze that Liz returned in kind.

"Liz Driscoll, Hermosa Beach PD and Archer. PI, retired LAPD."

The men nodded Archer's way and Levinsky asked: "Who was your chief?"

"Gates," Archer replied.

"Good man. Before my time." Archer nodded to show that the point was taken. He'd been marginalized as old guard.

"Archer knows the missing Hermosa woman," Liz said.

"Personal background's good," Arnson agreed. "What have you got on the Hermosa victim?"

Archer picked up the dialogue:

"The house is clean and we're going over the car. I'm running down phone calls, clients and meetings. There were a lot of people involved in the Hernandez trial that weren't happy with her."

"Understand. We checked it," Levinsky said.

Arnson offered an apologetic smile, "We only came on late yesterday, but we picked up what we could. Any thread you pulled that might unravel?"

"Not yet, but I guess we agree Hernandez is our guy," Liz piped up with a little too much enthusiasm.

Levinsky gave her the once over. "If he is, he's in our jurisdiction. No working at cross-purposes. We good on that?"

Levinsky flexed his cop muscle, and Archer was amused. Archer thanked his lucky stars he quit before he turned into Levinsky. Arnson was already tired, and probably planning his retirement considering the way he rolled his eyes at his partner's bravado.

"That's not to say we don't appreciate what you bring to the table." Arnson stepped in smoothly "Best we can tell, Hernandez has been out of touch about two weeks. Before that his parole officer says he was quiet."

"The PO doesn't seem to have been real attentive," Archer noted. "Hernandez could have been out of touch since the day he walked, for all we know."

"It happens. Martin's not the brightest bulb and his caseload is heavy. His superiors are having him go through his records with a fine-tooth comb," Arnson answered practically.

"Do you have any idea why he was calling Josie Bates? He sent letters to the others – victim's families, witnesses," Liz asked.

"Don't know. Make a note to ask," Levinsky directed Arnson.

Archer resisted the urge to point out that would be the first question Levinsky should have asked, and that Arnson should tell his pompous ass partner to stuff his note-taking comments. Arnson was a better man than Archer by far and actually took the note.

"How long has he been living here?" Liz turned in a tight little circle to give the place a once over.

"Six months." Arnson took a few steps just to move. This place made them all itchy. "We know Hernandez had three job interviews in the last four months. Cuwin puts his chances for real employment at minus ten on a scale of one to ten. Hernandez got out on compassionate release and is on all sorts of meds: blood pressure, heavy insulin. We have syringes. He reuses so watch yourself if you find one."

"Money's tight all around," Liz muttered as she joined Archer to look at the evidence bags laid out on the counter. "Quite a pharmacy."

Levinsky took over. "Seconal. Nembutal. Ketamine."

"Date rape drug?" Archer picked up the bag and looked at the powder. Levinsky took it away from him and put it back neatly.

"We call it a drug-facilitated sexual assault drug now," Levinsky responded.

"Behind the times, Archer," Liz snickered. "What did Cuwin say about this stuff?"

"The guy has sleep problems. Possible epilepsy."

"Possible?" Liz raised one of those pretty eyebrows.

Arnson shrugged, "Government doctors. Amazing those bozos kept him alive after the little fray inside. You know about that, right?"

Liz and Archer nodded.

"Anyway, they used the Nembutal to reduce the pressure on his brain when he was in the prison hospital. It doesn't explain why he has all this stuff. Then again, I was kind of surprised he didn't get the big sleep. Your friend must be one heck of an attorney."

"Hope we find her. I'd like to hear what she was thinking representing scum like that." Levinsky added his two cents. "Especially now."

"Maybe the government boy shouldn't have been in the ring with her." Archer came to Josie's defense, but before the discussion could escalate, Liz stepped in. She touched two of the evidence bags.

"These two are both strong enough to knock the victims out so they could be transported, but it would take a while to take effect. The Ketamine is fast acting, easy to administer. The women wouldn't remember a thing," Liz noted. "Was he cooking it?"

"If he was, he wasn't doing it here. Best guess, he helped himself at his last job. Raining Cats & Dogs Veterinary Clinic. It's illegal in the U.S. for humans, but you can use it on animals. He had the placement for two days before they fired him for being creepy," Levinsky said.

"And they didn't report anything missing?"

"Even if they knew he had taken something, they didn't want any trouble," Arnson replied.

"Is there a roommate? A girlfriend?" Liz again.

Levinsky barked a laugh. "Women aren't his favorite people."

"Then he's in touch with his feminine side," Liz drawled. "A set of high end kitchen towels? A spoon rest?"

"His mother," Arnson replied. They all looked at him. "That would be my guess. He borrowed her car a couple times. She gave him money. I talked to her yesterday. She doesn't know where he is."

"What did the car look like?" Archer asked.

"Big. Blue. It's an old Buick. A real classic," Arnson answered just as his eyes went to the bedroom door. A uniformed cop was waiting for a break in the conversation.

"I'm almost done here," he announced.

"Let's have you take a look before we close up." Levinsky and Arnson stepped back so Liz and Archer could go first.

"We've got a possible red mid-size seen in Hermosa. That is what we're looking for," Liz said and Arnson followed up with some small talk. Then they were in the bedroom.

A mattress and box springs were pushed up against the wall and into a corner. There was a small window sans shades or curtains. Clothes were draped over a chair with a fraying rattan seat. On the far wall was an old bureau and over that, thumb-tacked to a wall that could really use a scrubbing, was a big desk calendar. Neatly tacked to the calendar and taped to the wall were pictures, newspaper clippings and a book cover. A police photographer was snapping his last, for-good-measure shots and moved aside when Archer walked toward the calendar.

"Don't touch..." Levinsky began but a look from Archer silenced him. Liz followed up with a glance that said 'you asked for it' as she joined Archer.

In the old newspaper clippings, Daniel Young's quotes were highlighted in yellow marker, and Josie's picture was circled. There was a picture of Hernandez sitting in court looking over his shoulder. Archer looked closer. Hernandez cleaned up good. Archer never would have guessed this was the guy in the booking photo. Xavier Hernandez looked white, not Hispanic. His skin was pale, his features delicate. His eyes were keen but soft. He was one of those guys who could have been fifteen or twenty-five depending on who was looking. Two teenage girls wouldn't have seen beyond those pretty eyes.

Archer moved on.

There were pictures of Josie on the beach, taken within the last few months. Archer recognized the bikini she was wearing because he'd been with her when she bought it at a shop on Pier Plaza. They'd ended up at the tapas place for dinner. This guy had been stalking her even then. How could they have missed a guy like Hernandez pointing a camera at them? One of them might, but not both.

There was a picture of Erika Gardener in a torn t-shirt and cut-offs kneeling next to tomato plants that had been planted in beds that ran parallel to the driveway. He couldn't tell for certain if it was her place, but he'd have to assume. There was a basket by her side and a car parked to her left. Archer could only see a little bit of the bumper. Hernandez had tacked a dried Hydrangea on the wall. Archer tried to remember if he had seen purple ones in Erika's yard.

"She's wearing an engagement ring," Archer muttered to Liz.

There was a picture of Daniel getting into his car. No, that was wrong. Daniel Young was holding the door for someone. Archer didn't recognize the place, but Young looked happy. Whoever was holding the camera brought out his good side. The car was a red Toyota. Archer had seen a red Toyota in the parking lot of Young's building. The fishmonger at Quality Seafood thought the car he had seen was red. There was a torn piece of grocery bag with Daniel's name scrawled on it and an address that Archer assumed was Young's. And there was something going on in the living room.

All heads turned at the sound of scuffling. Since those heads belonged to cops, they did what came naturally. Levinsky was the first at the doorway, Archer had his revolver at the ready, and Arnson flanked Liz who stepped back to get a bead through the men's bodies into the living room. When she did, she was eye-to-eye with a shoulder cam.

Levinsky was the first to react.

"Oh boy." He rolled his eyes, looked over his shoulder at Arnson and lamented. "It's Smith." He turned back to the guy with the camera. "Smith, get out of here."

The camera lowered revealing a guy in his thirties with the reddest hair Liz had ever seen. He was grinning ear-to-ear and freckled from brow to chin.

"Come on Levinsky. Give me something. It took me forever to find you."

"Smith, you gotta stop following us."

"Nope, you and Arnson get the best stuff. Besides, the guy outside," Smith looked over his shoulder just in time to see Daniel come in. "Him! He told me this is Xavier Hernandez's place. You think people have forgotten about him, but they haven't. Come on. Give me something I can sell to the networks, or something really good for YouTube. I gotta make a living Levinsky."

"I told him not to go in the house!" Daniel skirted around the freelancer to stand with the cops.

"Who are you?" Arnson asked.

"Dr. Daniel Young. I testified in the Hernandez trial."

Liz turned into Arnson, "We brought him. Just in case he could help out if you had Hernandez."

"Jesus, what a circus. Amateurs," Levinsky lamented and Liz colored.

The camera was up on Smith's shoulder again. The little red light was on and Smith was yapping.

"Levinsky, why is a bad guy like Hernandez out of jail? And where is he? Has the LAPD lost a murderer? A child killer?"

"Get that out of my face." Levinsky whacked at the camera and Smith laughed. Here was a man who loved his job.

"Dr. Young says Hernandez is suspected of kidnapping two women. Are we going to see a repeat of what happened in the desert? Are you looking for bodies?"

Now Levinsky wasn't the only one tired of Smith. Archer elbowed through the cops and advanced on Smith who backed up with the camera going. Archer was quick but he knew there was going to be some good footage of him looking like a crazy man. He didn't care. One big hand went over the lens and another yanked the camera right off Smith's shoulder.

"Police harassment," Smith howled. "You better not break that. I'll sue the department. I'll..."

"I'm not a cop," Archer growled, stopping only when he had backed Smith to the door. Smith looked around Archer and back to Levinsky and Arnson. Both shrugged.

"He's not," said Arnson confirmed.

"Hey," Archer hollered. "You want the camera or not?"

Smith's head whipped around in time to see Archer dangling the shoulder cam from three fingers. He dashed for it and grabbed it just as Archer was about to let go.

"Not funny, man. Everybody's gotta make a living," he complained.

"You're not going to do it here," Archer said.

"Doesn't matter," Smith grumbled. "The local news will go for some of this stuff. I think there will be a lot of people interested to know you guys lost Hernandez." Smith raised his voice on the last for the benefit of the LAPD. If they were worried, they didn't show it.

"Get out of here, Smith," Levinsky called. "And you better tell whoever is feeding you info regarding our whereabouts that I'm going to find them and write 'em up."

If Archer could have kicked the redhead's butt on the way out, he would have. Instead, he just stood in the doorway to make sure the guy left as directed. When he returned to the others, Arnson was giving Levinsky the game plan.

"We'll talk to the public affairs officer when we get back this afternoon and let him know what's going on. Nobody's going to run that mess."

"Maybe not, but the networks aren't going to ignore the lead. Reporters will be nosing around for a bigger story soon," Liz suggested.

"They'll probably have it."

Everyone turned at the sound of Daniel Young's voice. Their attention trained on Smith, they hadn't noticed the psychiatrist move into the bedroom. He was standing in front of the bulletin board with his arms by his sides and his shoulders back. His eyes slid over to the cover of Reverend Wilson's book. His gaze moved from the bold foiled title, to the picture of Janey, and finally to the calendar.

"What are you talking about?" Archer asked.

"How long has Ms. Bates been gone to the best of your knowledge?" Daniel answered Archer's questions with one of his own.

"Best guess is two days," Archer answered.

"Janey and Susie were held, tortured, and then killed on the fifth day. We don't have long to find Ms. Bates and Ms. Gardener. And that, Archer, is more than my expert opinion."

He turned his head, looked Archer in the eye, pivoted and walked out of the room. If Archer didn't know better he would have thought he saw a spring in the man's step.

CHAPTER 28

An Outbuilding in the California Mountains

It took Josie a minute to realize the stealthy sounds outside the wall weren't a figment of her imagination. The two women had passed the day in silence. Erika's fear was catching and Josie had been infected. So when she heard noises, she got up, wanting to be facing the door when the man came for them.

Her still-bound hands hit the concrete block. Her head spun and she steadied herself as best she could. She wilted, caught herself and pressed up against the concrete. Erika saw what she was doing. Josie put a finger to her lips. Then Erika heard it, too. She crawled toward Josie, threw her back up against the wall, and flattened herself against the concrete. It was late afternoon and murky inside the hut, but both hoped that their positioning and the light would keep them hidden.

"It's him," Erika whispered. "Xavier."

Josie didn't move. She strained to hear despite the pounding of her heart. It was the wrong time. He came early in the morning or late at night. He didn't come now, not in late afternoon. Her lips, dry and cracked, burned as she formed the words:

"No, it's not."

Xavier Hernandez's Place, Los Angeles

Archer didn't take his frustration out on Daniel. Instead, he stood apart and watched everyone leave the house.

Daniel looked like he was trying to hold himself together. Testifying in court, talking to Hernandez in the controlled environment, writing his reports, making his pronouncements to reporters on the courthouse steps was antiseptic and powerful for the free man. Now the bad guy was free, and he was after people who'd done him wrong. Josie still didn't make sense, but Archer learned a long time ago that there wasn't much sense in crime. Daniel Young was learning that, too.

Levinsky came out with the uniformed cop and packed evidence bags in the back of the unmarked unit. Arnson and Liz walked across the yard where they huddled with Daniel Young. Arnson and Young were doing the talking. Liz listened.

Archer raised his head. The sun was a bright, shimmering ball of light. It was another scorcher. He looked back again, but Liz wasn't done. He wanted to be gone. There was nothing to be had here. Archer was almost ready to call a halt to the chitchat when something caught his attention.

An Outbuilding in the California Mountains

Slowly, Josie pushed herself off the ground, and with hope came strength. Caution was thrown to the wind and she called out:

"Hey. In here! We're in here! Help us."

Erika sat up. She got to her knees, tilting forward, straining to hear exclamations of shock from whoever was out there. Instead, they heard the leaves rustle as someone inched toward the bunker. A branch cracked under that person's feet. It sounded like a bomb going off. That was when all hell broke loose. Josie couldn't tell how many people crashed through the trees and ran through the leaves. Laughing and whooping, the people on the outside found all this fantastically funny.

"Hey, you shit heads...wait..." It was a girl's voice that rang out. Not exactly the kind of girl you'd want to bring home to mom, but it didn't matter. Josie didn't want to marry her, she wanted her to stay put.

"There's a reward," Josie screamed and in return she heard nothing.

Xavier Hernandez's House, Los Angeles

Behind her dark glasses, Liz Driscoll's eyes followed Archer.

"Detective Driscoll? Are you listening?" Liz turned her attention back to Daniel Young. He was a pushy guy.

"Sorry. What were you saying?"

"His family," Daniel said. "Xavier's mother was Caucasian and a citizen, his father was an illegal who took off soon after Hernandez was born. The mother controlled everything in his life because she recognized early on he was trouble."

"If she was that controlling, how come he was out on that highway alone?"

Young shook his head. "Little boys grow up and want some space. They came to an agreement. He could go anywhere he wanted as long as she knew where he was. Once he checked in, she turned her back and never asked what he was doing. What Hernandez came to realize was that his mother was wary of him; I don't think she was afraid but she knew enough not to push."

"So the mom exerted her power by letting him know she could take away money, food, shelter, and he fought back by refusing things she wanted like going to the doctor or staying put at night or not going to school?" Arnson asked.

"That's rather basic, but yes," Daniel agreed. "It was a male/female power struggle."

"Doesn't sound like a crazed homicidal maniac if you ask me. My mom usually had me by the balls when I was a kid, too." Levinsky had joined the group.

Arnson rolled his eyes. Liz smirked. The comment confused Daniel in the context of such a serious discussion. Daniel tried again to get serious.

"Xavier was an enigma, but he was sane. He killed those girls because he was bored and they presented an opportunity to alleviate that boredom and get back at his mother. It was Ms. Bates who elevated him to the status of a passionate man unable to resist the advances of a young girl. He never was that. There was no passion in him, just the need for sensations. I warned them against believing anything else."

"Kidnapping is a little different. That takes some planning."

"I never said he was stupid, I said he was bored."

"You think he could manage kidnapping two women given what happened to him in prison?" Liz tipped her head as if that would help her discern exactly what Daniel was saying because it didn't sound like he was saying much.

"How did he get his victims to the shack in the desert?" Levinsky asked.

"According to Hernandez, he tried to help and when they were willing to go with him to get out of the sun, he drove into the desert. He knew the area well enough to know that there were places like that shack all over. Xavier never admitted one way or the other what he knew about that location. He did like remote areas. He was very observant. When I spoke with him, he talked about watching people while they camped and while they slept. This time he went a lot further than watching."

Daniel eyed each of the people surrounding him, pausing just long enough to make sure all eyes were on him. He smiled slightly. He positioned his head just so.

"Ms. Bates convinced everyone that Hernandez did things spontaneously with no intent to harm. She made him sound almost simple, but he has a powerful sense of purpose. He has a plan here, and he is executing it the same as he did with Janey and Susie."

"Were drugs involved with Janey Wilson?" Levinsky asked.

Daniel shook his head. "No. The girls were clean and nothing was found at the scene. They had a little food. A few bottles of water were found in that shack. It was squalid. I wouldn't let an animal live in those conditions. It was a classic case of..."

"How did he kill them?" Arnson asked, not caring that Daniel wanted to discuss the psychology behind the crime. Daniel scowled, but answered the question.

"Susie was asphyxiated. She also had a head injury, but the investigators didn't find any object capable of delivering such a blunt force injury. That always bothered me. I don't think they looked very hard."

Daniel sniffed at the cops' ineptitude, and the three detectives exchanged glances. The two LAPD detectives seemed to be taking Liz to task for bringing this guy. Daniel was clueless, not noticing that he wasn't making any friends, he went on:

"In Janey's case, she died of a knife wound. Ms. Bates argued heat of passion. There was evidence of sexual activity. But Josie Bates was more insidious than that..."

Daniel dropped his voice to share his lascivious information. He put his fingers on Arnson and Levinsky's arms simultaneously, but the cops weren't interested. They all had a timetable and Liz was getting antsy, too.

"We've got what we need, doc. Right guys?" Liz suggested.

"But it's important to know his methodology. Details are so important," Daniel insisted as he tried to draw them back, but they were already dispersing. "I can give you a timetable for his actions. I can predict..."

"We got it," Levinsky assured him. "Isolate the victims, keep 'em and kill 'em."

Arnson, though, did pause. " Does he have ties to the desert? A job? Friends out there?"

"No. He has no friends, and he simply likes remote places." Daniel answered but it was clear he was pouting. Liz almost laughed. He must have been a piece of work to deal with on the stand. She almost felt sorry for Josie Bates. Cross-examining him would be like trying to sweep up Mercury.

"Does he have a special kind of remote place he likes?" Arnson asked.

"I could go back through my files and analyze..."

But Arnson and Levinsky were now done with him. Liz was part of the boys group, but Daniel wasn't.

"Guess we have our work cut out for us." Liz spoke over Daniel. They were wasting time and Daniel would drag this on if they let him.

"Yep," Levinsky answered. They turned to Liz. "You want to follow-up on the visitors Hernandez had inside and see what they know?"

"I already have a call into the woman who ran the literacy group. Hernandez never missed that one," Liz said.

"Good. We've got one of Gardener's neighbors saying she saw a car in the driveway around the time we think she disappeared."

"Could she identify it?" Liz again.

"Nope. She said it could have been a dark red but probably brown. It wasn't new. The reason she noticed it was because it was pulled all the way up to the garage and she wondered if Gardener had picked up a second car for some reason."

"Too much to hope for that she saw anyone getting in or out?" Liz asked.

Levinsky snorted at the ridiculousness of the question. At least Arnson put his hand out and shook Liz's.

"Appreciate your help, Driscoll. Let us know if you find anything on your end."

"Vice-versa, Levinsky."

With a nod, the men were gone, headed off to follow-up on what they had: Erika Gardener's address book, a warrant to run her computer for clues, and coming down hard on Cuwin Martin. Yep, there was a lot to do. On Liz's end, she just had to do it without Hagarty knowing.

CHAPTER 29

An Outbuilding in the California Mountains

"Kids," Josie whispered excitedly. "It's kids out there."

"Yes" Erika breathed. "Yes. Oh my God. Thank God. But they ran away."

"No. They're hanging out there waiting for something to happen," Josie answered.

"Try again," Erika urged.

"Help. Help us." Stronger now Josie jumped up and waved her bound hands as she called out. "Help us. We're here. Open the door."

Josie was screaming and Erika was scurrying fast on her hands and knees. She grasped Josie's ankle and tried to pull herself up, but Josie shook her off. She wasn't strong enough to hold both of them up. And it didn't matter anyway. Someone was coming toward them. It was only one of the four she had identified earlier, but that didn't matter. One was all they needed to open the door, and if they couldn't, it only took one to make a phone call.

Suddenly, it was quiet. There were no frantic hands on the door, no calls of assurance. Josie licked her lips and the cracks stung under the pitiful layer of saliva. She pounded her hands at the edge of the opening, wiggling her fingers in her desperation.

"My name is Josie Bates. I live in Hermosa Beach. Josie Bates. Do you understand? If you can't open the door, I need you to call this number..."

Josie's voice rose and cracked. A sob broke through the cadence of the numbers she called out. She paused and regrouped. The person outside had stopped moving but Josie sensed they were still listening. She began again, calling out each number like it was a bead on a rosary:

"310-862-3510. His name is Archer. Tell him where you found us. Please, open the door or call that number. 310-862-3510. There's a reward. There will be a reward."

Josie called the number again and again. Her voice rose to such a frantic pitch that she hardly recognized it. She made it through nine numbers. She called again and managed to call out six. When she started from the beginning, she was shrieking the area code and it frightened her. Who was this hysterical woman? Where was the tough attorney she used to be: cool under pressure, clinically objective. But Josie knew exactly where that person was. She was locked up, incarcerated, unable to fight for herself. She was like any other person who finds their options not just limited but nonexistent. It was a surprise, this weakness. How could she have been so arrogant, so sure of herself when, in reality, she was pitifully weak? From the corner of her eye, Josie saw Erika collapse against the wall.

"They're gone," she whimpered.

Josie sank to the ground just as Erika did her one better and rolled on her side, folded her hands under her cheek and closed her eyes. They stayed that way. There was no discussion of hope and no strategy rolling around in their heads. Whoever had been out there was gone now. The birds had stopped singing. The women inside the building seemed to have stopped breathing.

Josie's eyes went to her hands and even that took a great effort. She didn't want to die bound as she was. She didn't want to die like Erika, either: beaten and resigned. But, at that moment, it was too much to find the energy to rouse either her outrage or her spirit.

She leaned back her head, hoping to shut her brain down so that despair wouldn't take over. Instead, images rolled around inside. Hannah, Archer, Max. Strangely, it was the unfinished wall in her house that caused her to move. If she died, the house would be sold and she didn't want people thinking she hadn't finished what she started. If she died, Hannah would become a ward of the state and, again, Josie wouldn't have finished what she started. If she died, Archer would never know that she loved him from the bottom of her heart.

Maybe she wasn't arrogant after all; maybe she just had purpose in her real life. There was a difference, after all. Now this was her real life, so she had to find her purpose again. Gathering her energy, Josie scooted into the corner, crooked her knees and rested her hands. In the next second she was working on the knot again. Erika turned her head to watch, but Josie couldn't meet her eyes. There was nothing to say and the last thing Josie wanted was to see her own fear reflected in the other woman's eyes. It seemed Erika understood because she rolled over and faced the wall. It was then, when they had each decided how they would end their time in that hot, hard place, they heard a tentative voice ask:

"How much?"

CHAPTER 30

Xavier Hernandez's Place, Los Angeles

Levinsky, Arson and the uniformed cop were pulling out onto the street, and Daniel Young was already in the car when Liz realized Archer was nowhere to be found.

"Back in a minute."

She closed the door and followed the only path Archer could have taken. It ran between the pit bull's domain and Hernandez's duplex. The chain link fence that kept the pit bull corralled intersected with an old wooden one that ran parallel with the freeway. The wooden fence listed, not only because it was weather-worn, but because an ancient tree – the only living thing flourishing in this neighborhood – had grown at an unnatural angle, seeking light between the freeway pilings. There stood Archer, his lips moving, his eyes trained on the tree. Following his gaze, Liz saw a platform cobbled together and wedged precariously between one large branch and another that didn't look as if it could hold up a sparrow. A boy was crouched on the slats. He had a bird's eye view of the duplex where Xavier Hernandez had lived for the last few months.

Liz turned and went back to the car. Three minutes later, Archer followed and swung himself inside. He was fastening his seat belt when the little boy appeared and stared at the car. Archer raised his hand, but the little boy just looked through the windshield, his eyes taking in Liz, Archer, and Daniel in turn. He would be in a gang before he was twelve and in prison by the time he was eighteen, but for now he was just a wary little kid clinging to a chain-link fence.

"Let's go." Daniel touched Liz's shoulder then sat back and buckled his belt.

Archer looked over his shoulder. "You've got to get out more often if a little kid scares you."

"Give it a rest, Archer, he's right." Liz started the car and backed out in a cloud of dust. She headed to the freeway. "Did you get anything back there?"

"Not as much as I wanted," Archer admitted. "The kid thought I was INS. When I told him I was just interested in Hernandez it got a little easier. My Spanish isn't what it used to be, but I know that he thought Hernandez was loco."

"Was the kid scared of him?"

"No, just said he was crazy. He was always trying to pet that dog, walking into the street even if there were cars coming. He said Hernandez was confused and his eye didn't work right."

"Ocular damage from the beating probably," Daniel said, wanting to be part of the conversation.

"He also said Hernandez had visitors."

"That's interesting," Liz commented.

"A man came at least twice, and once there was a woman with him," Archer said.

"Cuwin Martin, I would assume," Daniel muttered, turning around to look back at where they'd been.

"I doubt Cuwin makes house calls," Archer scoffed. "He can't even find his way back to his office."

Liz snickered and took the on-ramp fast before shooting across traffic and landing them in the carpool lane. Archer glanced into the side mirror. Behind them the cars slowed. L.A. drivers could smell an unmarked unit a mile away.

"When was the last time someone was there?" she asked.

"Archer?" Daniel gave him a verbal poke. Archer took a deep breath. The guy was really beginning to get on his nerves.

"He saw the woman three days ago. She was in and out fast. She was carrying a small box when she went in and nothing when she came out. He hadn't seen Hernandez for a couple of weeks."

"And before that?" Liz cocked her elbow on the door and rested her head in her upturned palm as traffic slowed.

"He doesn't know. He remembers the last time he saw her because his mother and her boyfriend had a big fight, so he went to the tree and sat there until after dark. He said the woman was pretty."

"Could he identify her or the man? I mean, if someone had a picture of them and showed him, could he then?" Daniel asked.

Archer shook his head. "No, he saw her go in from the back, and it was dark when she came out. According to him, she was medium height, pretty, long brown hair, and skinny. For a kid like that, though, skinny and beautiful are relative. The interesting thing is she got into an old red car."

"That doesn't give us much, does it?" Daniel raised his voice. "There must be ten thousand red compacts in Los Angeles."

Archer swiveled and threw his arm over the seat back.

"But we're only looking for one, Daniel, and we can narrow that down some. There was a red compact in the lot behind your office. I remember what it looked like. I'd know if it I saw it again. I bet if I drove it up for that kid to look at, he could tell me if it was the same car he saw. You'd be amazed what people remember."

"In my line of work, I'm always amazed at what they forget," Daniel shot back. Archer eyed him a second and then turned back around.

"You're right about that, Doc."

Young made a great living pulling memories out of people's brains; maybe he even helped them create some new ones. Liz and Archer both had taken statements, sat through trials, followed up on leads based on faulty memories, but they had to start somewhere. There was an old red car in the parking lot behind Daniel's building. It was there the same day Daniel found that list in his car. Josie had been 'helped' into a red car. It was a point on the map, and it was getting bigger all the time. He didn't need Daniel Young's permission to buy into it or to pursue it.

"Liz, think you can pull some strings and get the records from the pay station at the pier parking structure?"

"Oh, yeah, right," she laughed. "Let's spend three weeks sifting through all those tickets looking for cars that were there within twenty-four hours of Josie disappearing. Then we have to run the charge card receipts – that's assuming the person we're looking for used a charge card instead of paying cash. I don't think those two women have that kind of time."

"And we don't have anything else," Archer answered sharply, hating the cavalier way Liz referred to Josie and Erika Gardener. "We know Josie was at Quality Seafood. Let's get a picture of Hernandez down there for a confirmation. We know she had a drink with a guy who fits his description. We know she was unsteady and needed help. We can make the assumption she was drugged, and we know he took her toward the parking structure. We know she got into a small red car. We know someone in a blue and white shirt was on the other side of the car helping Hernandez."

"Yeah," Liz admitted reluctantly. Archer was on the right track, she just couldn't spend all that time running this down without raising some eyebrows.

"And we don't have to check a twenty-four hour cycle. We know Josie was at Quality Seafood about four thirty. Get a range of tickets from two through five o'clock."

"It could be done," Liz admitted. "And it would just take a phone call. I'll follow up with the literacy teacher who worked with Hernandez, too. Will you take care of showing the picture around?"

"Not a problem," Archer said, grateful that Liz was getting on board. "Do you have someone who can run the credit cards?"

"Yep, as long as we're not talking a couple hundred," Liz agreed.

"Great. We get the names, we run them through DMV, come up with some registration information. If we get a hit with a red compact, we check it out. It's not like the pier is a hot bed of activity that time of day. If twenty cars went in and out I'd be surprised." Archer turned toward her. "Right? It's doable. Right?"

Liz swerved out of the high occupancy lane and back in again in one smooth move. She gained only three car lengths. That made her as ticked off as not thinking the car park through on her own. Some big-time detective she was. "Yeah, I'll see if I can pull in a favor from the city clerk. But, Hernandez won't have a credit card."

"Nope, but I don't think he's our man," Archer said.

"Don't be ridiculous. Of course he is." Daniel barked a laugh from the back seat.

Liz's eyes went to the rearview mirror, and Archer slid his own right to check out the traffic. He looked back just in time to catch Liz looking at him, and he smiled. Daniel was an acquired taste that neither of them was acquiring.

"You want us to drop you at your office?" Liz asked.

"Yes, if you don't mind," Daniel said but he wasn't to be deterred. "But I can't believe you don't think Xavier is your man. That's patently ridiculous given all we know about him."

"We don't know anything about him," Archer said as the freeway opened up. "And what you know about him is irrelevant. It's ten-year-old information."

"It's relevant. Believe me," Daniel sputtered. "I've already told you enough to fill a book about Xavier Hernandez."

"We're talking about a different Hernandez. First, he's impaired. Second, the place where he was living trumps your volumes of information you got from him behind bars."

"Really? Well, then, fill me in since you're the experts now."

Before they could answer, Daniel unlocked his seat belt and thrust forward. He reminded Archer of Max putting his snout between the seats when he and Josie were in the car. The damn dog didn't want to miss a thing and neither did Daniel Young. "This affects me, you know, and if you're thinking there's someone else in the mix, I have the right to know."

Liz raised a shoulder as if to give Archer permission to answer, but it was more to say 'he's got a point."

"It's what we didn't see in that place," Archer answered.

"Like what?" Daniel demanded.

"Like a yellow highlighter. A pen." Archer suggested. "Hernandez took some quality time making that list we found in the cars. What's he writing with?"

"People keep those things all over," Daniel scoffed. "A pen could be in the drawer or under the bed."

"LAPD would have bagged them if they found them." Liz shot that his way just as she swerved again.

"What about a camera?" Archer suggested.

"Not everybody owns a camera," Daniel came back.

"People who take pictures do. There are pictures of you and the two women." Liz threw that out for consideration. "Good pictures, I might add. "

"Maybe he has it with him." Daniel said. "Maybe the people who visited Xavier have the camera."

"Maybe the people who are visiting Xavier are setting him up," Liz said. "That's the point. Maybe Hernandez isn't the mastermind; maybe Hernandez is the dupe. You've got a guy who suffered severe brain trauma, he's on all sorts of meds and he's running around leaving a ton of clues for us to follow that point right at him? That is really strange."

"Stranger things have happened." Daniel insisted.

"We don't count anything out," Archer said. "The point is that you're in our territory. We'll put the current pieces together because they have more immediate merit. We might find that Hernandez's cellmate had something against Josie and Gardener. Could be there's a girlfriend out there thinking she can make a few bucks off this."

"That's a stretch. If it was ransom, we would have heard by now," Liz said.

"Point being, we need to give weight to what we can see and touch, not theories about how Hernandez will act," Archer countered.

"That I can't argue with." Liz lowered her hand and clipped the turn signal. She exited on Pacific Coast Highway, made a right and settled in for the surface street drive to Hermosa via Manhattan Beach.

"What's really bugging me is that list," Archer continued. "It was a no-brainer. Once it was found, anyone on that list would connect it to the Hernandez trial. He had to know the cops would put it together fast, find out he was on parole, and run down to where he was living. Then he leaves that giant bulletin board? Come on." Liz rolled her eyes.

"Hernandez was always arrogant," Daniel suggested.

"Someone is." Archer muttered. "Could be someone out there is playing us."

"That's a definite possibility," Daniel suggested as he slid back in his seat.

Archer looked over his shoulder. He nodded at Daniel Young. That was the first thing they had really agreed on so far.

An Outbuilding in the California Mountains

Erika's head shot up just before she pushed herself up on her hip. Josie was on her feet, using both hands to steady herself as she hurried to stand just underneath the opening. Suddenly the inside of the hut was electrified, sparking and crackling with disbelief and hope.

"How much? As much as you want," Josie hollered.

"We have money," Erika joined in.

"There are two of you in there? Shit." The girl's voice was filled with awe and it wasn't the kind Josie liked. She sounded like Billy Zuni, high and happy and hallucinating.

"Don't worry about anything except what I'm saying. Pay attention to what I'm saying," Josie said evenly. "My name is Josie Bates. I live in Hermosa Beach. Do you know where that is?"

"Sort of," the girl answered warily.

"Do you have a phone?"

"Yeah."

"Okay. Ready? Dial 310-862-3510. A man named Archer will answer. Tell him where you are. Tell him I'm here with you. He'll know what to do." Josie waited. "Do you have him? Did he answer?" Josie fought to keep hysteria tamped down, but it was getting more difficult. "Are you there? Dammit, did you call?"

Erika put her fingers on Josie's leg as if to temper her reaction, but the tall woman would not be calm.

"There's no reception," the girl said finally, and it sounded as if she were half asleep. Leaves shuffled. She seemed to sigh.

Erika whispered. "She's leaving."

"Don't go. Please. Please," Josie called. "We'll give you anything you want."

"I'm so messed up." The girl mumbled just as they heard her companions calling, shouting curse words and saying they would leave her if she didn't get her butt in gear.

"Shit. Shit. I'm coming!" The girl yelled and started to run.

"Stop. Please. You can't leave." Josie and Erika cried simultaneously.

But the girl could leave, and the girl did leave. When they were sure she was gone, Erika crawled to her corner and Josie lay down in hers.

"Don't worry. Someone else will come. Something will happen. I promise," Josie said, but she wasn't really trying to convince Erika Gardener. Hell, she wasn't even trying to convince herself anymore.

CHAPTER 31

Day 3
Hermosa Beach

The story of Xavier Hernandez was starting to niggle at the edges of big news again thanks to the freelancer who had tracked Levinsky down at Hernandez's place and sold a snippet of film to one of the local stations. At the same time, in a serendipitous moment, one of Hannah's flyers found its way into the hands of the local paper. The paper did a bio on Josie including a nice little history of the Hernandez trial and noted the fact that it was the ten-year anniversary of that particular 'trial of the century'. That article was read by the local CBS News at Five anchor who happened to live in Manhattan Beach. The freelancer made some bucks, the newspaper had a nice little bump in readership, and the CBS News at Five added some fuel to the fire with information on Xavier Hernandez's release from prison as part of the release of forty-five thousand felons to relieve prison overcrowding (which the California high court had decided was cruel and unusual punishment). Then they went a step further. They interviewed Daniel Young who, like an idiot, spilled the beans on the lists in the cars, speculated on why these two particular women were targeted, admitted he was also at risk, and offered to exchange himself for Josie Bates and Erika Gardener if Xavier was listening.

When Archer saw it, he was disgusted. When Liz saw it, she was pissed. The freelancer's clip showed her standing with Levinsky and Arnson clear as day. She could only hope Hagarty didn't watch T.V. When Hannah saw it, she was sad. On one hand, they were talking about a Josie she didn't know and wouldn't want to know; on the other hand they were reveling in the possibility that Josie had come to a bad end.

Hannah turned off the set, and took Max out for a walk. When the dog was bedded down, she picked up her big bag, locked and checked the front door, positioned herself at the end of the walk-street on the corner of Hermosa Boulevard, and waited.

Archer picked her up exactly on time. She climbed into the Hummer, put on her seat belt and listened to the radio. The host was accepting calls concerning the question of whether or not Josie deserved what she got because she had defended a scumbag in the first place. Calls ran fifty-fifty that she did, and ten-to-one that the good doctor was brave, a saint, and the only one who might have a chance to save these women. Archer flipped it off. He had no intention of listening to a Daniel Young love fest.

They drove the rest of the way in silence, the miles melting under the Hummer's tires. That Archer drove too fast when there was a break in the traffic was something Hannah understood. Every hour away from their search was an hour that further jeopardized Josie. It would be many hours before they got back because the Edleman

Children's Courthouse in Monterey Park was about as far from Hermosa Beach as you could get.

When they arrived, Hannah got out of the Hummer. She dragged her giant purse from the back seat and put it over her shoulder. The beach was hot, but Monterey Park was blistering. Archer slammed his door, came around and walked with her. It was a second before Archer realized Hannah had dropped behind. The heel of her shoe was stuck in the melting blacktop. Archer looked back just as she yanked her leg up and the heel released. The next step was the same. She yanked again. Then she stomped and yanked. She stomped once, twice, three…Archer went back and took her arm.

"It's okay, Hannah," he said quietly.

Her head snapped up. Behind the huge, gold-rimmed sunglasses, Archer could feel her green eyes turning to glass. That was always the first sign that her defenses were rising and her armor was clicking into place. Funny how well he knew her when all this time he didn't think he had been paying any attention at all.

"It's cool," he offered.

He tightened his hand on her arm, steered her toward a sidewalk, and gave her no time to count or argue. When they got there, Hannah pulled away. The fact that she didn't give him one of her 'looks' allowed him to take no offense. She leaned a hand against a stunted tree that, at one time, had probably been part of some long-forgotten beautification project.

Hannah raised her foot and peeled the black stuff off her heel. When she was done, she stomped the rest clean, and Archer turned away to give her some privacy. It was a ridiculous gesture considering they stood within a foot of each other, but he was embarrassed by her antics, unable to shake the idea that if she really wanted to she could control all the touching and counting. Yet a part of him also empathized. Hadn't he been uncontrollable when he was accused of killing his stepson? No one could have deterred his outrageous righteousness, so he let Hannah be. They were all on edge. If this is where she danced on the head of a pin, so be it.

Archer put a hand to his eyes and rubbed hard when he realized he was starting to count the heel-whacks on the concrete, too. When she reached twelve, she added a vocal.

"I should have gone with her. I should've." The words pushed themselves through her teeth so that they were shredded by the time Archer heard them.

He almost laughed, though, when he realized she had spoken eight words combined with twelve stomps, which brought her to her magic count of twenty. Archer wondered how she did that, decided Hannah must be some sort of savant, and then entertained the thought that she had lost a little of her mind.

"You couldn't go to work with Josie. That doesn't make sense."

Hannah put her foot down. The heel of her shoe still had some tar on it, but other than that she looked amazing. From afar she could be taken for an attorney in her crisp suit. Except that the skirt was a little shorter, her shoes a little too cutting edge and her hair a little too wild for an attorney. Still, she looked like she was ready to plead her case.

"I meant Mrs. Crane. If I had just let her send me to a foster home for a while, you wouldn't have to be here with me. You could be looking for Josie." Hannah let go of the tree and stood up. She shook her head back and set her jaw.

"Yeah," Archer mumbled.

"Really?" Hannah's shoulders pulled back, the set of her jaw softened but that was the only indication that some of the wind had been sucked out of her sails.

"Yeah about what you meant. If we weren't here, I could be looking for Josie," Archer answered. "But you shouldn't have gone with that woman, and you're not going today. You can't just leave with the clothes on your back."

"I packed my stuff." Hannah pushed her giant bag forward. It wasn't just a purse, it was her parachute in case she flew too close to the judicial sun and was cast down somewhere foreign. "I know how it works."

Archer pulled his lips together, considered the bag, and then took it off her shoulder. When she resisted, Archer gave her the look and she let go. It took him a minute and a half to go back to the Hummer, open the door, toss in Hannah's bag, and return. He didn't break stride when he came abreast of her, and she didn't hesitate when she turned on those very cool heels of hers to join him.

"You're not going anywhere," Archer muttered.

He hoped it was true. If he had to get the bag out of the back of the car it would be the longest walk he ever took.

Judge Leisinger's Courtroom, Edleman Courthouse, Montery Park

In the Edleman Children's Courthouse words like wretched, hopeless and desperate was the order of the day for attorneys, judges, clerks and investigators whose lot it was to take children away from their abusive and neglectful parents and put them into a horrendously flawed foster care system. There were other attorneys who fought to keep those kids home with drugged out mommy or fist-raising daddy. And there were the kids who didn't win no matter which way it went.

To mitigate the devastation experienced every day in this court, the building itself had been constructed as a testament to denial. The hall floors were carpeted; the walls were bright with pictures of cavorting cartoon characters and super heroes. Just off each courtroom was a playroom rather than a holding cell. The judges and staff spent part of their salary buying stuffed animals, gifts meant to give kids something to cling to when Child Protective Services whisked them away with nothing more than the clothes on their back. The door between the courtroom and playroom was soundproof so the children could not hear the testimony against their parents, yet it was made of glass so that they could see them.

In the courtroom itself, the bench was nestled into a well rather than elevated on a platform. The entire place was well thought out so that the little ones would be less intimidated. Archer and Hannah were far from intimidated, but they were uncomfortable: Archer was too big and rough for the place, and Hannah was too sophisticated and knowledgeable. She'd been in children's courts often enough to know that the trappings didn't change the misery.

The county attorney was there when they arrived, and it took no time for her to assess the situation. Her look said that these two were trouble. Hannah and Archer looked back and thought the same of her. The woman, if, indeed, that's what she was, was huge. From shoulder to knee, there was no break for a waist, no indication of breasts, no ballooning of hips. Her hair was short and swept haphazardly behind her ears. She wore neither jewelry nor make-up, and there was just a hint of a mustache on her upper lip. Her hands were beefy, her feet flat and wide. Her jacket and pants draped over her without any consideration of fit or style. She had to scare the hell out of kids; she scared the hell out of Archer.

Mrs. Crane joined them within moments of Hannah and Archer's arrival. Her ever-present clipboard was clutched to her breast. She wore a matching sweater set despite the heat outside, sensible shoes, and well-pressed trousers. Her single strand of pearls was as thin and tight as her lips, and as fake as her smile. She paused and bent from the waist as she drew alongside Hannah.

"You look so nice today, Hannah." Her tone indicated that the last time she had seen Hannah the girl looked like a slut.

She gave Archer a stiff 'hello' before joining the county attorney. They were all in place when the chambers' door opened and Judge Leisinger appeared. He was a gray sort of fellow: thick silver-grey hair, putty-grey shirt, and a metal-grey tie visible just above the neck of his robes. Even the black robes had a silvery sheen as if time was worn away the blackness and softened his judicial demeanor. He took his seat behind the lowered bench, picked up a file, flipped through a few pages and smiled at those gathered.

"Morning all." Murmurs of morning rolled back at him from the left side of the courtroom. Mrs. Crane sat and lowered the clipboard to her knees. The judge continued on. "We are here today to complete the petition for legal custody of the minor, Hannah Sheraton."

Judge Leisinger rested his eyes on Hannah. His gaze indicated that all those who appeared before him were children, so his expression registered no surprise at her appearance or comportment. "How are you today, Hannah?"

"Fine, thank you, Judge," she answered.

He smiled at her, but the big woman from the county lumbered up and captured his attention.

"Judge," she said, in a deep and gravelly voice.

"Good morning, Mrs. Rice." Judge Leisinger smiled, his greeting solving the mystery of the attorney's gender.

"Morning, Your Honor." She answered back as if such niceties could barely be tolerated by someone like her with so many important things to do on that hot, hot day.

"I haven't seen you in this court for some time, Ms. Rice. I thought Hermann was handling this."

"He was, Your Honor, but he's on leave,"

"I hope nothing serious," Leisinger noted conversationally.

"Heart Attack. He'll recover," Mrs. Rice said offhandedly.

"Then I suppose you're going to kick the can down the road until he returns?" His tone was that of someone who always hoped for the best.

"Not at all, Judge. We intend to..." Leisinger held up his hand.

"A moment, please. I'm not so quick on the uptake first thing in the morning." His eyes rested on Archer. "I assume you are representing Hannah, sir?"

Archer rose and addressed the court. "I'm here to support Hannah."

"Excellent. Mrs. Crane I know well, so we are all accounted for. Counsel? Now it's your turn."

"Your Honor, we have a situation," Mrs. Rice said.

An Outbuilding in the California Mountains

Josie hadn't meant to sleep so long, and now the cement cell was heating to an almost unbearable degree. She was sweating as she worked the hinges on the old metal door.

"What are you doing?"

Josie held up Erika's shoe without looking at the other woman, "I took it out of your closet. I'm glad you wear high heels."

"You're not going to get very far." Erika's voice had a dreamy quality that made Josie take notice. She stopped her efforts to work the hinge, sat on her heels and looked more closely at the other woman.

Erika Gardener was laying on her back, curling her hair around one finger, her eyes lazily moving from the hole in the wall to Josie and back again. She was obviously more interested in the small patch of outside that she could see.

"If he comes this morning, we should ask him for some toilet paper."

Josie couldn't help laughing. "Tell you what, when we get out of here we'll find a real bathroom, but first we have to get out."

Josie slammed the heel of the shoe up against the bolt that held the hinge tight. Rust fluttered over her bound hands. What she wouldn't give to be free of the rope.

"Want to help?"

"No, thank you," Erika answered lazily.

"Okay," Josie answered and hit the heel of the shoe against the metal so hard the shoe broke.

Edleman Children's Court, Monterey Park

"We don't deny Josie has gone missing. It's all over the news, Judge."

It was Archer's turn to speak now that Mrs. Rice had her say, and her say had been laced with ugly innuendo. "But to suggest she is willingly absent or unreliable is bull."

The judge raised one finger, a warning for Archer to watch his language. The big man rotated his shoulders under his jacket. He couldn't remember the last time he'd put on a jacket and tie, yet that morning he did it without thinking. In fact, he would have worn a straight jacket if that were what it took to plead Josie's case. When the jacket lay a bit more comfortably on his shoulders, Archer readjusted his language.

"Josie would have walked over hot coals to be here, and you don't have to take my word for it."

"Your Honor," Mrs. Rice interjected. "It is not a function of this court to speculate about why Ms. Bates is gone, only to establish that she is. Now we must analyze how that impacts the best interests and welfare of the child, Hannah Sheraton. We all know where statistics stand on matters like this. There's a greater chance that Ms. Bates, a single woman used to living alone, may have simply found the idea of being legally responsible for Hannah too much. There's a greater chance of that than of foul play."

"She didn't find the idea of defending Hannah from a frame-up too much of a bother. Or what about making sure she had a home to live in all this time, and a school to go to?" Archer retorted. Mrs. Rice glared at him, her eyes almost disappearing in the folds of her cheeks.

"The court isn't concerned with history," Mrs. Rice drawled.

"Your Honor, can I approach?" Archer asked. He was no attorney, but he knew the protocol.

Leisinger waggled two fingers. Archer stood in front of the bench and looked right into the judge's eyes. What the man was thinking was a mystery. The guy was good.

"Josie Bates is the most reliable person I know, but we can't change the fact she isn't here. But if she were, she'd be the first to say that all she wants is what's best for Hannah. I can tell you, leaving Hannah in Hermosa is what's best for her." Archer squared his shoulders. "You've got Hannah's file, and you know that history is the only thing important here. Hannah's had a hard life until Josie took her in. Staying in Hermosa gives her the stability Mrs. Rice is talking about."

He shot the woman a glance that withered her a bit but didn't knock her down.

"Judge, the people of Hermosa are worried about Josie, but they are also friends to Hannah. They are a family now. If you knew Josie, and knew the people I'm talking about, you'd know I'm right. No foster home could be better for Hannah than we are."

"Well, doesn't that argument just have a lot of holes in it? We don't even know if these people exist. We know nothing about this man, and I think that bears looking into. Also, why does he so desperately want to be responsible for this young girl?" Mrs. Rice cried.

Mrs. Rice had a dirty mind, which could be forgiven considering what she heard inside these courtrooms. Archer still didn't like the insinuations. He looked back at Leisinger.

"Retired LAPD, Judge. Private investigator now, and I do some freelance photography and-"

"And," the big, fat woman interjected. "Accused of killing his own stepson. Let's not forget that."

Archer gave her a long, hard look and this time she didn't flinch. Slowly he turned back to the bench.

"And exonerated."

"But they were charges of violence against a child. Exonerated or not, that cannot be overlooked. Transcripts show that he had no regard for the boy, and that he refused the mother's wishes that he care for the boy after her death. It doesn't matter if this man didn't actually kill anyone, it is his attitude toward children that is critical."

Archer wanted to strangle the woman. She was like a mindless animal. Her teeth were dug into something she shouldn't have a hold of, and she didn't know enough to let go. She added:

"Hannah Sheraton is, after all, a child."

Even the judge could not help himself. He and Hannah shared a glance. One side of the courtroom knew very well that Hannah was no child. But Leisinger was an old hand at this and the indication of his understanding was no more than a flicker in his eye, a barely perceptible twitch of his lips.

"Mrs. Rice, please. You know better than to try histrionics here." His time at Children's Court had given the judge the patience of a saint and the ability to reprimand like a parent.

"Then let me call Mrs. Crane, Hannah's case manager." Mrs. Crane rose in anticipation of her moment in the spotlight only to hesitate as Leisinger's ever so expressive finger pointed to Archer.

"I would like to speak to this gentleman." He gave her a look over the top of his bifocals. "You may sit, Mrs. Crane. You, too, Mrs. Rice."

The attorney heaved her great bulk to the left. She heaved to the right. She was unsure of which way she should turn now that the judge was rewriting her script. Finally, she plopped herself on the bench next to the caseworker.

"Thank you." The judge turned his attention to Archer. "It's time for twenty questions, sir. Let's begin with where you think Ms. Bates might be."

"No idea. We have her car. We have information that is pointing us to an old client who was recently released from prison."

Mrs. Rice rolled her bulk as if she was going to stand up. The judge waggled his finger and went back to Archer.

"How long has she been gone?"

"Two days; almost three."

"Do you live with Mrs. Bates?"

Archer hesitated for the briefest moment then answered, "No, Your Honor. We have separate residences."

"Who else lives at the home with Ms. Bates and Ms. Sheraton?"

"No one, Judge."

"So Hannah would be alone in the house if I disallowed CPS's request to remand her to their custody?"

"Yes. But…"

"Let's stick with the basics. What are your plans for Hannah should I release her to your custody?"

Archer looked over his shoulder at the girl. His eyes lingered on her while the filmstrip of their existence together ran through his brain. Hannah looked back, knowing Archer could go either way where she was concerned. She didn't try to sway him by look or word. He would do what he wanted, and it would be weighted in everyone's best interest, not just hers. Hannah could accept that. Finally, he turned back to the bench.

"Could you clarify, Judge?"

"Considering you are here, and you are speaking for Hannah, I would assume you arrived with a plan for her custody until the matter with Ms. Bates is resolved."

"I would check on her. I can always be reached."

"But she would be alone in the house?"

"There's the dog. The house has a security system. Hannah's been alone before," Archer answered.

That was just too much for Mrs. Rice. She tried to shoot out of her seat only to need an assist from Mrs. Crane. The drama of her outrage was lost in the moment.

"Your Honor, isn't that the point here? To show that the court has compassion? Place her, so she is not left alone."

"Placement is more alone than being in Josie's house."

All heads turned. It was Hannah who responded to Mrs. Rice's argument and her retort was sharp and honest. No one spoke, no one tried to hush her, but they all judged her. To Mrs. Rice Hannah was a widget on the assembly line, to Mrs. Crane she was an uppity brat to be beaten down, to the judge she was a refreshing curiosity, and to Archer she was Josie's protégé, a young woman who now spoke for herself fearlessly.

Hannah's long-fingered hands were crossed in her lap, resting quietly, her tapping and counting was perhaps forgotten but probably just controlled. She was poised and confident, but all one had to do was look a little deeper to see that her green eyes smoldered and her jaw was clenched. She spoke to the judge.

"Have you ever been in a county home?"

"I've visited many times, yes," the judge answered.

"No, I mean, have you ever lived in one?" she pressed.

The judge shook his head. Hannah looked at Mrs. Rice and Mrs. Crane. Both had the good sense to lower their eyes.

"Well, visiting is different than living in one," she went on. "If you're lucky, it's just lonely in those places. If you're not so lucky, you have to fight for food or fight off some guy who says he's your foster father and he needs some love. Sometimes the women beat you. Sometimes you have to take a beating, so they don't do it to the little kids. Even if you have a good house, the foster mother won't remember your face a year later. These people aren't real parents; these women aren't real mothers." Hannah looked over at the two women. "Why don't you all go stay a week in a placement, then come back and tell me I have to go."

When Hannah was done and there was no response, she looked just long enough at the two women to underscore her challenge, and then turned her eyes back to the front of the court. She couldn't look at Archer for fear she would be tempted to beg him to save her. She didn't look at the judge because he was one of them, one of the three arbiters of the state's idea of justice.

"It is not a perfect system, Hannah," Judge Leisinger said quietly, "but it is what we have. Should the court find placement preferable, I will take your comments into consideration and personally review the situation."

Mrs. Rice had the decency to lower her voice when she caught the court's attention. She fumbled through her papers and came up with what she wanted.

"Your Honor, I would like to introduce a letter from Hannah's mother. She objects to the proposed custody of her daughter by Josie Bates. She loves her daughter dearly and does not -"

"That's rich," Archer sniffed. He leaned forward like a man on his third shot of whiskey wanting to argue a critical call in the World Series. "Her mother is a murderer. She tried to have this girl take the rap for what she did. Hannah's mother is at-"

"We believe in rehabilitation in this state," Mrs. Rice interrupted.

"Then you must believe in Santa Claus," he muttered.

"That's enough," the judge ordered, his anger presenting itself as annoyance. "I am fully aware of the history of both mother and daughter. Step back, sir."

The judge would not allow a parent – murderer or not – to be disparaged. This was children's court, and even a child like Hannah Sheraton would not be subjected to more pain than she already carried if he could help it. He motioned for Mrs. Rice to step forward. She handed him the letter. He read it, sent it along to his clerk, and turned his attention to Hannah.

"Ms. Sheraton, your principal is concerned about you," he said.

"I haven't missed one class, Judge. I'm on the honor roll. I lied to Mrs. Manning about where Josie was because I didn't want her freaking out. Josie is important now, not me. Please, I need to be home when she comes back. She'll need my help."

Hannah's head dipped. Her cloud of hair hid her face briefly. When she raised her head, tears glistened in her eyes, one spilled over her lashes and coursed down her cheek but her gaze never wavered and her voice did not break when she said:

"Please, don't make me leave my home."

The judge did Hannah the courtesy of watching her a minute longer before he turned to the county attorney.

"Mrs. Rice? Do you have anything else?"

"Yes, Your Honor. I'd like to give Mrs. Crane a few moments."

"Go ahead."

He picked up a pencil and tracked Mrs. Crane's precise steps. Archer sat down next to Hannah. As he did so, his knee touched hers, his shoulder bumped against hers.

They faced forward, but that second of contact, that moment of connection, changed everything. Hannah knew she had a champion, and Archer understood why Josie had needed to rescue this girl. What he loved about Josie, he could admire in Hannah: determination, strength in the face of fear, and an absolute belief that right, not expediency, should prevail. Now the only thing that prevailed was Mrs. Crane, and her voice was filled with the constipation of county crap.

"Your Honor, Ms. Bates' residence is acceptable in terms of the physical layout. Hannah has her own bedroom, and the home is clean and well taken care of. She has been attending her meetings with her psychologist. And, indeed, she is an excellent student." Mrs. Crane took a deep breath so that her energy would be high when she launched into the bad stuff and, indeed, what came out of her mouth was bad. "But, Your Honor, there are obvious problems that even you cannot ignore."

"I will do my best to follow you," he answered evenly.

"Well, I took it upon myself to look a little further into the environment Ms. Sheraton finds herself in. She spends much of her free time at a restaurant/bar called Burt's by the Beach. Hermosa has problems with public intoxication and young people are greatly affected. In fact, just last year the statistics for alcohol related crimes – both misdemeanors and felonies – among minors was alarmingly…"

"Do you have those statistics," the judge broke in.

"Of course." She minced toward the bench, handed over her research with flair.

"Anything else?" he asked.

"Yes. There is another child named Billy Zuni. He also seems to have difficulty at home. He and Hannah spend quite a bit of time together. We cannot have children watching out for children. I've already started an investigation into Billy's home situation and, if need be, I will ask the court to remand him to county custody, also."

"No, you can't do that!" Hannah shot straight out of her seat and was at the judge's bench before anyone could stop her. "Are you going to let that bi-"

"Be careful," the judge warned even as the two women gasped.

"I'm sorry." She put her hands up in apology and took two steps back. When her hands came down again, she took two steps forward. "It's just you have to understand. Everyone in Hermosa looks after everyone. We're not out getting drunk every night."

"Billy Zuni has been arrested for truancy," Mrs. Crane added.

"And half the time he isn't in school because he's with his mom who's hung over. What's wrong with that? He's taking care of her." Hannah shot back. "Why don't you let me talk?"

"I think that would be a good idea, Mrs. Crane. You can sit down," Leisinger directed.

Hannah stood up straight and put her hands by her side. Archer saw her index finger start to tap her thigh. The heel of her left shoe was being raised and lowered almost imperceptible. It took everything he had not to speak for her, but that wouldn't help. Hannah had to have her say.

"Your Honor. Judge. I'm only sixteen, but I've been around. Not like those women want you to think, but I've seen a lot. One thing I know is that adults screw up and make bad choices, and kids have to pay for them; kids screw up and make bad choices and they get creamed. I never had one person looking out for me, and now I've got a whole little city worried about me and Josie. You don't know how worried everyone is, and how they are all trying to help. I may have screwed up with the posters, but I was trying to do the right thing. Maybe that wasn't the right thing, but I have to tell you there's one thing I can do that nobody else can."

"What would that be, Hannah?" Judge Leisinger asked.

"I can wait. I know how to keep my eye on the door. If I'm not there, Josie will know. If I am there, she'll come back to me eventually. Waiting always brought my mom back, and she didn't even care about me."

Nobody could argue with what Hannah brought to the table. In that final sixteen-year-old argument for independence, was a message of hope and faith and love that was both an uplifting explanation of her own strength, and a devastating commentary on the system.

"Judge?" Mrs. Crane cleared her throat, and it sounded like she was singing too loud in church. "That was quite lovely, but we have to also point out that it is this person," she half turned toward Archer, "a man who has been Ms. Bates' significant other who appears to be offering himself as interim guardian to Hannah."

Mrs. Rice lumbered up beside her counterpart in a show of solidarity. Her sweater had bunched up on her substantial hips; her arms were akimbo instead of at her sides because of her bulk. She couldn't help but add her two cents.

"It would be one thing if this gentleman was in a committed relationship with Ms. Bates, then we could argue that he was a father figure within the household. But this relationship is casual, and that is hardly the optimal situation for Hannah. She will be a young woman alone in an environment that this man has access to, day or night."

Outwardly, Archer didn't flinch; inside he was boiling. It was a good thing this woman wasn't talking that kind of trash in Burt's bar. Archer would have decked her in a minute, wiped that self-righteous piggy purse off her lips. Hannah, though, started. He pressed his shoulder against hers and felt the tension in her body.

"We're good," he whispered.

"Thank you for that input, Counsel. Mrs. Crane." The judge took thirty long seconds to consider the paperwork on his desk.

"Your Honor," Mrs. Rice didn't know when to quit. Judges could be like sleeping dogs, better to let them lie. The expression Leisinger showed to her was less than pleased. She didn't notice and kept poking at him. "Please also consider that Ms. Bates is known to have been attorney of record in some quite notorious defendants. Even this man." She indicated Archer. "Even he admits that they are tracking one of her clients as the possible perpetrator of her disappearance. But he is not the only possibility. No matter what has taken Josie Bates away from Hannah Sheraton, it boils down to the fact that there are only two choices – the situation she finds herself in is dangerous or she is selfish. "

Archer was on his feet. "You don't know what you're talking about."

"Sit down," The judge snapped. "Now."

Before Archer could settle in his seat, the judge who had heard enough nonsense, made his ruling.

CHAPTER 32

Josie Bates' House, Hermosa Beach

"Totally awesome, Hannah! Come on, you gotta admit it. Three patties on those burgers is way awesome. And fries? And onion rings? And pie?"

Billy Zuni balanced on the low wall that separated the Strand from the sand. Every fifth step he threw out his arms, pretending he was going to fall, but Hannah didn't bite. She walked a few steps ahead, her thumbs crooked in the pockets of her low cut jeans. Her sweater was tied around her waist because it had been too hot to wear a sweater in the first place. She had thought it would be okay since it was made of an open weave cotton that she figured the breeze would go right through it, if there ever was a breeze. It was the heat that made her even more edgy and impatient with Billy. The burgers were awesome, but she wasn't going to go on like some fool about them. Besides, Billy was ignoring the fact that Burt was treating them like kids whose parents were divorcing.

"He gave you a deal, Billy. Burt doesn't charge twenty bucks for all that food," Hannah sniffed.

"So?" Billy jumped down from the wall, his flip-flops slapping on the concrete. He ran ahead of her and turned around to walk backward. "Doesn't mean that they weren't awesome, does it?"

"No," she muttered.

"And maybe he just wanted to celebrate that the judge let you go. I know I want to celebrate. Man, you beat the whole system."

Hannah couldn't argue with him about Burt's generosity so she didn't try. She just didn't like overt kindness. It bothered her, made her skin itch, made her think there was another shoe that was going to drop if she gave in to comfort. Burt had put his hand over hers as he passed on his way to give an order to the kitchen. She had smiled at him even though she didn't like people touching her. When he stopped to ask if there was anything she needed at the house, he didn't take no for an answer and promised to send over some ready-made meals. She would have preferred he accepted her word that she was fine. When he didn't, it made her feel like he thought she was lying. And when he went about his business, greeting other patrons and filling their orders and that made her mad too. She didn't want anyone to be doing business as usual. Nothing was usual.

Then she saw his mangled legs, trophies from that horrid motorcycle accident. He had almost died but he worked his way through the pain and terror and come out the other side, business as usual. That's when Hannah got up to leave. She didn't mind working through the pain and terror, she just didn't want to be more mangled when she reached the end of the journey. So she left the restaurant and Billy followed. He caught up with her, but knew better than to actually touch her as she walked. He fell behind for a while, then for a while he walked in front of her. All Billy really wanted was to help.

"Bet Archer was glad you didn't have to go to a foster home, too."

Hannah's eyes lowered, and she couldn't help smiling. She and Archer had both been jazzed when they walked out of court, leaving the two county witches to stew over the fact that they hadn't cast the proper spell on Judge Leisinger. Archer had even managed a smile. It wasn't big and it wasn't wide, but Hannah saw it.

"Forty-eight hours isn't much but it's something," Hannah said, not wanting to voice what she really thought.

In her soul, Hannah took this as a sign that everything was going to be all right. She had tried to thank Archer, but he got back in the Hummer like he hadn't heard her so she didn't try again. The morning had turned to afternoon by the time he dropped her back at Josie's. The last thing he did was reach in the back for her big bag. He gave it to her and said:

"Put that stuff away."

He took off, needing to catch up with Liz Driscoll and check his messages hoping the people he was tracking had called him back with information that could lead to Josie. It was Archer's twenty that had bought them the feast at Burt's, and now Hannah was getting antsy. She wanted her phone to ring. She wanted to get home to see if there was a message on the house line. She wanted Max by her side because he made her feel like she was home for sure, but Billy was sticking to her like glue. He was walking backward again, jabbering as he always did about nonsensical stuff, hardly noticing that Hannah wasn't just lost in thought, she had come to a dead stop.

"Hannah, want to go over to..."

A few steps later, Billy figured out she was mesmerized by something she saw over his shoulder. He stopped, too, and shook back his blond shock of hair.

"Hannah? You okay?"

Without a word, she put her hand out like a sleepwalker and pushed him aside. Billy followed. He didn't see anything, yet it was clear that Hannah did. She walked slowly at first, and then picked up the pace until she was running. That pretty sweater unwound from her waist and dropped to the ground as she ran. Billy scooped it up and followed after her.

"Hannah," he called, but she didn't stop until she was at the 'T' where Josie's walk-street dead-ended into the Strand. Billy pulled up behind her.

"Shit, dude," he breathed.

Shoulder-to-shoulder, they stood looking at the people surrounding Josie's house. There were a hundred of them, maybe more, holding candles whose flames didn't flicker in the hot, still evening. On the far side of the crowd, traffic crawled on Hermosa Boulevard as drivers gawked. One driver who had obviously had one too many slowed to a stop, lifted his middle finger and hollered something that Hannah could not hear but knew to be vile.

There was a television truck illegally parked against the curb and a blond woman was speaking earnestly into the lens of a huge shoulder cam pointed her way by a big guy wearing a green t-shirt. When sirens sounded in the distance, the commentator picked up the pace. Hurriedly, she finished speaking, and then shouldered her way through the crowd, raised her hand and pushed her microphone up toward the man standing atop the low wall that Josie had built. His arms were outstretched like Christ on the cross, and he was talking trash to the faithful and the fools.

An Outbuilding in the California Mountains

Erika tore a piece of her skirt off, wrapped it around her bound hands and rubbed her face. She rubbed and rubbed. Her skin was raw, but Josie had given up trying to make her stop.

"How's this?" Erika asked, and for the tenth time Josie looked up.

"Yeah, looks good."

Erika smiled. "Great. Okay. Your turn. If we make ourselves look nice, maybe it will make a difference. God, I wish I had a comb."

"Hmmm." Josie was half listening because the knot of the rope around her hands was starting to give. She stretched her finger as far as it could go and wiggled it under the knot, but she couldn't get enough leverage.

"Erika, come here. Quick. I can't hold it too long." Erika did as she was told, crawling toward Josie who was holding her wrists up. "Look, see, it's giving. Can you work one of your fingers underneath?"

Silently Erika bent to the task. She straightened her pointer finger and worked it under the rope. Josie held her breath, but Erika breathed hard with the effort. Slowly the rope gave. Neither woman uttered a sound and certainly not a word of delight. Superstition was the order of the day inside that hut. Don't speak of hope because God might hear and dash it. Don't wish for water because it might rain outside and they would have none inside.

Don't talk of their lives before this, because they might never get back to them. So, when that little loop of cotton rope jiggled, when Erika crooked her finger underneath, when the end of it popped through that loop, they dared only look at one another.

Erika bent again and pinched the remaining knot between thumb and pointer finger. She worked the rope back and forth, back and forth. Impatient, Josie contracted and expanded her wrists. She wriggled them, and the work became frantic. Erika giggled, and Josie barked a laugh.

"Oh Jesus. That's it. That's it." Josie rejoiced. In the next second the rope fell away and blood rushed to her extremities. She rubbed her wrists, she wiggled her fingers, and looked at her hands as if she had never seen them before. Then she heard:

"Josie? What about me?"

"Oh, Lord. I'm sorry. I'm so sorry."

Josie reached for Erika's bindings, but the other woman pulled her hands away. She wasn't smiling anymore. She seemed peeved.

"I mean, what about me?" Erika said again. "Do I look nice?"

Josie Bates' House, Hermosa Beach

Hannah heard all she needed to hear. The man on the wall, the guy who looked like an undertaker, was calling down God's wrath on Josie Bates and it pissed Hannah off.

Without thinking, she tore through the crowd, pushing aside the candle holding idiots and flew at the man in black, knocking him off the wall. There was a collective gasp. Someone hollered. A woman screamed. All Hannah heard was the sounds of commotion; all she saw was the man in black. Hannah was over the wall in the blink of an eye, pushing him back into the small yard. She was younger and faster than he, and she straddled him before anyone knew what was happening. Her fists flew and the fact that he made no effort to protect himself enraged her even more.

Some people called for her to stop; some implored God to intervene; someone was calling out a play-by-play. The moment had turned into an event, but Hannah didn't care about any of it until she felt a man's hands on her shoulders. She wriggled out of his grasp.

"Back off," she screamed. "He can't say those things. He can't."

Hannah was sobbing now. The blows she delivered were soft with despair and exhaustion. Soon she couldn't raise her arms any more, and she collapsed on the man in the black suit.

The crowd hushed. In the fading light of day, in the glow of the flickering candles and the light atop the shoulder cam, Isaiah Wilson put his hands atop Hannah Sheraton's thick black hair as if he was blessing her.

In the next moment, the man who had tried to pull Hannah away grasped her shoulders again, but the preacher's arms encircled Hannah even tighter. Lying on the ground, holding the sobbing girl as if she were his own, Isaiah Wilson looked at the man who would have taken her away. He smiled. He said:

"Hello, Daniel."

CHAPTER 33

"Is she alright?"

Reverend Wilson looked up as Archer and Daniel Young came into Josie's living room.

"She'll be okay."

Archer didn't break stride as he walked across the room, took the picture Isaiah was holding, and put it back where it belonged. It was Josie's favorite: her and Max when she first found him, sad and hungry and abandoned under the pier. Archer put it back next to a picture of Hannah standing in the framing of the arch between the living room and dining room.

Isaiah Wilson's lips tipped, and Archer knew the expression for what it was: a smirk, a look of superiority, and a mocking expression. The man was getting everything he had come for, the opportunity to gloat over Josie's misfortune and another limelight to bask in. When this was over, Archer was going to have Josie's place fumigated.

"Praise the Lord," Isaiah said offhandedly. "I would never want to see a young girl hurt."

"I think it's yet to be seen how Hannah will weather the shock she had today." Daniel put in his two cents.

Archer wasn't sure if he was voicing his concern or just wanted to get in the preacher's face.

"She won't die, will she?" Isaiah tilted his head as if to say if Hannah were alive she was doing better than his Janey.

Knowing that the point had been taken, Reverend Wilson pulled at his black slacks and sat down on Josie's sofa. His socks were black silk and his shoes spit-polished. But Archer was focused on the shine of blood that had seeped through the fine fabric at his knee. The injury underneath the cloth was pretty bad if Archer could see the burgundy blood on the black fabric. Not that he cared, because the guy deserved everything he got for the stunt he pulled. He would have grabbed the sucker himself if he'd been there.

"You are a bastard..." Archer began, but Daniel stopped him.

"Archer, please," Daniel said. "He didn't come here to hurt Hannah."

"I only wish I had been praying for that girl all these years. Obviously, being Ms. Bates' child is trying."

"You know she's not Josie's kid," Archer muttered. "She may never be after what happened today."

"God's will, Archer," the reverend answered. "But Ms. Bates has been blessed. Hannah fought as fiercely for her as any daughter would have. Ms. Bates could learn from her: fight for a cause and not a paycheck."

"Christ, that trial was ten years ago. Drop it."

Archer exploded, unable to listen to this talk. What was with this guy anyway? Why bring God into all this like God had a side. Yet when the reverend turned his cool eye on Archer, the burly man immediately understood the import of what he had said. He wasn't sorry, but he understood.

"I'm not saying you shouldn't grieve for your daughter, but Josie didn't kill her," Archer argued.

"No, she did not. At least not literally," Isaiah agreed. "All those lies about Janey, all the insinuations, that was just business, an investment in her career, wasn't it? And now, it seems, she is being paid a dividend she didn't expect."

"So you came here to pray that she's going to die? What kind of religion is that?"

Archer glanced out the living room window. Some of Wilson's flock had found their way back and their candles were lit once more. When Josie got home he'd talk to her about curtains. He caught sight of Paul Rothskill in the crowd. The whole gang was here – Daniel, Paul, Isaiah Wilson – and that put Archer on his guard.

"It's the oldest kind of religion." Isaiah turned Archer away from his distraction. "An eye for an eye. I don't seek it, I simply point out that God's laws cannot be broken without the consequence. He sees, he waits, he allows free will to take its course, but always His hand is there for final justice."

"But in this case justice isn't being handed out by God, is it?" Archer challenged. "There's a real, live, breathing human being who took Josie and Erika Gardener. God may work in mysterious ways, but he doesn't snatch women from their homes or their cars."

The preacher put his fingers on the knee of his pant leg and probed the ever- growing stain of blood as if he wasn't listening. He did not wince or pull his hand away.

It was as if he were detached from all the pain and worry except for that which he carried in his heart and soul.

"Josie Bates stood between God and Xavier Hernandez; now God will not stand between her and him."

"Isaiah, please." Daniel sat down opposite the reverend. "You must listen to me for a minute."

"Really Daniel?" The reverend said mildly just before his eyes slid toward the doctor as if he didn't even deserve that much attention. "I value my time and I believe it has been established that even if one were to listen to you, there is no reason to take what you say to heart."

"Insults won't help. I did what I could."

"And I did not come here to speak with you. In fact, I am surprised to find you here at all. It seems odd that you kept up with Ms. Bates considering."

"I didn't keep up with her. We are tied by circumstance. It was a fluke that I saw you on the news tonight. I had plans, but I came here instead. I thought I could help."

"You can't." The reverend cut him off. "You never could."

Though there was no room for Daniel to maneuver, he tried anyway. He clasped his hands and bounced his fist up and down as if that would help him find the right words to say. Archer almost stepped in but changed his mind. There was a blush of anger creeping up the back of Young's neck and a pale disdain on Wilson's face. One would have thought these two would be compatriots. Daniel was trying hard to be.

"Isaiah, do you know why God has not healed you?" Daniel asked.

"No. Do you?" Isaiah's brow rose but his surprise was mocking. Daniel, the buffoon, pushed on seemingly unaware that he was being played.

"Those resentments you hold toward Ms. Bates have poisoned your life. Not only would God not want this, Janey wouldn't."

"You don't know anything about my Janey's mind. You were incompetent ten years ago, and you are irrelevant now."

"What happened in that courtroom had nothing to do with competency. You know that as well as I do."

"Really?" Isaiah baited the shrink.

"Yes, really." Daniel's voice lowered, ready for the debate. "Both of us had issues with Josie Bates. And both of us find ourselves here. I am on that list of Xavier's and so are you. Did you know that?"

"Actually, yes. This gentleman brought the news."

"And do you know why Xavier considers me a threat?" Daniel posed the question but didn't wait for an answer. "Because I saw inside his head, and because I knew that he was a sane, calculating, and vicious man. But Bates? What reason did he have to hate her? None, and she was still taken on a perfectly beautiful afternoon, drugged and whisked away without so much as a hair left behind to prove he did it. We are facing true evil, Isaiah. Evil that does not differentiate between us. You always thought you were above it all. You weren't. You aren't. I promise you that. In fact, I guarantee it."

"Your pronouncements were always so absolute, Daniel. Black and white. Dr. Young's opinion above everyone else. I admired that surety at one time." Wilson shrugged to indicate his dismissal. "Now it is just unfounded arrogance. You are like a braying donkey, Daniel."

Archer's interest went to the Reverend. He had not been shown the list with the pictures next to each name, so the analogy was worth noting. Seeing the two men locked in their tug of war gave Archer notice that there was more to learn.

"I'm not the fool. What you did here tonight will make things worse for everyone concerned. I guarantee that, too."

"You thought you could guarantee a conviction, Daniel." Without breaking eye contact with Daniel, Isaiah called out to Archer. "Did you know that the good Doctor here is a fraud, sir?"

"That's stiff." Archer moved toward the two men. The bad blood between them ran almost as deep as the hatred they both had for Josie.

"Not really. It was your Ms. Bates who exposed him." Isaiah looked away from Daniel to Archer. "Look at the transcript of his testimony. He probably hates her just as much as the rest of us."

"Don't try to change the subject, Isaiah. My problem with Josie Bates was public. I suffered it, and I moved on. I have a thriving practice. I'm brought into this because Xavier Hernandez is a shark, trolling until he finds prey. He found Erika Gardener and Josie Bates. Maybe I'm next. Maybe you are."

"I will pray for Ms. Gardener, but for Ms. Bates there can only be one outcome."

"That sounds like a threat, to me," Archer said. "And with stunts like you pulled tonight, you've all but given permission for Hernandez to do whatever he wants to

Josie. At least Young is being proactive. At least he's got some real balls."

Daniel turned slowly and looked at Archer. He blinked as if coming out of a deep sleep, but Isaiah and Archer didn't notice. It was between him and the preacher now.

"Unlike a courtroom, Archer, here truth is what is important. And the truth is that Josie Bates lied about my daughter. "

"I haven't read the transcripts. I don't know what was said, but I know Josie. Whatever she did, it was done to represent her client to the best of her abilities. That was her job."

"And, my job as a father, and a believer in God's justice, is to represent my faith and my daughter. I have lived all these years waiting for that woman to get what she deserves. I hope she dies. I hope Josie Bates stands at the gates of heaven, and St. Peter turns her away with my Janey looking on."

Isaiah Wilson put his hand in his pocket, but before he could make another move, Archer was across the room. The big man towered over Wilson as he put one hand on the couch arm and another on the cushion. He got in the craggy face of the pricey preacher. There was a smell that came off the man; a smell like mothballs or an old woman's house, or rotting leaves or food left in a hot place too long. It made Archer gag, but he didn't turn away.

"Maybe you got tired of waiting for God to do his business, *I-say-ah*. Maybe you took Josie and Erika and put them somewhere because book sales are down, or because you just wanted some attention, or because you wanted to be the one that did them in. I don't know why you'd want to hurt the Gardener woman, but the way you talk about Josie sounds like a confession to me. So where are they? What have you done with them?"

Isaiah held Archer's gaze for a split second, but before he could answer a movement in the doorway distracted him. Archer backed off and all three men looked at Hannah who was leaning against the unfinished archway that led to the dining room. That exhausted, beautiful, tortured young girl's fingers frantically tapped the bare two-by-four, her lips moved, and she had eyes only for Isaiah.

"Why is he still here?"

"I was just leaving, Hannah." Isaiah rose. The right leg of his slacks was pasted to his knee with the dried blood. He made no attempt to free it. "I have what I came for."

"Exactly what was it you got?" Archer demanded.

"I made people remember why Ms. Bates finds herself in this position. It is because of what she did to my Janey."

Isaiah Wilson pulled together his lips. He walked slowly toward Hannah. For a second it seemed that he was going to touch her, instead he confided in her.

"She killed my daughter a second time, Hannah," the preacher said quietly. "That woman pointed the finger at my Janey and called her a harlot. She condemned my daughter to hell, and she elevated that man who killed her to an unwitting victim of her lust. She said my daughter deserved her death; I say Josie Bates deserves the same."

Before Archer could step up and take out the guy's other knee, before Daniel could reach into his psychologist's bag of tricks, Hannah spoke.

"You're going to hell for wishing that. And you know what, your daughter is turning her back on you in that heaven you think you deserve."

In the silence, all anyone heard was Max's nails clicking as he came to rest beside Hannah. Deliberately, she reached for the dog, hunkered beside him and buried her face in his fur as if to say she preferred the comfort of a dumb animal to the company of the God Isaiah Wilson represented.

"I'll leave this for you, Hannah. Perhaps, after you read it, you will understand."

Isaiah Wilson put the papers he had taken from his coat and left them on the hall table. Archer followed Wilson out the door. As he did, he took the papers with him. The only way Hannah would ever read what went on in that courtroom was over his dead body.

CHAPTER 34

Hannah sat with her knees together, her elbows crooked, her face cradled in her upturned palms. Her index fingers tapped and tapped, paused and tapped. The sleeves of her jacket had fallen away from her wrists and pooled at her elbows. As Hannah watched herself attacking Isaiah Wilson on television, Daniel Young watched her.

She was used to men looking at her, but not the way Daniel Young did. It was as if he was trying to decide what to do with her. The fact that he was still in the house annoyed her. Or, maybe she was just aggravated that Archer insisted that Daniel sit with her like a nanny while he regrouped. She had looked out the window twice to see him sitting on the low wall. Both times he was talking into his phone. She knew one of the calls would be to Faye, because what happened was probably going to get child protective service's panties in a knot. Archer wouldn't be able to keep Hannah out of custody; they were going to need a lawyer. She figured the other call would be to Liz Driscoll to see if there was anything new on her end. But now it was just her and Daniel Young, and she wished she were alone. At the very least, Hannah wished she hadn't sent Max out to be with Archer.

"What?" Hannah demanded without bothering to look Daniel's way.

"I beg your pardon?" Daniel answered.

"You're staring at my arms."

"No," he answered. "I was just thinking."

"Bet you're thinking it would be cool to cure me." Hannah sat back, not liking this tall man in the well-pressed clothes.

"I don't recall saying I thought you were sick."

"That's rich," Hannah snorted. Her eyes were still glued to the television. The news anchors were laughing, and there was a picture of a duck in the corner of the screen. At least it wasn't a picture of her.

"I am curious about you and her, that's all."

"What do you want to know?" Hannah's eyes flickered his way. "I'll tell you, and then you can go home."

Daniel laughed, lazy and long before his voice just sort of blew away. He shook his head like a parent who had heard it all. His patients must hate it when he did that.

"I'm not some gossipy neighbor, Hannah."

"And you're not a friend. You're just someone Archer is supposed to be protecting."

He laughed again. "No, I don't need protecting. I know things about Xavier Hernandez that..."

He never finished his thought. Hannah stood up so abruptly that he was stunned into silence. She turned her back and started to walk away.

"I was speaking to you, Miss."

Hannah looked over her shoulder. It was her turn to laugh, but she didn't. She just smiled slightly.

"Wow. That was weird."

"And what you did was rude," he suggested in that ever-so-patient way of his. Hannah tilted her head. She narrowed her eyes. Something had crept into his voice that made her think twice about getting in his face.

"Okay. Sorry," she said. "Do you want something to drink?"

"No. Thank you."

"Then you can go if you want. I'm good."

"I'll wait until Archer comes back in."

"Suit yourself, but I don't need a babysitter."

"Then do you mind if I look around?"

Hannah pulled up short again. He might as well have asked her to drop her drawers. This was Josie's place and even Hannah didn't take liberties yet.

"Why?"

"Maybe something will jump out at me." Daniel stood up and wandered toward her. "You live here so you might not see certain things. I'm trained to notice, to read into clues that people leave subconsciously."

"Cool. Like a pile of rocks that will point us to Josie?" Hannah widened her eyes, mocking him. "You must have been a Boy Scout."

"You never know. Sometimes you don't see what's right in front of your eyes. That's the funny thing about human nature, you see what you want to." Daniel was neither insulted nor deterred by Hannah's defenses. "Wouldn't you be sorry if there was something that you missed? Wouldn't you hate to live with that knowledge the rest of your life? What if there was one small thing you didn't see that might have saved Josie?"

"I thought you didn't like her," Hannah said warily.

"It's not about her, it's about me," he said as he held Hannah's gaze. Then he smiled broadly. "It's all about me, Hannah."

He came closer. He touched a lamp. Hannah didn't want him to do that. Not without touching it more than once. One more step and his shin was against the coffee table.

Hannah's eyes swept over Daniel as she tried to figure out what made her wary of him. He seemed to be growing in stature, taking up more room than he should and Hannah backed up a bit. Yet it wasn't his physical presence that bothered her, it was something else. Then she figured it out. There was something under Daniel Young's skin that he was refusing to scratch.

If it had been her, she couldn't resist touching, probing, and exploring the boundaries of whatever it was that caused her anxiety. She wanted to understand everything: the bad and the good. This guy was too eager for something and Hannah didn't want to know what it was.

"Yeah, whatever," she said abruptly.

Hannah turned on her heel and went into the kitchen, cupped the curved rim of the counter with the heels of her hands, let her fingers tap the cool granite top, and scanned the walk-street before looking out toward the ocean.

Wherever Josie was, Hannah hoped she could see the ocean. It was with that peaceful, wishful thought that the house erupted with a noise that seemed to come straight from hell.

A Rental House, San Fernando Valley

The girl sat on one of the dilapidated lounge chairs strewn around the backyard of the house she shared with her boyfriend and his friends. She smoked a joint and tried to relax. She didn't have to be at work until eight, so she had all day to catch up on her sleep. But she couldn't relax, and she couldn't sleep because every time she closed her eyes she thought about that place in the woods.

Her boyfriend told her she was tripping. Her boyfriend laughed at her. Finally, her boyfriend told her to forget about it. Last thing they needed was any trouble with the law. Still, she argued, it was only a phone call to some guy. Her boyfriend got mad, called her a couple of names and then wanted to screw around. She didn't like that one bit, so out she went to the yard where she stayed all night. Now it was another evening and he had gone off to his part-time job and she was supposed to be doing laundry. Instead she was watching the sun make its way across the sky. She was stoned and lazy and the thought that he was probably right about all that shit drifted in and out of her mind like the smoke to her lungs. She raised the joint to her lips, inhaled, and held it.

Yeah, he was right.

She should forget about it.

She was working on it.

Josie Bates' House, Hermosa Beach

Hannah dashed through the house toward the sounds of Max's barking and snarling, only to stop in the doorway of Josie's bedroom and cling to the jamb. Archer stood with his legs splayed and his back bent over so he could hold on to Max who was straining to get at Josie's closet.

"What the hell are you doing?" Archer growled.

Hannah pushed off, wanting to see what Archer was seeing. Knowing you didn't run headlong into trouble, she made a wide circle and stood behind him. What she saw was Daniel Young cowering in Josie's closet, half buried in her clothes, clutching a shoe like a club.

"Get that animal away from me!" Daniel's scream made Max bare his teeth and snap all the more. Spittle flew from the dog's mouth, and Daniel turned his head away. His escape was blocked on all fronts. Young's arms flailed over his head, his knees were pulled into his chest as if he could save himself by getting small. He screamed again. "Put that animal away."

Archer hollered back: "I should let him go."

"Archer," Hannah said quietly.

She touched him. Touched him again and again on the arm that quivered with tension of holding the big dog. A second later, he handed the growling dog off to Hannah.

"Put him in the kitchen."

The tone of his voice left no room for discussion, so Hannah took Max and spoke gently to him as she led him out of the room. She would have been gone in another second, but Daniel Young defended himself at her expense.

"She gave me permission. It's her fault."

Hannah whipped her head back. The old dog, sensing a change in attitude, strained toward Daniel once more.

"I never did, Archer," Hannah insisted. "I didn't tell him he could come in here."

"Go on, Hannah," Archer said, making it clear he didn't put much stock in Daniel's objection. He grabbed for Daniel. "And you. Get out of there."

Before Archer could touch him, Daniel stood up, pushed aside the clothes, and dropped the shoe in an attempt to regain his dignity.

"I'm sorry I upset you," he said as he eased his way around Archer. "I thought I might find something you and Hannah overlooked. Something that might lead us to understand what convinced Ms. Bates to meet with Hernandez."

"Do you think we wouldn't have noticed something out of place?" Archer demanded.

"No, but you might not think that something you see everyday could hold a clue. No one is completely open about their lives, Archer."

"Josie is," He grumbled and went to the bed and sat down. He was tired. Physically and emotionally exhausted. The last thing he wanted was for his mind to be muddled. Young was slick and he muddled minds for a living.

"No, Archer, Josie isn't any more honest than any other person. I'm not saying she has lied to you, I'm saying there are things that are personal to her. I was just going to look through the book at her bedside when that dog came at me." Daniel swiped at his slacks but inclined his head toward the nightstand. "Do you know what she's reading?"

Archer shook his head.

"Just because you don't know doesn't mean she has lied to you about something. It only means the subject hasn't come up in conversation. But it might mean something to me. Xavier was a voyeur. Did you know that? He loved to watch women. He would go into houses and take things from them. They probably never knew their things were gone they were so inconsequential."

"Why didn't you tell me that before?" Archer asked, peeved that this kind of information was withheld.

"We've been busy, and as I recall you preferred me to speak only when spoken to." Daniel sat on the opposite side of the mattress. "In forty-eight hours you've assaulted me and dismissed me. You're angry with me for talking to the press. I would at least have expected a thank you for helping Hannah when Isaiah came, but I'll give you the benefit of the doubt on that one." He laughed a little. "I must say meeting you has been a challenge, Archer. I didn't expect you at all, but I do understand. Now I need you to understand me."

"Yeah. Okay." Archer gave a grunt and a nod. He looked around the room. "So did you find anything?"

Daniel reached for the book and fanned the pages. Then he put it back on the table and looked around the room.

"No. I suppose you were right. There's nothing special here. Nothing special at all." Daniel sighed. "I would have expected more of Ms. Bates. Something more interesting."

Archer had enough. He stood up. He had things to do, but Daniel wasn't finished.

"You have to prepare yourself for the eventuality that she may never be found."

Archer shrugged him off.

"I don't give up, Young, and neither does Josie."

"Perhaps denial is best for now." Daniel looked at his watch. "Just remember, I'm here for you if reality rears its ugly head. Now, I suppose I better be going."

Daniel was almost out the bedroom door when Archer called to him:

"What did Josie do to you?"

Daniel turned around. He smiled as if he was pleased. Archer was finally beginning to realize that Josie Bates was not the woman he thought her to be.

"Are you sure you want to know?"

"Yeah," Archer answered.

"She discredited me. Josie Bates questioned my integrity and my standing as a medical doctor. She found old records that indicated I had not finished my graduate work and she presented this information to the jury as if that made me a charlatan. I lost my standing with the media, the ethics board reviewed me, and it took me three years to straighten things out. By that time Josie Bates had moved on and made her fortune, and my practice was in a shambles."

Daniel tilted his head and watched Archer. If he was hoping for sympathy he didn't get it. If he was hoping to see Archer's appreciation for Josie waver, he didn't see it. Daniel took a step closer to the big man.

"Paul Rothskill? The young man who went for help that day? Josie Bates got him on the stand and pointed out to the jury that he was a convicted sex offender. In reality, he was a young man serving his church, and trying to help the teenagers in his charge. She painted him with the ugliest of brushes. She ruined his life."

"Was he a pervert?" Archer demanded.

"When he was eighteen he had sex with his sixteen-year-old girlfriend. Her parents brought charges. Josie Bates smeared Janey Wilson with her diary and with the fact that she had traveled to Mexico with a young man who had sex with an underaged girl. Josie Bates drove Isaiah Wilson to near madness. Josie Bates made Susie Atkins look like a little whore." Daniel paused, seemingly surprised at the passion in his story. He pulled back; he twisted his neck. He calmed himself and lowered his voice. "You know, now that I think of it, she and Xavier were well matched. They looked for weakness, and when they had the opportunity they exploited it. There is some skill in that; there is something to be admired about that ability. I suppose, though, someone is just better than she is at it now. Somebody smarter found her weak spot."

"Xavier." Archer said.

Daniel blinked.

"Xavier, of course. But as you and Detective Driscoll speculated, there may be someone else. It could be anyone. In truth, I just don't think there are a lot of people who love Ms. Bates the way you do."

With that, Daniel left Archer sitting in Josie's bedroom. He was too tired to move, too worried to know which way to turn. Then he heard the doorbell ring, his name called out, and he was re-energized. By the time he got to the living room, Daniel Young was gone and Liz Driscoll was waiting, grinning like a fool.

"Let's go, cowboy!"

CHAPTER 35

An Outbuilding in the California Mountains

Josie broke off the edge of the energy bar and held it out to Erika, but the other woman's eyes were glued to their tiny window on the world. The sun was starting to go down. The heat had settled beside them like the fat relative at a small Thanksgiving table.

"Erika!" Josie picked up the blonde's hand and put the piece of food into it.

Erika put it in her mouth while Josie rewrapped the oatmeal bar carefully, intent on preserving any fingerprints that might be on the plastic coated paper. That would make two pieces of evidence if they were lucky. When she was done, she leaned back against the wall and nibbled at her own little chunk.

"He's coming tonight," Erika said.

"Yeah?" Josie said.

"He is," Erika insisted. "Tonight is going to be different. I think it's getting close to the end. I think this was all some kind of joke or a test or something."

She pulled her eyes away from the small hole in the wall. Her skin had a pink tinge, the color of the sunset. She smiled at Josie as she scooted back to rest against the opposite wall. Josie smiled back. She couldn't take her eyes off Erika Gardener whose own were bright with excitement.

"You know, we might be on television or something. Like a reality show."

Josie nodded.

This was not good.

Sepulveda Boulevard, Torrance

"Arnson called. Him and Levinsky are stuck at a triple homicide, so he thought we could check this out and let him know what we find."

Liz's eyes darted left and right to monitor the traffic. She wanted to get where they were going, and she wanted to get there fast. There was only one problem. No one got anywhere fast once you got out of the beach areas.

"Don't get your hopes up. We may not find anything," Archer warned.

"Yeah, yeah, I know. But it could be something. Hell's bells, I didn't even think about asking if Hernandez was monitored. It's amazing what they can do with those things. They've got GPS technology on those ankle bracelets."

"But why didn't Cuwin Martin tell Arnson and Levinsky that Hernandez was wearing a GPS when they first caught the case?" Archer asked.

"Because it wasn't him who spilled the beans. Cuwin's supervisor took his files because he's been out on sick leave."

"More like putting his head in the sand," Archer countered.

"Either way, he wasn't exactly doing a bang up job on the follow-up of Hernandez. The darn monitor went off like Fourth of July fireworks in the last month.

Hernandez wasn't staying put, but the monitors only reported his movement half the time and half of that time Cuwin blew it off. He put most of the reports in the round file, if you know what I mean. He's a lazy son of a bitch," Liz decided. "Anyway, Levinsky is going to run down the movement in 90036 zip to see if Hernandez was anywhere near Erika Gardener's place. It made sense to send the South Bay tracking our way. So, we're going to check out this place in El Segundo because the GPS put him there within the last week."

"How is Hagarty hanging?"

"What he doesn't know won't hurt him, Archer." She put a skinny finger to her lips and then laughed from her belly.

"Just watch your butt so nothing comes around to bite it," he warned.

"I could get down with that depending on who's doing the biting," Liz quipped as she slid her eyes his way. Archer couldn't help but laugh. There was no way Liz Driscoll could look enticing, but he admired her for working with what she had. He would truly hate to see her go down. Liz Driscoll was one of the good people, and it was clear she was sticking out her neck for him, not Josie.

"What did they tell you?" Archer asked as they came to a stoplight.

"Hernandez was on the Westside, he's been down here and around Hollywood. I'd bet you anything he was in the hills. That means he has transportation and mom's car is out. He didn't have money for his own. Even if he did, nobody was going to insure him." The light changed. She hit the gas. "Anyway, that's how he got the photographs."

"He took them with a car?"

"Funny." She grimaced. "I tell you shit's going to hit the fan if we don't find those ladies alive. Parole is already in a helluva of a lot trouble these days-"

Archer only half listened to Liz's litany of screw ups by the parole board and their minions. Liz didn't have a clue her off-handed comment was anything personal and he couldn't blame her. Archer had been where she was, wanting a break, a big case, a spotlight bust. Still, in her excitement, she was losing sight of the human element, and that meant Liz Driscoll might make decisions that weren't in the best interest of the victims. It wasn't for him to point this out because he walked the other side of the road: the victims were all he cared about and that made for its own slippery slope.

"There it is." Liz glanced to her left and eased into the median. She cut her eyes Archer's way, and her grin faltered as she noted his expression. "You okay?"

"I'm good," he assured her. "And so are you. Let's do this."

"You got it."

Liz turned away to attend to traffic, but her smile was gone. Archer was right. It was time to get serious.

They were on the border of Torrance and El Segundo, waiting to make a left that would let them cross the wide and busy highway. The flush at Liz's jaw, the sparkle in her eye, did not escape Archer's notice. Pleased with his validation, Liz turned the wheel and the car bounced over the railroad track that still serviced a run from L.A. to Santa Monica. She drove past the big, high gates and finally stopped in front of the office of A1-Storage.

The California Mountains

He loved the wind in his hair. It was a long way to go, but he was taking a leisurely ride this time. He liked that it would be dark by the time he arrived. His presence would be unexpected. He would surprise them once more. Gaslight them. Why not? Tit-for-tat the way they had done to him all those years ago. He would wake them up and make them play. Twenty questions was his game. It would be a cross examination combined with a journalist's interview. He had packed prizes. If they answered his questions correctly, they would each get one.

Maybe.

If they didn't, well, wouldn't he just show them that he could play hardball, too.

A-1 Storage, El Segundo

The A-1 Storage facility was deceptive. From the street it looked like a few garages sitting on a patch of land between an abandoned body shop on one side and an empty lot on the other. Now that Archer and Liz were behind the gates, the landscape changed: hundreds of storage units radiated across acres of land. Row upon row of freshly painted, identical steel buildings lined wide, paved lanes. You could get a flatbed back here, and the units were big enough to store a good-sized boat. There was no landscaping, nothing that would entice anyone to waste a minute more here than was necessary.

Liz cut the engine and pulled on the emergency brake. They opened their respective doors simultaneously. It was dusk now and the spotlights atop each unit were lit but ineffectual. When it was dark, the place would look like Stalag 13.

"There's got to be a hundred of them." Liz was looking around even as she came to stand with Archer.

"We only need one to cough something up," Archer noted, quietly hoping they wouldn't find two dead bodies.

Liz led the way; Archer was close behind as they walked up the three wooden steps that led to a door marked 'office'. The 'office' was nothing more than a converted storage unit, changing out the rollup to double glass doors. Inside was cool, narrow and basic. There was a desk, a couple of filing cabinets and a guy who looked like he should be selling insurance instead of sitting in a little metal box watching television.

"Hey." He greeted them without taking his eyes from the screen. "Just a sec. They're going to have the reveal any minute. You wouldn't believe what this woman used to look like. She was butt ugly. I mean b-u-t-t ugly. Coyote ugly. Here she comes. Oh, God! She looks worse. What a dog."

Archer looked at Liz. Liz shrugged just as the man turned an absolutely delighted face their way. He didn't seem to mind that they hadn't uttered a word.

"These make-over shows are incredible. *What Not To Wear* is the best. That Windy person's show isn't bad, but this one – what's her name, the cook lady with the talk show? Come on. Big chic." He looked at the two as if they should know. Suddenly he snapped his fingers, totally delighted with himself. "Corrine something. Yeah. She does the worst ones. Ever watch it?"

Happily he looked from Liz to Archer, but Liz caught his attention when she pulled out her I.D. The guy behind the desk was not really impressed and definitely not nervous.

"Why didn't you say so?" He grinned wider.

"We wanted you to have your moment," Liz answered. "You done?"

"Oh yeah. Show's over. What do you need?" The man rearranged his face into an expression of concern, but when he furrowed his brow his eyes seemed to cross. Archer thought it looked painful.

"We're looking for a guy named Xavier Hernandez. Five seven. Good build. Black hair. We had him here about a week ago according to his monitoring. Maybe he rents a unit," Liz suggested. "Want to see a picture?"

"Nope. I see people who rent these units for like five minutes while they fill out the paperwork. I never see them again after they get their key. I'd be hard pressed to remember what any of them look like."

The man rolled his chair away, spun around and landed expertly in front of the smaller filing cabinet. Archer wondered how many hours he had spent perfecting the move between waiting for someone to walk through the door and the next makeover show. He whipped open the drawer. Behind him someone on TV was still gushing and Archer couldn't resist a look. The guy turned back and caught him in the act.

"A dog, right? Huh? See what I'm sayin'?" The man's head bobbed up and down.

"I've seen better," Archer admitted and then he stepped forward. "What have you got?"

"I'm really not supposed to show you this without a court order. Privacy stuff and all that." The man said it like it was no skin off his nose if someone squawked.

"I can get one," Liz offered, "but this is a life and death thing. I'd hate to waste any more time than we have to. So, maybe you could just chat with us a little bit. We'll start by assuming Hernandez rented a unit here because you are holding a file."

"Yeah, you could assume that. Good customer. He's been with me since-" The man cracked the lips of the folder like he was peeking at a Christmas present, "-1997."

Archer and Liz looked at one another.

"Really? Were you here then?" Liz asked.

"Yep."

"You sure it was him that rented the unit. Not a woman?"

"Nope. It was him. I would have had to see his I.D.," he assured them. "Unless he was on that chick's makeover show. Some of those makeovers look like guys when they're done." He guffawed, pleased with himself. "I'm tellin' ya. Know what I mean?"

"Yeah, we got it." Archer tapped his temple. "Is there anything in the unit?"

"Hey, I don't stick my nose in," he objected. "Besides, not my job. Trucks are in and out of here all day. He rented that space like 8 years ago."

"Seven," Liz corrected.

"What?"

"Seven years ago."

"Seven, six, eight. All I know is the bill gets paid every month, and that makes me happy 'cause I don't have to make those reminder calls. Hate those damn calls."

"How does he pay?" Liz asked.

"Check."

"Got copies?"

"Naw, we changed over to electronic about three years ago." He twirled his chair around again. Archer would bet he was singing along to *Stayin' Alive* in his head. He bounced in his chair, happy as a clam to have someone to talk to. "I can track it down, but for that I'm going to need an order for sure."

"Can we take a look inside his unit?" Liz asked, but it sounded more like an order.

The guy shrugged. "Am I going to get in trouble if I show you?"

"I think you were probably concerned that you smelled smoke and opened that unit to check it out. We just happened to be here to offer our assistance to a citizen."

"Okay. Sure."

He put his nose in the air like he was sniffing. He got it. He grinned. He was having fun. He hopped up, grabbed his key, double checked his records and led them out the door and into the facility.

Behind them, the television host continued to gush.

Mrs. Rice's Apartment, West Los Angeles

Mrs. Rice, a woman of sour disposition even when she was at home, ate her dinner early on a T.V. tray in front of the television. Her husband worked nights, and that was fine with her since she always brought home a lot of work.

Tonight she was lamenting the fact that she had left Hannah Sheraton's file at the office. Given what she was seeing on the local news, the girl was completely out of control. No doubt the video would go viral. The public seemed to have an insatiable appetite for beautiful young girls acting out. Mrs. Rice had never done anything like that in her entire life. Then again, if she had, no one would have noticed. She had never been beautiful and even she doubted she had ever been young. Still stinging from her defeat in court, Mrs. Rice was sure she would vindicate herself with this proof that Hannah Sheraton was living a permissive existence in a beach town whose notoriety stemmed from annual volleyball tournaments and drinking contests. Add to that her attack on a man of God, and this was just the fodder Mrs. Rice needed to revisit the forty-eight hour ruling Judge Leisinger had handed down.

That kid was a loose cannon. She had to go, and she had to go as soon as possible.

CHAPTER 36

A-1 Storage, El Segundo

Unit 244 was down the main path and over one at the end of the row just in front of a high wall that was topped by curling barbed wire.

"Is there only one way into these units?" Archer asked as he eyed the wide rolling door that was closed and padlocked.

"Yep. Once your stuff is in there, the only way to get it out is through this door."

Satisfied, Archer moved closer and to the right. Once they opened it there was no telling what could happen. If Hernandez was behind the door, there was going to be a fight. Archer would assume he had weapons. If so, no one wanted to be directly in the line of fire. If he didn't have anything and he tried to run, he would have to get through three people in order to make his escape. Make that two. The manager, Archer figured, would be pretty useless.

He was unlocking the unit and starting to roll the door up as Liz eased her gun out of her holster and inched to the left. She held it casually by her side, but Archer knew if anything came out of that unit too fast it was toast – including Xavier Hernandez. He only hoped Liz was a good shot and downed him. The last thing they wanted, however, was a dead guy who couldn't tell them where Josie and Erika were. Archer did not draw his weapon. The last thing he needed was to be involved in a shooting with an officer at his side; the first thing he wanted was his hands around Hernandez's neck.

The door rose smoothly, riding its rails with a slight, well-oiled rumble. Inch by inch it went up, revealing nothing initially. Six eyes squinted through the gloom of the setting sun into the black cave-like interior of the storage unit. The manager, so fond of reveals on television makeovers, had latched onto the fact that Archer and Liz were looking for something that might not be all that cool, so he had moved behind Archer and was ready to duck if he had to. The door stopped moving, the motor stopped whirring and the three people stared into the unit. A dozen heartbeats were shared between them as they waited.

Nothing happened. Josie did not call out. The stench of death did not hit them broadside. A frantic Hernandez did not rush them.

"Is there a light in there?" Archer asked.

"Want me to turn it on?" The man whispered.

"You're just checking to make sure everything's okay, right?" Liz suggested.

"For God's sake. Flip it," Archer barked.

"Right. Right." The manager wrung his hands, swallowed hard. Taking one giant, Mother-May-I step forward, he reached around and flipped a switch, stepped back and put himself against the wall next to the door.

"Holy moly." Liz whistled as she stowed her gun and rested her hands on her hips. "You ever see anything like this, Archer?"

"Nope," he said.

The manager poked his head around the corner, saw what they were seeing and laughed with giddy relief. All thoughts about privacy rights and the need for a warrant flew out of his head.

"I'll be damned," he whistled and walked right on in.

He squeezed his skinny body past the towers of toilettes: white, pink, blue, beige, high boys and elongated seat models. There was even one that was painted with flowers. All of them were new and stacked to the ceiling, packed into the place from one wall to the next. Curious as a kid in a corn maze, the manager kept up a steady stream of chatter as he picked his way into the unit. When he came out again he was grinning from ear to ear.

"Look what Hernandez had in the back."

Here came that laugh again. The guy sounded like a honking goose as he held up his treasure. Archer rolled his eyes. Liz stifled a chuckle. Plastic, life sized, blow-up dolls were draped over each of the man's arms. One was dark haired and bore a striking resemblance to Betty Boop. The other was blond. Both had lips like blowfish. It would take a whole lot of hot air to puff up the rubber babes, but it didn't look like they'd been inflated for a while. Archer had a funny feeling that the manager was going to take some liberties as soon as they were gone. At least someone would get something out of this.

"What's your name?" Archer asked the man who was carefully inspecting his rubber friends.

"Benny," he answered offhandedly. "Think Hernandez would notice if one was missing?"

Archer gave himself a mental checkmark for reading the guy right.

"Think your wife would notice she had competition?" Liz pointed to his wedding ring, and Benny appeared crestfallen.

"Come on, I'm talking a joke. You don't think I'd really, well, you know."

"'Course not, but curiosity can be powerful, Benny. Besides, we couldn't let you steal. Just wouldn't be right," Liz went on.

"We're obliged you took a look inside," Archer mumbled as Liz holstered her gun. As much as he was relieved, it was still a huge disappointment not to find some clue that would lead them to Josie. Hernandez's profile was getting weirder by the minute.

"Hey, my pleasure. That's the most fun I've had in a long time." Benny stuffed the plastic dolls into a toilette. "Your guy sure has an interesting inventory."

"I didn't think Xavier was kinky that way. Thought he preferred the real thing," Archer noted. Benny stepped out and hit the switch. The door started to come down.

"Who's Xavier?" Benny asked.

"The guy who owns this unit," Liz reminded him.

"Nobody named Xavier on this docket. It's Havier Hernandez. Havier," he insisted, snapping his head between Liz and Archer. "I'm sorry, I guess I wasn't listening."

"Geeze," Liz breathed, chancing a look at Archer who was none too pleased.

He turned away, disgusted that they had wasted more than an hour on a wild goose chase. He kicked at a stone and headed toward the car. Behind him, Benny continued to apologize as Liz continued to assure him anybody could have made the mistake. That was a lie Archer wouldn't have told, but that's what women brought to the force. Peacemakers, dammit. Lost in his thoughts, trying to decide which way to turn next, Archer only half-registered the rest of the conversation between Liz and Benny. The other half of his brain was noting that they weren't alone on the lot.

About fifty yards down, a man was working a unit lock. He was short, light skinned and dark haired. Archer paused. He tilted his head. The man looked familiar, and in the next second he knew why. He had seen this man in his dreams and carried his image with him every waking minute since finding that note in Josie's Jeep.

Xavier Hernandez had finally made an appearance in the flesh.

An Outbuilding in the California Mountains

It took him longer to get there than he had anticipated since he wasn't driving the old car, but it had been a lovely ride nonetheless. So it was quite dark as he hitched his pack and picked his way through the forest. He had been feeling a little blue, a little lack-luster until that afternoon. Then the girl had made such a fuss, a wonderful fuss for the television people. Boy, didn't she get everyone's attention? Her method was a little awkward but her intent was spot on. That's really what it was about, wasn't it? A little recognition of the harm being done to so many. Well, that and a little retribution, and retribution was just another word for payback and that was just another word for justice. She was just too young to know how to exact her pound of flesh with grace and creativity. He had the advantage of time, hindsight and maturity to plan, and execute a plan, and that plan was going better than he ever could have imagined. Soon he would pull the PR trigger and he would be back in the game. And the women? Well, they'd be back home safe and sound but he would always be there, in their nightmares. That was perfect justice. Make 'em sweat forever.

He chuckled. Then he laughed, and his laugh carried through the quiet mountains, and he loved the sound of it. It had been so long since he felt so good about himself or seen the future so clearly.

A-1 Storage, El Segundo

Archer pushed off just as Hernandez shot upright and bolted for the front entrance. He had fifty yards on Archer, and Archer had fifty pounds on him. The fifty pounds would hold him in good stead if he caught the guy, but it wasn't doing him any favors now. Hernandez was in good shape, slim and quick and afraid. It was the fear that made Hernandez faster than Archer would have anticipated; but Archer's emotional inventory gave him a shot at getting his man.

Seeing what was happening, Liz ran to the car, threw herself in, grabbed the radio, called for officer assist, and gave their location over and over again. Behind her, Benny screamed questions, swore he didn't know who that guy was, and then screamed just for screaming sake. This was probably the most exciting thing that had ever happened to him. If he didn't die of a heart attack, Benny would, no doubt, swear that it was he who fingered the bad guy and caught him after a grueling chase. He would be on TV. He would be the reveal, the transformation, just like one of his makeover shows. For his part, Archer didn't care who took credit. All he wanted was to catch Xavier Hernandez. When he had him, when he knew where Josie was, he was going to kill the son-of-a-bitch. First, he had to catch him.

As Archer ran, the wide road down the center of the A1-Storage property seemed to lengthen and narrow. His foot hit a rock and his ankle buckled, sending him smashing into one of the roll-doors. The thing shook and rippled and trampolined Archer back on track. Pain registered in his shoulder, his ankle may need some looking after, and his lungs weren't those of a thirty-year old cop anymore, but none of it mattered now. Hernandez was almost at the gate.

Archer saw that traffic on Sepulveda was at a dead stop. Headlights cast a kliegish glare north, and red brake lights haloed the southern exposure. Archer had no idea how long the traffic had been stopped for the light, but he hoped it turned green soon. If that happened, Hernandez would be no match for commuters trying to get home. They would just as soon run over him as stop. But Hernandez didn't try to shoot across the eight lanes north and south. He grabbed the post of the gate and swung himself right with the grace of a pole dancer, landed on the sidewalk and shot off again.

He looked behind him to gauge Archer's progress and saw the big man closing. Xavier's blank expression surprised Archer. He expected more: fear, loathing, triumph. No matter, that connect was enough for Archer to drill into the man's brain. Hernandez's had only one, simple objective: get away. Archer wasn't about to let that happen.

He pumped his arms and legs and picked up speed, shooting through the dark, sensing drivers taking note as he, too, grabbed the fence and redirected himself. Behind him he heard a car door slam and tires screech. Liz was giving chase but she had come to an abrupt halt, the way blocked by the stopped cars. She opened the door and slammed it again as she took off after the two men on foot.

When Archer made the turn, it took no more than a millisecond to figure out why the cars weren't moving. The twice-a-week train was making its run. Archer's eyes went to the train then back to Hernandez and back again. He measured the speed of the locomotive and Hernandez's trajectory. The man was going to have to make a choice sooner than later. There were two: veer left and scramble over the cars that were nosed up against the crossing arms, or go right to a miles-long straight away that ran past local businesses.

Archer stepped it up, guessing Hernandez would go right. That wouldn't be good for him. A right turn meant the person with the most stamina would win, and that person wasn't Archer. The only chance he had was to catch Hernandez before he got to the crossing and made the turn.

Breathing hard, sweating like a pig, Archer stepped it up. Close. Closer. He was now so close he could hear Hernandez panting and see the sweat on his shirt. Archer's right hand shot out. His fingers scraped the man's back then he lost contact. Hernandez was within his grasp but every time he thought he had him, Xavier found another spurt of energy. Archer drew his gun though he knew there would be hell to pay if he used it. But he knew a good defense attorney, and he would happily put his life in her hands. If she wasn't around to defend him, then he didn't care what happened after his bullet found its way into Xavier Hernandez's head.

Archer fell back a few steps. He could hear Liz's shoes pounding the pavement behind him, and he could only hope that the backup she called for was spreading out to catch Hernandez whether he went left or right. But that's not what he really wanted; he wanted Xavier Hernandez in his hands; he wanted to bring him down. One handful of shirt would be enough to do it. The gun in his hand was heavy and sweat made it slick to hold, so Archer stuffed it in his belt. Both hands free again, he made that one last heroic effort to catch up to the younger man, but Hernandez wasn't turning left or right. He was heading straight for the train. With superhuman effort, Archer sprinted.

"Hernandez! Stop! Stop!"

Archer reached out, extending his arm until he was sure it was going to pop out of its socket. He stretched his fingers. He was so close, a prayer away. All he had to do was knock the guy off his feet and roll him away from the train, but it was too little too late. Hernandez bolted past the red and white striped barriers and was airborne. For a split second he was alternatingly bathed in the glow of the red and white lights. His knee was raised, his arms extended as he vaulted in front of the locomotive.

Archer saw it all: the conductor swearing, his expression going from shock to fury, his shoulders pulling back as he strained to brake. Archer thought he heard people in the cars gasping in shock, lamenting in dismay, shouting out with hope. Liz was calling behind him. They would lose Hernandez unless…

That was when Archer did the unthinkable.

He catapulted over the barrier; positive he could hit Hernandez hard enough to push them both to the other side of the tracks. In a split second he was airborne too and his hand clamped down on Xavier Hernandez's shoulder. For one miraculous moment, Archer had his man. The last thing he saw was Xavier Hernandez turn his head to look, not at the train, but at Archer's hand on his shoulder.

CHAPTER 37

A-1 Storage, El Segundo

It took an hour and a half to get traffic moving again on Sepulveda. Commuters had gone from curious to cross to downright irate as the cleanup effort went on too long. They barely waited for the last of the emergency vehicles to clear the road before they revved their engines and went on about their business.

Liz hung out long enough to give a blow-by-blow of what went down to the investigating officer, offer some words of exoneration to the shaken conductor and watch as Xavier Hernandez and Archer were stabilized and loaded in to separate ambulances. When that was all done, Liz headed back to A-1 Storage, only to stop as she stepped over the tracks. The uniformed guys had missed something, and she didn't want them to have it. She bent quickly and swiped up Archer's revolver. Looking over her shoulder, seeing no one was paying any attention to her, she stuffed it into the inside pocket of her jacket and went on her way. Liz wished she'd stuck around to help clean up when she saw Benny waiting for her. He rushed up to her so fast that he overshot and had to retrace his steps to catch up.

"Remember, you said none of this was going to be my problem? Remember you said that?"

"There will be an officer around soon to take your statement," Liz said wearily.

"Well, I'm ready. I'll give him a statement. I'm going to tell them you forced me to do it, to open that unit. Flashing that badge and everything. I only opened it 'cause you told me I would be doing my civil duty."

"Civic, Benny. Civic duty," Liz corrected.

"I don't care. I'm just saying there was some duress there, right?"

"Sure, Benny. No worries. You tell 'em I threatened to hold your head in one of those toilets if you didn't do everything I said. You tell 'em that, Benny." She raised her hand over her head. Smart man that he was, Benny fell back and didn't follow. Had he kept up that nonsense, Liz would have taken him out.

On her own, Liz made a beeline for the unit Xavier had been trying to get into. Pausing in front of it, she took stock: the lock was off, and the door was partially open. Liz hitched her pants, got down on her hip, rolled onto her back and stuck her head under the corrugated roll-up. The tangential light from outside was enough to show her that no one was inside, dead or alive. She scooted back, stood up, looked for a switch, realized this must be an older unit and heaved the door all the way up manually. Given the circumstances, she had probable cause to search, not that it would have made any difference if she didn't.

"Hey!" Benny was yelling at her. "Don't go in there. I'll call my boss. I'll call the cops. Hey!"

Liz looked over her shoulder. Benny was framed in the office door, watching her every move, looking like he needed to pee bad as he moved from one foot to the other. Her first instinct was to flip him off. Instead, she ignored him and flipped on the light.

Inside, the unit was exactly like Xavier Hernandez's except it wasn't filled with toilets and inflatable dolls. In fact, it wasn't filled with much of anything but the stuff that was in it was more than interesting. Liz went to the center of the space, planted herself and did a slow three-sixty. There was a bed: frame, mattress, sheets and a pillow. It was neatly made and better than you'd get in lock up, but that wasn't saying much. Still, it struck her as odd since his place in L.A. was a mess

Check on the bare walls, too. His montage in L.A. had been meticulously created: photos mounted with care, pins piercing the exact center of the prints, Isaiah Wilson's book cover spread out neatly and a calendar with uniformed red X's across the days of the week. If Hernandez was so fixated on the players in his trial, why live here for weeks with nothing to remind him of his loathing?

"Why leave the notes?" she said aloud.

Liz turned and put her hand on her hip and muttered to herself. Why didn't he just take the women, kill them and be done with it. He didn't advertise when he took Susie Atkins or Janey Wilson.

She walked over to some storage boxes that were open and stacked on their side to create a make shift bureau. There was a kit with insulin in the top one. She picked up a prescription bottle. It was his seizure medicine. Liz put it back exactly as she found it. In the next one there were a few t-shirts, some socks and underwear.

None of this was making any sense. Hernandez had laid a trail with boulders, not breadcrumbs, to his place in L.A. Tracking his movements once they found out about the GPS wasn't rocket science. So what did he want them to see? What did he want them to do once they found all this? Perhaps this was a trap, and they had been seconds away from tripping some wire. But there were no weapons, no booby traps, nothing that looked out of place here or in the L.A. house.

Then again, could he simply have been taunting the three who received the notes? He probably counted on the ineptness of the cops to keep him safe. The system, after all, had proved to be filled with fools: reduced charges and a walk on compassionate release gave him good reason to assume they were all idiots.

The *why* of Bates and Gardener, though, was still out of reach. Liz couldn't come up with one good reason why they were snatched. Targeting Daniel made marginal sense, yet he was just one of many witnesses. Still, if Hernandez was fixated on people that supposedly did him wrong, why not take Daniel or Isaiah first? Either of those guys would have been easier than taking out a tough cookie like Josie Bates. Maybe the men on that list were teasers, highlighted for no other reason than to throw off the authorities. Hernandez had killed two girls; now he had taken two women. Could it be as simple as that?

"Find anything interesting?"

Startled, Liz pivoted, shoving back her jacket to show the gun at her waist. She stopped short of drawing it, straightened, rotated her shoulders under her denim jacket and tried to look cool.

"Geeze. You're taking a chance, Captain," Liz said, unable to make eye contact with Hagarty.

"That's funny coming from you."

He was dressed in a sport shirt and jeans, hardly the sharp togs of a man on duty, and that meant he'd been called away from family time. Everyone in the office knew what family time meant to Hagarty, so Liz stayed quiet while he walked into the unit, checking out everything inside except her.

"So, did you find anything?"

"What you see is what you get. Bed, camp toilet." She pointed to the back of the unit. "Hot plate. Some food. All the comforts of home."

"Charming," Hagarty muttered.

"It's better than the place he was living in -"

Liz caught herself, but it was too late. Hagarty looked over his shoulder and raised a brow. She had been told to step down long before touring Xavier Hernandez's place. She felt another big, black demerit mark foul the space above her head.

"Clothes. Extra blanket." Liz held up a blanket, trying to distract Hagarty. "Like he would need it in this hot box. Still has a tag on it. I can run that down and see if anyone remembers him buying it."

Hagarty stood over the stacked packing crates. "Lot of medication here."

"Hernandez has some problems."

"Five bucks and change," Hagarty muttered. "He liked to read."

"Yeah?" Liz walked over to join him.

"Wouldn't call it literature." Hagarty poked at the book. It would have been kind to call it erotica, and honest to call it porn.

"No accounting for taste." Liz said.

"Paper? Pencils? Pens?"

"Nope," Liz answered.

"Okay, then." Hagarty blew a breath through pursed lips. He stuck his hands deep into his pant pockets. He kept circling like a dog trying to find just the right spot to flop.

Liz barely breathed. He wasn't going to engage, and whatever was coming wasn't good. When he faced Liz, she looked right at him: chin up, shoulders squared, thumbs hooked over her belt. Liz wasn't defiant; she was just steeling herself for the rumble. Any other time Hagarty would have been amused. He liked Liz Driscoll. She was an arrogant little fighter, and that actually made her a good cop; just not the cop he wanted on his force. Hermosa Beach was too small for someone determined to work outside the box, and this wasn't a made for TV movie where everything was sure to work out in the end.

"How much do you know?" Liz asked.

"I know this has gotten out of hand," Hagarty said. "And I know I was clear that I didn't want you pursuing the matter. Arnson and Levinsky are excellent detectives, and they have the resources. We are no match for that kind of LAPD strength, Driscoll."

Hagarty walked a few more paces, turned and leaned back against the cold, metal wall. He looked at her like a father would, or at least the way Liz imagined a father would.

"I had a big case when I was just five years into my stint as a detective in Riverside. It was incredible: media all over me, brain working overtime, leads piling up and making no sense. I'd be up at night pacing, trying to figure it all out." He snuffed a laugh as if to underscore that he had once been a reckless buck and hindsight wasn't pretty.

"Did you figure it out?" Hagarty's eyes went to hers. His expression softened. He was grateful she asked.

"I did. Got my man, and I thought I was invincible. It was a hell of a feeling, Driscoll. It was like I had the world on a string, and that feeling doesn't end with the collar. There's the trial, the interviews, the knowledge that the starry-eyed kid who walked into the academy dreaming of fighting for justice was actually a warrior." Hagarty sniffed. "My wife said I wasn't the man she married, and she was right. I thought I was better than that man."

"That kind of thing can really get under your skin," Liz commiserated. "The investigation, not your wife."

Hagarty smiled at the qualification.

"It wasn't the investigation that nearly screwed me, it was my ego. My wife had to cut me down to size real fast, or I would have been telling the same story every night at the local bar, resting on some rotting laurels, and been divorced. Thank God I married a smart woman."

"But you understand what I was doing," Liz interrupted, taking her last shot.

"Sure, I get it," Hagarty answered.

"Great. Good. Okay, then I'll get to the hospital. I want to see if I can talk to Hernandez."

Hagarty stopped her. "No, you won't. Los Angeles is sending an officer."

"But Hernandez is mine," Liz insisted.

"No, he isn't," Hagarty answered. "He never was."

"But you said you knew what it was like. You just told me."

"The difference is, Liz, that case was mine. I had the blessing of my captain. Now I'm captain, and it's my job to run my department. You had your orders, you chose to ignore them, and people got hurt. One of those people is the guy who could tell you where those women are."

"That's why I want to see this through. I've got to make amends," Liz pleaded.

"What's done is done, Driscoll. It's over."

"You're firing me?"

Hagarty shook his head, "It's not that easy. But I like the book, Liz, and the book says you were insubordinate. I want your badge and your gun."

"Aw, come on, Captain," Liz lamented. Her thumbs unhooked from that belt of hers. Her arms rose and fell, her head swung right and left. Those pretty eyebrows of hers pulled together in frustration. "Come on. I've towed the line ever since you hired me. Give me a break. Just one."

Hagarty pushed off the wall. His hands were out of his pockets. Memory lane was being left behind.

"Tomorrow you will collect anything in your office apropos to this case. You will messenger it all to Arnson and Levinsky. You will leave your badge and your weapon in my office, and you will stand down until I have a chance to review the situation. Until then, you're on paid leave."

Liz started to object, but Hagarty was quick with a raised hand and a warning.

"The next words out of your mouth better be thank you. If not, I would suggest you do not speak and do as you're told. Do it quietly, Driscoll."

Liz fell back a step and closed her mouth. He was right. She egged his house and he was still offering her the last treat in his candy bowl.

"Seal this place, advise the manager that Arnson's people will be down here to take possession, and then go home. Am I understood?"

"Yes," Liz mumbled. As he walked past she reached for him. He paused and looked at her. "I am sorry, Captain. Really."

"So am I," he said sadly, and then he was gone.

Liz stood in the glare of the bare light listening to nothing, staring after her boss, hating herself and wondering if two women were going to die because she was a screw up. She took one huge breath, and then another one to keep from crying. When that didn't do the trick, Liz Driscoll hung her head, swiped at her eyes, and pinched the bridge of her nose. Finally, she pulled up, and took another look around. There were a million questions running through her brain, not the least of which was who was helping Hernandez? Arnson would be the one to find out, not her. Fingerprints, trace evidence, there was so much that could be recovered in here. All she really needed was to find out who rented that unit. She picked up Xavier's book and absentmindedly started to fan the pages when she heard:

"Hey." Benny was back and ready to rule the roost.

"What?" Liz snapped but her edge was gone, she sounded whiney.

"Your boss says you're not supposed to be here."

Liz narrowed her eyes. Benny was starting to really annoy her.

"Give me a minute."

Even Hagarty had cut her some slack. He could have taken her badge then and there and he didn't, so good old Benny was going to toe the respect line, too.

"I'm going to time you," Benny threatened. "One minute."

"Yeah, yeah," she muttered.

Liz fanned the pages so that they ruffled loudly. She hoped it irked him. She was about to do it again when her eye caught something. Quickly, she turned to the inside cover. There were three phone numbers listed in Hernandez's distinctive printing. Next to one was a happy face. Printing and avatars, just like the list found in Bates' car and Young's, too.

"Thirty seconds!" Benny yelled from outside.

Liz made a face, ignored the weird feeling that was crawling up her spine and grabbed her phone. Fast as she could, she snapped a picture of the phone numbers written on the flyleaf. She was about to put the book back where she found it when a red-faced Benny ripped it out of her hands.

"Hey."

He fell back slightly when Liz turned on him, but managed to stand his ground.

"Do you think I'm stupid? I saw you pick it up here. Right here. Captain Hagarty said to leave everything the way it was." Benny stomped over to the bed and put the book back exactly where Liz had found it.

"Yeah, and now your prints are all over it, and that's proof that you knew what was going on here. I'm going to have the LAPD look at you real close, Benny."

Liz made her ridiculous threat hoping the man would fall apart, but all she did was make a dent in his outrage. He cocked his head and tried to look imposing, but a man in a cheap, short-sleeved dress shirt couldn't pull it off.

"I have to lock up. Now."

"You're an upstanding citizen, Benny."

Liz gave him a tight-lipped smile, walked out of the unit into the hot night, and got back in her car. Instead of starting it, she took out her phone, and dialed the first number she had photographed. She got a canned message. Liz hung up without leaving a message of her own because she didn't know who was on the other end. She dialed the second number. This time, she got Daniel Young's office, and that really didn't surprise her all that much. Xavier had obviously been making plans. This time she left a message.

"Daniel, it's Driscoll. Xavier Hernandez is in the hospital. You can breathe easy for now. Call me as soon as you get this."

Liz called Daniel's cell and left the same message. There was no urgency now. Xavier was the catalyst and he had been taken out. Even if Xavier had someone helping him, the plan would be in disarray. She would leave Isaiah and the others on the list to Levinsky and Arnson, but Liz had a weird soft spot for Daniel. Maybe it was because, behind his bravado, Daniel was just like her. Neither of them would ever be the really cool kids on the block.

Liz dialed the third number and got a pizza parlor. She hung up just as Benny walked by. She got out of the car and followed him into the office. The T.V. was off; Benny was packing up to go home. He was not amused when he saw her.

"I just wanted to apologize," she offered her best girl-smile.

"Sure you do," Benny mumbled.

"No, really. I know we put you in a tight spot, but it was for a good reason."

Benny slammed a magazine into his pack.

"Okay. Apology accepted."

"Great. Then have a good one," Liz said just before her finger went to her lips, and she looked back at him as if she had just thought of something. "Hey, one last question, Benny. Who actually did rent that unit? You know, the second one?"

Benny wasn't having any of it. Fool him once but not twice.

"That's for me to know and you to find out." Benny grabbed his keep-things-cool lunch bag and walked past her. He slid open the door and Liz gave up. She couldn't argue with a third grader.

"You could have been a hero, Benny."

When the man didn't yield, Liz left. She walked down the three little wooden steps, got back into her car, adjusted the air-conditioning and pulled out of the lot slowly just to make Benny mad. She made a right, bumped over the railroad tracks, and took note of a couple of burned out flares her compatriots had left.

The only good thing now was that she still had her badge, her weapon and a lot of hours before she had to turn them in.

An Outbuilding in the California Mountains

"We'll play a game. I have prizes."

His whispered words were crystal clear, and Josie hung on every one hoping to identify his voice. It could have been Xavier Hernandez, but it had been ten years since that trial and even then he had only spoken when necessary. He didn't haunt her memory, she didn't dream about him. She never thought of that trial once it was finished. And now? Now she was nearly out of her mind with exhaustion, hunger and thirst. For all Josie knew, she might be hallucinating. Even if she was, being engaged in something was preferable to wallowing in the despair that had settled over her and Erika.

"What kind of game, Xavier?" Josie asked.

"Savior? That is funny." He chuckled. "Yes, call me Savior."

"Savior, let us out please." Erika called out, eager to please.

Josie reached for her and took her hand. She squeezed it in a gesture of solidarity. They waited like schoolgirls hoping to be released from detention. Finally, the answer came.

"No."

"What do you want?" Erika asked.

"To make you sorry,"

"For what, you sick bastard?" Josie demanded. She was about to raise her voice again when Erika yanked on her arm. Josie clamped her lips together. Erika was right. They were in no position to fight. She tried again and modulated her voice. "We never hurt you."

"You did."

He sounded like a man delighted with his performance in bed even though his partner lay cold beneath him.

"I'm sorry," Erika offered. "We're sorry."

"Tell me for what?"

He was hugging the outside wall, slithering closer to the opening. Josie's skin crawled and her eyes were riveted on the opening. Soon he would be able to look down on them. Out there the landscape was different somehow, because it gave him an advantage they didn't have. She hated that advantage. Look her in the eye, that's all she wanted. Don't show a face covered with glasses; don't shine a blinding light obscuring your face. Just level the damn playing field. That she could deal with. Suddenly, something scraped against the cement and the women jumped.

"He has a knife," Josie said. "He killed Janey with a knife."

Indeed, he was dragging something metal across the wall; dragging it right up to their little window. He stopped and started again. Erika looked left. He had changed positions and was dragging it along the shorter wall. The women pulled closer to one another. Josie wrapped her arms around Erika Gardener who had begun to tremble. 'Round and 'round he went making that horrid sound. And, as he passed under the little window, he pushed through a piece of paper.

It fluttered to Erika. She caught it, but it was too dark to see what was on it. Josie put her chin atop Erika's bowed head and listened. He was going faster now, almost running as he giggled and dragged the metal. On the second pass, he dropped something else through. Erika picked that paper up, too.

"We're sorry for making you do this," Erika said as she held the paper up for Josie to touch. It was slick and oblong. Photographs.

"That is a stupid thing to say."

He chuckled and dragged the sharp thing over the bricks three times right under the window. Back and forth and back it went as if he were honing the edge of a carving knife.

Suddenly, Erika relaxed and shook off Josie's embrace. Something had changed. Erika got to her knees. When she spoke again, it was with wary exhilaration. She knew something, but it was clear she wanted to be sure.

"I'm sorry for what I did. I don't know what Josie did, but I was cruel. I should have seen how much I meant to you."

Rising to her feet, she touched the top of Josie's head. It was a triumphant little gesture that gave Josie hope.

"And what did you do?" The man asked.

Erika said, "I didn't believe in you."

The knife crisscrossed over the cement in an angry, ugly, frenetic trail.

"Josie Bates? Confess, bitch."

Scritch, scratch, scratch, scratch, scratch. He was moving upward, standing on whatever allowed him to reach the opening, but Josie wasn't paying attention. Erika's lips were on her ear. Josie leaned closer to hear.

"I know who it is," she whispered and then she kissed the lobe of Josie's ear. "I can get us out of here."

CHAPTER 38

Torrance Memorial Hospital, Torrance

"Hey."

Liz walked toward the bed where Archer lay, but she spoke to Hannah who was keeping vigil. Bathed in the soft glow of the light box that allowed the nurses to check vitals while their patient slept, Hannah looked ethereal and exhausted.

"Hi." Hannah smiled as the older woman pulled up a chair next to her.

"Have they got him knocked out, or is he just sleeping?"

"Knocked out." Hannah shrugged casually, but Liz saw beyond her pretense. The girl's hands were tightly clasped, her eyes didn't leave Archer's face, and she leaned toward him, not away. Hannah said: "Thanks for calling and letting me know he was hurt.

"No problem. I thought he needed a friend," Liz said. "Sorry I couldn't pick you up."

"It's okay. Burt drove me down. He had to go back to the restaurant. He's going to pick me up later."

"I can take you home," Liz said.

"No, it's okay. I'll wait for Burt. He'll come back after he closes."

"It's only nine-thirty, and Burt doesn't close up until two," Liz reminded her.

"I don't mind. I want to be here. He stayed with me when I needed him."

Liz looked at Archer then back to Hannah. She got it. Burt and Archer were family; Liz was only cop. In a few hours she wouldn't even be that.

"Did Hernandez get away?" Hannah asked.

"No, he's here." Before Liz finished Hannah all but bolted out of her chair.

"You've got him? He told you where Josie is?"

Liz caught her arm and Hannah tensed. "He's in ICU, Hannah. We don't even know if he's going to make it. I'm really sorry."

Hannah sank back onto her chair. Still beautiful, still young, she looked so tragic and vulnerable that Liz would have changed places with Archer just so Hannah would have someone to lean on.

"What if he dies?" Hannah asked, her voice so quiet Liz could barely hear it.

"Then he dies, and we keep going. We know there was a woman who visited him. We know there was a man who came with her. We know a small car was seen at the pier and at Erika Gardener's place. I have phone numbers to check. We've got stuff going on. We do, Hannah." Liz's bottom lip disappeared under her top teeth. She bit hard hoping to squeeze out the right words, but Liz never had kids and never had much reason to talk to one unless they were stumbling out of Sharkeez drunk as skunks.

Finally, she simply gave it her best shot. "I'm not going to give up. You shouldn't either."

There was nothing more to say so they kept their eyes on Archer who was as still as death. Occasionally, the silence was broken by a beep from one of the machines, the rumble of a cart being rolled down the hall, nurses speaking in hushed tones just outside the door. The two women didn't notice. Each was lost in thought.

Hannah thought Archer looked old in the limp hospital gown. It had fallen off one shoulder and she could see the heart monitors. His hair was messed up, his big body pierced with IVs, his boxer's face slack and his face pale. It was only three days ago he had found her in his apartment, two days ago when he had been so forceful and sure of himself. He took command of the search for Josie, he stood up for her in court, and he actually smiled when the judge ruled in their favor. Archer was the next best thing to Josie, and Hannah could do nothing for either of them.

"A lot of people say they'd throw themselves in front of a train for someone they love. I always thought that was a saying."

"Josie's lucky," Liz muttered, surprised to find she didn't begrudge Josie Archer's affection any more. She tilted her head. "You know, he doesn't look so bad considering he mixed it up with a train."

"You haven't seen the other side of his face," Hannah joked, only to turn serious again. "Another second and they say he would have probably lost his leg."

Liz nodded, but she wasn't really thinking of Archer's leg. She was thinking of that second Hannah mentioned. If Archer had jumped one second earlier he would have cleared the train. If he waited one more second, Hernandez would be free but easily tracked down. One second of hesitation would have left Archer on the right side of the train and Liz wouldn't be facing review. A second and they would know where Josie Bates and Erika Gardener were right now.

One damn second. It didn't seem fair to any of them. Still, what Archer had done was amazing and selfless and heroic. Whether Liz remained a detective or not didn't matter much in the grand scheme of things. Whether Archer and Josie Bates and Erika Gardener survived, did. Still, one lousy second and Liz could have held on to what she had, too.

"Do you have someone to stay with tonight?" Liz asked.

Hannah shook her head. "No, but it's cool. I'd rather just go home. Max is there. I'll be near the phone. I'd rather be alone."

"You got it." Liz started to get up, but Hannah stopped her.

"The county is going to take me into custody if I don't have someone to supervise me."

"I know." Liz put her hand on Hannah's shoulder and patted it. Instead of shrugging her off, Hannah touched her. The girl's fingers tapped gently.

"Maybe you could, you know, stay and make it look like you're going to take care of me. I mean when they come, I could tell them that a detective is going to be responsible."

Liz hesitated, wanting to say yes in the worst way. Instead, she slid her hand off Hannah's shoulder.

"I can't. I'm sorry."

"I get it. It's asking a lot," Hannah said.

"It's not that. It's – work." Liz couldn't even bring herself to tell this girl she'd been disgraced. Once more, Liz Driscoll was letting someone down.

"You're right. I'd rather have you looking for Josie. I wouldn't care normally, it's just that I know they won't tell me when you find her," Hannah said.

"I'll try to run some interference." The false promise was out of Liz's mouth before she could stop it. Maybe she was just trying to convince herself that she'd find a way out of this mess. "Gotta go, Hannah. You hang in there."

"Will you try to talk to Hernandez?"

"I'll poke my head in, but I doubt either one of these guys will be doing much talking tonight. Get some rest."

"You, too, Detective Driscoll," Hannah answered, her eyes back on Archer.

There wasn't anything left to say, so Liz left Hannah as she found her. It was only a few minutes later when a nurse came into the room. Hannah didn't even notice her until she leaned close and whispered:

"What would you like me to do with his things?"

An Outbuilding in the California Mountains

"Help me. Let me see," Erika hissed.

Excitedly, she motioned for Josie to help her. Afraid to make too much fuss, Josie balanced on one knee and planted her other foot solidly on the hard earth. She cupped her hands and nodded when she was ready. Erika put one foot into the saddle Josie created. There was a presumed count to three, and then Josie lifted Erika high enough to put her other foot on Josie's knee, raised tall enough to see through the little hole in the wall.

Josie's head fell back. Her arms and body shook with the effort. She didn't know how long she could hold Erika, but the other woman didn't notice. Josie's head fell so that her brow rested against Erika's calf. She leaned forward, and that helped to stabilize her a little.

"Look at me." Erika spoke to the darkness in a girlish and inviting voice. "You're looking for me, aren't you? Aren't you looking for me? Come on. Show me your face."

Josie closed her eyes, anticipating the name that was to come.

"I see you. Come closer, you sanctimonious…"

Josie looked up, she whispered: "Hurry. I can't hold you much longer."

Erika nodded as she clutched at the edges where the brick was missing. She glanced down and Josie thought she might be smiling. Then she raised her head again and Josie heard her say:

"Shit."

As Erika fell backward instinct took over. Josie reached out hoping to catch her or at least break her fall. But Josie's reflexes were slow and Erika's body was heavy and awkward in the small space. Her arms flailed, but when her head crashed into the opposite wall and Josie heard the crack of her skull, she knew it was bad.

"Erika! Erika!"

Josie's hands roamed over the other woman, touching Erika's legs, her torso, her hair that was wet with blood. Then she touched something solid where Erika's throat should have been. Before she could identify what it was, the interior of the hut was illuminated. Josie grunted and threw her hands up. The light hurt her eyes as much as it frightened her. Suddenly it started to strobe. Every movement she made became a fractured frame for the entertainment of the man outside. Josie's eyes turned away from the light only to recoil at the sight of Erika Gardner dead, a knife sticking out of her throat.

Sick with shock, Josie looked back trying to look past the light to the man outside as she asked:

"Why?"

CHAPTER 39

Day 4
Josie Bates' House, Hermosa Beach

Max slept. Eventually, Hannah would, too, but first there were chores to do. Despite the late hour, Hannah watered the plants inside and outside the house. She remade Josie's bed because it was still messed up from when Archer and Daniel Young sat on it. She put the dishes in the dishwasher away. When Josie came home, she wanted her to see that she had cared for the house as if it were her own.

Finally, Hannah opened the plastic bag the nurse had given her. She took out Archer's clothes and laundered them even though they would never be worn again. His pants had been cut off him in the emergency room, his shirt was missing buttons and was torn at the elbow, there was blood on his socks and there was only one shoe in the bag. Hannah could no more have left his clothes in that condition than she could have left Josie's house without checking the lock on the door.

When the laundry was started, Hannah dug back into the bag and laid the rest of his things on the dining room table: money, keys, ID, and cell phone. She counted

Archer's money. Ten dollars: a five and five ones. The I.D. wallet had his driver's license on one side and his state investigator's ID on the other. The investigator's ID had a better picture than the driver's license. She adjusted the license so that it was perfectly centered in the plastic sheath. Finally, Hannah reached for the phone. Under the table, the heel of her right foot started to bounce, and she counted silently. There were three messages, two of them from his clients who were upset that he was not on the job and one from Peter Siddon. The man was on a rant. Hannah shut it off. She couldn't listen to another word spoken against Josie.

Then Hannah stopped touching, stopped shaking her foot, and decided to go to bed. It was very late. Tomorrow was going to be a big day. As much as she would like to go to the hospital and sit with Archer, she would simply call for an update. There was no way of telling when Mrs. Crane would be coming for her, but there was no doubt she would come.

After she finished packing her things, Hannah got into bed. Max rolled into her. She put her arm around him and fell asleep wishing she believed in God. If she did, she could pray for a miracle because that was the only hope left.

Hermosa Beach PD, Hermosa Beach

It was after midnight when Liz Driscoll walked into the office. It didn't take long to realize exactly how pathetic she was. The desk officer greeted her like a mortician at a viewing, and Liz was the one in the casket. The night dispatcher studiously attended to his board even though there were no calls. Even the cleaning crew stepped aside to let her pass. They should have just screamed 'dead man walking' and be done with it.

She tossed her jacket on the extra chair in her cubicle, plopped herself down and put her head in her hands. She cursed the burger and extra large order of fries she'd eaten because she thought it would make her feel better. It made her feel like a cow. The damn food was sitting right in the middle of her gut. Maybe it wasn't the burger upsetting her stomach, maybe it was that gluttonous serving of crow she had with it.

"Damn. Damn." She whispered, her curses directed at no one but herself.

Liz sat heavily in her chair, rolled up her sleeves and pulled three files to the middle of the desk. In the first was background on Bates. In the second were the trial transcripts Isaiah Wilson had given to Hannah and Archer had given to Liz when she picked him up to check out A-1 Storage. She opened the third and found her investigation notes from the interviews at the pier, discovery notes on the Jeep, phone calls to make and follow up on. She set it aside and rifled through her inbox, delighted to find the preliminary report on the Jeep.

Sitting back, Liz put her feet on the desk and crossed them at the ankles. The report looked formidable, but it was just like reading a medical history. There were lots of little boxes to check off and then a few spaces for notes.

Liz's eyes trailed down the little boxes noting the ones that were checked. A partial fingerprint had been found and it might match to Hernandez. They were following up. Liz thought it was wishful thinking. No D.A. was going to bring cause based on a partial. Hair samples had been found. They were short and dark and came from a female.

The only thing of interest was a piece of fiber. More than a couple of strands of thread, but less than an actual piece of fabric, had been found on the frame beneath the driver seat and was identified as black and white and blue. It had been sent to another lab for fiber content analysis. Liz would have those results the next day – which really was today – which didn't matter because Liz wasn't on this case anymore.

Liz dropped the paper, swiveled and fired off an email to have the lab send results to Arnson with a copy to her at her personal email. Hagarty was going to have to deal with that if he found out.

She opened the second file and did a quick scan of the transcripts from the Hernandez trial, then she settled back to read it in earnest. There were fifty pages and Isaiah Wilson hadn't been kidding when he said Josie Bates was vile and relentless. She was also a damn good attorney.

On the stand, Josie had reduced Isaiah Wilson to tears, confusing him in his grief about what he did and did not know about his own daughter, her sexuality and her sexual experiences. She did the same with Peter Rothskill, using his standing as a sex offender to paint Janey as a teenage harlot. The mitigating circumstances of Rothskill's situation would have allowed for jury sympathy, so Bates blew him up under cross and left it to the prosecution to try and put him back together again. But it was Daniel Young's testimony that was really interesting.

Expert witnesses were usually grilled relentlessly in the hopes of tripping them up, discrediting them or simply making their testimony look foolish and irrelevant. Josie destroyed Daniel Young with a clean, surgical strike. She pointed out that Young, psychiatrist to the stars, expert witness extraordinaire, was a charlatan. With a few pointed questions, she puffed him up like a peacock spreading his tail feathers, and with a few more equally brilliant questions, slaughtered him when she revealed he had never finished his graduate work. His board certification was a fluke, a lie, and a sham. He was no more an expert on the state of Xavier Hernandez's mind than she was. In fact, everything out of his mouth should only be taken as seriously as the braying of a donkey.

"Ouch," Liz mumbled.

She tossed the transcripts on the desk, and went back to her file. The latest paperwork was an update from Arnson on his contact with the prosecutor from the Hernandez trial. Arnson found the man happily retired after making a fortune in private practice and investing wisely. There had been no notes in his car, no strange phone calls and no one hanging around his house. He knew no more than anyone else about the people on the list or why Hernandez would target Erika Gardener – a lovely woman who had rejected his advances. She had been engaged. Josie Bates? He could understand anyone but Hernandez trying to take her out.

There was a report on Isaiah Wilson's activities during the last week. He had been absent from the church for two and half days. He lived alone, so there was no one to vouch for him in the evenings.

Liz Driscoll closed the folder. She would send it over to Arnson just to make Hagarty happy. The one person who was still an enigma was Paul Rothskill. Out of curiosity, Liz turned to her computer and typed in the name. It was not unique and she pulled up an author in England, a lawyer in Oregon, and a podiatrist in California. She clicked on the lawyer, saw that he was a portly guy in his seventies and clicked out again. Scrolling once more, wasting time because she didn't want to leave this place she considered home, Liz found a reference to Paul and the Hernandez trial.

She clicked on that, and pulled up the same picture Archer had seen. Paul had been a handsome young man. Liz clicked out and was back to the Google listing. She was about to close out when the name Peter Siddon caught her eye. It was linked to Paul Rothskill and the link was to the High Desert News in Palmdale, California. Liz leaned closer to the screen.

A local daycare had been shut down because of allegations that the owner was married to a registered sex offender. An anonymous tip led to the alert that Peter Siddon, once known as Paul Rothskill, was married to Laura Siddon, owner of A Child's Place. Rothskill, notorious for his part in the events that led to the killing of Janey Wilson…

She hit print, walked down the hall, took the copy out of the network printer and walked back to her office. There she made a note for Arnson:

Check out ASAP. Called Bates' office multiple times. No message. Angry. Will have message slips from her office forwarded.

Then she made a second note, putting the Post It on the transcript:

Bates refers to Young as braying donkey. Check for references to clown (See copy of list left in cars/avatars).

She tucked the transcripts in the second folder, bundled it up, made out the routing information and then checked her phone. It was almost two in the morning. She hoped Burt had managed to get Hannah home to bed. Liz clicked over to her photo file and looked at the numbers she photographed in Hernandez's book. She looked for messages, but Daniel Young had not called her back.

Snapping her phone shut Liz got up, put on her jacket and walked down the hall to Hagarty's office. She didn't bother to turn on the lights when she walked in. Instead, she took the four steps she knew she had to take to reach his desk. Once there, she took her weapon out of her holster, discharged the clip, and put it on his desk. She unsnapped the badge from her belt and put that down, too.

Then Liz Driscoll turned her back and left the office, happy she had not turned on a light. There were a few things she couldn't bear and seeing her badge surrendered was one of them.

An Outbuilding in the California Mountains

Josie Bates could not stop trembling. Intellectually Josie knew she was in shock, but intellect was no help anymore. This nightmare had turned horrific. Josie had passed the night with a dead body, the memory of Erika Gardener's face, and the knife stuck in her throat. The man who killed her had kept the strobe light shining inside so long that Josie couldn't decide if he was enjoying his handiwork, or if he was as shocked as she to see what he had done.

She had decided he was pleased, and that knowledge destroyed the last of Josie's bravado.

She curled into her corner, and kept her back to Erika. But out of sight was not out of mind. Josie thought of what would happen as soon as the sun rose. She would see Erika dead again. At noon the heat would work its ugly fingers beneath Erika's skin. One full day, maybe two and the decomposing body would create a hell on earth. Whoever had done this to them would have been kinder to bury Josie alive. But kindness was not in the cards, nor was humanity or hope. Even faith was gone. She had believed Archer would find her. He had not. Josie was determined not to look at Erika again. She decided not to move from her corner. She decided to die as quickly as possible.

Yet, when that first grey light came through the small opening in the wall, she turned her head and looked at the body, the dried blood, and the white film over the woman's once blue eyes. And there was something else. The pictures Erika had been holding were now on the ground.

Josie reached for the first one. It was a snapshot of a cat in a well-kept backyard. There was a stone statue of a grinning frog. She set it aside and reached for the second one, inadvertently touching Erika's cold skin.

Josie raised the picture, looked at it and, in the next instant, began to keen. Head thrown back, neck arched, she clutched the picture to her breast, the picture of Hannah standing next to the half-finished archway in Josie's own house.

CHAPTER 40

Torrance Memorial Hospital, Torrance

"Hey there, cowboy," Liz whispered.

Archer blinked, disoriented by everything: the room, the drugs, pain and Liz Driscoll sitting by his side.

"How about you wet your whistle." She got up and took the pink plastic cup with the Sippy straw and held it for him. He took a drink without raising his head. That was as long as it took for him to remember.

"Hernandez?" he rasped.

"He's breathing, but that's about it. LAPD is going to put a guard on him as soon as he shows signs of coming around." Liz offered him the water again. Again he sipped. "Oops," Liz reached for a tissue and patted Archer's chin dry when the water dribbled out. "How you feeling?"

Archer closed his eyes and pulled his brows together.

"Figured." Liz sat down again and pulled her chair close to the bed. "Archer, listen."

"Find anything?"

One side of Liz's lips tipped. Even in this state he wanted to be on top of things. Not that it mattered. No matter what she told him, Archer wouldn't remember two days from now. She told him the truth anyway.

"Not much. Got some phone numbers that were printed in the front of a book we found in the unit. Same block printing. No car. No keys in Hernandez's pockets; nothing in his pockets at all. Everybody's focusing on figuring out who's helping him. "

Archer raised his hand, the one with the IV in it, and motioned to the water. Liz was up again.

"You want something to eat, too?"

He shook his head.

"Erika Gardener's picture," he said.

"Yeah? What about it." Liz sat again but stayed close to the bed. It was taking everything Archer had to talk.

"Picture in Daniel's office. Check," Archer said. "Her house. Check pictures. Purple dress."

"Sure, I'll take a look," Liz answered.

"Car in the lot?"

Liz chuckled, she had no idea what he was talking about, but it seemed important to him so she answered as best she could.

"Not yet. They should have it this afternoon."

"Good. Good. Erika's picture. Parking."

"I'll stop by Daniel's office. I promise. But I'm not…"

Liz never finished her thought. Archer was drifting off again.

"Okay, Archer. I'll check."

Liz Driscoll stood up and looked at him. He was a really good man, she decided. Taking a minute to rearrange Archer's hospital gown so that it covered both his shoulders. She did that gently so he wouldn't wake up. Liz didn't really want to see Archer's face when she told him that she'd been suspended. She also didn't want to hear him suggest that she back off on this thing. He wouldn't want her to jeopardize the chance of keeping her job, but Liz knew she couldn't go back to the job unless she had done her best for Archer and Hannah and Josie. Liz had started this for all the wrong reasons; now she was going to finish it for the right ones.

Liz gave Archer's shoulder an extra pat, and then she did something that surprised the heck out of her. She kissed his forehead. Archer would never know she lingered, but she would carry the feeling of her lips against his skin to her grave.

Christian Broadcast Complex, Orange County

"There are three requests for interviews, Reverend. *Good Morning America's* producer has been most insistent that she speak directly to you. I've done the best I can, but I'm afraid I'm not really very good at this."

The young girl with the very long hair and the very loose floral dress and the very, very sensible shoes, who only two days ago had stood guard against Archer, was now gatekeeper once again. This time she was charged with keeping the media at bay until Reverend Wilson was ready to deal with them. As devoted as she was to Reverend Wilson, she was not happy with her new role. She much preferred greeting the worshipers who came in the hopes of praying with the reverend, or to leave a card or flowers or drop off their checks so the ministry could flourish.

Since that horrible incident with that devilish black girl, all hell (for thinking this she apologized to God with a quick prayer) had broken loose. Faith would have to take strength from Isaiah Wilson whose demeanor had not changed one bit. This only made her love him more – as her spiritual leader, of course.

"You're doing an admirable job, Faith. I greatly appreciate it in this time of my need."

"I only wish there was more I could do," she said quietly.

"I promise to call on you if it becomes necessary." Isaiah's assurance was laced with undertones of admiration and gratitude, yet he never looked at her directly. Instead, he considered the messages she had given him and handed her back two. "Please tell *Good Morning America* I would be happy to speak with them if they can come in three days. I'll clear my schedule."

"Three days?" Faith blinked. "But, Reverend. That will be six days."

"Is there some significance?" Isaiah asked.

"Your daughter?" Faith was not quite sure how to phrase her concern so she just blurted it out. "Well, everyone says it was five days before she died. People believe that's when Mr. Hernandez will kill these two women," she said tentatively. "Perhaps a word of forgiveness from you would change things?"

Isaiah leaned forward and Faith was drawn to him as she always was.

"This is God's move, Faith. Do you not believe those women's fate is in God's hands now?"

"I do," she breathed. "Yes. You're right."

"And you do not believe I know anything more than God, do you?"

"No, Reverend."

"And why is that?" Isaiah pushed.

"Because you are only a man, and they are only women, and it is God's plan."

"That is correct."

He held her gaze and Faith clutched her hands in front of her. Just before she was about to speak again, the phone rang. Isaiah tilted his head and she shook hers. It was always a hypnotic experience to be in Isaiah's presence, but to speak with him so intimately was euphoric. Faith snapped out of it, she took up the receiver and turned away from Isaiah.

"Reverend Wilson's ministry. Faith speaking. How may I help you?"

Faith listened and then she put her hand over the receiver.

"It's a hospital. They say Xavier Hernandez has asked for you."

CHAPTER 41

The California Mountains

He rode back as fast as he could. He rode for miles and miles thinking about what had happened. He killed her. KILLED. K-i-l-l-e-d. The word went through his mind in psychedelic permutations. There must be a name for this incredible feeling. It felt as if the word itself was going to engulf him.

He sped through the city not bothering to stop at the lights, not noticing when he cut off a car. He panicked when she threatened his plan. Erika should not have done that. There was a timetable and, had she stuck it out, she and Bates would have been saved. That had been the point. Punish them, humiliate them and save them. Xavier would have been blamed, there would be another trial, Xavier would be back where he belonged and he would have his life back. Janey would be put to rest. It would have been perfect and now look. Erika was a nosey stupid bitch. Too smart for her own good.

He rolled into his drive. The surrounding buildings were dark. He dug into his pants for the key and that's when he felt it. There was a small hole in his pocket. It would have to be fixed. He let himself in, locked the door, and went straight to the bathroom. He showered for a very, very long time to calm his mind. He prayed for a plan. God must have heard because by the time he was drying himself he was able to consider his options. Once he was dressed, he realized there was only one: he had to leave Josie Bates where she was.

Pity that, especially considering Hannah. Just as a child should not be taken from a parent, a parent should not be ripped from a child. Still, it couldn't be helped. He would make it up to her. As God was his witness, he would make up for this mistake.

The Beach, Hermosa Beach

Hannah sat on the beach watching the water come in and go out. It was the first time she had sought out the sand and the water for herself, and it wasn't just because Josie loved this place. Hannah wanted to be there because it would be a good long time before she saw the ocean again. Hannah calculated that she had about five hours before Mrs. Crane came to get her.

Judge Leisinger wouldn't want to rescind his order, and he would make Mrs. Rice cool her heels for an hour or two. Then he would call Mrs. Crane in and between the video presentation of Hannah attacking Reverend Wilson, the news reports of Archer's hospitalization the night before, Hernandez's injuries that kept him near death, and Josie's continuing status as a missing person, they would convince him that foster care was the only option for Hannah Sheraton. After all, who else was there to watch her? A barkeep with bad legs? A dope smoking kid whose own mother barely let him in the house? Faye whose daughter needed her and, when push came to shove, would choose blood?

So here Hannah sat with Max by her side. She wasn't supposed to have the dog on the beach, but no one would call her on it. She put her hand on his head and let it slide down to his jowl. He loved that she petted him there because he always leaned into her caress. When she was gone, Hannah would miss him a lot, but the worst part was that he would miss her. Since Josie's disappearance Max was disoriented and moving more slowly. Now that Hannah would be going and Archer wouldn't be able to take care of him, she hoped he would survive to see one of them come home. It was hard enough being abandoned when you were young; to be abandoned when you were old would be horrible.

Leaning over Max, Hannah took out her phone and used him like a pillow while she dialed Josie's number. It rang and when it picked up, Hannah held the phone to the dog's ear so he could hear Josie's voice. She hung up, and put the phone back in her pocket.

Archer had submitted a tracking request to the phone company, but now the LAPD would have to follow-up. Since no one would think to tell her anything, Hannah would just keep dialing until the day Josie answered or the battery gave out. Eventually, there was nothing more to do.

"Come on, Max."

Hannah stood up, and dusted off her rear. She took the dog by the leash and grabbed the bag she had brought with her, pausing only long enough to look at the ocean one more time. It really was beautiful. She wished she could tell Josie she had changed her mind about the beach.

Max pulled on the leash. He wanted to go home, but Hannah tugged the other way. Together, they walked slowly to Burt's By the Beach. It was only eight in the morning, but already the place was doing a brisk business. Burt's famous pancakes brought them in, and his free coffee refills kept them there.

Hannah smiled at a few people she knew, and paused to let anyone who wanted to pet Max do so. He was a good boy and patiently let them, but Hannah saw in his eyes that he wanted to go home. She did, too, but they would both have to suck it up. She slid onto a stool at the counter and Burt came right over.

"Hungry?" he asked.

She shook her head.

"How about Max?"

"I already fed him."

"So?" Burt leaned on the counter. He was a good listener. Nothing fazed him. Hannah didn't know if this would.

"Max needs somewhere to stay. I was thinking you could take care of him for a while. Until Archer is better and Josie comes home."

"I figured last night would cause some problems for you," Burt sighed. "How's Archer doing?"

"Good. The doctors are really surprised. They think another couple days in the hospital." Hannah said. She looked down at Max. "So, will you take him?"

"Sure thing," Burt reached for the leash. "But maybe we could come up with something. I know a lawyer who could stand in for Faye."

Hannah shook her head. "Thanks, Burt, but it's not worth it. When Josie's back, she'll come find me."

"So will Archer, kiddo."

"I know. But Josie first."

Hannah slid off the stool, handed over the bag with Max's dish and food, took the dog's face in her hands and leaned in for a kiss.

"It won't be long," Burt said. "You'll be back, and so will Josie. It will be like it always was."

"Sure, Burt," Hannah couldn't help but smile at his lie. It would never be like it always was. Her fingers itched to tap, and her mind was dying to count, but she didn't want her distraction to be the thing Burt remembered about her. "See you soon. And tell Billy bye for me. Have him tell Mrs. Manning at school what happened."

"Sure thing, kiddo," Burt assured her sadly.

She walked out the door and counted her steps all the way back to Josie's empty house. There she finished packing the things she would need when Mrs. Crane came for her. The last thing in the bag was the picture of Josie and Max. When that was done, the house seemed truly empty.

Torrance Memorial Hospital, Torrance

He heard the whispers in his wake and, though he didn't smile outwardly, inside Isaiah Wilson rejoiced. He had thought his notoriety was limited only to the faithful, but now he was once again in the broader public eye. Even though it was preordained that he should be a man of consequence, there had been moments in the last years when he wondered if God had turned his grace away.

He had asked after Archer and been directed to his room. There Isaiah Wilson stood at the foot of the bed, hands crossed at his crotch, eyes on the big man who looked much less intimidating than the last time they met.

Isaiah was a patient man and had waited until Archer opened his eyes to speak.

"I am here to pray for you. You do not deserve to be in the path of His retribution against Josie Bates."

"Screw you," Archer whispered and then he managed to push the call button. By the time the nurse arrived Isaiah Wilson was gone, and Archer wished he could take a bath and wash off the blessing he had dared to utter.

Isaiah took the elevator up to ICU. There, his presence was not noted with the same enthusiasm as it had been at his first stop. That was understandable. ICU nurses and doctors were intent on their patients, those poor souls lying precariously close to death. Most were only a breath away from seeing their savior or the devil.

Isaiah stopped to ask the way to Xavier Hernandez's room. He was directed to it, but was told Xavier had fallen back into his coma. Still, Isaiah went on his way and was surprised to find that there was no one to guard the man in the bed. Given the urgency people felt about finding Josie Bates and Erika Gardener, one would think they would have an officer posted to listen to any utterance Xavier made.

In the room, Isaiah found himself thinking that it was a pity there wasn't more privacy. He would have liked to be alone with this man. He would have liked to squeeze one of the tubes that ran into this person who killed his child; or ease a pillow from under his head, put it over his face and rest his weight upon it until Xavier's soul fled his body.

Instead, he stood close and looked down upon Xavier's handsome face. In repose, he looked quite beautiful. Mounting his daughter, his knife at the ready,

Isaiah was sure he had looked like the devil. But now the topic was not Janey or that long ago atrocity Hernandez had visited upon them; now the topic was Josie Bates.

Isaiah leaned down and put his lips near Xavier's ear.

"You have served your purpose, Xavier. You've done well."

With that, Isaiah Wilson straightened up and left the hospital. He had seen with his own eyes that Xavier Hernandez would never speak to anyone ever again, not about Janey nor Susie and definitely not about Josie Bates.

The Office of Daniel Young, Manhattan Beach

Liz sat on the floor for an hour and a half before anyone came. Finally, a woman stormed down the hall looking beautiful, chic and pissed. Her jeans were tight, her filmy blouse rolled off one shoulder, her heels were high and that hair of hers was cut with surgical precision so that the bangs fell exactly to the bottom of her brows. Upon closer inspection, though, Liz decided she wasn't all that pretty. Her anger hardened her lips; the high color of her emotion stained the right side of her face like a birthmark rather than coloring it prettily.

"Hi." Liz pushed herself off the floor and adjusted her jacket, trying to look presentable.

The other woman's shadowed eyes swept over Liz as she said: "Doctor Young won't be in today. Come back some other time."

"I'm Liz Driscoll, Hermosa PD." Liz said this so convincingly the woman did not ask for identification.

Instead, she unlocked the door, pushed it open, and rested her weight on one foot.

"Well, he's not coming in for anybody. I don't think I can be plainer than that."

The woman twirled and stormed into the office, tossed her stuff on the reception desk and started to open drawers.

"No problem," Liz said as she followed, closing the door behind her.

"Look, I don't know what I can tell you. There haven't been any phone calls. There haven't been weird people hanging around. I'm sick of hearing the name Josie Bates. So, I don't know what else you want from me."

"I'd like to see some pictures Daniel has here."

"There aren't any pictures," Gay put her hands flat on the desk and glared at Liz. "And I've got a ton of appointments to cancel. I don't know why he even bothered to make them until all this stupid mess is over with."

"Well, can I look around?" Liz asked.

"Sure. Just don't touch his desk. He's really funny about people touching his desk."

"Okay. Thanks." Liz walked toward the inner sanctum, pausing before she went in. "I left a message for him last night and haven't heard from him."

"Don't worry about it. He's a prick. He only calls when he feels like it. If there's something better to do than call you, he does it. I don't mind telling you, I'm just a little tired of this whole thing."

"What whole thing?"

"You know. Booty call? For a while I thought we had something really good going. Wrong! How stupid can I be? After everything I've done for him. I've bent over backwards."

"He's got a lot on his mind," Liz commiserated.

"Then I wish he'd tell me about it. You know what I mean?" She took a minute to catch her breath and look at Liz. She wasn't going to cry, but there was hurt behind her eyes. "He was so cool for a while. You'd think I'd know by now."

"Know what?" Liz asked.

"That all men are psycho. All they do is think about themselves."

Liz had never been good at girl talk, and couldn't exactly discuss the psycho assertion with any real authority so she didn't try. Psycho was relative, but Liz could sort of see why Gay – she finally had a name – put the label on Daniel Young. It was never a good idea to sleep with your boss, but to sleep with a guy as anal as Daniel was really stupid. Liz had a hard time having him around in the last couple of days; to have him follow her home at night would be too much.

Liz left Gay to her phone calls and checked out Daniel's office. The man might as well have installed a spotlight over his desk. She took a look at the desk, but didn't touch anything. There really wasn't anything to touch, anyway. No pictures. Then she turned around and saw the vanity wall.

The framed magazine covers were all old, but Daniel had been quite the darling of the media for a while. There were pictures at formal events. Liz admired the way he wore a tux. There were luncheon photos: Daniel with Mayor Riordon, Daniel on a movie set, a headshot of a well-known actress on which she had scrawled 'thanks for saving me from myself'. Then she saw the picture of Daniel surrounded by women in evening gowns. This was what Archer wanted her to see: Daniel and Erika Gardener. His arm was around her instead of reaching out to encompass all the women. Erika did not look happy. Liz knew a relationship when she saw it and this was a relationship. Daniel should have told them.

She took the picture from the wall and walked back to the reception room. Gay was on the phone, her voice sweet and concerned as she cancelled an appointment and thanked Mr. Bond for understanding that even doctors have sick days. She looked at Liz, fingers poised to dial again.

"Do you know her?" Liz held out the picture. She didn't even have to point at Erika Gardener because Gay's eyes went right to her. She grimaced. She looked at Liz.

"Yeah, I know who that is. Daniel's fiancé."

Chambers of Judge Leisinger, Edleman Courthouse, Monterey Park

"And you've spoken to Mrs. Crane? She agrees with this?"

"Given all that has happened, given that the man who you thought should take custody of Hannah Sheraton is no longer able to, given that her birth mother is in jail and her guardian, Josie Bates, is still missing, yes, Mrs. Crane agrees a placement is the only course of action."

Leisinger didn't bother to look at Mrs. Rice when he said: "A simple yes would have sufficed."

He picked up a pen and hesitated. Leisinger was a man who expedited that which had to be expedited, but this time it felt like a criminal action. Pity that in this case chronology put Hannah in harm's way via an intractable system. He would rather have ten Hannahs running around than Mrs. Rice and Mrs. Crane partnering up. Still, there was no choice now. He put his signature on the order remanding Hannah Sheraton to the care of the state.

"When will Mrs. Crane be picking her up?" Leisinger asked.

"She's already called Hannah to let her know she'll be coming as soon as she has the paperwork."

"That's kind of her," Leisinger said.

"She wanted to make sure Hannah would be ready. You can't waste time in these matters," Mrs. Rice answered.

"Pity that," Leisinger noted. "Good day, Mrs. Rice."

The Home of Cory Cartwright, Westminster

Detective Arnson sat in Cory Cartwright's home on a small chair covered in a fabric stamped with big, pink roses. The place screamed old maid, and yet Cory Cartwright was far from it. Old, sure. She was probably in her sixties, but the woman knew how to take care of herself. She had a bod that just wouldn't quit and, for a married man like Arnson, just thinking about it made him feel like he owed his wife an apology. It didn't help that she was wearing some kind of yoga stuff that made her look like she was forty.

"You know," she said as she walked back into the room after taking a little powder break, "there was no reason you should have come all this way. You could have just asked me about Xavier over the phone. Not that I don't love company, you understand."

She reclined on a sofa that looked none too comfortable and smiled at him. Caps, he decided. Nobody had teeth that perfect.

"We like to do things in person when possible," Arnson answered.

"So you can look a body in the eye and know if they're lying? That is so CSI."

"Actually, yes." Arnson colored under her scrutiny. "I understand you ran the literacy program at the prison. I was hoping you could tell me if Xavier Hernandez's work ever referenced his trial for the murder of Janey Wilson. I'm specifically interested to find out if he mentioned Josie Bates or Erika Gardener."

"I don't follow," Cory answered. "He read a lot. In fact, I remember him because he was a voracious reader. He wasn't really one to discuss the things he read. I never engaged the inmates in discussions of their crimes even if they wanted to. That wasn't my job."

"No, I'm not talking about his reading habits. I wondered if you might still have some of the stuff he wrote. You know, did he write stories or a journal or what?"

Cory Cartwright threw back her head and laughed.

"What he wrote? Xavier had a learning disability. He couldn't write if his life depended on it."

A Rental House, San Fernando Valley

"Come on. Hurry it up. I gotta get to work!"

The girl's boyfriend hollered at her through the closed and locked bathroom door. Sometimes she thought she should get rid of him, get out of the house, and change her life around a little. There just had to be a better way to live. Her, him, his friends and one bathroom just didn't add up to a really fine situation. But this morning, he was just going have to wait to take his ten o'clock dump because she finally decided what she had to do and she was going to do it – as soon as she remembered the number.

CHAPTER 42

Josie Bates' House, Hermosa Beach

Daniel Young knocked on the door and was surprised not to hear the dog bark. He hated that dog and the dog hated him, but he was ready to face the animal. So when Hannah opened the door and the dog didn't appear, Daniel figured his luck was turning.

"Nobody's here," Hannah said when she saw him.

"I know. I heard what happened to Archer and Xavier," Daniel said. "Can I come in?"

"I guess." Hannah held open the door. "I'm not going to be here very long."

"Where are you going?" Daniel asked, noting the suitcase by the door.

"Everyone heard about Archer. I'm being placed." Hannah followed Daniel into the living room. "Don't make yourself comfortable. They'll probably be here soon."

"I am sorry, Hannah. I had no idea the disappearance of one person could create such misery for so many. It's rather like a house of cards, don't you think? The way we are all interlocked." Daniel laced his fingers together to illustrate his point.

Hannah sighed. She was getting pissed. "What do you want?"

"I want to help you."

Daniel dropped his hands. Irritation flickered under his smile. She wasn't fooled There was no reason he should want to help her when he hated Josie. He was just looking for attention.

"You want to take care of me?" Hannah smirked. "I don't think the judge would go for that. Besides, I don't think we'd get along."

"No, nothing like that." Daniel shook his head. "I wanted to offer my professional services. Given everything that's happened, I doubt Ms. Bates will be coming home. I thought you might want to prepare yourself for that. I thought I would reach out to you. Someone needs to now."

"She'll get back," Hannah snapped. "And she'll find me. And if she doesn't Archer will. He'll come get me."

Hannah walked back to the door and put her hand on the knob. The house was too quiet and she didn't like Daniel sharing the silence, but Daniel had an agenda. He wasn't going anywhere until he met it.

"Neither of those things will happen, Hannah," Daniel said gently. "It would be better to face the facts now. I read your history. I know how you clung to the notion that your mother would love you and care for you. I know the danger you put yourself in because of that delusion. Don't put yourself through it again. I know…"

"Just shut up. You don't know anything about Archer and Josie," Hannah said angrily. She didn't have to be nice to him, and she didn't want him spoiling her last minutes in this house.

"I do know about Josie Bates, and you know, too. Look at your hand. You can't help yourself. Your anxiety is reflected in your compulsiveness. You may say you believe she's coming back, but you're already grieving. Let me be the one to help. Please, Hannah."

Daniel Young walked toward her, but Hannah barely noticed. She was looking at her hand, and she was fighting the numbers running through her head. It wasn't until the tips of his shoes came into view that she realized how close he was. Her head snapped up. He looked bigger and broader than he had when she first met him; he was frightening and threatening because he seemed to be looking through her.

"I could save you, Hannah."

"I don't need saving." She backed off and pulled open the door.

"You will," he insisted.

"No, I won't. And you better go now."

Hannah wished Max was there or Archer or anyone. Where was Billy when she needed him? She didn't want to be alone with Daniel Young, but he wasn't listening to her. He looked at her as if trying to decide whether he should do what she wanted or what he wanted. Before he could make that decision, a phone started to ring. They looked at each other and then they looked toward the dining room.

LAPD, Detective Levinsky's Desk, Los Angeles

"Yep. Yep. Sure. Thanks. Okay." Levinsky made a few notes, hung up on the caller and immediately dialed Arnson. "We got the fiber content back on the strands found in Bates' car. White/black/blue. Consistent with sportswear microfibre. Yeah. You know, all that fancy stuff that breathes."

He listened for a minute.

"Could be Bates'. I'll call and have the kid check her closet. Yeah. Yeah. Maybe not. It's all in the file."

Levinsky was about to hang up when Arnson told him that Hernandez couldn't write. Levinsky was surprised. That definitely meant someone else was in the mix.

"Think those broads are still alive?" Levinsky asked. He listened for Arnson's answer then said: "Naw, me neither."

He hung up and thought it was a damn shame they'd probably be finding a couple bodies one of these days. What a waste. Both those women were lookers.

Liz Driscoll's Car, Hermosa Beach

Liz knew she should go home, but home was a long way away from Hermosa Beach, and she just wasn't ready to let go.

She had done what Archer asked and found the picture of Daniel and Erika Gardener, faxed the info of their engagement to Arnson and asked him to check in Erika Gardener's house for anything that might connect the two currently. She suggested he also check the long ago restraining order that had been granted to Erika Gardener. It would be interesting to see if Daniel Young was named. Liz called the hospital on her way back from Manhattan Beach. Archer was doing better, but there was no change in Hernandez. Now she was sitting opposite Josie Bates' house wondering if she should stop in and see Hannah. There were a zillion reasons not to – the first being that Liz would eventually have to admit that she was off the investigation. There was only one good reason to knock on that door and the reason was that Hannah was a kid.

"Aw, hell," Liz muttered. She didn't have anything else to do. She'd go and sit with Hannah until they came to get her, but first there was one more call she had to make.

"Morgan?" Liz said when her contact at the city clerk's office picked up. "It's me, Driscoll. Got anything on the parking garage? Excellent. Hold on." Liz pulled her notepad out and got ready to copy. "Okay, shoot."

"Ten in the time frame you gave me," came the answer. "I already ran the names on the cards through DMV. I came up with four red ones: two Toyotas, a Cadillac and a Mountaineer."

"Don't care about the Cadillac. Give me the Mountaineer and the Toyotas."

Liz started to write. The mountaineer was registered in Santa Ana so Liz discarded it. The first Toyota was to a man named Forest Kempmeir and the second was registered to a Gaylene Sheff, one resided in Manhattan Beach and one resided in Orange County."

That, Liz thought, was promising. "Give me the addresses of the last two."

Liz took them down. When she was done, all she could do for a second was stare at the information. In the next minute, she was dialing Arnson.

"You won't believe this. The red Toyota? It's registered to Daniel Young's secretary but the address is his place."

San Diego Freeway South

Isaiah Wilson adjusted his Bluetooth earpiece. He would never get used to wearing such a thing, but it did have its place. Peter Siddon's voice was coming over loud and clear.

"Yes, Peter. I think it's a good idea to go home. No. Don't wait for me. I've seen Xavier, and there's nothing to worry about. Josie Bates? No, I doubt she'll bother either of us ever again. All will be well. I promise."

Isaiah signed off. For the first time in many years he was at peace. Now there was only one last stop to make. There were two ladies he wanted to see one more time.

CHAPTER 43

Josie Bates' House, Hermosa Beach

Hannah dashed for Archer's phone, and Daniel Young was following after. She caught it on the third ring.

"Hello?"

"Who is it?" Daniel was so close Hannah could smell him. She turned away and put hand over her free ear.

"Yes. Yes. Okay. I don't care. Just tell me as best you can." Hannah turned back to Daniel and whispered: "Do you have something to write with?"

Daniel had a pen. He rushed into the kitchen. Hannah heard him rummaging for paper, and he heard Hannah begging.

"No, don't hang up. Just say it once more. Please." Daniel was back, pen and napkin at the ready. "Okay. Yes. The Santa Monica Mountains. Does it have a name? Okay. Okay." Hannah motioned to Daniel and he started to write as she spoke. *Mile marker 3. A turnout by the rock with the purple graffiti.* Then what? *Walk in a ways. Straight. If I hit the river it's too far.* That was it. The woman on the other end of the line was done.

"Who are you? What's your…" Hannah asked, but the woman had hung up. Hannah twirled on Daniel.

"She said she spoke to Josie and to the other lady. They're in some kind of little house or something up in the mountains. Oh my God, this girl talked to them. They're alive."

"It can't be? Really?" Daniel grabbed her hands and Hannah let him.

"Yes. Yes. We've got to call someone. Call Detective Driscoll," Hannah said as she disengaged and picked up the phone again. Daniel put his hand on it before she could dial.

"I know the place. I know the rock. I cycle up there. Come on, I'll take you."

Hannah pulled back, "No, we need to call Liz."

"A minute could make all the difference. My car is right outside. We'll call her on the way," Daniel insisted.

"Okay. Okay."

Hannah left everything behind. She forgot about Mrs. Crane as she rushed out of the house. There was only one thing on her mind: Josie.

"Where? Where's your car?" She called to Daniel and he pointed just down the street as he grabbed her wrist.

"This way."

He pulled her along as they ran then flung her toward his car. She threw herself inside, closing the door as Daniel fired up the engine. While he checked traffic, Hannah used Archer's phone to dial Liz's number but the line was busy. She rang off just as Daniel Young made a U-turn at the light and sped off toward the freeway unaware that his speed and his car had been tagged.

Liz Driscoll's Car, Hermosa Beach

Liz was still on the phone when the car went by her. She wouldn't have given it a second thought had she not seen Hannah sitting in the passenger's seat. Though she couldn't see clearly, it looked as if Daniel was driving.

"Idiot," Liz muttered. She couldn't believe he was helping Hannah run from the county people. Hannah made a big mistake dragging him into this, and she wasn't doing herself any favor either. Liz didn't have Hannah's cell number, so she called Daniel's as she pulled out into traffic.

He answered on the first ring.

Daniel Young's Car, San Diego Freeway, North

"Yes?"

Daniel Young put his hand to his Bluetooth and pushed it further into his ear. He glanced at Hannah who was busy with Archer's phone as she redialed the woman who had called.

"Detective Driscoll. Yes, we know where she is. Santa Monica Mountains."

Hannah looked up, those green eyes of hers so hopeful. Not only was Daniel her white knight, but the cavalry was coming, too. He smiled at her then looked back to traffic and eased over into the carpool lane. It was the perfect time of day for this to all end and he was the perfect person to make it happen. He had almost forgotten Liz Driscoll on the phone. He touched his earpiece again.

"It's the 3-mile marker near the graffitied boulder. Yes. Yes. That's the one. We'll see you there." He ended the call, smiled broadly and said to Hannah. "Looks like you were right. You're going to see Josie Bates."

"I can't believe it. Thank you so much. Thank you," Hannah breathed.

Unable to reach the woman who had called, Hannah started to dial again, punching in Josie's number, positive that this time Josie would answer. All she had to do was push the button and Hannah would tell her they were coming.

Hannah put Archer's phone to her ear and listened to Josie's distinctive ring. It echoed not just in her ear but all around her. The sound was coming from the back seat of Daniel Young's car.

Liz Driscoll's Car, San Diego Freeway, North

Liz tossed her phone on the seat beside her. She couldn't believe what had just happened. Young hung up on her. She put the pedal to the metal and kept Daniel Young in sight.

Forest Lawn Cemetery, Orange County

Isaiah Wilson walked across the green lawn, past the headstones and toward a mausoleum. Well, hardly a mausoleum but a monument to Janey nonetheless. To the left of Janey's monument a modest headstone inscribed with the name Susie Atkins.

This was his last stop. He needed to be here with his two girls who would have been women today if Xavier Hernandez had not happened upon them.

"Josie Bates can't hurt anyone anymore," the reverend said to the gravestone and the monument.

Then Reverend Wilson began to cry. Retribution was not all it was cracked up to be.

CHAPTER 44

The California Mountains

Daniel was not happy. Hannah should have been slower given the backhand he dealt her when she recognized Josie Bates' ringtone. Oh, he had tried to explain, but Hannah Sheraton was no dummy. She attacked him, endangering them both. He had to hit her. It felt right and good because it ended any pretense.

Between the woman who called Archer's phone, this little slut, and Erika, this whole thing had just gone to hell in a handbasket. How could he have been so stupid? He had taken Josie Bates' purse and briefcase out of the red car and thrown it into the back of his own so Gay wouldn't see them. Now Bates' stuff was jumbled up with his personal accouterments: his bike, his helmet, his flashlight and backpack. Thinking about that miscalculation made him so angry he hit Hannah again for good measure a second later.

Luckily, they were on the freeway when he did. Cars were going too fast for anyone to really see what happened. Even if they did, this was Los Angeles. Drivers would leave Mother Theresa bleeding on the shoulder rather than get involved.

At the turn off, Daniel hit the gas and took the road to the 3-mile marker in record time. He careened into the cul de sac under the rock and slammed on the brakes. Flinging himself out of the car, he ran to the other side, ripped open the passenger door and went after Hannah as she tried to get over the back seat. He pulled one leg; she kicked with the other. He dragged her a few inches; she screamed and railed and clutched at the headrests and the slick leather upholstery.

"Get out of there. Let go!" he ordered.

Daniel grabbed her jeans and yanked her backward with one hand. With the other he pried her fingers off the back of the seat, aware of her smooth, young skin, the scent of her hair, the flash of her eyes. Oh, he was an exceptional man to be able to appreciate these things even now, in the heat of battle, in this epic war of wills. Dazed as she must be, he had to admire that she still fought, grunting, grappling and kicking as she tried to stay out his reach. But she was simply putting off the inevitable because Daniel was tall, strong, and truly ticked off.

"Damn you. Stop it." With one last lunge he had her, lifting her high as he pulled her out of the car. Holding her tight, Daniel slammed the door shut with his foot.

"This won't work," Hannah snapped.

"Oh, yes it will." Daniel pushed her and she staggered off the road and into the forest. "I'll take the chip out of Archer's phone. No one will know that woman called. Liz Driscoll doesn't know where we were going…"

"She does. I heard you tell her," Hannah cried.

"You are stupid," he muttered. "I was talking to dead air. She doesn't know anything. When you disappear I'll tell them you were hysterical about being put in foster care, and that you were screaming about finding Josie Bates. I'll tell them you were delusional and that it wouldn't surprise me if you hurt yourself. Everyone knows you're a cutter. They'll believe me."

"Archer won't. Billy and Burt won't!" Hannah whirled on Daniel. Facing him was preferable to being herded in front of him. "Is Josie alive? Is she?"

"Why don't we just go see?"

Daniel Young raised his arm and pointed. When Hannah didn't move he drew back as if to strike her again, and Hannah scrambled away, walking backward, watching for an opening to make her escape.

"Why did you do this?"

"Because Josie Bates ruined me," he said flatly. "Turn around."

"No!" Hannah screamed and then she screamed again. "Help me. Somebody help me."

Hannah bolted, hoping to lose herself among the trees, but Daniel was faster still. Scooping up a big branch, he hit her as she cried out. Again and again she screamed for help; again and again he struck her. When Hannah was on the ground, lying in the leaves, rolling over thistles and into the undergrowth, she fell silent and put all her energy into warding off the blows.

"I was someone and she took it all way. She deserves what she got and worse," Daniel raged.

"You're crazy!" Hannah found her voice and reached for his club at the same time.

"Shut up!" He swung again and the wood cracked against her forearm.

Hannah cradled her arm as she pulled into a ball. As long as he didn't hit her head, she had a chance; if she could keep him engaged, she had a chance.

"Why Erika Gardener? What did she do to you? " Hannah cried.

She hunched her shoulders, flinching as she readied herself for another blow. It never came. The mention of Erika had given him pause.

"She didn't want to marry a liar. I wasn't a liar. Josie Bates made it seem like I was. She found a mistake on my university records that showed I hadn't completed my last courses. She said I was a fraud. She said whatever came out of my mouth should be given no more attention than the braying of a donkey. The judge let her attack my character and my intelligence. I loved Erika, and she left me because of what Josie Bates said in that courtroom."

As quickly as Daniel had fallen into his reverie, indulged in his self-pity, he snapped out of it and remembered where he was. His handsome face hardened, his eyes narrowed. He grabbed Hannah and yanked her to her feet.

"I wasn't an expert anymore; I was a laughing stock." Daniel pushed her. "That way."

They pressed on. Hannah looking for any opportunity to escape, and Daniel knowing he would never allow that. Finally, he called 'stop'. Hannah blinked. There was nothing but trees in front of her. She stared, unsure of what he wanted her to see. Using his piece of wood to push the hair away from her ear he whispered:

"It's not exactly a beach house, but I think Ms. Bates got used to it."

That's when Hannah saw it: the ancient cement building with the locked metal door. Her stomach lurched. Slowly she looked over her shoulder, unable or unwilling to acknowledge the horrid truth until Daniel grinned at her. That's when she understood that Josie had been locked away like an animal.

"You're sick," she whispered.

"No. I'm smart."

That was it. Hannah couldn't look at him any longer. Raising her hands, she pushed Daniel Young as hard as she could and ran.

"Josie! Josie!"

Hannah cried out, praying to hear any sound from inside that place. All she heard was Daniel's cry of rage as he caught her by the hair and pulled her off her feet.

"You killed her. You did kill her," she sobbed, her own hands covering his as she tried to alleviate the searing pain at her scalp.

"Maybe. Maybe not."

Dragging her across the rough ground, through the dry leaves, and over the rocks, Daniel pushed her down and planted his foot on her chest. Working fast, he took away the metal rod that locked the door from the outside, reached down, and wrapped his arm around Hannah's neck. She seized the moment and drew her long nails down the side of his face while she buried her teeth in his arm.

Daniel howled in pain, but instead of letting go he rammed Hannah's head into the steel door. She crumpled at his feet. With all his might, he pulled the door open and threw Hannah Sheraton inside like a piece of trash.

Slamming the door shut, he put the bar in place, and scurried to the little berm to look inside. What a pity he didn't have his cycling helmet with the light on it so he could see better and she wouldn't be able to see him. Then he realized it didn't matter if Josie saw him, and that was a wonderful epiphany. He tiptoed up, he grinned, and called:

"Hello in there! Hello! It's me, Daniel!"

Liz Driscoll's Car, The California Mountains

Liz leaned over her steering wheel, driving slowly, keeping an eye out for Daniel's car. She cursed herself for losing him on the turns, but she'd never been good at tailing anyone. Two miles later, she turned around and headed down the mountain again. That's when she saw the car. The overhang near the boulder had shielded the cul de sac going up the mountain, only to expose it on the way down. She pulled over to the side of the road, took out her phone, and called Arnson. She gave him her location, what she had observed, and a heads up that Hannah might be a hostage. She cut him off just as he warned her to wait for backup. Liz knew she wouldn't. Not because she wanted the glory of the collar, but because lives truly were on the line.

Not knowing how far off the road Daniel and Hannah were, Liz entered the woods cautiously. There was a hint of a path and she walked it carefully, inching herself forward, knowing if she made too much noise she would further jeopardize the women she hoped were still alive. She needn't have worried. Daniel Young was making enough noise to cover any that she could create.

An Outbuilding in the California Mountains

With the last of her strength, Josie had moved Erika into the corner of the hut opposite the door. She had not touched the knife in the woman's throat so that evidence would be preserved. Then she collected the pictures, the food wrapper, and the Xerox with the shadow printing on it, and put it all beside the body. Once that was done, she crawled to her corner.

Half conscious now, she thought she was dreaming when she heard someone calling. Looking up toward the little window, Josie saw a man's eyes. They were crinkled like he was smiling. She put her hand over her own to shade against the sunlight, and tried to raise the other one to wave at him. But she was weak and that hand fell back down. It didn't hit the ground. Instead, her hand fell onto a pillow of glorious hair. Josie turned her head and prayed she was hallucinating.

"Hannah?"

The California Mountains

Liz hunkered down behind a stand of trees that was surrounded by brush and rock. She watched Daniel Young balancing himself on the berm as he called into the hut. Hannah was nowhere to be seen, so Liz reached the only conclusion she could: the women were inside.

Carefully, she reached into her pocket and withdrew Archer's revolver. Gun in hand she listened, knowing she would have to bide her time if everyone was going to get out alive.

"Josie Bates!" Daniel laughed. "Now you know how it feels to have someone take everything away from you. It's kind of like dying except I didn't die, did I? I'm the one who survived. I'm the best. I'm the smartest. I'm the one they should have listened to, not you. Say something, you bitch."

An Outbuilding in the California Mountains

Josie heard Daniel Young's tirade, but she couldn't respond. Her last energy would be used up caring for Hannah. She pushed aside the girl's hair, she put her cheek against the girl's head, and she cried. Josie hadn't wanted to die with her hands tied, but better that than to die with them free and wrapped around this girl she loved.

When Daniel called out again, when he mocked her and reviled her, when he castigated her for the sins he perceived she had committed, Josie barely heard him. She was listening to another voice, a closer voice.

"Don't worry, I'm here now," Hannah whispered and Josie stopped crying.

The California Mountains

Liz's patience was rewarded sooner than she expected.

Tired of talking, frustrated by the silence in the hut, Daniel Young backed away, picked up a stone, and threw it against the cement wall. Two more times he threw things. He was like a bully wanting one more lick. Finally, he did a few turns, realized there was nothing more to do, and started back to his car.

Liz flattened herself on the ground, and he walked past without notice. There was a spring in his step. She hoped he enjoyed the rest of his day, because she was going to have him booked by the end of it.

Pushing off, staying low, moving fast and quiet, Liz went straight to the door and pulled off the metal bar.

"Hannah," she called. "It's me, Liz. Hannah, push! Push on the door!"

The door opened like the portal to hell. The stench of human waste and despair and death slammed up against her, but Liz ignored it. All she could do was stare at Erika Gardener's body, the wraith that was Josie Bates, and a bloodied Hannah raising her hand. Liz started to smile at the girl only to realize that Hannah wasn't greeting her, she was pointing toward the forest. Liz looked just in time to see two things: Daniel Young and the huge piece of wood he was swinging at her head.

Liz ducked and crouched as she tried to avoid the attack. It wasn't a perfect maneuver, but it was enough so that she endured only a glancing blow. Thrown back, she landed on her wrists, rolled through the leaves, and came up on one knee with Archer's revolver still in hand. But Daniel was determined, and psychotic, and the branch swung again. Liz ducked and rolled once more. She raised the gun but she was off balance, and the revolver was heavier than her own weapon. Once more the branch came down and this time it was too close for comfort. She scrambled, but Daniel had tired of the game. With a roar, he threw himself on top of her.

Liz brought her knee up, but it did no good. Her leg was wedged between her body and his; her effort to subdue him had been ridiculous and futile. He laughed and pinned her arm to the ground, wrenching the gun from her hand. Hoping to move just enough to keep him from getting a good grip on it Liz thrashed, tossing her body as best she could, but she was small and no match for him.

Suddenly, a bloodcurdling cry sounded as Hannah rushed at them and threw herself into the mix. Spread-eagle, she landed atop Daniel, but she was a slight girl and disoriented by the beating he had given her. With a roar, Daniel threw her off. Hannah hit the ground so hard the breath was knocked out of her. Liz bucked, praying Daniel would be distracted by the two-prong attack, but it was Liz who was distracted. It was reflex that made her turn her head, and instinct that made her seek out eye contact with Hannah. Both things were mistakes.

In that split second Daniel Young grabbed the gun, Liz tore her eyes away from Hannah, and the girl rose to reach for the man's arm. In the next instant, Daniel Young lay hard on Liz Driscoll, put the gun against her head, and pulled the trigger.

Blood and brains sprayed over Hannah's face. Paralyzed by shock, Hannah couldn't move even when Daniel looked her way. Even when he began to giggle and then laugh, she simply stared at him. Peeling himself off Liz Driscoll, mesmerized by her dead body, he finally stood upright again. It was only when he looked at Hannah's horrified face once more that he understood what had just happened.

Covered in Liz Driscoll's blood, Daniel's chest rose and fell not with remorse but with triumph. He felt like God; he was God. There was no longer any need to play games. No more talking. Now he knew that he could silence any voice that spoke against him. He turned toward Hannah as he raised the revolver.

"Beg," he said.

Silently, awkwardly, unsure of what to do, she scooted back away from him.

"Beg!" he roared.

Hannah shook her head. Her heart had seized up. Her voice wouldn't work, but Daniel didn't believe she was afraid. He knew her kind. He saw defiance in those damn eyes of hers and disdain in the set of her lips. It would be a pleasure to wipe that look off her face.

"I could have helped you." He raised the gun just a little higher.

"In your dreams," Hannah spat back.

"I can live with that," he said as he put both hands on the gun and pointed it at her face.

But before he could pull the trigger, Josie Bates rose up behind him. With all her strength, she took the knife she had ripped from Erika's throat and shoved it up into Daniel Young's neck, the tip of the blade finding its way into his very expert brain.

CHAPTER 45

Day 8
Josie Bates' House, Hermosa Beach

"Thanks."

Josie took the tea Archer offered and cupped it in both hands. Four days earlier she couldn't imagine being alive much less wanting a hot drink. But she was home now, the weather had broken, and the beach towns were shrouded under a chilly fog.

Archer took a chair next to her on the patio. She glanced his way, taking in the walking cast on his leg and the scabbing on the side of his face. Her eyes flicked to Hannah who was sitting on the wall with Max at her feet. The girl's jaw was still swollen and bruised. Josie imagined that there was some damage under her clothes, too, given the size of the branch she had been beaten with. No one would ever know Hannah was hurting, though. Hurt was something she just didn't share easily. Josie took a drink and reflected on what a battered threesome they were. Still, they had all found the strength to do what they had to in order to survive.

"You sure you don't want to go in? The doctor said you should rest," Archer suggested just as Josie's thoughts were roaming to Erika Gardener.

"No, I'm good." Josie smiled at him.

Archer didn't insist because he understood her reluctance. It would be some time before Josie was comfortable behind locked doors or surrounded by four walls. Even her beloved house wasn't the haven it should be. The minute Josie fell asleep, she dreamed she was back in that hut with Erika Gardener; the moment she opened her eyes she saw Daniel Young's face, not Archer's, next to her. Hannah suggested Josie go with her to see Dr. Fox, but Josie declined. A shrink was the last person she wanted to see.

Archer leaned over and kissed her shoulder. She put a hand on his head and drew it down his face. Her skin was warm from holding the mug. He grasped her hand and kissed her palm. He could not get enough of her.

"Here they come," Hannah called.

Josie smiled. Time for her and Archer would have to wait. Hannah had risen and was facing Hermosa Boulevard. Josie followed suit and then helped Archer. She was cadaverously thin but not weak; Archer was awkward but still strong. Max got on his hind legs and put his front paws on top of the wall as they came together. Hermosa Boulevard had been closed to traffic since early morning, people began gathering by eleven, and now the first patrol car in the funeral procession was turning onto it.

Archer put his arm on Josie's shoulder; she put her hand on Hannah's. Car after car rolled slowly by. One of their own had died in the line of duty, and all of law enforcement had turned out to honor her: LAPD, Sheriff, Marshalls, Hermosa, Redondo and Manhattan Beach PD. Fire engines from surrounding areas had joined in. They couldn't see the hearse carrying Liz Driscoll's body yet, but the three people on that patio were thinking about her.

"He almost got away with it, didn't he?" Hannah said softly.

"He would have except for Liz," Josie answered. "I don't think I'll ever come to grips with the fact that she died for us."

"He would have killed all of us if he could have." Hannah glanced over her shoulder at Josie, but Archer answered.

"Maybe. If he had to. But that wasn't the plan in the beginning. The cops found files full of information on Josie and Erika and Isaiah Wilson, all of it organized and detailed. Daniel had been stalking you and Erika off and on for years. Erika knew about it. That's why she had the restraining order in place, and that's why she moved so often. She didn't think to tell anyone involved in the trial because she thought it was personal.

"He probably didn't know what he was going to do with it until Xavier's release was announced. Once that happened, the plan was simple. Kidnap Josie and Erika, blame Xavier, then Daniel would claim expert knowledge and lead the authorities to the hut at the right time. He would be a hero. Xavier would be arrested and sent back to prison. His brain injury left him pretty much without a reliable memory or decision-making skills, so he did whatever Daniel told him – including living in a storage unit."

"But wait. Go back. Daniel knew all along that Xavier had been released?" Hannah asked.

"He made a big stink about not getting the letter, but he had. I can't believe I bought his outraged act," Archer said, disgusted that he had been so easily duped.

"But how did he find Xavier once he was out?" Josie asked as she moved into Archer. She was shivering partly from the wet-cold of the fog and partly because of the memory of her ordeal.

"He went in through the back door and offered to conduct a psychiatric examination of Xavier before he was released. He told the prison health officials that he wanted to help Hernandez acclimate once he got out. Daniel asked that they advise him of where Hernandez would be living and his medications. That was one thing Cuwin Martin actually did right. He sent all that information to Daniel and then forgot about Xavier. Cuwin figured he was taken care of."

"God, that was smart," Josie muttered. "Daniel never showed up on the visitor's list but he had access to Xavier."

"I still don't get it." Hannah turned toward them. Her fingers were tapping, but not as frenetically as they had in the last few days. "Daniel was doing okay. People had forgotten about what happened."

"He hadn't forgotten," Josie answered. "Neither had Isaiah Wilson or Peter Siddon."

"So Daniel just took advantage of everyone and nobody figured it out." Hannah raised her green eyes and Archer almost smiled. She had an amazing way of boiling things down.

"Yep," Archer answered. "We all cut him slack because he was on the list. Problem was, he made the list. He played us every step of the way."

"Is the lady who worked for him going to get arrested?" Hannah asked just as Max tired of looking over the wall. He got down on all fours, turned a few circles and curled up at her feet.

"Gay? No. He used her, too," Josie said. "She was in love with Daniel and was so impressed with his compassion. Gay made the calendar with the pictures on it because Daniel told her it would help Xavier remember his past. He never told her who was in those pic..." Suddenly, Josie lost interest in what she was saying. She nodded toward the street. "Look."

A contingency of officers on horseback was making its way slowly and solemnly down the street. Looking majestic and ghostly, they cut through the fog that muffled the clopping of the horse's hooves.

"Liz would have loved this," Archer noted.

"She deserves it," Josie said.

"She deserved better," Hannah sighed. "But I know she's seeing it all."

Josie smiled and dropped her hand from Hannah's shoulder. Given all the things that had happened in this girl's life it was amazing she still had that kind of faith. That Hannah couldn't pinpoint where her faith lay didn't matter. She simply accepted that it was there as her mind went back to Gay and the choices women make.

"How could Gay be so stupid?" Hannah insisted.

"How could she not?" Josie laughed. "Daniel convinced her he loved her. When he signed over the red

Toyota to her and registered it to his address, she thought he was getting ready to make the relationship permanent."

"She sold out for an old car?" Hannah said. "That's lame."

"She just heard what she wanted to hear." Josie shook her head in solidarity with that woman. She and Gay had a lot in common. During Hernandez's trial, she thought nothing of using words that would be interpreted to suit her defense rather than discover the truth. It was a game; it was a challenge; it was wrong.

"We all did the same thing," Archer admitted. "I just thought he was a buffoon. I'm so sorry, Jo."

"No worries," she assured him before her gaze encompassed Hannah and Max, too. "I'm home now. We all are."

Archer kissed her, pulled her back into him, and wrapped his arms around her.

"I hope Gay realizes how lucky she is. Her fingerprints were on the photos and calendar, her car was at the pier, he drove her car to Erika's house. Daniel could argue that she was jealous of Erika and wanted vengeance on Josie for hurting the man she loved."

"He might even have killed her if he thought he needed to," Josie noted.

"It sounds stupid," Hannah said.

"It sounds crazy," Archer agreed, "but it was also kind of brilliant when you think about it. He averted any suspicion by admitting he was near the pier with his bike group the day Josie disappeared. I never asked if he finished the ride – which he didn't. He veered off, hid out in the underground parking garage and waited for Hernandez to meet Josie. Once contact was made, he went up to put the list in the Jeep – that's when he ripped his bike shorts – then hustled back to the parking garage to act as a Good Samaritan. He helps Hernandez get Josie in the car, locks the bike, drives Xavier back to the storage unit, switches to his own car and takes off with Josie unconscious beside him. He comes back later and loads the bike in the SUV. The Toyota is at his place where Gay can get it if she needs it, and she's none the wiser. She was used to them switching off cars by this time.

"Next it's Erika's turn," Archer continued. "Daniel has Xavier handle the wine glasses, drives to her place alone, somehow talks his way in, they have a drink, he plants the glasses in the trash, and that's it. He's back in the office by the time I burst in like an idiot. There were so many things that should have tipped me off."

"Maybe your radar wasn't working because you were worried out of your mind," Josie chuckled.

"Who told you that?" Archer murmured and pulled her closer.

"But why did you go to the pier in the first place?" Hannah asked Josie.

"I'm assuming Xavier called," Josie said. "I would have met him if he asked because he had been a client. I probably would have met Daniel if he called. The truth is, I don't remember anything other than waking up in that building."

"What was Daniel going to get out of all this?" Hannah pressed.

"Star status. He would be given credit for rescuing Josie and Erika before Xavier killed them," Archer answered. "And the two women he hated most in the world would live out their lives beholden to him."

"But when he panicked and killed Erika, his plan changed," Josie said. "He had to leave me where I was. Then Liz called about Xavier, and Daniel thought he was home free. If Xavier died, everyone would assume he took the secret of our whereabouts to his grave. Daniel would simply be back where he started. No harm, no foul."

"What about Peter Siddon and Reverend Wilson?" Hannah insisted.

"Someone had tipped the local authorities to Siddon's history. He thought it was me. Reverend Wilson? That poor man just never got over his daughter's death. My disappearance gave him reason to resurrect her memory and broadcast his grief. Everybody blamed me for ruining their lives." Josie put aside her tea and looked over at the procession. "I'll never stop blaming myself either."

"It was a long time ago, Jo," Archer said, kissing her lightly, breathing in the scent of her hair. "You did what you were supposed to do. You were just smarter than the rest of them."

Hannah looked over at Josie and their eyes met, but Josie really wasn't seeing Hannah when she said:

"No one should be that smart."

With that, she turned to watch the hearse carrying Liz Driscoll's body disappear into the fog.

THRILLERS BY REBECCA FORSTER

The Best-Selling Witness Series

HOSTILE WITNESS (#1)
SILENT WITNESS (#2)
PRIVILEGED WITNESS (#3)
EXPERT WITNESS (#4)
EYEWITNESS (#5)
FORGOTTEN WITNESS (#6)
DARK WITNESS (#7)

BEFORE HER EYES
THE MENTOR
CHARACTER WITNESS
BEYOND MALICE
KEEPING COUNSEL
(USA Today Best Seller)

To contact me and to see all my books, visit me at:

RebeccaForster.com

66594415R00215

Made in the USA
Lexington, KY
18 August 2017